The King's Way Home

Hidden Scrolls Series

The King's Way Home

Hidden Scrolls Series

Thomas Pizur

Illustrated by L. Sue Baugh

Second Edition 2023

For permission to reproduce any part of the work, contact Thomas Pizur at www.thekingswayhome.com

ISBN 978-0-578-85092-4 (Print)
　　　978-0-578-36652-4 (ebook)

Printed in the United States of America

Illustrations: L. Sue Baugh
Book design and layout: Jericho C. Hernandez
Chapter border art: Susan Gavin
Book cover artwork: 1106 Design studio

"Fiction reveals truth that reality obscures."
—Ralph Waldo Emerson

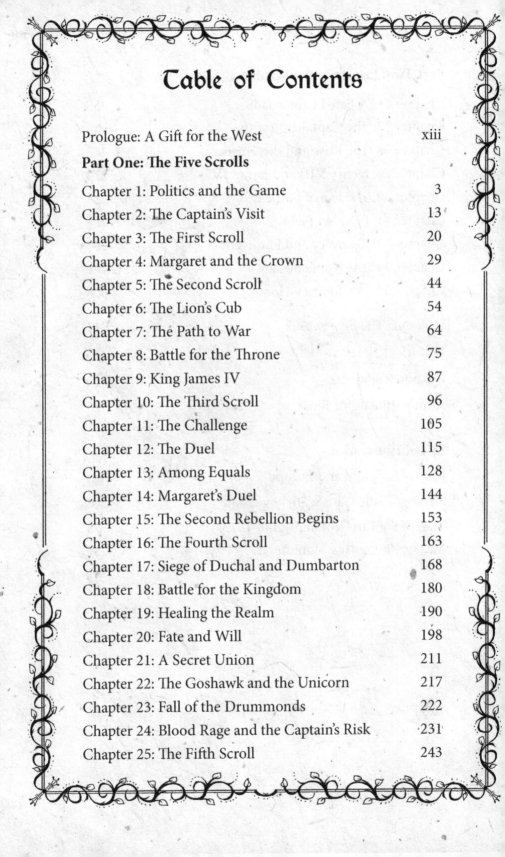

Table of Contents

Prologue: A Gift for the West   xiii

Part One: The Five Scrolls

Chapter 1: Politics and the Game   3

Chapter 2: The Captain's Visit   13

Chapter 3: The First Scroll   20

Chapter 4: Margaret and the Crown   29

Chapter 5: The Second Scroll   44

Chapter 6: The Lion's Cub   54

Chapter 7: The Path to War   64

Chapter 8: Battle for the Throne   75

Chapter 9: King James IV   87

Chapter 10: The Third Scroll   96

Chapter 11: The Challenge   105

Chapter 12: The Duel   115

Chapter 13: Among Equals   128

Chapter 14: Margaret's Duel   144

Chapter 15: The Second Rebellion Begins   153

Chapter 16: The Fourth Scroll   163

Chapter 17: Siege of Duchal and Dumbarton   168

Chapter 18: Battle for the Kingdom   180

Chapter 19: Healing the Realm   190

Chapter 20: Fate and Will   198

Chapter 21: A Secret Union   211

Chapter 22: The Goshawk and the Unicorn   217

Chapter 23: Fall of the Drummonds   222

Chapter 24: Blood Rage and the Captain's Risk   231

Chapter 25: The Fifth Scroll   243

Part Two: Legacy of the Scrolls

Chapter 26: A Fated Crossroads   255
Chapter 27: The Captain's Promise   259
Chapter 28: The Rose and the Thistle   266
Chapter 29: Henry VIII and James IV   274
Chapter 30: The Eve of Battle   282
Chapter 31: Flodden Field   288
Chapter 32: Recovery and Forgiveness   295
Chapter 33: The King's Legacy   302
Chapter 34: The Journey Home   308

Epilogue: The Five Scrolls   311
Historical Notes   315
Acknowledgments   323
Author/Illustrator Bios   325

List of Illustrations

Map of Scotland and Europe   xxi
Stirling Castle Gate & Stirling Castle   6
Map of Stewart Scotland: 1488-1513   88
Master Zheng He's Monastery   257

List of Characters

STEWART FAMILY

James IV, eldest son of James III and king of Scotland from 1488 to 1513.

King James III, father to James IV. James III is the only king in Scottish history to be overthrown by his son.

Thomas Cochrane, hated leader of a group of "familiars," or commoners, who influenced King James III to the detriment of the nobles

Jamie and John, James IV's younger brothers, who played only minor roles in James's court

JAMES IV'S SUPPORTERS

Robert Hume, childhood friend and courtier to James IV. He carried on the Five Scrolls, given to him by James.

Captain Jacob van Horn, Dutch sea captain and teacher of James IV; a student of Master Zheng He of China

Master Zheng He, a famous Chinese sea admiral and diplomat/warrior in Emperor Yongle's court. He received the Five Scrolls from a wandering monk and gave them to Captain van Horn to pass on to someone worthy of them in the West.

Wullie Fraser, servant to the Gray family and then to the Stewart household

Lord Gray, weapons master and military leader, teacher of James IV

Lord Montrose, teacher and military leader under James IV

Lord Argyll, teacher and military leader under James IV

Sir Lennox, captain of the king's knights under James IV

Lord Ross MacLean, Highland chief who becomes a supporter of James IV

Lord Angus Douglass, nobleman who switches sides easily until finally becoming loyal only to James IV

Lord Haile, regent over James until he comes of age, although he has little influence over the boy king

Admiral Andrew Wood, Scottish naval hero who clears the North Sea of English pirates during the reign of James IV

DRUMMOND FAMILY

Lady Margaret, beloved of James IV, second daughter of Lord Drummond

Lady Sibylla, Margaret's younger sister and beloved of Robert Hume

Lady Euphemia, Margaret's older sister, wife of Lord Fleming

Lord John Drummond, father of Margaret and her sisters

Lord Fleming, Euphemia's husband, who does not support James IV

Lady Aileen, cousin of Margaret and her sisters

ENEMIES OF THE DRUMMONDS AND MARGARET

Lord Crichton, who resents the Drummonds' influence

Lord MacKenzie, co-conspirator who hates the Drummonds

Lord Jameson, a former rebel lord who resents the Drummonds

LEADERS OF THE 1489 REBELLION

Lord Crichton, leader of the second rebellion of 1489

Lord Forbes, supports Crichton and others in the second rebellion

Duke of Bothwell, brother to Lord Angus Douglass and a rebel supporter

Lord Jameson, leader in the second rebellion along with Crichton and Forbes

Lord Lyle, supports Crichton in the second rebellion

ENGLISH FORCES AT FLODDEN FIELD

Earl of Surrey, leader of the English forces

English infantry, archers, and artillerymen

ENGLISH TUDORS

Henry VII, king of England, who signs the Treaty of Perpetual Peace with James IV

Henry VIII, the son of Henry VII and enemy of James IV and the French King Louis XII

Margaret, Henry VIII's 13-year-old sister, who marries James IV and has a surviving son, James V. This son becomes the father of James VI, who rules over a united England, Wales, and Scotland—modern-day Great Britain—as King James I.

FRENCH ALLIES

King Louis XII, who renews the Auld Alliance with James IV, binding Scotland and France to help each other should England attack either one of them

Anne of Brittany, queen of Louis XII; she calls on James IV for help against England

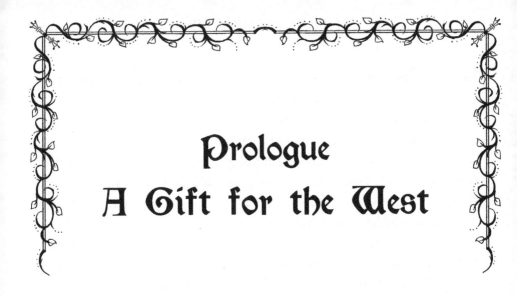

Prologue
A Gift for the West

Year: 1482
Port city of Mombasa
Kenya, East Africa

The night Captain van Horn's life changed forever began in a most unpromising way. By midnight he had lost all his money in Mombasa's gambling dens. Without even rickshaw fare in his pockets, he stumbled through the city's narrow, crowded streets to the inn where he was staying. Even in late evening, the air was thick with cooking smoke; the rich smells of spices, seared meat, and camel dung; and the salt tang of the Indian Ocean.

As he entered the inn lobby, the clerk greeted him with unwelcome news.

"There is a Chinese gentleman waiting in your room, Captain. I told him you wished no visitors, but he said he had an appointment."

Van Horn, who was having trouble keeping the clerk in focus, grunted in disapproval. His usually florid face was even redder from drink, and he was in no mood to see anyone.

"Who is he? What name did he give?"

"Master Zheng He, he told me. Well-dressed. I would say one of the upper-class Chinese, maybe even royalty."

"Master Zheng He!" the captain said, astonished. The man was a legend in China, a renowned explorer of the seven seas and a member of the Chinese emperor's own court.

"What does he want with me?"

"Perhaps he needs another ship captain," the clerk said.

If so, this was an unexpected bit of good fortune. Even Asians at times hired Dutch captains—the most reliable navigators and sailors in the Western world. And van Horn would need money to pay his debts before he left Mombasa.

But as he climbed the stairs to his room, the effects of his drinking bout began wearing off, and a familiar guilt stalked him.

It whispered, *You should be doing more with your life than this.* That voice arose whenever he had a quiet moment—one reason he kept carousing when on land. Strong drink blotted out the emptiness within, though it was always there to greet him in the morning.

Well, what should I do, he thought, *become a priest?* That ludicrous idea made him laugh out loud and startled a Hindu couple passing him in the corridor. He was creating a bad impression of Europeans in their eyes. He swept off his captain's hat and made an exaggerated bow.

"Pardon me, your graces. I'm not myself tonight."

The captain put his hat back on and watched them walk away. He had a sudden moment of honesty.

I've not been myself for a long time.

That only made him angry, and he flung open the door to confront his visitor, potential client or not.

He stopped in the doorway as if struck by a yardarm.

Master Zheng He was sitting by the curtained window, his thin, sensitive features illuminated by candlelight. The man radiated a benevolent power that went straight to van Horn's soul—as if everything the captain had ever done was laid bare before this man.

"Jacob van Horn." The low, cultured voice carried easily across the room. "I have been looking forward to this meeting for some time."

The master gestured to the chair next him. "Please, join me here."

Van Horn drew near and saw the creased lines in Master Zheng's face, which spoke of considerable age. Yet his eyes shone with a strong, youthful light. His long silk jacket and tunic were embroidered with dragons that seemed to move in the flickering light. Van Horn was most surprised to see a cross of gold on a thin chain around the man's neck. Was he Christian? It seemed doubtful.

"I see you have noticed the cross." The creases around Master Zheng's eyes deepened as he smiled. "I am Confucian, but I also honor the Nazarene from the Middle East."

At van Horn's confused look, the master continued. "Nearly eight hundred years ago, a monk from Syria brought Christianity to China, and the religion has survived there since that time. However, given the politics of my country, that may not always be so. Already the signs of intolerance are rising, and many have fled to other countries. It is time for the sacred knowledge that has resided in the East to be carried to the West."

Master Zheng peered intently into the captain's eyes. "Yet before we proceed further, Jacob van Horn, I must ask you a question. Answer not only from your mind but from your heart. What is a man's greatest treasure: power, wealth, knowledge, or love?"

Each word struck van Horn deeply. Wealth he had known and lost several times over. He had power as captain of a ship, absolute lord over the crew, but it was fleeting, gone when the ship docked. Knowledge, of course, was valuable; no one would deny that.

But love was the one thing that had eluded him. In fact, when his sister and her daughter—the last of his family—had died of the plague, love seemed to vanish from his life. He often wondered bitterly, *Where is God's love in that cruelty?*

But now, under the spell of Master Zheng's question, he thought only of how much he had cherished his sister and her child, how much they had loved him.

Tears welled in van Horn's eyes. He spoke slowly, "I would say love is the greatest treasure, Master Zheng. Of all things, it gives us the most."

Master Zheng sighed gently and leaned back, smiling. "My spirit chose you the moment I saw you on the dock, Jacob. Now your answer. has confirmed my choice. I have something to offer you, something that you have hungered for all these years."

"And what is that?" the captain asked, his heart beating hard.

"A way to fulfill your soul, to live a life that blesses."

A warmth slowly filled the captain's chest. With all his heart, he wanted what this man offered.

"What must I do?" he asked, his voice hoarse with emotion.

"Stay here with me for a while. I will teach you what you need to know."

"But I have debts—"

Master Zheng raised his hand. "I have already paid your debts. And there are one or two ship captains who would be happy to take over your vessel. Am I correct that you have nothing drawing you back to your Dutch country?"

The captain hung his head, ashamed he had no one waiting for him. "Yes, that would be true."

"Then it is settled." Master Zheng drew a card from his sleeve and handed it to van Horn. "Meet me at this address tomorrow morning at nine o'clock. We will begin."

When the captain appeared at Master Zheng's home, the sage quickly ushered him into a side library and closed the doors behind them.

"Not even my servants must know what I am about to show you."

He led van Horn to an ornate table where a small wooden chest waited. Its twelve square panels were beautifully decorated with carved and painted vines and cherries, the figure of a sailing vessel and a palm tree, and a bronze lock set in what looked like a metal compass rose.

Master Zheng unlocked the chest and slowly lifted the lid. Inside, five small scrolls, each tied with a silk ribbon, lay on a cushion of golden silk.

"These Five Scrolls carry the condensed wisdom of the Nazarene's words. They have been kept in the East since the ninth century. Now the wheel of fate is turning toward the West, and they must go to your part of the world."

He closed the lid and locked the chest again. His eyes searched the captain's face.

"You must take them there."

"Me?" van Horn said. "But surely you are the one—"

"A Chinese mandarin among Europeans? I doubt they would listen to me. It must be you, Captain," Master Zheng said firmly.

Seeing the concern still on van Horn's face, he smiled gently. "Don't doubt your worthiness, Captain. You will be adequately prepared before you set out. I will see to it."

Over the next few weeks, the captain began to study the wisdom of the Five Scrolls and the healing arts and sciences of the East, including the complex energy system of the body and the use of medicinal plants, tinctures, and potions. Van Horn proved so apt a student that Master Zheng bestowed on him a Chinese name—Lao Shan, meaning "old, wise mountain."

The weeks stretched into months, the months became two years. At last Master Zheng declared him nearly ready to depart on his mission to bring the Five Scrolls to the West.

"However, there is one more skill you need to develop, one that will give you an unusually accurate means of judging character. You have no doubt heard of a game we call *chwee wan* in China. I believe you call it golf in the West."

Van Horn stared at him open-mouthed. How in God's name had golf found its way to China? And why did Master Zheng consider it on par with the other ancient arts?

The captain stammered, "I—I have played the game a few times in Amsterdam. But forgive me, Master Zheng, I fail to see how this will help me on my mission!"

The sage smiled. "Let me tell you the story of this mysterious game and how it got the best of me when I was younger. I was at the time a member of the Emperor Yongle's royal court and filled with pride at my own prowess and success. Then an itinerant monk calling himself Wulu Yong appeared before the emperor, carrying a bag of what he called 'clubs.' He told the emperor he desired to teach the young princes and other members of the court a game that would strengthen their character and develop their skills.

"We were all eager to learn this game, so the emperor commanded a course be built. The monk showed us how to hold and swing the club, strike the ball some distance, and use finesse to hit it into a small hole in the ground. I was used to excelling at sporting games, and I was sure I would best all others within a short time.

"Alas, such was not the case. The game defeated me at every turn. My long shots fell short, my shorter shots fell long, the ball possessed a devious mind of its own. And worse, all my self-control deserted me. I became short-tempered, envious of others' success, and driven by a desire to win at all costs. I abandoned my other duties and my friends and became obsessed with mastering the game.

"The monk Wulu Yong finally took pity on me and pulled me aside. 'Zheng He,' he said. 'You have lost yourself in this game. The solution to your dilemma is obvious. Remember who you are.'

"His words pierced me like a sword. In one instant, I understood what he meant. The Christians would have said I had forgotten I was a beloved child of God. The Daoists would have said I had forgotten that I was the spirit dwelling in the body. I had become lost in anger and fear, engaging in endless warfare with myself and others.

"When I realized this, I was bitterly ashamed." Master Zheng paused, as if the memory still had power over him.

"What happened next?" the captain asked.

Master Zheng smiled. "I remembered my true self, a being divinely loved, and I apologized to the court for my disgraceful behavior. The game now taught me patience, perseverance, grace in winning or losing, and most of all, how to let my soul or spirit guide my life. When Wulu Yong saw the changes in me, he showed me the chest with its Five Scrolls. The monk instructed me in their meaning and charged me to find the right person to take them to the West. And so, Captain van Horn—Lao Shan—we find ourselves here today!"

At that moment, a servant knocked and entered the room, carrying a tray with two small cups and a bottle of rice wine.

"Ah, just what we need." Master Zheng gestured to the servant to fill his cup and van Horn's with the gold-colored liquid. He lifted his cup. "To those who recall us to ourselves!"

Van Horn quickly raised his own. "As you have done for me, Master Zheng. I was also lost in this maze of a fallen world. You are the one who led me back to myself. May my skills match your teaching!"

For the next year, Master Zheng taught the captain every nuance and skill he possessed in the game. Van Horn discovered for himself how this pastime could challenge a man's character—frustrating his every attempt to master it.

In response, Master Zheng showed the captain how to let his Soul guide him, until in the end, no matter what obstacles the game presented, van Horn remained equitable and calm. His skills even surpassed Master Zheng's.

Master Zheng then instructed him in the deeper lore of the scrolls and added, "You must not only give the Five Scrolls to the right person, but mentor the person along the path where the scrolls lead them. This will be a crucial part of your mission."

"I've never fancied myself in the role of teacher," van Horn said. "But then I never thought I'd end up here! As you say, Master Zheng, my Soul will see to it."

"I must occasionally visit the West, so I will be able to meet you now and then and discuss what you must do. You will not be alone."

When it came time for van Horn to set sail for Europe, Master Zheng accompanied him in the rising heat of morning to the Mombasa dock where a ship bound for the Netherlands awaited him. Master Zheng clasped van Horn's hand warmly.

"You have been a blessing to me, Captain. I couldn't have asked for a better student. God protect and guide you. A great deal depends on your success."

Van Horn hastily wiped his eyes, surprised at how keenly he felt their parting. He remembered an old saying he had heard once on his travels. "A master can become closer than a mother and father."

"You have my deepest gratitude for all you've taught me, Master Zheng. I promise you, I will find the right man."

The captain boarded the ship, and as they made for open waters, he stood on deck until he lost sight of Master Zheng. Only then did he retire to his cabin and read over the list of royal princes the sage had given him. Of each one, van Horn would ask the fateful question. What is a man's greatest treasure: wealth, power, knowledge, or love? The answer would determine which man would receive the scrolls and their teaching.

He glanced through the names: Prince Alejandro of Spain, Prince Charles of France, Prince John of the Netherlands, Prince Edward of England, and Prince James, the Duke of Rothesay of Scotland.

Scotland. A chilly, backward land where the national pastime seemed to be fighting among themselves or betraying each other to the English. They were barely able to keep a king on the throne.

But they do play the game of golf there, he reminded himself. *Even if it's been banned by the king.* The game might exert a civilizing influence on the people. Besides, he knew a few of the Scottish noblemen through his trade and shipping connections.

Still, it was an unlikely place for the Five Scrolls to find a home. He would start with Prince Alejandro of Spain. With any luck, he wouldn't need to deal with the Scottish court.

Part One

The Five Scrolls

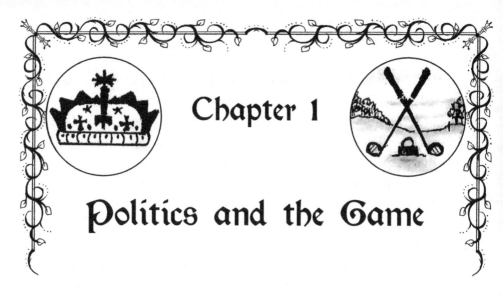

Chapter 1

Politics and the Game

Five Years Later: 1487
Mid-summer before dawn
Stirling Castle, Scotland

The stealthy rasp of a key turning in the bedchamber door brought young James Stewart sharply awake. Heart pounding, the boy slid a hand under his pillow and grasped the hilt of a dagger his weapons master, Lord Gray, had given him. Lately, dark plots and intrigues against the crown had swirled around the halls of Stirling Castle like malevolent spirits.

Had someone been sent to kill him? The words of Lord Gray rang in his ears.

"They'll come in the hours before dawn, when men sleep soundest. Let them draw close. Then be quick! You'll have only a moment to strike."

In the pre-dawn light, James could see the door open slowly and a dark figure step silent as a shadow into the room. The boy gathered himself under the blanket. At fifteen, he was tall and strong for his age and a good hand with a knife. The intruder crouched slightly and moved forward, his footsteps soundless. James's grip tightened on the dagger. Just three more steps, and the assassin would be within striking range.

Then a rough, low voice broke the silence. "If your dagger isn't pointed at me, Your Grace, I'll be insulted as your teacher."

For a moment, James was too surprised to answer. Then "Lord Gray!" He exclaimed. He flung off the covers and jumped out of bed. "Another step, and I would have stabbed you!"

Lord Gray smiled, "Good to see my training hasn't been wasted, Your Grace."

"But why steal into my room at this hour? Our lesson isn't until after sunrise."

"I've come to show you a secret that many know but few speak of. It's the reason I persuaded the king to leave you behind while he journeyed north." He held out a bundle he had been carrying, "Put on these clothes and follow me, Your Grace."

A sudden suspicion stayed the boy's hand. What if Lord Gray had been corrupted by those who plotted against the crown? After all, just a year ago, one of his father's closest allies had tried to betray the king to the English.

And before that, his father's own brothers had plotted to remove him from the throne. One of them had escaped, but the other had been executed. If blood kin could prove traitorous, why not a weapons master?

James asked, "Where are you taking me, Lord Gray? Why must I go in disguise?"

"Good," the man grunted in approval. "Wise to be cautious, Your Grace. But for now, you must trust me. Dress quickly, before the castle wakes."

James unwrapped the bundle to find commoner's clothes. He threw on the rough tunic and summer cloak and pulled on a pair of soft-soled boots that would make no sound on the castle's stone floor. He followed Gray into the corridor and saw by the dim torchlight that the man wore a short sword under his cloak and carried a walking staff in one hand.

"Lord Gray," he said quietly, "people will see I'm not at Mass in the chapel. That will raise suspicion."

"My nephew will be there, disguised as you. The old priest is so addled, he'll never notice the difference."

James grinned at the image of Father Ian addressing Gray's nephew as "Your Grace." As they moved down the corridor, the torchlight fell across the boy's face, revealing his deep-set eyes, straight nose, and broad, generous mouth—the Stewart look that already had the nobility scheming to present their daughters at court.

Among the men, he was known for his insatiable curiosity, athletic strength, and uncanny ability to learn languages. Even at fifteen, he already knew English, French, Latin, Greek, Spanish, Italian, and some Danish. It was rumored that he was learning the old tongue, Gaelic. There were those who whispered the line of Stewarts had its crowning achievement in this boy.

Lord Gray led the way toward the side entrance of Stirling Castle, one used mainly by the kitchen servants. The man was alert to every sound. When they approached the end of the corridor, he flung out an arm to stop James. An old servant carrying a basket of bread had just turned the corner toward them. James's heart dropped. The servants all knew his face, whatever clothes he might wear.

To his surprise, the servant seemed blind to the two of them and announced in a wheezy voice to the corridor at large.

"The gate's been left open . . . should anyone care to use it."

The Lord Gray grinned broadly. "Good man, Wullie. We'll be back before the bells strike ten. What about Sheriff Duncan?"

The servant moved passed them without a glance and began singing in his wheezy, reedy voice, "All the sheep are grazing in the glen, in the glen-o . . ."

James, mystified, started to ask what it all meant, but Gray raised a hand for silence. James followed him down a narrow staircase, through Wullie's gate, and out the side of the castle.

"Wullie Fraser once served my uncle," Gray explained. "He'll tell no one about you leaving the castle this way."

"But why was he singing about sheep—"

"You'll see soon enough, Your Grace."

Stirling Castle Gate

Stirling Castle

Any other questions James might have asked disappeared as he stepped into the startling beauty of the summer dawn. Rolling blue-green hills spread out below the castle's western side, their valleys silvered with mist that rose like smoke in the sun's warmth. The sheep pastures in the hills glowed brilliant yellow-gold in the first slanting rays. Two falcons circled overhead in the brightening sky, buoyed by the rising winds as they hunted. James smelled the sharp scent of cook fires and heard sheep bleating far in the distance.

The boy turned and looked back at Stirling Castle just as the rising sun struck the walls and rooftops. The castle stood above the city of Stirling like a monument of Scottish strength, having been won from the English in battle a century ago. The dawn light gilded its walls a deep gold as the king's crimson pennant fluttered in the glowing dawn. Mountains rose up in the west like ancient sentinels watching over the castle.

Not for the first time, the boy felt the bright stirring of ambition, of what it would mean to be king of this land and all it held. He would do such deeds! His only sadness was that his mother, who had died two years ago, would not see him take the throne.

"This way, Your Grace," Gray said. "Mind your step. It's a rough, twisting trail."

James followed the man into a thick wood, pushing through deep underbrush and half-tripping over rocks that turned treacherously underfoot. Twice James saw red deer bound away, startled by the sound of their approach. Ravens cawed harshly among the trees and followed them in a noisy escort overhead. Tough, bristling thistles grew in patches of sunlight. The barbed plant made a fitting symbol for the crown and country of Scotland.

Finally they emerged into a small clearing where two horses had been tied. As they left the castle farther behind them, Lord Gray seemed to relax and became more talkative.

"These are dangerous times, Your Grace. Your father seems determined to alienate even his allies. He is pushing the nobles toward civil war with every outrage he commits against them. In the coming tempest, you will need to know who are your friends and who are your foes.

"That's why I'm taking you to learn the game your grandfather and father have banned throughout the kingdom. When you ascend to the throne, you'll find it a valuable tool to have as king. On the playing field, men can speak to each other freely and, often, as equals."

The game! James felt a jolt of excitement. The boy knew that if violators of the king's ban were caught by the sheriff, they would have to pay a heavy fine or lose a prized warhorse, a bitter punishment for any nobleman or knight.

He had heard the king say many times that the game threatened Scotland's military readiness, that it "required neither strength nor skill." But James had never seen the game himself, as he had been kept close to the castle for most of his life. He had heard only that the strongest fighters in the realm were among those accused of playing. Perhaps it was a secret dueling game.

At last they reached the edge of a wide meadow. James saw three men waiting for them under a gnarled oak tree. Even from this distance he recognized them as the Earl of Montrose, the Earl of Argyll, and the knight Sir Lennox, all men loyal to the royal court. Each of them carried a walking staff like Lord Gray's.

Gray dismounted. "We'll tether the horses here, Your Grace. We can't have them trampling and fouling the course."

As they crossed the meadow, James noticed all the grass and wildflowers had been cropped close to the ground in a space the size of a goodly pasture. He recognized a sheep-grazed area when he saw it. So this was what Wullie had been singing about.

Lord Gray called out, "Good morrow, lads!"

"Good morrow!" Montrose called back. "We see you've brought our apprentice to the noble game."

As James greeted Lord Argyll and Sir Lennox, he overheard Gray murmur to Montrose, "Have you heard that the king has seized Lord Gordon's estates?"

Montrose replied as quietly, "Yes. We must discuss this outrage later with the others."

Lord Gray asked more loudly, "And where have you lads sent the king's sheriff this time?"

Argyll's grin split his bearded face. "We have him running like a witless hound, first into the arms of a buxom lass I know at the Oxhead Inn, and then to Foxfarrow Hill at dawn. I believe he's about to arrest a herd of the king's deer."

"Ah, my fondest time," Sir Lennox said, "was when he surprised Abbott MacHugh and his monks on pilgrimage to Edinburgh! The abbot made him do so much penance we didn't see his face for a month."

Montrose said to James, "Now, don't think this paltry meadow is our real course, Your Grace. With the sheriff on our heels, we have to move about. So we pay for sheep to graze only a small plot. If we want to play a real game, we have to go north out of the king's reach, or over to Flanders or the Netherlands."

Sir Lennox added, "'Tis worth the journey. The Dutch have easy courses in their flat country, and we can often win the cost of our voyage from them." He pulled out a flask of whiskey and handed it to James. "To your health, Your Grace."

The whiskey burned a pleasantly fiery path down James's throat before he passed the flask to Argyll.

Gray asked, "So when will Captain van Horn join us? He said to gather four days after Mid-summer's Eve, and unless I've missed the mark, that's today."

Argyll shook his head. "I've had no word from him. But then, the captain comes and goes like a fey spirit these days. He's been visiting the royal courts of Europe for the past few years but won't say why. So, I say we start without him and see if he appears in our path. Who has a club for our young prince here?"

James was about to ask who was Captain van Horn when Lord Gray held up what the boy had thought was his walking staff. Now he saw that the staff tapered to a strange rounded end with one flat side. Gray handed it to him.

"This, Your Grace, is called a play club, or as Captain van Horn would say, a driver."

James grasped hold of it. He could feel the weight of the rounded end. This was a club?

"How do we fight with these?" He asked.

The men smiled, and Argyll clapped him on the shoulder. "You've spirit, Your Grace! Would that your father had more of it. The rebellious barons and the English would not be so bold on our southern borders."

Gray winked at the others. "We do battle with these clubs, Your Grace, against the most cunning, formidable foe you will ever meet."

"The English?" James asked eagerly. "Or is it the Spanish?'

"Why, our very own selves," Sir Lennox replied. "And," he pointed to the meadow, "Great Nature herself. Every day she challenges us to overcome her."

"And every day you must master your own inner demons and keep a cool head," Gray said. "This game shows a man's character. That's why I want you to learn it."

James's face glowed with sudden understanding. "Golf! You're going to teach me golf. Am I right, my lords?"

Argyll laughed. "Right you are, Your Grace. And we have a bag full of weapons for this game."

Sir Lennox added, "For now, Your Grace, the one you hold will do. You'll have to learn how to wield it before you can use the others. Lord Gray, why don't you show the prince how it's done?"

Gray bowed to them. "By your leave, my lords."

He shed his cloak and pulled out from his kit objects that looked like hen's eggs. He held one up between his thick fingers.

"Wooden balls painted white to show up against the grass. We set one down on a little block, like this."

Lord Gray cleared a small space in the ground and then pushed the shaft of a small wooden block deep into the soil. The top of the block had a shallow indentation where he placed the ball. James frowned, wondering what in God's name Lord Gray was going to do next.

The man straightened and pointed to the far side of the meadow. "You see that striped stake set in the ground, Your Grace?"

"Where?" James squinted, searching the meadow's edge. "Ah, I see it now!"

"That's our target. Now let's see how close we can come to it."

Lord Gray took a step back from the wooden block, his body facing the ball and his eyes fixed on it. He grasped the club handle in a strange grip, one hand folded around the other, and touched the flat head of the club to the ball. He planted his feet and seemed to sink his weight.

Lord Gray's head moved only slightly as he swung the club up and back past his shoulder, and then with a great whipping force, swung down and through, twisting his whole body. James heard a hollow *thwock* as the club connected with the ball; it soared in a high, curving arc like a white bird flying. At that moment, without knowing why, the boy felt his heart flying after it.

"Good one, Gray!" Lord Montrose cheered.

Sir Lennox shaded his eyes. "A fine, straight shot, right at the stake."

"Your best yet," Lord Argyll said. "The young prince brings you luck!"

James stepped forward quickly. "Let me try, Lord Gray."

Gray moved aside. "Plant yourself where I stood, Your Grace, and I'll show you how to do it. It's good you're willing to learn from others, unlike your father."

Gray adjusted the boy's hands on the club handle, getting him used to the strange grip.

"Elbows straight, shoulders and hips squared, just so. Now, take a few swings—that's it, that's it. You've a natural feel for this, Your Grace. It took Lennox days to master it. He kept wielding the club like a sword!"

Lennox protested, "Not so, my lord. More like a blacksmith's hammer."

As the men laughed, Gray set another ball on the block. "Now, touch the flat part of the club to the ball, take your swing, and try to hit that ball as straight and true as you can at the stake out there."

James felt as if the club were a living thing under his hands, able to sense what he wanted. He gazed across the meadow at the striped stake set in the ground. He looked back at the ball with an image of the stake clear in his mind. Straight and true. He swung back, gathered the power in him, and released it in one fluid, downward sweep. He heard the club connect solidly. The white ball flew far down the meadow—

—and headed straight for a stranger who stepped onto the cropped grass. The man seemed to materialize out of thin air. The boy yelled, "Look out, sirrah!" and the man neatly sidestepped the ball.

"Captain van Horn!" Lord Gray shouted over the distance. "You're right on time, my friend! Come join us!"

Chapter 2

The Captain's Visit

Captain van Horn heard the warning shout and saw the ball at the same time. His sailor's reflexes saved him from a nasty bruise on the leg.

"*Door de heiligen!*" his rough voice proclaimed. "That was a fair shot—nearly half a furlough!"

The captain had traded his seafaring clothes for a suit cut in the Flemish style, with broadcloth breeches, a linen shirt, a dark felt jacket, and a felt hat decorated with gold trim. Stout walking boots came up nearly to his knees, and over one shoulder, he carried a large leather bag with several clubs.

Van Horn waved to the four men calling to him. "God save you, good sirs!" He shouted.

The captain shaded his eyes against the early morning sun and peered at the five figures standing near the oak tree. Even at this distance, he could pick out James by his slight build.

"Master Zheng," the captain mused, "this young man has virtuous strength and aim. I pray to God he will be the one we seek."

It had been nearly five years since he had embarked from Mombasa to find a worthy candidate for the Five Scrolls. One by one, the princes of Europe had proven disappointing—either too egotistical, too reckless, or too lost in worldly pleasures to provide the right answer to the question Master Zheng had given him.

This Scottish Prince James was the last name on the list. It had been a harrowing voyage to reach the Scottish shores, fighting a fierce storm at sea and dodging English pirates up the eastern coastline. If he failed here, there was nowhere else to turn.

As Van Horn drew near to the men, he studied James more closely. His hopes rose at what he saw. Although the young prince was dressed in commoner's clothes, he had an unmistakable air of royalty about him. His confident bearing and his clear, high forehead and perceptive eyes spoke of someone who faced the world as a leader, an explorer.

The captain guessed this young man would not follow a role assigned him, royal or not.

Van Horn greeted the men warmly. "God's peace be with you, my lords and Sir Lennox."

"God save you, Captain." Gray brought James forward. "And this is our Prince James Stewart, the Duke of Rothesay, heir to the throne of Scotland."

Van Horn bowed. "Your Grace, an honor to meet you."

"Welcome to our country, Captain," James said.

Gray said, "The captain has sailed most of the world's oceans, Your Grace, and traveled as far as Cathay, which some now call China."

James brightened. "I have heard of Cathay from the Venetian ambassadors in my father's court. I confess, some of their tales seem fantastical. I hope to learn the truth from you."

Their eyes met, and for a moment van Horn had the distinct impression the boy was silently weighing his character. *This young prince is older than his years. An auspicious sign.*

"I am at your service, Your Grace," van Horn said. "Cathay is the origin of our Netherlands version of the game."

He withdrew a club from his bag. "As I saw myself, Your Grace, you made a fine shot, but this club might allow you to make an even better one."

The other men drew close to examine it. James studied the rounded end and noticed at once that the flat side was angled slightly.

Van Horn pointed to the improvement. "This, gentlemen, is

based on the measurements you gave me the last time we played. See how the club face slants a bit backwards as you specified, Lord Gray? You were right on the mark. It lengthens the ball's flight by some yards."

He handed the club to James. "I invite you to test it yourself, Your Grace."

James hefted the club to get a feel for its weight and length. This club seemed to have more authority and strength than the one Gray had given him. It didn't wait to do his bidding so much as it seemed to be his partner in the game. James stepped up to the ball, swung back, and whipped the club down and through.

The ball sailed out in a high, long arc, bounced once, and rolled to a stop.

"Farther, indeed!" Gray cried.

Each took a turn with the new club, and even Sir Lennox hit the ball farther than he ever had before.

Captain van Horn clapped his hands in admiration. "Gentlemen, you have given the club its proper baptism. In my bag is one for each of you, compliments of a grateful ship captain and his Asian counselor, Master Zheng. Your Grace, the club you hold is my gift to you, made by the finest woodworker in the Netherlands."

James flushed with pleasure. "Many thanks, Captain. As a newcomer to the game, I appreciate all the help given me."

He turned to Gray. "With the king still absent for another fortnight, could we not invite Captain van Horn to stay at Stirling Castle? I'm sure he has much he could share with us."

Lord Grey grinned broadly. "Well, we should make that offer a condition of a wager! Let's challenge the captain to come within a hand's breadth of the stake."

The other three joined in. "That's a fair challenge!" "I'd wager on such a bet". "Five guineas that he falls short."

The captain bowed to them all. "I accept your challenge, gentlemen. If I lose, I'll sleep in the royal stables. Allow me the indulgence of using my own ball."

He pulled a white ball from his bag and set it on the wooden block. When he addressed the ball, club in hand, James saw a change come over him.

This was no longer the jovial captain but someone who called on a power that seemed to rise from the ground beneath his feet and course through his body into the club. The power gathered like a coiled spring as van Horn swung the club back—and then unleashed as he swung down and through.

The ball soared over the meadow and then, as if guided by an invisible hand, struck the stake and knocked it sideways.

A wild cheer went up from the men. They crowded around van Horn, vigorously shaking his hand. But James met the man's eye, and a kind of knowing seemed to pass between them, as if the captain were acknowledging in some way what James had perceived in him.

James stepped forward. "You have earned the hospitality of Stirling Castle, Captain, for as long as you wish to stay."

Van Horn bowed more solemnly than the occasion required. "I am honored by your offer, Prince James. Perhaps I can express my gratitude in a practical way."

He turned to the others. "Have you shown the prince the finer points of the short game?"

"Not yet," Argyll replied. "We'd only just begun the long drive."

Van Horn hefted the leather bag onto his shoulder. "Then if you would give me leave, my good sirs, I'll introduce the prince to the subtle art of the green."

Montrose laughed. "Your Grace, you couldn't learn the art from a better man."

Van Horn inclined his head and gestured toward the far end of the meadow. "If you will come with me, Your Grace."

James eagerly fell into step beside van Horn as they crossed the meadow toward the striped stake where five white balls lay within a circle of greener grass. He could barely make out a small hole set off-center in the circle. The boy was burning with questions for the Dutchman now that they were alone.

"Captain, what did you mean when you said that Cathay was the origin of your Netherlands game? Didn't your countrymen, like ours, invent it themselves?"

"*Zegen mij*, bless me, no, Your Grace, though there are plenty that will claim it's true. No, the fine art arose in China some five hundred years before a single club arrived in the Netherlands. It traveled along the Silk Road and various sea routes to the Italian ports. Through our commerce with Venice and Genoa, we heard of the game and picked it up. It turns out that a similar form had arisen among the Scots. The Dutch and Scots have shared the game ever since. I must say, given the war-like nature of this land, I'm surprised at how well the game has taken hold here."

James shook his head, grinning "My grandfather and father both banned it. I think that made the men take it up. We Scots can't abide being told what to do."

The captain cocked his head at the boy. "Your Grace, you've a perceptive eye for one so young, if you don't mind my saying so."

"I don't mind at all, Captain," James said steadily.

Once again, van Horn felt he was being appraised not by a boy but by someone far older in a boy's frame. With his heart beating fast, he sensed now was the time to ask the question he had posed to the other princes.

He tried to make his voice casual. "Your Grace, you've grown up in the royal court and seen all manner of things. Tell me, what do you think is a man's greatest treasure: power, wealth, knowledge, or love?"

James heard not only the question but the weight behind it. For some reason, the answer seemed to mean a great deal to this seafaring Dutchman.

"Power?" He mused. "I've grown up with men of power, not just my father the king, but every duke, earl, and baron in the middle country. They abuse it freely, warring against each other. My own father has neglected justice in his drive for power. Many now hate him as little better than a tyrant."

James glanced at the gold trim on the captain's hat. "And wealth?

Those in the noble ranks, including the Stewarts, have wealth. But too often, they can't be sure of the loyalty or love of anyone around them. I remember the Duke of Abbington, who devoted himself to acquiring lands and money but ended up alone with only his servants for company. In truth, I rarely see my own father, who is often away trying to seize more money and lands for his treasury.

"Knowledge . . . well, that's my own passion, Captain. What could be better than learning? Yet I've seen scholars at court discuss how to deceive and cheat others as coolly as they discussed matters of art and music and how to increase the yield of barley."

The captain said quietly, "Which leaves love, Your Grace."

James thought of the two secret desires that burned in his heart. One was the longing he bore for Lord Drummond's second daughter, Margaret. He had not dared speak of that desire to anyone in the court, only to Robert Hume, his closest friend.

The other longing was more difficult to put into words. It was like yearning for a home he vaguely remembered yet had never seen, one that pierced his heart whenever he thought of it. There was no word in any language he knew for what he felt. Yet this feeling drew him deeper into the world and made him believe anything was possible.

James sensed if he could solve this mystery, he would have the courage to meet every challenge in life, and even declare his love for Margaret.

He answered out of that feeling, unaware that his face seemed lit from within.

"Love must be the greatest treasure, Captain. I believe without it, power earns only hatred, and wealth buys an empty room. And knowledge . . . knowledge proves cold and heartless."

The captain challenged his answer. "But without wealth and power, Your Grace, love can wither."

James thought for a moment. "Yes," he said at last. "I suppose so. Yet I have seen wealth and power destroy people far more thoroughly. I stand by my answer."

To his surprise, the captain's eyes filled with tears; the man laid his hands on James's shoulders. "Your Grace," he said, his voice thick with emotion, "I believe you are at last the one we've been seeking."

As James stared back at him in wonderment, the captain fumbled for a handkerchief and blew his nose, rubbing it hard.

"Forgive me, Your Grace, it's been a long voyage. I shouldn't have spoken so. Come, I'll show you the short game."

He started to move on, but James stopped him. "What did you mean I'm the one you've been seeking? Seeking for what purpose, Captain?"

Van Horn said, "Later in Stirling Castle, Your Grace, I will answer all your questions. But the answers are for you alone and not for anyone else in your circle. You will understand why when you see what I have brought."

"What will I see?"

"Something that no one in the West besides myself has ever viewed. Now we must attend to the game at hand. It will aid you in what you are to hear tonight, I assure you."

James said nothing, torn between belief and disbelief. He was acquainted with charlatans at court who spun fantastic tales, but he sensed truth in the captain's voice and manner.

"I may not have a man's experience, Captain, but I will accept your word as you give it. Later, then, at Stirling Castle. Now . . . about this short game you spoke of."

Van Horn picked up one of the white wooden balls lying in the grass. "You have seen what power can do with this little object, Your Grace. Now I'll show you what subtlety can do."

The captain dropped the ball back onto the grass and pulled a club from his bag. The end of it looked more like a short, thick blade, but it was angled, like the driver. He tapped his white ball toward the hole cut into the ground. The ball curved toward the hole as if it had eyes to guide it, hesitated at the edge, and then dropped in without a sound.

The captain leaned on his club. "And that, Your Grace, is the subtlety of the short game."

Chapter 3

The First Scroll

The mid-day sun was high overhead when James and the others returned to Stirling Castle. As the only Stewart family member present, James wanted to impress the Dutch captain with the royal castle's hospitality. Lord Gray cautioned James to hold the noon meal in the royal private quarters, where the men's talk would be overheard only by trusted servants.

As they entered the room, sunlight streamed through the tall windows of the Royal Chambers and illuminated the rich banquet spread on the king's table. The castle steward had outdone himself in preparing the meal. Servants brought in a parade of breads and cheeses; roasted eel, pork, beef, and venison; boiled leeks, beans, and fine summer peas made the rounds of the table accompanied by French wines from the seaports.

The three earls feasted on one side of the table, with van Horn and Sir Lennox on the other. James sat at the table head and urged his guests to try every dish. The captain had brought small tins of tea from China that he passed around to the others. When James brought one tin up to his face, the scent of flowers bloomed in his nose.

Van Horn also astonished the men by showing how deftly he could slice meat without a knife by using a pair of eating utensils he called chopsticks. James marveled at how dexterously he could flex the two sticks to pick up any food he desired. Sir Lennox tried using the chopsticks to cut his own meat, only to send a piece of pork flying across the table to land in Lord Montrose's wine glass. The men roared with laughter.

"By the saints," Gray shouted, "a hole-in-one!"

The conversation shifted to the changes stirring on the Continent, the recent invention of a printing press in Germany, and the race among nations to find a new route to India. Some believed the world was round and the new route would be discovered by sailing west instead of east.

Argyll asserted, "The country that wins the race will rule the continent, perhaps the world whether 'tis round or flat."

Ancient Greek and Roman texts, sent from the Middle East and translated into Latin, had been stimulating new ideas in science and the arts. Montrose exclaimed, "The ancients declared that human reason can discover the laws of nature. We've some catching up to do."

James said eagerly, "Gentlemen, the next time you travel abroad, bring me copies of all the texts you come across. I wish to learn the knowledge they contain."

At the end of the meal, the servants brought in platters laden with pastries, fruits, and candies. Captain van Horn then entertained the company by telling James how golf had run afoul of the government in the Netherlands.

"We Dutch have been dabbling in the game for nearly a century, Your Grace. But the Scottish king is not the only one to ban the game. We players are required by law to keep a goodly distance from the cities."

"Why is that?" James asked, tearing a piece of bread off a loaf. "Is it interfering with the country's armies?"

"Armies? Bless me, no. Nothing of the sort." Van Horn held out his glass and a servant stepped forward to replenish his wine. "At the start, we played with a club and ball anywhere we pleased. But the game itself set us at odds with the local citizens. As you saw today, Your Grace, a good driver can send a ball at great speed and range right at a hapless passerby!"

James's face reddened. "My apologies. In truth, you seemed to spring out of the ground."

"Twas my fault entirely, Your Grace," the captain replied. "In the old days, we Dutch used to try to strike a distant target in three shots. But in the Netherland cities, passersby are everywhere. No need to aim, you'll hit one, guaranteed! And that was the problem. Hats knocked off, ladies' hairdos ambushed, horses frightened into a gallop, and, I'm afraid, a few windows broken."

The captain sipped his wine. "Well, it was all too much for the citizenry, and soon there was a clamor to throw us and our clubs into the sea. As players, we were naturally upset by this. A good club costs a great deal!"

Argyll raised his glass as the others laughed. "In our country, Captain, the king and Parliament complain that we prefer the game to military pursuits such as archery, drilling our men, and artillery practice. And if it's not treasonous to say so, by God, it's true!"

"Spoken like a patriot," Montrose agreed. "Who wouldn't prefer to play the game in the early morning mist rather than slog through marshes with sullen farmer-soldiers and fire cannon at dull-faced sheep? In contrast to these blunt endeavors, the game sharpens the wits and strengthens the character."

James turned to van Horn, remembering the new club he had shown them. "But Captain, obviously you didn't stop playing. You have craftsmen improving your game."

"You've gone straight to the mark, Your Grace. It took some time, but through skillful negotiating, we reached a compromise that more or less satisfied all sides. Golf was banned in the cities, but we were allowed to construct special courses on outlying land where we now play unhindered. And in the spirit of international relations, we invited our Scottish trading partners," he gestured at the men across the table, "such as these fine gentlemen here, to join us. They, in turn, have made our game more interesting, adding the short game with its holes that I showed you this morning."

Argyll helped himself to another pastry and said, "God's truth, the game has had unexpected benefits for both countries, Your

Grace. Many a trade agreement has been struck while players waited for a turn at the course."

Gray leaned forward. "Why, on the last trip, I obtained a merchant's assurance that he will press only one heavy hand on the scale instead of two when weighing the Flemish cloth he sells me. I, in turn, promised to put only one stone instead of five in the wool bundles I sell him!"

James joined in the laughter, but he was noticing something else as the men spoke. The four Scotsmen would ordinarily have been fighting over land boundaries, personal slights, shaky alliances, and family feuds. Yet here they were, sitting at the same table as comrades and playing off one another's memories of their time on the course.

Unity. The word came unbidden to his mind, a concept that so far had eluded Scottish lands.

James felt as if he had grown older in the span of a few hours, that he was not sitting in his father's place but forging a place of his own. Perhaps the game was a way to lead people away from the national pastime of fighting one another and toward greater union for the benefit of them all.

James saw the captain watching him carefully throughout the meal, as if studying something only he could see. The boy sensed a striking difference about this man compared with the others sitting at the table. Whereas the earls and Sir Lennox felt like tangled balls of wool to him, the captain felt like a well-ordered pattern woven into cloth. It was a difference that intrigued the boy.

"Captain van Horn, tell us something of Cathay—I mean China—and its people. I know little about them, though one trader swore to me their spices are extracted from dragon's blood."

The captain chuckled and downed his glass of wine. "You are wise to seek the truth, Your Grace. No, their spices are grown and harvested in natural ways—on trees and bushes. No blood is involved, except that shed by traders who brave desert bandits on the Silk Road or the many pirates at sea."

James leaned forward. "And what of the story of golf in China? That seems a good tale to know. Was it a gift from their gods?"

The captain put down his chopsticks together and placed them across his plate. His reddish face was bright with humor. "Alas, the game's true origins are lost in antiquity, so we will never know if the gods were involved."

Van Horn gestured for more wine. "My own mentor, Master Zheng, tells me the Chinese have a mortal record of the game in a book called *DongXuani*. It was written during the Song Dynasty, about four centuries ago as calculated by their sages. This volume describes a game called *chuiwan*."

"*Chwee wan*," James repeated, savoring the sounds on his tongue. He imitated the words' rising and falling tones, something he had never heard in all the languages he had learned.

"Excellent, Prince James," van Horn said. Again, James felt the man's penetrating gaze. "*Chuiwan. Chui* means 'to hit' and *wan* means 'ball.' The game was played with different clubs inlaid with jewels, jade, and ivory. One club had a flat side and was called *cuanbang*, what we term a 'driver.' Another club was called *shaobang* and was used to hit the ball shorter distances. The book even tells of a nobleman's daughter digging a hole in the ground for him to hit a ball into. It was a game only the emperor and his nobles could play."

Montrose laughed and nodded at Sir Lennox. "While we let any whey-faced dragoon who can wield a club into our company!"

James waited for the men to grow quiet again and then asked, "But tell me this, has the game improved their rulers? Has it tempered them in any way toward the people?"

A moment of silence greeted his questions. James was surprised to find everyone, not just the captain, staring at him. He didn't know quite how to interpret their silence.

"What I mean is, a king ought to serve as well as rule, don't you think? He has to use power, that's certain, rising above those who would threaten the crown and the kingdom. But he must also use subtlety, I think, having regard for the nature and benefit of his people. When I am king," he added decisively, "I will see to it!"

The weighty silence continued. He saw the men exchanging glances among themselves and felt his face getting hot. He became acutely aware that he must have sounded like a bragging boy.

Finally Gray said, as if speaking for them all, "When you are king, Your Grace, you can count on us to support such a rule."

Something told James the gathering was best ended on that note. Any more of this talk, and it would feel he was speaking near-treason against his own father. James stood up, indicating the banquet was over.

"Your health, gentlemen. May God watch over and protect you. My thanks for a memorable time."

Argyll bowed to James and to the Dutchman. "Captain van Horn, we shall inform you of where we next play. Our thanks for your generous gift."

The four Scotsmen bid James and his visitor farewell. Captain van Horn was making rather a business of drinking the last of his wine, finishing his dessert, and collecting his small tins of tea. By the time he was done, even the servants had gone, and he was alone with James.

The boy gestured toward the door. "If you wish, we can continue our conversation in my private chambers."

The captain smiled. "Your Grace, I think you will find what I have to say worth the wait. Also, begging your pardon, I've taken the liberty of having a certain small chest delivered to your bedchamber."

James eyed the captain but said nothing. This man was full of surprises.

The small chest, as promised, was waiting for them on a side table as they entered James's rooms. The slanting sunlight from the window shone on the chest's reddish wood and ornately painted panels. James knelt down to examine it more closely.

"Captain," James said, "is this what you have been carrying for so long?"

"Yes. It contains a treasure that is centuries old, Your Grace. With the exception of myself, you are the first European to see it."

The captain took out a key from his waistcoat pocket, inserted it carefully into the lock. James heard the dry click as the lock yielded. Van Horn slowly lifted the lid, and the scent of aromatic cedar filled James' nostrils, evoking images of a desert land in his mind.

James's throat went dry with excitement. Perhaps the chest contained a rare jewel from the Orient, an exquisite ivory carving, or an elixir of life.

Instead, five plain parchment scrolls, tied with silk ribbons, lay on a gold silk lining inside the chest. James glanced at van Horn, half hoping that the scrolls hid something more impressive.

But the man was gazing at them with a mixture of awe and reverence. "These Five Scrolls represent a hidden wisdom passed on through Master Zheng. I was sent to find the one person in the Western countries who could receive the scrolls."

James turned to the captain. "That's why you asked me that question when we were alone in the meadow."

"Indeed, Your Grace. And you answered as we had hoped."

Van Horn carefully lifted out the first scroll from the chest. "The scrolls have been translated from the ancient tongue of Aramaic, the language of Palestine, into Latin, the Western scholars' language."

He paused. "Read this carefully, Prince James. It is important that you grasp not only the words but what lies behind them. When knowledge of this scroll is part of you, then you can move on to the next one. Think on what I told you this morning about the long and short game, Your Grace, and what you yourself said about being king. Power and subtlety may seem to be contradictory qualities, yet they complement one another."

The captain held out the scroll to James, who took it with slightly shaking hands. The boy pulled the ribbon and carefully unrolled the parchment. He bent his head and began to read.

THE FIRST SCROLL: The Soul and Divine Love

The Soul descends from Divine Love,
Dwells within our Earthly body, and fills it with light.

But as we embark on this Earthly life,
The Great Forgetting begins,
And the Soul's light dims.
We become lost in desires, trapped in fear and anger,
Waging endless war with ourselves and others.

Yet the Soul is never lost.
When you remember who you are,
All wars cease, and the Soul's light of peace
Is radiant within you.

You are a Soul filled with the love of the Creator.
Through you, Divine Love dwells on Earth.

I will remember who I am. Where I come from. Where I will return.
I will express Divine Love in all I do.

James felt his body growing hot and then cold as he read. Part of him understood not only what the scroll was saying but something more than the words could express. This explained that longing for home he had felt, and his depth of feeling for the world, as if it were a veil hiding something more real. Those moments, he knew now, were meant to awaken the memory of the Soul within him.

James had no sense of how long he had been reading, yet he had never felt so clear and alive. When he looked up, the captain met his gaze and smiled knowingly. "Does it ring true?"

"Aye, that it does," James said, his voice husky. "More than anything ever in my life."

"Keep this knowledge to yourself for now until it has set deeply within you. You might think of it as a seed that's been planted and must be protected and nurtured until it can withstand the harsh elements of nature."

James said, "But I have many questions. What does it mean to 'express Divine Love in all that I do'?"

The captain laughed softly. "We will talk about that later. For now, Your Grace, simply read this scroll until you have memorized it. Let it sink deep into your mind and heart."

James said on impulse, "When I am king, I want you to come live with me at Stirling Castle. And I will invite your tutor Master Zheng to come as well. He seems like someone whose knowledge could never be exhausted."

The captain bowed. "I am honored, Your Grace. I will stay for another a day or two." His eyes glinted with humor. "After all, we have work to do on that short game of yours. But I am afraid it is not yet destined for me to live at Stirling, much as I would wish it."

James felt a stab of disappointment. Then he asked, "Is it destined for me to become king?"

"Oh, yes," the captain said. "You will be king."

Before James could ask more, van Horn said, "I must take my leave of you now, Your Grace. There are several nobles I must visit while I am here. Lord Gray will call on you again early tomorrow morning, and I will meet you with the others on the course. In the meantime, make sure no one sees this scroll. No one, Your Grace. I will take it with me when I leave for the Continent in a few days."

"But what about the other scrolls?" James asked. "May I not read them as well?"

The captain locked the cedar chest once again and picked it up. "In time, Your Grace, you will read them all, I assure you."

A sudden affection for the Dutchman flooded James's heart. "What can I say, Captain? My thanks are too poor for the gift you have offered me."

Van Horn replied gently, "Read . . . and remember who you are, Prince James. That is thanks enough for me."

Chapter 4

Margaret and the Crown

The next morning, James was dressed and ready before Lord Gray arrived at his door. Once again, they passed Wullie in the corridor, who sang in his wheezy voice, "the sheep are a'grazing in the hills, the westerly hills-o . . . " to let Gray know where they should meet the others and the captain.

James took advantage of the ride to ask about van Horn. "How long have you known the man, Lord Gray? And why have I never seen him in my father's court?"

"I met van Horn, well, it must be eight years ago. He is one of a handful of Dutchmen sailing under the Portuguese flag. If a seafaring man wants adventure, Portugal is the place to go. Their empire is expanding into Africa and the Far East, and they look to find a new route to India by sailing west."

Gray's face darkened. "As to why you haven't seen him in your father's court, well, it's doubtful such a man would be welcome. He's helped make a few of us nobles and barons a little richer in the purse, something your father wouldn't approve of. And he brings knowledge of the world with him. Again, something your father wouldn't approve of."

James said nothing. The anger in Gray's voice reflected the boy's own frustration. Gray ducked under a low-hanging branch and turned his horse toward an open field at the edge of the woods.

His voice was calm again when he spoke. "I've heard it said that van Horn was a hard-living man until he met a Chinese master, this Master Zheng, in Mombasa. After that, he changed."

James pushed another branch aside. "Changed . . . in what way?"

"It's hard to explain. More disciplined, I'd say, more . . . master of himself. There was always a fire in him, but now it seems he's learned how to use it."

James asked, "Can I trust him, Lord Gray? Can I believe what he tells me?"

"Believe him? Yes, Your Grace, and more . . ." Gray studied James for a moment. "You can trust him with your life."

When they joined the others, James noticed this time the nobles and Sir Lennox stepped back to let the captain teach him. James was glad, for yesterday he had memorized the first scroll, and it had left him with vexing questions. He had the odd sense of being more at home and yet more isolated than he had ever felt. The paradox left him suspended between his life before the captain's arrival and his life now.

He was about to ask his first question when the captain asked him one instead, "Tell me, Your Grace, which way is the wind blowing?"

James hesitated. What was the man up to now? He decided to play along and studied the trees swaying around the course, their leaves bending in only one direction.

"The wind's from the southwest, Captain."

"And the temperature of the day?"

The boy was sweating lightly, even in the early morning. "Warmer than usual, with moist air."

"And the grass before us, what condition is it in?"

James looked out over the course. It sparkled in the sun's slanted rays. "Soaked with dew, but perhaps the wind and heat will dry it soon."

"Rightly noted!" the captain said, pleased. "All these things will influence the ball's flight and its movement on the ground, Your Grace. You need to know the conditions that Nature provides and adjust your play accordingly. Let's see what you can do."

James approached the ball and gauged the direction and force of the wind. If he hit the ball high and straight for the marker at the far end of the course, the wind would carry the ball to the right. If he hit it lower and slightly to the left, the wind would likely push the ball toward the center of the field. A wet ball would travel more slowly over the grass, so it might end up farther from the green.

The captain, behind him, said quietly, "See the shot with your inner eye, Your Grace. Then let the ball follow that path."

James touched his club head to the ball and imagined, as clearly as if he had hit it, the white sphere flying in a low-curving arc and the wind pushing it where he wanted it to go.

He swung up and back and whipped through the swing, ending with his body turned and his right leg anchored only by the toe of his boot. The ball, as if predestined in its flight, followed his imagined arc over the course until it struck the ground and rolled onto the green.

"Excellent, Prince James," the captain said.

Sir Lennox shouted, "A true shot, laddie—pardon, Your Grace! Couldn't have done better myself."

Montrose, Argyll, and Gray began betting among themselves who could match or better the drive.

"Gentlemen," the captain interrupted. "I ask your indulgence. Allow the prince and myself to finish the play before you take your turns. I wish to show him a few more tricks of the game."

"Sail on, Captain," Gray said. "We need to hatch a plan to distract the sheriff tomorrow morning. The wool-headed, dung-filled scone is beginning to see through our ploys. We have to be more devious now."

The captain shouldered his bag and gestured toward the green. "If you please, Your Grace."

James set out with him across the meadow, where the rising

sun cast their long, thin shadows over the grass. He smelled the sweet scent of clover on the wind and heard sheep bleating close by, perhaps the flock that had grazed their course. Now was the time to start asking his questions.

"Captain, if the game is rooted in Earthly life, how does it help us remember who we are?"

"Admirable question, Your Grace. Think back on what we just did. Do you not see a wider principle at work?"

James reflected on the qualities of nature the captain had made him notice. The wider principle seemed to be about shifting his focus from a narrow task to the wider conditions around him and then adjusting his actions. But a good farmer or shepherd did the same thing, marking the wind, the conditions of the fields, the tracks of predators who might threaten livestock. This principle didn't seem related to the Soul.

James felt a mounting frustration. What exactly did the captain want him to see?

Van Horn gazed ahead of them, where James's ball stood out against the green.

"Ah! Your lay is fortunate, young prince," he said.

James started to speak, but the captain held up his hand. "Now, before you ask me any more questions, I challenge you to sink that ball in one stroke. Surely," he said, with an odd emphasis to his words, "a Stewart prince can do this one small task."

The captain handed James the second club for the short game. James studied the lie of the green. The grass was still wet, and the green slanted both uphill and to the left from where his ball lay. But farther out, the green slanted to the right and slightly downhill to the hole.

The complexities of the shot began to multiply in his head. How could he sink the ball in one stroke? It would take a miracle of skill. His hands were sweating on the club shaft, making it hard to get a good grip. What did the captain mean by saying, "Surely, a Stewart prince can do this one small task."

The words now sounded mocking. Anger burned inside James, his Stewart pride pricked by fear of making a fool of himself. Perhaps the captain was having fun at his expense. He suddenly wanted to strike the ball and send it flying into the woods and then send the Dutchman packing.

At that moment, the words came to him *"trapped in fear and anger, waging endless war with ourselves and others . . ."*

Appalled, James straightened and looked over at van Horn. The man smiled slowly, the expression on his face one of deep understanding. It was clear he knew what James was feeling.

Without a word, the boy turned back to his task.

I will remember who I am.

Anger and fear faded. James looked at the green with a wider, clearer vision. Near the center was a smooth, relatively flat section he hadn't seen before. If he could hit the ball there, he would have a clear shot at the hole. It would be two strokes, not one, but James sensed that the captain's challenge had never been about numbers.

James swung the club back a foot or two and struck the ball with just enough force to send it uphill. It reached the level area, slowed, and stopped. He walked in silence up to the ball, aware the captain was watching him as he lined up the next shot.

A path seemed to appear in the grass leading from where he stood to the hole. He lined up the club and gently struck his ball. It rolled slowly along the path until it reached the very edge of the hole and then stopped.

James and the captain gazed at one another, a quiet understanding flowing between them.

James said, "The game helps us remember who we are by showing what happens when we forget."

Van Horn walked over to the ball and tapped it lightly into the hole. "Well played, young prince," was all he said.

Fourteen-year-old Margaret Drummond leaned out the Drummond Castle window, waiting to catch sight of the first carriages coming to attend a feast her father was giving later that day. The bright sun highlighted Margaret's fair skin and high cheekbones, her green eyes, and dark brown hair that curled around her shoulders and cascaded down her back. In this unguarded moment, her face seemed childlike and full of wonder.

Then the sound of carriage wheels caught her attention, and her features sharpened in dismay.

"It's Lord Haile and Lord Angus—enemies of James the Third!" she called back to her two sisters in the bedchamber. Her older sister, Euphemia, was choosing which necklace Margaret should wear to the feast. Since their mother's death, she often helped her sisters dress for formal occasions. Her younger sister, Sibylla, was trying to decide between a blue or white gown for herself.

Margaret demanded, "Why would Father invite these men to dine with us when Prince James will be here?"

Euphemia replied sharply, "Father doesn't need your approval for his guest list."

"Lady Margaret, please come sit down," her lady in waiting, Lena, begged. "I have to braid your hair, and you've yet to choose your gown for the feast."

Another maid showed Euphemia a pearled necklace, but she waved it aside and pointed to a single emerald necklace for Margaret instead.

She said, "Prince James is too young to worry about who is for or against his father. Lord Fleming says that he is frivolous and spoiled and thinks only of his own pleasure—"

"He is none of those things!" Margaret snapped, her eyes bright with anger. "He is generous, quick-witted, and genuinely pious! And he has more sense than Lord Fleming ever will!"

Euphemia's mouth thinned in anger. "I am weary of you insulting my husband, Margaret. I will talk with you later when you are more civil."

As she left the room, Margaret leapt down from the window seat and shouted after her, "And I will talk to you when your husband is a better man!"

"Margaret, Father will hear you!" Sibylla warned.

Margaret settled into her chair before the dresser mirror, her arms folded tightly across her chest.

"Let Father hear us," she said. "Lord Fleming is too cunning by far, and you know it, Sibylla. There is a worm of ambition eating at his heart."

"Yes, but there's no need to fight with Euphemia."

Margaret's face softened. Her sister's gentleness reminded her painfully that before Lord Fleming, she and Euphemia had been close as sisters.

Margaret studied her reflection in the mirror as her lady-in-waiting, Lena, fastened the single emerald with its gold chain around her neck. She had often used her youth and gender to camouflage her fascination with the game of politics played by her father and the other noblemen. When the nobles visited Drummond Castle, she moved her needlework frame to a room nearby and listened carefully. Who would notice a girl working on her needlework?

Now she sensed that her father and the men he had invited were planning something that centered on James. It made her fearful for the prince.

"Margaret," Sibylla said, smiling, "I know which gown you will wear." She held up a green velvet dress with gold cord decorating the sleeves and neckline. It was one of three gowns on the bed.

"And how do you know this?"

"Because Prince James said green was his favorite color."

Margaret's face flamed bright red as the other women laughed.

"Aye, sister, 'tis true enough," she admitted. She pointed to Sibylla's blue gown. "But his good friend Robert Hume favors blue."

Sibylla reddened as well, but her voice held a trace of sadness. "I wear the color for him, even if he still travels with the king. You are lucky to have James here."

Margaret said darkly, "You should tell Robert to stay away from the king's company."

"Why?" Sibylla asked. "Do you think Robert's in danger?"

"My lady," Lena pleaded with Margaret. "Please be still so I can finish."

Margaret faced forward again, enduring Lena's hands braiding her long hair. "Yes, I fear for those close to the king. Resentment against him grows stronger every day. I hear the nobles talk of little else but their anger at his rule. And one day it may spur them to action."

Lena wound a gold ribbon through her braid. With her hair up, Margaret looked older, like Euphemia. Right now, she felt like the oldest one in the family, including her father.

Things would be different if their mother were still alive. She had a shrewd mind that could see through the deceptions and flattery of the nobles. But she had died shortly after arranging Euphemia's wedding, and her absence still weighed on the three sisters.

Margaret said slowly, "Sibylla, I think of Mother at times like this. Don't you feel her hovering close to us? It makes me wonder if there is not more to our Earthly life than what we can see or hear or touch."

"There is Purgatory," Sibylla said, "and the heavenly realms—"

"That isn't what I mean. Don't you think there is another world behind this one? I see it as a place familiar and wondrous and close."

"No." Sibylla smiled at her. "You think of the strangest things, Margaret. As if you're dreaming while awake."

Yes, Margaret thought, *but which part of it is the dream?*

When James saw the invitation to the feast at Drummond Castle, he exclaimed to the captain: "You'll come, of course! It says here that Lord Drummond has assembled the local noblemen and some of the most learned men in the region—plus the finest musicians. And you will meet his three eldest daughters, who are considered among the most beautiful women in our country."

James felt his face get hot as he said this.

"How can I resist such an offer?" van Horn said. "I would be honored to accompany you."

James busied himself finding the right clothes to wear and kept asking his valet to fetch him another tunic, a different doublet, a better set of shoes, worried he would disappoint Margaret. With all the people at the feast, he would be able to talk with her openly, something he could rarely do as a royal prince.

Finally, in desperation, he asked the captain for his opinion. The man did his best to keep a straight face, seeing how anxious James was, and declared of the boy's latest attire, "Your Grace, a royal prince of China could not look any more elegant."

Only then did James agree to start for Drummond.

By the time they reached the castle, most of the guests had already arrived. The dining hall had been lavishly decorated for the occasion. Woven tapestries depicting scenes of Scottish folklore and history decorated either side of the room. The banquet table shone with the castle's china and crystal, a reflection of the glittering nobility who gathered around the table.

Then James caught sight of the Earl of Angus, leader of the Douglass clan, and Lord Haile. He frowned. These noblemen had been urging greater union with England and were strong critics of his father, the king.

At that moment, the captain leaned forward and murmured in James's ear, "Tell me, Your Grace, which way is the wind blowing?"

James glanced sharply at the man, and then sudden understanding blossomed in him. When he turned back to the gathered company, his vision seemed to have altered, as if he were looking at the group from above.

The group itself seemed to have altered as well. The men appeared to be bound by lines of force into alliances that could be seen only with his inner vision. Lord Gray, to his surprise, was allied with Haile and Angus, while the earls of Montrose and Argyll, along with lords Crichton and Lyle, stood apart from them.

The knights were allied with their lords, but Lord Drummond seemed to have alliances with both sides. The lines of force radiated from him in both directions.

James gazed in wonder. Was this inner perception a quality of the Soul? Perhaps it was the "wider principle" the Captain had urged him to grasp—to see what was visible only to the awakened eye.

And then his eye fell on Margaret.

She hadn't seen him yet; her attention was turned on her two sisters. They were laughing at something Margaret had said. She looked up at that moment, and her face glowed with pleasure when she saw him. His heart stirred at the smile that lit her face, at the way her dark brown hair, bound up in a gold ribbon, caught the light, and at the forest green of her dress. She had never looked so beautiful.

Lord Drummond came striding toward them with a broad smile of welcome. He had always voiced strong support for the Stewarts, eager to see his daughters accepted into the royal circle. He had not encouraged the bond between James and Margaret, but he had not interfered with it either. The family already boasted two queens of Scotland in their line.

Drummond bowed first to James and then to the captain. "Welcome to Drummond Castle, Your Grace, Captain van Horn. We are honored to have you attend."

James said, "Lord Drummond, I would like my guest to have the pleasure of meeting your daughters. Captain van Horn should know the flower of Scotland before he departs on the morrow. Surely you can arrange to seat us beside them."

Lord Drummond beamed. "Of course, Your Grace. I'll see to it. Follow me."

A few quietly spoken words to the servants, a rearranging of chairs, and Captain van Horn ended up between Euphemia and Sibylla. The younger sister turned to James as he sat down. "And how is your friend Robert Hume, Your Grace? Is he well"

"Aye, that he is. And I'm sure he is sorry to miss this banquet."

The captain, seeing that James was chafing to talk with Margaret, kindly intervened. "If I may offer my poor self as substitute, Lady Sibylla, I have something from the exotic East that may delight you and the rest of the company gathered here."

The captain produced a flowing, embroidered silk jacket from his rucksack. He created a small sensation around the table as he donned the garment with a flourish. The green silk cloth was festooned with red poppies between black and white cranes, whose eyes were of red coral and wings tipped with gold.

The captain announced, "My lords, items like these from exotic Cathay are all the fashion in Venice. Every family of nobility pays a small fortune for such luxury. But this is more than an elegant garment. Observe!"

He astonished the group by whipping his arms about so rapidly the silk sleeves made a thunderous sound like great wings beating. As the cloth flashed, the cranes on his jacket seemed to take flight.

Margaret watched in admiration, then turned to James, her green eyes bright with humor. "Can you match his skill, Your Grace?"

James smiled at her boldness, one of the qualities that had attracted him from the start. They had known each other all their lives, and she had never been intimidated by his standing as crown prince.

James glanced down at his velvet sleeves and moved his arms rapidly as the captain had done. The purple cloth merely stretched a bit. "I'm afraid not. But I do have a skill with languages."

"And what can you say in them," she asked, "that I might want to hear?"

"Well, I might say in Gaelic, *a ghrá geal or a chuisle mo chroí.*"

"What would be the meaning?"

"Something best expressed in private," he said, and was pleased to see her blush. It wasn't often he could catch her off guard.

Margaret then raised her wine glass to her mouth and said so softly that only James could hear, "You were invited here for a reason, James. Be careful who you trust."

James smiled and reached for the bread in front of her, speaking as softly. "Why are the king's enemies at this table?"

Margaret whispered, "They want something from you. My father plays both sides, for and against the king. He thinks I don't see it."

Before James could reply, the Earl of Angus called out, "Your Grace, how goes the king's journey north? I hear he is visiting several clan territories as well as towns."

James nodded. "I received a letter from him a fortnight ago. The journey goes well, although not all the nobles are welcoming. The power of the crown is something they resist."

Angus cocked his head at this and glanced at Argyll and Montrose before answering. "Begging your pardon, Your Grace, but if the king would attend more to the needs of his people, perhaps the nobles would have more respect for the power of the crown."

There was a muttering of approval around the table at this, although Montrose, Argyll, and Crichton glared at Angus.

James felt his Stewart temper rising but kept a tight rein on it. "What needs do you refer to, Lord Angus?"

Angus leaned forward. "The need for justice is one, Your Grace. Every petty laird and nobleman can set up his own court and make his own laws. For stealing a loaf of bread, a man might get a simple fine in one place. In another, his son is taken in servitude or the man is jailed. The crown could put an end to such inequity by instituting laws of the land."

It was a point James had argued hotly with his father many times. In his travels with the king over the years, James had seen for himself the injustices Angus spoke about. If his father could change it, why didn't he?

His feeling toward the man softened. "You are correct, Lord Angus. It is something I will attend to when I am king. The people must believe the law is motivated by fairness, not by whims. Injustice breeds many ills."

Angus smiled and leaned back in his chair. James noticed that even Montrose and Argyll nodded at the earl, and the feeling around the table seemed to become more harmonious.

James asked, "What other needs of the people do you see being neglected, Lord Angus?" He looked around the table. "Or do any of you see?"

The men glanced at each other, as if inviting their companions to speak. Then the Earl of Haile said, "The king also neglects the expertise and wisdom of the noblemen close to him, Your Grace. He listens more to the commoners he's gathered, such as his groomsman, than to his advisers and counselors. How can we influence the affairs of state if we have no influence with the king?"

The man spoke the truth. Even James had seen his father consult more with his groomsman about foreign matters than with Lord Angus, who was an accomplished statesman. James paused before answering, trying to assess the purpose behind this thread of conversation. With these men, there was always a hidden motive.

Remember who you are, the words whispered in his mind.

He said at last, "A king should make use of his wisest counselors, which are usually the most learned and experienced men of the country." He turned toward Angus. "Although, my lord, I should warn you I would not hesitate to take the advice of my groomsman," he smiled at Angus's dark look, "regarding my horse."

Laughter rippled around the table, and Lord Gray raised his wine glass in salute. "Well played, Your Grace."

He felt Margaret press her foot against his but resisted the urge to respond. Instead, he gazed thoughtfully at the group. Was this what they wanted from him—to know what kind of king he would be? Why? He was only sixteen and his father would likely rule for many more years. Or were they already seeking to influence him as they could not influence his father?

The captain's warning came to mind. *Which way is the wind*

blowing? He focused inward and shifted his vision again briefly. The lines of alliance had brightened, but he was surprised to see the focal point was now himself. Yet he could also sense a dark undercurrent flowing through those lines.

Then Haile's voice intruded on his thoughts. "Your Grace, I hear that the king has taken your two younger brothers to Scone to see the ancient site of Scottish coronations."

James felt a stab of jealousy. The king had never taken him to Scone, where the Stone of Destiny had once been set before it had been stolen by the English two centuries ago. Why did his father grant his brothers this favor?

"Indeed," Lord Angus added, "it's said he favors your youngest brother, which is another mark against him. You are by far the most accomplished son, Your Grace."

Lord Drummond said, "I observed the same inclination last Candlemas, Prince James, but didn't wish to speak of it. The king gave your brother the highest place at the table and left you in his shadow!" Drummond stuck the table with his fist. "An injustice, Your Grace! One that made those who support you burn with indignation. You would think he was grooming the least able son to be king."

These words played on James's deepest fear—that one day, in the heat of their arguments, his father would disinherit him and make one of his brothers king. Was taking them to Scone a first step in that direction? Perhaps that was why the king had agreed so readily with Lord Gray to leave him behind for this journey. James vowed that when the time came, he would be crowned at Scone and nowhere else.

After all, hadn't the captain said he was destined to be king?

His hand curled into a fist as he said hotly, "My father now scorns knowledge and feels no need to learn the languages of Europe. Yet what better monarch can a country have than one who is highly educated?" He was nearly shouting now. "My father may have shown my brothers Scone, but they will see it only as princes, *while I will see it as a king!*"

To his surprise, the company rose to their feet and shouted their approval. Only then did James realize he was standing. Their massed support was like a fire feeding his ambition, and for a moment, he tasted the power of the crown.

He avoided looking at the captain. *We wage endless warfare . . .* Right now he wanted war to wipe out the anger and hurt that burned in him. Then Margaret gently pulled his arm. At her touch, his anger banked and cooled. He sat down again, and the company sat down as well, the men talking excitedly among themselves. James no longer cared—he was lost in Margaret's lovely eyes.

She said quietly, "You showed them what they wanted, James. Is it what you want as well?"

"To be king? Yes . . . above all else."

"Many of the nobles here want you to marry an English princess and not a Scottish lady. What if that's the price of their support, James? What will you do then?"

He leaned toward her and spoke from his heart. "I will be myself, a *chuisle mo chroí.*"

"Don't mock me," she whispered. "What does that mean?"

He covered her hand with his. "It means you are the pulse of my heart."

It was the second time he had made her blush. "This could be dangerous, James. Some of the nobles at this table will never accept the daughter of a Scottish earl as queen."

She was right. Ever since his birth, a faction of Scottish nobility, including his father, had tried to wed him to an English princess for their own political ends.

James tightened his grip on her hand. "Never worry about that. When I am king, they will accept whatever queen I choose."

Across the table, the captain gazed at the two of them with grave concern. *Tread carefully, James. There is treachery here.*

Chapter 5

The Second Scroll

James hoped the captain would overlook his outburst of anger and jealousy.

That hope lasted until the two of them climbed into the royal carriage for the ride back to Stirling Castle. One moment the captain was smiling and waving at the noblemen as James said a reluctant farewell to Margaret. The next moment, James was startled to find the captain staring at him with the grim expression of a judge.

The man leaned forward, but instead of delivering a reprimand, as James expected, he said urgently, "There is much I must tell you before I leave, Your Grace. It's clear that a storm of rebellion is brewing in Scotland. What I heard tonight confirms it. Some of the nobles even infected you with their anger."

James squirmed at the memory but did not back down. "I will not endure my brother being put on the throne, Captain. I will not!"

The captain said dryly, "Fortunate for us, then, that Lady Margaret was on hand to call you back to yourself. She has a calming way about her, don't you think?"

At this James fell silent. Her touch had done more than calm his anger. For a brief moment, he had realized how the nobles had played on his feelings about his father and brothers. His ambition had quickly swept that realization aside, but now the cheering of the men at his words seemed hollow and contrived. They had manipulated him like a witless schoolboy.

James threw aside his traveling cloak in frustration. "How can I remember who I am if I'm blinded by what I feel? Margaret will not always be there to calm my passions. If we are the Soul, as the first scroll says, then why is it so hard to remember that? Every passing desire sweeps it aside!"

The captain's gaze softened. "I know it's hard, Your Grace, but you are not alone on this path. I believe you have the depth of character and judgment to succeed—and if Master Zheng knew you, he would feel the same, I'm sure."

James crossed his arms and stared out the carriage window. Resentment burned inside him. First the captain and this mysterious Master Zheng give him an impossible task, and then they assure him he can do it—all without telling him how! This business with the scrolls was beginning to feel more frustrating with every word, like a trick puzzle with no solution.

The captain spoke to the boy's stubbornness. "You have experienced the pain of forgetting who you are, Your Grace. But tell me this: What happens when you remember, as you did earlier today?"

The question caught James by surprise. He looked hard at van Horn but could detect no judgment or mockery in the man's face. Chagrined, James tried to recall as clearly as possible what had happened on the green.

"I . . . I felt strangely at peace. I could see the shape of the green and knew exactly where to hit the ball. On the second shot . . . a path seemed to appear in the grass, and I merely hit the ball to follow it."

"And how did you know these things?"

James shook his head. "I'm not sure, Captain. The knowledge just seemed to be there."

The words of the first scroll came back to him with new meaning.

When you remember who you are,
All wars cease, and the Soul's light of peace
Is radiant within you.

He looked at van Horn in silence. The man smiled slowly, a warm light in his eyes.

"I do believe you are ready for the second scroll, Your Grace. We will need a secure place to speak."

"At this hour, that would be Stirling Chapel, Captain. No one will disturb us there."

Van Horn helped James light the rows of candles in the small chapel, whose stone walls and thick oaken door would be proof against royal spies and overly curious servants. James knew no one would attend the chapel until the midnight Mass. The old priest, Father Ian, might even sleep through until morning, as he had done on more than one occasion.

Wullie sat watch in the corridor outside, pressed into service as their guard. The old servant wheezed, "I'll sing 'Our Lord Comes' should anyone appear, Your Grace."

James suppressed a smile. "Good man, Wullie." He closed the door and threw the bolt in place.

In the silence, James could feel the weight of decades of prayers and supplication for the Stewart family in the chapel around them. Here was a fitting place to learn of unearthly matters. The captain set the small chest carefully on the altar. In the flickering candlelight, it seemed to glow with a light of its own.

Van Horn seated himself on one of the wooden pews and gestured for James to join him. "Before I give you the second scroll to read, Your Grace, perhaps there are a few questions you'd like to ask me."

A torrent of words burst from James. "If we are the Soul, why do we need a body? What is this Earthly life for? And why—*why* is it so easy to forget who we really are? It causes so much suffering and pain!"

Van Horn raised his arm as a shield and half-joked, "Have mercy on an old seaman, Your Grace!"

"But I want to know! How else am I going to do as you ask?"

"Sit down. Sit down, James," the captain said. "That's it. Now, I will do my best to answer you. What do you desire to know first?"

"The Soul—what is it exactly?"

"Hmmm." Van Horn closed his eyes and pinched the bridge of his nose briefly, then blinked to clear his vision. He could feel the passionate, inquisitive mind behind James's dark eyes. *The boy will not be put off by easy words or simple descriptions. Master Zheng, how do I explain the ineffable to him?*

"You want to know exactly, eh? I must tell you, this was the first question I asked Master Zheng when I read the scrolls myself."

"What did he tell you?"

"Let me answer this way, Your Grace. Do you think all people fear death?"

James blinked at the question. "I—I suppose so. From what I have seen, it is the one fear everyone shares."

"It is natural to do so. But the fear exists only while you are on Earth. It does not extend to the Soul or the realm of Divine Love."

He sighed and shook his head, muttering, "How can I help you grasp this?"

The captain began again, speaking carefully. "Once you leave this Earthly life, you cross a kind of threshold, and all fear drops away. Someone will meet you—either those who have gone before you or others who serve as guides. You enter a realm of infinite compassion and peace. I cannot say how, but you know beyond any doubt that you have existed forever and are cherished beyond imagining."

James gazed at the captain in awe. The man's face seemed to reflect the realm he spoke of.

"You have seen this place?" James whispered.

"Yes, I have seen it. Master Zheng showed me long ago."

"Can . . . can you show me as well?"

The captain shook his head. "Your mind is not ready yet, James," he said quietly. "It would overwhelm you--like taking a man from deepest darkness into blinding light. I barely endured the sight myself, and I had a year or two of preparation."

"Then why do we have to leave this wondrous place and come to

Earth? Why take on a body that suffers disease, old age, and death? Look at Wullie. The poor man can scarcely speak without wheezing like a bellows."

Van Horn threw one arm over the back of the pew and regarded James steadily. "Once again, you've gone straight to the heart of the matter. I asked Master Zheng this as well. In fact, I have asked this question of every sage, magus, and spiritual master I've encountered in my life."

James could feel his heart beating fast. To know this mystery! "And what do they say?"

"That our Earthly life is part of a great cycle of Creation. The Soul descends from this wondrous realm and takes on a body the way a caterpillar takes on a cocoon. The body is a place where the Soul can emerge in its full glory."

"But how can the body, something so frail, serve in this way? We've been taught it is a source of corruption and death."

"Ah, yes. The body is greatly misunderstood." The captain leaned forward, his hands clasped between his knees. "Tell me, Your Grace, on the course, did your mind or your body know how and where to hit the ball?'

James reflected. "My body. My mind had no answers."

The captain nodded. "Quite so. Contrary to what you have been told, the body has a great purpose. It can receive and anchor the Divine Love within you. It can help you remember you are the Soul."

"Yet my anger swept everything away—as if I had never felt anything else. How can we hold onto the Soul when our own feelings conspire against it?"

"You have asked for my help, and you shall have it." Captain van Horn walked over to the altar. He unlocked the small chest and drew out the second roll of parchment.

"I won't say another word until you've read this, Your Grace."

James took the scroll, pulled the silk ribbon, and unrolled the parchment.

THE SECOND SCROLL: The Soul's Sanctuary

The Soul seeks a sacred place to dwell within you,
A sanctuary where it can remain,
Despite the storms of desire, anger, and fear.

Build this sanctuary in your heart.
Here the Soul can deepen your Love for
The Creator, for others, for yourself.

Each time you remember who you are,
You strengthen this sacred place within you,
Allowing the Soul to fill your life with Divine Love.

I will remember who I am. Where I come from. Where I will return.
I will build within me a sanctuary for the Soul.

Even as he read, James could feel inside him the faint presence of such a place. Perhaps he had already started to build it; perhaps he had been building it every time he felt a longing for his true home. It was as if he had stumbled across a sacred place deep in nature, like a natural shrine, and it had entered his heart.

"Tell me, can anger or fear or other desires destroy this place?"

"No, Your Grace, they cannot, though they can obscure it from your sight for a time." The captain laid a fatherly hand on his shoulder. "I can assure you from experience that once you build this sanctuary, you will always have it."

"But you're leaving soon. How can I do this without your guidance?"

"I will help you before I leave. You have a talent for these matters, Your Grace." Van Horn laughed. "Besides, it may sound a bit mad to say this, but I urge you to use the game to practice the second scroll! Without the distraction of an opponent, you will face your own demons directly, as you did on the green. The deeper and stronger you make that inner sanctuary, the more you will remember yourself when faced with a challenge."

His expression sobered again. "And make no mistake, James, you face some formidable challenges ahead."

"Given how we Scots fight each other, perhaps I should travel with you to learn more before I become king."

"Nothing would give me greater pleasure, but I fear events are moving too quickly. You must build your sanctuary in the midst of your life here at court. As for those who are eager to fight, I can tell you that the Highland chiefs in the north will support the king as they always have, but those in the central and southern regions are beginning to talk about forcing him to step down. They follow the earls of Angus and Haile. And you are square in the center of this storm, Your Grace. A damnably tricky place to be. You will have to be light on your feet."

An icy cold filled James's stomach. "You must have weathered many such storms in Europe, Captain. What advice can you offer?"

"Here is where you will need all the insight and knowledge your Soul can give you. It will help you know when to speak and when to remain silent—a valuable skill in navigating court intrigues. If you have to fight, it will tell you why—to curb aggression, to prevent a greater loss of life, or to end a conflict quickly. The Soul can tell you how to end a war so you don't start the next one."

Van Horn looked earnestly into James's eyes. "Trust that it will show you the best path not only for yourself but for all those around you. In the future, it may help you put an end to the constant warfare in your kingdom and allow your people to prosper and thrive."

A silence fell between them. James could hear the tower bells chiming ten. He realized in sorrow the captain would be leaving in only a few hours. He felt suddenly small and alone.

"Captain," he said. "I know I am sworn to secrecy, but could I, perhaps, tell one other person about the scrolls . . ." He saw the answer in the captain's eyes even before the man replied.

"It is too great a risk, Your Grace. In the troubled times to come, it will be hard to tell friend from foe. If your enemies knew about the scrolls, it would be easy for them to claim you had fallen under dark influences. They might try to deny you the throne or even accuse you of witchcraft. You must not give anyone such a weapon against you."

James stared at his feet—how much he wanted to tell Margaret about all this. If not her, at least Robert Hume.

As if reading his mind, the captain said, "But you have true allies, Your Grace. Margaret Drummond has a sailor's eye for dangerous conditions. Trust her to help you."

James asked, "And what about the men around me—the nobles and my father and brothers? How do I manage them?"

"Family is always a far harder challenge, no doubt of that. But you had a taste of what to do in Drummond Hall, Your Grace." The captain's eyes gleamed. "Ask yourself '*Which way is the wind blowing?*' That should take you to your sanctuary right away!"

James grinned. "I will keep that in mind, Captain." He hesitated. "There's one more thing I would like to ask you. It's about something that happened at Drummond Castle. It seemed to occur without any effort on my part."

"What is it?"

"When I first entered the great hall, I found my sight had changed. I could see something, like lines of force, joining men who shared the same beliefs. It happened once or twice more and gave me a knowledge I would not have had otherwise."

"Indeed!" Van Horn raised his eyebrows. "This is unusual to happen so soon, Your Grace, but not uncommon. As Master Zheng explained to me, when you remember who you are, other senses, like a second sight, may also awaken. This can be very useful when you want to know the truth at any time."

Before James could ask more, the captain spoke briskly, "Now, memorize that scroll until you can recite it by heart. For now, I will show you a way to build your sanctuary to make it strong and solid within you."

Over the next hour, van Horn had James focus on the faint feeling of a sanctuary he already had within him. When the boy had a clear sense of it, van Horn baited him with the comments the nobles had made until James could feel anger rising again and burning inside him.

"Slow your breath, Your Grace . . . That's it, drain all power from the emotion. Think of something you love or of someone whose love you can feel. Call on that higher quality—anchor it in your sanctuary."

The captain's voice struck a deep chord of affection in James's heart. The man's presence felt like a steadying arm thrown over his shoulders. *If only my father could be like this!*

At last the tower bells struck twelve midnight. By then, James could summon the Soul and its higher qualities at will. As the final tone quivered into silence, they heard Wullie's muffled voice croaking through the door: "Our Lord comes nigh/Arise, ye mortals . . ."

Apparently the old priest and his acolytes would not be sleeping through this night. The captain returned the second scroll to the small chest, and they snuffed out the altar candles. In the gloom, James led the way out through the chapel's side door.

The next morning, the pre-dawn light found the two of them standing by van Horn's carriage, which groaned under the weight of his luggage. James knew that tucked somewhere among the bags and trunks was a priceless cargo.

The two lingered together, reluctant to part. At last, the captain embraced James, his seaman's face a bit redder than usual.

"Guard yourself well, Your Grace, and that beautiful young woman you fancy. I want to see you both when I return."

"God speed, Captain, and thank you for all you have taught me." James's throat tightened painfully, and he found himself unable to say more.

"I will return as soon as I can, Prince James . . . when you will need me the most." His keen gaze seemed to peer into James's Soul as he said softly, "Remember what I showed you. Each day . . . go to your sanctuary."

The captain stepped into the carriage and leaned out the window to keep the prince in view. The driver cracked his whip, and the horses lurched forward. Van Horn watched as James's slender figure grew smaller and smaller in the castle gateway. The sight caught at his heart. The Five Scrolls had come to James at a critical time.

There's a great storm bearing down on that boy, Master Zheng. I'll pray for him as if he were my own son.

Chapter 6

The Lion's Cub

James watched the carriage disappear around a bend in the road, and a sense of abandonment descended on him. He hadn't felt anything like a father's love and care for years, and it was hard to let the captain go.

It didn't help when Lord Gray sent a message saying he and the others had to attend to the king's business that morning. There would be no golf practice either.

At moments like this, he sorely missed Robert Hume. Though James couldn't show his friend the scrolls, he could have discussed the questions they raised. Robert had a quick, lively mind that would explore any topic with the tenacity of a dog gnawing on a bone.

Then James recalled his promise to practice building his inner sanctuary, and his spirit revived. The task might help him understand more deeply the two scrolls he had memorized. He sensed there were layers of meaning he had only begun to touch.

On his way to the chapel, a royal courier caught up with him to deliver an urgent message. James saw the royal seal on the folded parchment, and his heart dropped like a stone. Something must be wrong for the king to send a message like this. He broke the seal and read:

"*Rumors of rebellion among certain nobles have reached us here at Dunsmore. We have decided to return to Stirling Castle immediately. Expect us within three days.*"

It was signed with a curt *"King James III."* No expressions of courtesy or affection for his own son, James thought. A familiar anger stirred within him.

The message had taken nearly a whole day to reach Stirling Castle. That meant James had only two days left until the king arrived. He had better strengthen that sacred place within him before then.

Early the next morning, Lord Gray arrived to take James to their new meeting place for golf. James told him about the king's message as they rode through dense woods. Gray listened in silence and then nodded.

"I'm not surprised. Unpopular as your father may be, he still has a good network of spies. And Lord Angus and Lord Haile have never been subtle about their dislike for the king, nor about gathering allies to their cause."

James asked, "Lord Gray, do you sympathize with Angus and Haile?"

Gray turned sharply to face him. "What makes you ask?"

"At Drummond Castle, you and those two lords seemed to be in agreement—"

Gray laughed shortly. "Ah. You caught that, did you? You've a sharp eye, Your Grace."

The earl rode in silence for a moment, and then said, "There's a difference between supporting the crown and supporting the man who wears it. Montrose and Argyll—indeed, many other nobles like Crichton and Lyle—will support whoever sits on the throne. The authority of the crown is what matters to them."

"And you? Which do you support?"

"I've always supported the man who wears the crown." Lord Gray's expression grew more severe. "But when a man abuses the power it gives him, then I must support another who is more worthy. A king should not be allowed to abuse his people, no matter who he is."

James said, "You can't mean for people to choose their own king. If so, every family and clan will seek to gain the throne. Such a contest would tear Scotland apart, as it has in the past."

Gray turned a searching gaze on the boy. "Unless there is someone already considered worthy of the crown. That choice could unite the country."

James said nothing, remembering the captain's words, *You are squarely in the center of the storm.* He understood now the captain meant more than being caught between warring nobles. He might end up caught between a father determined to remain on the throne and a rebel force equally determined to overthrow him—and perhaps give James the crown? The idea disturbed the boy more than he cared to admit. Despite everything, he still loved his father.

Gray's voice broke into his thoughts with a forced heartiness. "But let's put politics aside for now, shall we? We've arrived, Your Grace!"

He pointed to the wide, rolling landscape in front of them. "This is Black Douglass land clear to the horizon. The sheriff doesn't dare set foot here, or he'd end up as a ghost patrolling the countryside. Take a look at what this clan has built."

James stared in amazement. The gently rolling hills had been cropped by sheep and cut by scythe to carve out nine fairways and greens that covered several acres of land. It was the first time he had seen anything close to a proper course—an ideal place to do the work the captain and Master Zheng had given him.

They joined Argyll, Montrose, and Sir Lennox, who were already at the first fairway. James thought he detected a slight coolness between the three men and Lord Gray, yet they remained cordial. The four of them seemed willing to set aside their politics for now.

James joined in the talk, but the king's message had upset him more than he showed. When he tried to slow his breathing, it only made his heart race faster. *Family is always more of a challenge,* van Horn had said. In fact, the threatened turmoil in the country seemed to have lodged itself within him as well. He kept pacing back and forth while waiting for the others to finish their play.

When it was James's turn to drive, he closed his eyes for a moment and tried to feel the peace of his inner sanctuary. It was no use. He swung the club and sent his ball curving into the rough grass off the course.

"Ah, bad luck, Your Grace," Sir Lennox said. "Still, it's only one shot in the game."

It was an omen of things to come. That morning, the game seemed determined to test James almost beyond endurance. He could do nothing right. He drove the ball into brush, trees, thickets, and a flock of sheep. On the green, he watched his ball hop in and out of the hole, skim over its top, roll around and out, sail past, or stop only a hair's breadth from falling in.

James began to think that when the captain had left, he had taken all of James's skill with him.

By the fourth hole, the men were united again in their efforts to help James. The superstitious Sir Lennox tied a small cross on James's club to ward off the evil eye. Argyll and Montrose gave him advice about his grip and his stance. Lord Gray adjusted his swing.

Nothing helped.

By the sixth hole, the men turned away when James stepped up to the ball to spare him the embarrassment of witnesses. They stared at the sky and speculated on whether rain was coming or whether drought might settle in.

When James missed the ball completely on his first swing, all composure deserted him. Montrose, standing with his back to James, cocked an ear as the boy finally unleashed his Stewart temper.

"He's swearing in French, gentlemen . . . now Italian . . . ah, there's Danish, or I miss my mark."

"Only three languages?" said Gray. "He's got a few more—"

Argyll exclaimed, "Now Latin!" His eyebrows raised in mild

shock. "God's truth, he'd have to do penance for that phrase if a priest overheard it."

The men turned in time to see James hurl his club toward the green. It flipped end over end until it hit the ground halfway to the striped marker.

"Good throw, Your Grace!" Lennox called.

"Two more like that," Argyll encouraged him, "and you'll put the club in the hole!"

James stared after his driver in despair and shouted to the field: "The devil curse this game!"

Lennox gazed inquiringly at the earls. "What say you, gentlemen? Will he stay the course or quit?"

Gray said, "I wager he'll stay."

But when James saw the fairway at the seventh hole, he dropped his club and almost walked away. A large pond cut across the course, blocking their path to the green. To him, the water stretched wide as the Red Sea. He could already imagine his ball sinking to the bottom.

Lord Montrose laid a hand on James's shoulder. "Now the trick to a water hazard, Your Grace, is to ignore the water. Just take your shot."

James shook his head and stepped up to the ball. *Ignore the water,* he thought bitterly. *Might as well tell a man whose cloak is on fire, "Ignore the flames."*

One last time James tried to find the sanctuary within and felt nothing. *I will remember who I am . . .* The words rang hollow. Finally, like a drowning man going under, he gave up. He had failed the captain and disgraced himself.

He touched the head of his club to the ball, his mind mercifully blank as an empty parchment.

And then, without warning, it happened. The quiet of the Soul seemed to descend on him. He could no longer distinguish between himself and what lay outside himself—everything had blended into one. When the wind stirred, he could feel it move inside his chest.

He seemed rooted between Heaven and Earth, held in an

immense compassion. It was so far beyond what he knew as love that his passion for Margaret was like a small flame overwhelmed by the sun's blinding rays.

He slowly raised his head. Every leaf, every blade of grass, every object seemed burnished to a brilliant hue. His mind was utterly awake for the first time. There was no need to strive for love, or peace, or wisdom—those higher qualities were now simply part of him.

James looked down at the club in his hands and found himself unable to tell where his hands left off and the wood began. When he drew the club back and over his shoulder, it was an extension of himself. And when he swung down, he never felt the club connect with the ball. He saw only the small white sphere sailing over the water to land near the green.

The men behind him cheered, but he no longer cared whether the ball landed fair or foul. The deep joy that filled him was all that mattered.

When he looked over at the men, something about his face moved Lord Gray. He murmured to Sir Lennox, "Our prince has conquered his first kingdom—himself. We were right to think he will make a great monarch."

For the rest of the game, James continued to play with a sense of detached wonder. He was astonished to find the sheltered sanctuary within him was now vivid and clear, allowing him to hold on to his Soul with ease and to let go of everything else. After hitting the ball on the green, he would often walk away, not even watching as it fell into the hole.

The men gradually fell silent, feeling themselves in the presence of something far beyond the ordinary. Whatever had taken hold of James, no one wanted to break the spell.

By the time they were riding home, the power had faded enough for James to feel himself separate again. But his body still rang with the force of what had happened as if he were a bell struck by heaven; it was good to know he had justified the faith that Captain van Horn and Master Zheng had placed in him.

When the group reached the woods near Stirling Castle, the men parted from one another without a word. James rode on alone toward the castle gate. Everyone along the way, from the women and children gathering berries in the field to the men walking the road or driving carts toward the town below, smiled and bowed to him. The world seemed to breathe a universal goodwill.

As he neared the gate, James gazed up at the tower ramparts where the royal banner was flying in the morning light. He suddenly pulled his horse to an abrupt halt. As if to complete his joy, he saw a red-haired figure leaning over the wall and waving down to him. Robert Hume, the friend James most wanted to see, had returned to Stirling Castle.

James rode quickly into the courtyard where Robert was waiting. He leapt off his horse, and the two friends embraced, pounding each other on the back. Slightly shorter than James, Robert was more thickly built and almost lifted the prince off his feet. His clothes were covered in dust and darkened by the sweat of his horse.

A wide grin lit up James's face. "It seems a year since you left, not just a few weeks. But why are you here ahead of the king? I thought you were with him at Dunsmore."

Robert laughed. "I feigned illness, and the governess sent me packing. You know she can't abide sickness around her." He stopped and held James at arm's length, looking at him more closely. "Something's different . . . you look older somehow, or like you're about to join the holy orders. What's happened since I've been gone?"

James threw his arm around Robert's shoulders. "Some things I can tell you, some I can't. Let's go out to the gardens where we can talk, and you can tell me the real reason you came back early. I want to hear everything you learned while you were with my family."

Robert grew serious. "There's something I need to warn you about before your father arrives."

All laughter died out of James. The two of them walked through the courtyard into the walled gardens attached to the castle. The roses and phlox were in full summer bloom, standing out vividly against the deep-green hedges that surrounded the flowerbeds. James sat down on one of the stone benches, as Robert glanced around them to make sure they wouldn't be overheard.

He spoke quietly, his blue eyes squinting against the sun's glare. "You know how the king always consults with astrologers? Well, he found one in Dunsmore that he believes more than all the others. I happened to be in the king's chamber when they were talking, and I heard this soothsayer give a dire prediction. He said, *'In a year's time, the lion will be devoured by one of its cubs.'* You understand the meaning?"

James frowned. "The lion is clearly the symbol of the king, but 'devoured by one of its cubs'? Is my father mad enough to think any of his sons would harm him?"

Robert shook his head. "Not any of his sons—only you, James."

"What?!" He said hoarsely. "When did I ever give him cause to believe such a thing? That's madness!"

"Madness or not, after the soothsayer's prediction, the king lost his appetite and began to stay up nights conferring with his commoner friends. When I left, he was talking about putting your brother John on the throne, not you."

The words hit James like a rush of ice water, leaving him breathless. It was one thing to hear rumors about this; it was quite another to find out they were true. The news drove him to his feet, and he began pacing in front of Robert, intensely grateful now for everything the game had put him through.

With a strong act of will, he slowed his breath and shifted within. The sacred place offered him refuge against the powerful pain and anger that threatened to overwhelm him.

Gradually the harsh emotions subsided. In their place, he felt a deep sadness and sympathy toward his father, as if seeing him from a distance. *Why does he hate and fear me so much?* To believe that your own son would harm you—how tormented the man must be!

James sat down again, his mind clear and firm.

"I'll speak to my father straightaway when he arrives. There must be no chance for this poison to fester between us. What about my brothers? How are they taking this prediction?"

Robert said dryly, "Jamie still has no interest in the throne. You know he'd rather hunt and carouse than be burdened with anything that smacks of work. As for young John, he's basking in your father's attention."

"Yes," James mused. "John would do whatever the king wants with no thought of what it really means to be king. When my father is gone, the nobles will lead him around like a blind sheep. His reign would weaken the power of the crown and give that power to the nobles. Poor Scotland would be much the worse for it."

Robert looked at him in awe. "I'll ask again, what has happened since I've been gone? You are different, James. Before you would have been in a towering rage to hear this about your father. Now . . . well, if I were pressed to describe it . . . I'd say you're talking like a king." He half-joked, "Maybe your father is well advised to be wary of you!"

James smiled and clapped Robert on the back. "He has nothing to fear. I'll put his mind at ease. But I'll tell you this—I'm fortunate in my friends. You risked your place in the royal entourage to bring me this warning, and I'm grateful, Robert. To cover your lie to the governess, we'll have to tell her you had a miraculous recovery on the way to Stirling."

Robert waved his words away. "We're talking about the fate of the crown. I couldn't sit idle at Dunsmore with this knowledge." He eyed James shrewdly. "But if you feel yourself in my debt, you can pay it off by telling me if Sibylla Drummond has had any new suitors while I've been gone."

"She has not," James assured him. "I was at Drummond Castle only two days ago, and she is still waiting for you."

Robert flushed in relief. "Good, good," he murmured, and studied his boots carefully. "I don't suppose you can arrange for us to see each other soon?"

"There's usually a banquet to welcome the king home. A letter to Lord Drummond inviting him and his daughters should do it."

Robert glanced up at him. "How is she, James?"

James was about to reply with a jest. Then he saw the look in Robert's eyes and answered seriously, "She's as kind and beautiful as ever. You couldn't set your heart on a better lass."

"And what about Margaret?"

James, suddenly nervous, plucked a phlox blossom and started shredding its petals. "Well, she's beautiful, quick-witted, of course. But she's always giving me advice, whether I want it or not—"

Robert laughed and punched his arm. "She's your match, James. Admit it."

James grinned ruefully and tossed away what was left of the flower. "That she is. But I can't show my affection too much in public. And I would ask you to keep silent on the subject as well."

Robert frowned. "All right, I will, but why is this necessary?"

"As Captain van Horn would say, in these times, even love can be dangerous."

"What do you mean? And who the devil is Captain van Horn?" Robert asked, irritated.

James stood up. "I'll tell you later. Right now we have to prepare the castle to receive the king. Thanks to you, I know what to expect from him."

Robert said, "I pray you can persuade your father of your loyalty, James. Many in his court support you, but others would gladly see your brother on the throne to advance themselves."

"Then we'll have to know which way the wind blows, won't we?" James asked.

A movement in one of the castle windows caught his eye. For a fleeting instant, he thought he saw Wullie's face. But when he looked again, the window was empty.

Chapter 7

The Path to War

The next day, James and Robert worked with the castle steward to prepare for the arrival of the king and his Stirling knights. James wanted everything to be perfect when his father's retinue appeared. By nightfall, the two friends felt they had walked several miles throughout the castle.

James dismissed the servants from his private chambers and sank gratefully into a cushioned chair. Robert filled their mugs from a pitcher of ale and began devouring the bread left over from the evening meal.

"All right, James, now tell me what's been happening since I've been gone."

James regarded him thoughtfully and then asked. "Before I tell you anything, answer me one question. What is a man's greatest treasure: power, wealth, knowledge, or love?"

"I can choose only one?" Robert asked. When James nodded, he said decisively, "Power!"

"Why?"

"Well," Robert said, talking around the coarse bread in his mouth, "journeying with the king, I've seen what it's like not to have power. You get trampled by everyone above you and live in constant fear, like those poor wretches bound to their clan chiefs. With power, you can defend yourself and make sure anyone who wrongs you is punished. Power protects you."

"What's to keep you from misusing it?"

"Well, that's a risk, of course, but if you're a just person, you won't."

"My father once thought he was just. Now he uses his power to squeeze money out of people, and he's hated as a tyrant."

Robert stopped eating and cocked his head quizzically at James. "What's this all about? Does it have something to do with your Captain van Horn?"

James fell silent, a little unnerved that Robert had struck so close to the mark. He would have to be careful what he said.

"In a way." He told Robert about sneaking out of the castle with Lord Gray to learn the game ("You've got to teach me!" Robert exclaimed) and meeting the captain ("Why don't these things ever happen when I'm around?").

He told Robert that van Horn had shown him some of the finer points of the game and explained that it was a true test of character.

"You have no opponent but yourself and the course. What happens is all up to you."

Robert looked doubtful. "And this is harder than archery or swordplay?"

"You have no idea," James said darkly and refilled his mug. "But it's more than that. I saw men who ordinarily would have nothing to do with each other, or who would be fighting among themselves, united in the game. They have established an etiquette of play that would amaze you."

"I don't know. It doesn't sound Scottish," Robert tore off another piece of bread. "Our national game is fighting each other."

James set his mug down hard on the table. "Yes, and it's keeping us backward and poor compared to other nations. It would help if the king lifted the ban on this game. Maybe we would learn more self-restraint. Maybe the country would prosper, and good men like your father would still be alive—"

He broke off when he saw Robert's face.

"I'm sorry. I shouldn't have said that, forgive me."

Robert shook his head. "I wish with all my heart it were true."

After a moment of awkward silence, Robert said, "Maybe I should help you spread this game. If it's turning you from a prince into a king, maybe it would turn me from a courtier into an archbishop!"

James laughed. "It could improve your chances with Sibylla. I hear she admires a man who shows self-restraint."

Robert slapped the table. "Then I'll learn! Now, tell me, what else did this Captain van Horn teach you? I can't believe he traveled here just to show you how to hit a ball."

The prince stared into his mug. "He came here on business as well."

"James. I know that look. You're hiding something."

He set his mug down. "I can't tell you, Robert. I swore to keep the knowledge he shared secret for now."

Robert flinched as if wounded. "I thought we were like brothers to each other. You always said as much."

"We are . . . but Robert, when I'm king, I'll need men loyal to me even when they don't know my reasons for doing things. As my closest friend, as my true brother, I need you to be the first among those men."

He could see Robert struggling with the choice. At last he said, "All right. I'll help you keep the secret by not asking you any more questions. But the moment you can tell me—"

"You'll know everything, I promise." James added silently, *And by then, God willing, you'll understand the captain's question.*

Near noon of the third day, the watchtower guards alerted the castle that the king and his knights were approaching. James led the royal household to the courtyard and lined up with the steward, guards, and castle serving staff to receive the king.

James felt himself sweating with more than the heat of the

summer sun. He still hoped his father had awakened from his fear and would greet him in the old, familiar way.

But the moment the king dismounted, James could see the coldness in his eyes. He looked pale, his face lined with fatigue, and there were dark shadows under his eyes. James knelt with the others as the monarch approached, bowing his head as an added gesture of obedience.

He watched his father's booted feet pass him by without stopping, only to hear him greet the castle steward and other servants in the receiving line. The snub pierced James's heart. He had to work hard to shift into his sanctuary and feel, again, compassion for the king. *Family is indeed the hardest challenge.*

As he rose to his feet, his gaze fell on his brothers, Jamie and John, who followed in their father's wake. Jamie grinned at him and passed by, indifferent to what had just happened. It was doubtful he had even noticed it at all. But the younger John ducked his head, his cheeks red with shame.

James watched as the king disappeared with his retinue into the castle. The royal staff and servants were glancing at James and murmuring among themselves. With a sinking heart, he knew the king's public snub of him would spread rapidly to every baron, duke, and lord within a hundred miles. The news would please the lords Angus and Haile most of all.

James didn't have to wait long for the chance to speak to his father. Within the hour, a courtier arrived at his door to announce the king wanted to see him in the throne room.

Robert said grimly, "The saints be with you, James. I hope the king is in a mood to listen."

James felt his stomach twist into a knot as he followed the courtier through the hallways to the king's throne room. Even the meeting place was chosen to set a distance between them. Before this, the king had always received James in the family's private chambers.

He calmed himself as best he could, but his heart still pounded despite his efforts. When the throne room doors opened, James took in the scene with his awakened eye. It told him a great deal.

The king was sitting back in his throne, his hands gripping its arms and his head lowered like a lion waiting in ambush. Twelve-year-old John sat beside him, perched on the edge of his seat, a sign he was decidedly uncomfortable being there.

Thomas Cochrane, the king's favorite commoner, sat on the other side of the king. He was the only one relaxed and half-smiling at James.

He likes the way things are going, James thought. He saw that both men were wearing daggers on their belts. It wasn't unusual for men to carry arms, even at court, but it wasn't common practice between James and his father.

He decided to concentrate on the king and ignore the other two. He would have to handle this without giving away what Robert had told him. James approached the throne and knelt down on one knee.

"Sire, have I offended you in some way? Your greeting to me was not the customary one of a father to his son."

"Nor was yours," the king said sharply. He leaned forward. "Cochran rightly pointed out you couldn't look me in the eye—as if you had something to hide. Do you?"

For a moment, James was too astonished to reply. His gesture of respect had been completely twisted. He resisted the impulse to look at Cochrane and instead held the king's gaze steadily.

"Father, I meant merely to show obedience to you in a time when rumors of rebellion have been stirring up the country. People should see that the royal family is united."

At that point, Cochrane leaned over and murmured something in the king's ear. The monarch nodded coldly. "You show your loyalty in odd ways, James. Attending a banquet of rebel lords at Drummond Castle, for instance."

James felt a mix of anger and fear. *Cochrane has a spy at*

Drummond! He fought to remain calm and said, "We had visitors at Stirling, Father, and Lord Drummond offered us his hospitality. I cannot answer for the company Lord Drummond keeps."

"When you saw who was in attendance, you should have walked out of the hall."

James rose and stepped closer to the throne; out of the corner of his eye, saw Cochrane close his hand over the hilt of his dagger.

Again James ignored him and spoke in urgent plea to the king. "Father, I don't know why these suspicions have come between us, but let's mend this breach before rumors of it reach those who are your enemies. We must not give them any false hope that we are divided."

The king rose. "Your own words condemn you!" His anger struck James like a blow " '*My brothers will see Scone only as princes, while I will see it as king!*' You have always thought yourself better than your brothers—better than your father!"

"No, I—"

"Don't deny it! You have disputed and disagreed with nearly every step I have taken as king. And now it appears you think you have waited long enough to take the throne."

"No, Sire, that's not true—"

"I have been warned about you. '*The lion shall be devoured by one of its cubs!*' "

James blurted out, anguish making his voice loud, "Sire, the only thing devouring you is your fear!"

"NO!" the king roared. "No. I have been warned, and I intend to heed that warning. From now on, I'm setting Cochrane as guardian over you. He will act in my absence to make sure you do not consort again with enemies of the crown!"

Cochrane spoke for the first time, a note of triumph in his voice. "Prince James, be glad the king is taking this step and not arresting you for high treason."

Sudden rage nearly blinded James, and he was about to step toward Cochrane when something stopped him like a hand at his throat. He heard the captain's voice: *Remember who you are*. He took a deep breath and exhaled slowly.

The king stepped close to James, fury blazing in his eyes. "Your ambition will be thwarted in the very thing it desires. I will make your brother John successor to the throne. Now, LEAVE US!"

There was nothing more James could do. He backed slowly away from the king until the guards shut the throne room doors in his face. For a long moment, he was unable to move, as stunned and bruised as if he had been beaten. His tunic was soaked through with sweat.

Only one thing was certain: If ever he had expressed Divine Love in what he did, it had been in that room.

"Cochrane turned your father against you?" Robert's face was a dangerous shade of red. "Waylay that devil and run him through with a sword! You can best him, James, you know you can."

"No!" James rounded on him. "Am I to lose you to this madness as well?"

"But he's robbed you of the crown! You're the rightful heir—"

"He's robbed me for now. That doesn't mean it will remain so. Don't you understand? I can't keep following an endless cycle of revenge and killing—I have to find another way."

"James, if you don't go after Cochrane, you'll look weak. You know that. You can't fight human nature."

"Human nature? We've forgotten what that truly is."

Robert said nothing. James was beginning to understand more deeply the task set before him. He would have to *show* why another way was better. Talking about it wasn't going to convince anyone.

If Cochran had tested James in the throne room, it was nothing compared to what he did over the next few months. The man seemed driven to become James's personal devil. He replaced the prince's valet with his own servant, making it hard for Robert and James to be alone in the royal chambers, and set some of his men to watch the prince's every move.

James wanted more than anything to contact Margaret and make sure she was safe, since it was obvious to him that Cochrane's spy at Drummond Castle was watching the family. How else could he have known James's exact words? But he didn't dare. If his message was intercepted, it would put the entire Drummond family in great danger. He had to be content with hearing about her from Lord Gray, who visited Drummond regularly.

As the weeks wore on, Cochrane began to tighten his control not only over James but over every aspect of royal life at court. He alone decided who could see the king, extorting hefty bribes from people for even the briefest audience with the monarch. This practice infuriated not only the nobles, but the commoners who sought to present petitions for the king's judgment.

And Cochrane made sure James was not allowed to see his father at all. But the man's outrages had an unexpected effect. James began to discover he had allies in the castle he didn't know about.

Lord Gray's nephew, who looked uncannily like James, agreed to don the prince's clothing and act as decoy during morning Mass while James and Robert sneaked out with Lord Gray. Cochrane's men were none the wiser when James came back into the castle and changed places with the nephew.

James also began to encounter an unusually clumsy Wullie in the corridors and stairwells of the castle. Several times the old servant lurched into the prince, or James had to catch the old man as he stumbled and nearly fell. Later, James would find a message from Lord Gray stuck in his belt or cloak.

Other servants kept interfering with Cochrane and his men, coming to them at all hours of the day and night with alarming stories of spies spotted in the kitchens, in the stables, around the castle grounds. They whispered rumors of impending attacks by the nobles or hinted there might be night raids on the castle armory.

As the land fell into the full grip of winter, James began to feel almost sorry for Cochrane's men, forced to stand guard on the freezing ramparts or in the castle grounds, watching for an enemy that never came.

The king could do little to help Cochrane and his men. James III often left Stirling for weeks at a time, trying to rally support for the crown even as he worked tirelessly to increase the wealth of the Stewarts. These twin goals often clashed, as the very people who might have supported the king found that portions of their lands or wealth had been seized in the name of the crown.

As tensions in the country rose higher, lords Gray, Montrose, and Argyll strove to negotiate a compromise between the king and the nobles, only to have their efforts thwarted by the wall Cochrane had erected around the monarch.

James tried to help Gray and the others when he could, but by spring, he could see their efforts were failing. The final blow came when the king arbitrarily seized property and wealth belonging to the Homes clan in order to build a monastery for his archbishop.

The king's action sent a wave of fury through the central and southern families of the country, a wave that rippled even to the Highlands. If a monarch could do that to one noble's estate, what would prevent him from doing it to others? It struck at the heart of a tradition of independence and freedom central to Scottish life.

To make matters worse, England took advantage of the weakened crown to invade Scotland's southern borders. James III compounded the insult by making the hated Cochrane commander of the army and its artillery rather than appointing nobles to defend the region.

Pushed too far, a few nobles decided one fateful night to strike against the king in a way that would wound him the most.

James had no idea what they had done until the next morning, when the captain of the guard and four of his men at arms suddenly burst into his rooms. He and Robert sprang to their feet in stunned surprise as the captain stood rigidly at attention and recited, "Prince James, we are here to arrest you in the name of the King—"

"Why? What mad thing does my father think I've done?"

"—for committing high treason against the crown. You are to be confined to the tower until the king decides your fate."

"I've committed no treason!" James shouted.

The captain recited, still in his official voice, "Last night, Your Grace, the king's advisor, Thomas Cochrane and the king's closest companions were hanged on Stirling bridge by the men of lords Angus and Haile. The king charges you with conspiracy in this treasonous crime."

"That's a lie!" Robert shot back. "He has had no contact with—"

James raised his hand. Behind him, Robert sputtered and fell silent. James briefly closed his eyes. He needed wisdom more than ever now. The king, deprived of his inner circle, would be half crazed with grief and fear and all the more dangerous for that.

James opened his eyes and calmly faced the captain. "I am deeply grieved to hear of these killings, but I had nothing to do with them. As for suspecting me . . . my father is not in his right mind. Surely you see that, Captain. You have been with him for years. Has he ever been this way before?"

He looked at the other men at arms. "Can any of you honestly say the king has been himself these past months?"

The four men shuffled nervously and glanced at each other, unsure how to respond. The captain's official demeanor slipped, and for a moment the man James had known most of his life appeared before him.

"Your Grace," he said, his voice thick with emotion, "I cannot go against the king's orders. You must come with us to the tower."

James felt inside a silent command from his Soul to yield, and he trusted the impulse. "All right, I would not want you and your men to run afoul of the king. Allow me to gather a few things."

As he turned away to collect a few books and spare clothes, he mouthed silently to Robert, "*Tell Wullie.*"

Only then did James let himself to be escorted out of his chambers by the captain and his men at arms.

The moment they were gone, Robert rushed to find Wullie in the kitchens. They had to get James out of the tower before the king returned.

Everyone knew the charge of high treason carried a death sentence.

Chapter 8

Battle for the Throne

June 11, 1488
Sauchieburn near Stirling

"You're sure the king has confined James in the tower and not in the dungeon?" Lord Montrose asked.

Lord Gray nodded. "That's the message Robert sent through Wullie here." He gestured to the old servant who was seated by the door. Argyll and Montrose had ridden to Lord Gray's estate, one of the places they could meet in safety.

"That makes rescue more difficult," Montrose said. "There is a hidden passage into the dungeons but none to the tower."

Argyll kept clenching and unclenching the hilt of his sword, his face tight with worry. "I saw the king after Cochrane's death. He is certain the prince seeks to assassinate him and take the throne. Such madness in his voice . . ."

Lord Gray drained his cup of ale. "Lord Haile's spies say that his majesty is already preparing for war. He will surely execute the prince before he strikes."

"Pardon, Lord Gray." A servant stood hesitantly in the doorway. "There is a Captain van Horn to see you—"

"Send him in!" Gray exclaimed.

The three men greeted the captain warmly as he strode into the room, looking drawn and tired.

"*Gode Gud*, I heard the news when I docked at Dundee." He handed his dusty hat and traveling cloak to Wullie. "The prince still lives?"

"Yes," Gray answered. "That's the last word we have."

"Saints be praised." The captain mopped his forehead.

"But for how long, no one knows," Argyll added.

"Ordinarily we could bribe the guards," Montrose put in, "but the king's personal soldiers are watching James. They would likely kill the briber."

Gray leaned on the table. "There is no way to enter the tower by stealth. It would take an army to storm it, and James would be dead before we reached the top."

The captain mused in silence, rubbing his jaw as he pondered these grim facts. Then he spotted Wullie shuffling in with a tray of scones and sudden inspiration lit his face.

"Perhaps, gentlemen, one man can do what an army cannot. I have an idea that might work to our advantage." He turned to Lord Gray. "Tell me quickly, what skills of warfare have you taught the prince?"

Margaret crushed the note after reading it, her hands shaking.

"What is it?" Her sister Sibylla hurried over to her. "Has something happened to Robert?"

Margaret handed her the note without a word and moved to the window that faced Stirling Castle; her heart raced with fear.

Sibylla smoothed the parchment. "*James arrested by his father for treason. He is alive, but I fear the king means to hang him. What do you hear at Drummond? Robert*"

"This cannot be!" Sibylla exclaimed. She glanced around them and lowered her voice to an anguished whisper. "Why would the king do this?"

Margaret whirled, anger surging through her now. "The foolish monarch is determined to bring about his own downfall!"

She sat down at her writing desk and drew out a piece of parchment.

"The nobles wish to put James on the throne. You saw that at the banquet. Father told me the king knows this—he will surely have to—" She could not bring herself to say the words. "Robert must get all the help Heaven and Earth can provide. They have to save James!"

Margaret wiped her face furiously and reached for another parchment. Tears had smeared the ink on the first one. This was no time for weakness. Only within did she beg, *Mother of God, keep him safe! Please, please keep him safe!*

After the hanging of James III's companions, the king shed all restraint. Enraged, he declared war on the rebel nobles and sent out a call for all men sworn to the crown to assemble near Stirling. Only a handful of loyal nobles and the Highland clans responded, sending 15,000 men to the king's service.

The rebel nobles in turn gathered their own armies, nearly 20,000 strong, and marched to Sauchieburn, a few miles southwest of Stirling. There they pitched camp and awaited the crown's forces.

James watched helplessly from the tower as more and more troops arrived, swelling the king's encampment. Their clan banners fluttered near the royal insignia like hands raised in support. Whenever James demanded to see the king, or at least send a message to him, the guards outside the tower door merely laughed.

"His Majesty has nothing to say to a traitor," one of the men said.

James hoped desperately his father had not arrested Robert as well and that his friend had been able to get a message to Lord Gray.

Thrown back on himself, James devoted some of his time to practicing what Captain van Horn had taught him. To connect to the Soul, he drew on his love for Margaret; his feelings for the Captain and Robert; and the joy of the game when it flowed through him.

He found the sanctuary within growing more vivid, like a garden beginning to blossom. Even when the sounds of soldiers drilling for war, of drums and pipes, and the clash of weapons penetrated the tower, his quiet peace remained.

But as the time stretched on, restlessness stirred within him. It was in his nature to act not endure idleness. He paced from one tower window to the next, growing more frantic to escape with every passing day.

There were no bars on the windows. None were needed. The windows, barely wide enough for him to fit through, were more than fifty feet above the ground. Guards constantly patrolled the courtyard below.

On the eighth day, the sound of hammering woke him. He stumbled over to the window on the courtyard side and froze in shock. They were starting to build a gallows, pounding the timbers in place for the platform and steps. Planks and crossbeams lay on the ground, a coil of rope beside them.

The prince leaned his head against the window's stone casement, his throat suddenly dry with fear. He had seen his father hang traitors before and remembered well the agonized faces of men twisting and strangling at the end of a noose. James recalled the look of fury and hatred in his father's eyes when they last met. But until this moment, he had not truly believed his father would hang him.

All men fear death.

Never had his own death loomed so real. In his imagination, he had always died gloriously, defending the crown, or repelling invaders, or saving Margaret from English knights. Not like this. Not this terror that crawled in his bones and robbed him of breath. It left a bitter, metallic taste in his mouth and made the pulse of his heart pound in his veins. Sweating and light-headed, he slumped on the bed.

"*I will return when you need me most,*" van Horn had said. Well, he desperately needed the man now. What good was the Soul or his sanctuary if he died here on the gallows?

Pulse of his heart—the phrase echoed in him. What had he said to Margaret? You are the pulse of my heart. Her face suddenly appeared in his mind, her features as clear and vivid as if she were standing before him. James could feel her hand in his, warm and light. Through that touch, her love suddenly poured into his body with astonishing power. He had never felt anything like it.

His fear of death dropped away as if he had stepped across a threshold, and a profound peace and compassion swept over him. He knew with utter certainty he would live, no matter what happened. If he suffered Earthly death, he would simply return home. If he remained here, he was destined to become king and to fulfill his Soul.

The lines of force he had seen at Drummond Hall now seemed to connect him to everyone he knew and loved. He could even feel the clear presence of the captain, as if he were coming to meet him—

Rude laughter from the guards outside his door disrupted the feeling. James straightened up, wondering what had provoked them. Even so, his mind remained clear and calm.

"Look at the old hunchback!" one of the guards said. "A strong breath would knock him over."

"An' it please you, sirs," a familiar voice wheezed, "I bring food for Prince James."

Wullie! The poor man must have climbed over a hundred steps to reach this room. As if in response, Wullie uttered a harsh, hacking cough like a death rattle.

"God's blood! Let the old crow in before he dies at our feet."

James heard the key turn the lock. The guards pushed Wullie with his basket of bread into the room. James was alarmed to see a large hump on his back. If the king's men had beaten the old man—

Wullie shuffled over to the table in the far corner, out of the guards' sight. He waved James over and lifted off his thin cloak. James stared in disbelief. He was wearing a long rope coiled many times over his shoulder. James helped him lift it off and threw it under the table.

Wullie pointed at the spare clothes on the bed and then to his shoulder. James understood. Wullie had entered the room with a hump on his back. He couldn't very well leave without one. They stuffed the clothes under his cloak until he was a hunchback again.

Wullie then pointed to the darkest loaf of bread in the basket, and James nodded.

"God save you, Your Grace," Wullie rasped. He shuffled to the door again, rapping on it.

One of the guards opened the door and snarled, "Come on, get out of there, old man!"

The moment the door was locked again, James tore open the dark loaf and pulled out Lord Gray's message.

"*At two bells, Robert will be waiting below. Remember what I taught you.*"

That night at two bells, the guards changed. James took advantage of the noise to make his escape. He tied the rope around one of the bedposts and leaned out the window on the darkest side of the tower to make sure the way was clear. Moonlight flooded the ground below, but he couldn't see Robert anywhere. The soldiers who usually patrolled the area were mysteriously absent as well.

He couldn't hesitate now. James flung the rope down the side of the tower, looped a coil around his body, and rappelled down the stonework, as Lord Gray had taught him. It took only a few moments to reach the ground.

As soon as he dropped the rope, Robert emerged from the shadows with two horses and threw the reins of the second mount to James.

"Hurry! The king's men are close!"

James leaped onto his horse's back. "Where are we going?"

"To the nobles' camp near Sauchieburn. Let's go!"

They whipped their horses through the castle gateway. They had barely reached Stirling Bridge when a great shout erupted and suddenly the king's knights were riding hard behind them. Arrows hissed by James's head, and three struck the saddle on Robert's horse. They leaned forward, urging their mounts on faster, and gradually left the knights behind.

Mile after mile they raced through the moonlit countryside. James could feel a growing resolve within him, rooted in his deepening sanctuary. He must do everything in his power to save his father's life. There was no place in his heart for murder.

A faint light was appearing in the eastern sky when they finally spotted the white tents and flickering watch fires of the nobles' encampment. Robert and James rode across the wide meadow, pulled up their sweating, lathered horses at Lord Gray's tent, and found themselves quickly surrounded by a cheering crowd of nobles, knights, and soldiers.

In the dawn light, James saw the familiar faces of Lord Haile, Lord Angus, and a relieved Lord Gray. He jumped off his horse and raised his hands for quiet. The cheering dropped away.

"First, my thanks to you all, and especially to Robert, who knows how to pick a fast horse!"

Another cheer went up at this, but James shouted over it, "Do you have word when the king plans to attack?"

Lord Angus replied, "Aye. In two days, Your Grace. Our spies tell us he has readied his men to march against us. It will help our cause to have you in our camp."

James's mouth thinned into a grim line. "Then gather all the nobles. There is a price I will ask for my support."

Within the hour, Lord Gray's tent was crowded with every noble riding against the king. James stood by the camp table and spoke to the assembly with all the authority he could muster.

"You have just grievances against the king, and I know you do not take arms against him lightly. I, too, fear for the rights and liberties of Scotland, and for this reason I have agreed to join you.

"However . . ." James looked steadily at the men. "The price I ask is this: a sworn oath from every man here that the king will be captured, not killed. I am sure that no one desires to have the crime of murdering a king on their conscience. Some among you may already have the deaths of his companions on your souls."

An uneasy silence fell, and James was quick to notice that Angus and Haile avoided his eyes.

"But Your Grace," Lord Haile protested, "as long as the king is alive, he remains a threat to you, to us all."

"Nevertheless," James fired back, "he is not to be harmed! We must fight for the right reasons, my lords, not simply for revenge!"

A storm of protest greeted his words. Anger at James's father was high among the company, and they began reciting the number of insults and injustices they had received at his hands. James found himself arguing for some time, trying to persuade the nobles.

Finally, exasperated, he shouted for silence and gave an ultimatum. "*If you do not agree, I withdraw my support!* Do you want to slaughter each other for the crown? Would you bring that bloodbath on Scotland?"

The men fell silent at this. It was clear most of them were appalled at the prospect. James asked for parchment, wrote out the oath, and laid it on the table for the men to sign. He was gratified to see that Lord Gray was the first to step up to the table and affix his signature. The others slowly followed suit.

Robert stood in one corner, watching the scene unfold. Most of the men here were far older than James, and some towered a full head or more over him. But the young prince had been able to bend them all to his will. Robert began to realize just how ready James was to lead Scotland.

Lord Gray found armor for James and Robert and lent them two of his warhorses.

James described how Wullie had helped him escape. "I think the rope weighed more than he did! One of my first duties as king will be to reward him for his courage. He'll never have to climb a staircase again!"

Gray said, "I must tell you, Your Grace, Captain van Horn was the one who came up with the plan."

"I knew it! I could feel him near," James said. "Is he here in camp? I owe him thanks for more than my life."

"Gone to the coast, Your Grace. King Henry of England is sending warships to attack our Scottish frigates. The captain knows the shoals and eddies of the North Sea as few men do. He's sailing with our own Admiral Wood and his ship, the *Yellow Caravel.*"

"I'm sure he's needed by the admiral," James said, "But in faith, I would like him here with me."

Robert heard the sadness in James's voice and wondered, with a slight pang of jealousy, what hold this strange captain had on his friend. Perhaps reminding James of Margaret would break that hold.

"We must send a message to Drummond Castle," he said. "Margaret and Sibylla need to know we're safe."

James reddened, furious with himself for not thinking of her.

Lord Gray smiled. "Write your message, Your Grace, and I'll see it's delivered."

On the morning of June 11, James rode with the nobles and their armies toward the battlefield at Sauchieburn. The cavalry took the front lines, with thousands of men stretched behind them, row after row of infantry bristling with sharpened pikes and longbows.

One of Lord Gray's men carried the red and gold royal banner ahead of them all. It would be the first image to greet the king's eyes.

James could only imagine what his father would think when he realized the prophecy he had feared was fulfilled, despite all his efforts to thwart it.

Lord Angus, the most experienced warrior, led the rebels as they took the field. Banners displaying the nobles' coats of arms snapped in the wind, waving defiantly at the king.

The king's forces, lined up by clan, were already facing them in a wide line that stretched from one side of the field to the other. Sunlight glinted off their armor, and James heard the jingling of bridles and the impatient snorts of the warhorses, eager to charge.

In the lull before battle, James turned to Lord Gray and asked quietly, "What of Sir Lennox and lords Montrose and Argyll?"

Gray kept his eyes on the opposing army. "Sir Lennox fights with us, Your Grace, but Montrose and Argyll must fight with the king."

"Then I pray for their safety."

"It's good you do, Your Grace. Should the worst happen, it's likely they've made no provision for who gets their clubs."

James flashed a grin at him, and then had a sudden thought. "It's a pity, Lord Gray, that we could not settle this affair on the course and spare good men on both sides."

Gray nodded slowly. "A bonnie idea, Your Grace. But for today, we must shed blood. We'll see you're well defended. The king will send his men straight at you. The last thing he wants is for you to wear the crown."

At that moment, the king rode out from his men on a great gray charger. Even from a distance, James could see his face red with anger.

His father's voice rang across the open field between them. "Traitors of Scotland! You have among you a traitor son who would be king! God will see that victory is ours and all traitors sent to a fiery hell!"

Lord Angus roared back, "God will give no victory to a king who is tyrant over his people! He gives strength to the side of freedom and justice!"

At these words, the king drew his sword and with a roar, led the charge across the field. At the same moment, Angus raised his sword, and the nobles and their men leaped forward as one.

James felt the power of his warhorse as it surged after the others, and caught up in the fray, he drew his own sword. The two royal standards bore down on one another like two warships closing.

The moment the armies clashed, James lost sight of his father in the tangled confusion of horses and men, the ringing of swords against armor, and the battle cries of thousands of warriors. He had vivid impressions of knights fighting to keep the king's men away from him, the maddened screams of wounded horses, and the sharp, acrid smell of blood. His sword glanced off a shield and struck a knight's helmet; the man's returning sword thrust barely missed

James's leg. As the knight raised his sword to strike again, one of Lord Gray's men stabbed him in the chest.

The struggle seemed to go on forever as James's warhorse wheeled and turned to block anyone who tried to approach.

Then Lord Angus bellowed, "TO ME! PRESS HARD, PRESS HARD!"

James saw the tide of the battle had turned. They were charging again, this time after the fleeing Highland clans. James could see skirmishes to the right and left, but the nobles' forces were sweeping the field clear of the king's men.

As they rode forward, James looked desperately for his father, but could catch no sight of the gray charger or the king's royal standard. He prayed with all his heart that in the heat of battle, the nobles had not broken their oath.

For the next two days, James and Lord Gray and his men searched the battlefield and surrounding countryside, but they found no trace of the king. James was in an agony of suspense until, late on the third day, Lord Gray came into his tent, his eyes streaming with tears.

James felt a cold hand seize his heart and knew before Lord Gray uttered a word that his father was dead.

"It appears the king fled from the battlefield. At some point his horse must have thrown him, but we could find no one who saw what happened." Gray hesitated, his face pale and drawn. "I'm sorry to tell you this, James, but the king was found dead at the roadside with no one to attend him."

James felt a wrenching pity for his father. What a bitter end, he thought. Deserted by everyone, as alone in death as he was in the last days of life.

James gave orders for the king's burial but had little time to mourn his father. Almost at once, Lord Angus and the others urged him to claim the crown and begin the coronation rites.

"Forgive me, Your Grace," Lord Angus said, "but you must prevent any further threat of civil war. If you act quickly, the Highland clans will rally around you, despite their enmity toward us."

Lord Gray added, "I've already heard from Montrose and Argyll pledging their support. The fact we won the battle so easily means the Highland clans didn't have their hearts in the fight."

James looked at Robert, who nodded his agreement. James took a deep breath, and with an effort pushed aside his sorrow.

"I must bow to your logic, gentlemen. We will send messengers throughout Scotland and to King Henry in England, along with all the European heads of state. We must advise them that James III is dead, and his son James IV will ascend the throne." James turned to Lord Gray. "I want the coronation to take place at Scone. How quickly can it be done?"

Gray said, "We must notify the archbishop, ready the grounds at Scone, and prepare the coronation procession. Two weeks at the earliest, Your Grace."

"Press everyone you can spare into service. This ancient site must be a rallying point for all of Scotland." James moved to the opening of his tent and stared out at the battlefield, still stained with the blood of men and horses.

Robert came up beside him. "I'm truly sorry about your father, James. I wouldn't wish such a death on anyone."

James stared at the bloody field, his eyes dark with anguish. "I wished to see Scone as king, Robert . . . but not like this." He beat his fist softly against the tent post. "Not like this. I must find a way to change things!"

Chapter 9

King James IV

That evening, James wrote a brief message to Margaret before meeting with the nobles.

"*. . . My father, much against my wishes, died after the fray and is to be buried in Cambuskenneth Abbey in Stirling in a fortnight . . .*"

The torchlight in his tent flickered, and James paused. Shadows like restless spirits moved across the canvas walls, sending a brief chill through him. Then he shook himself, impatient at such fears and bent to his writing again.

"*Soon after, I am to be coronated at Scone on June 26, the anniversary of Robert Bruce's victory over the English at Bannockburn. The Drummonds and other loyal families and clans must be at Scone to show their support. I wish with all my heart you were here with me now . . .*"

It was a strange feeling to seal the letter with the king's signet ring, something he had watched his father do countless times.

He told the courier, "See that you put this letter in Lady Margaret's hand and hers alone." The thought of someone else reading his expressions of love made him sweat with embarrassment.

Margaret's reply arrived the next day.

"*My Dearest James, It was a great relief to hear you are safe and the rebellion is over. I must tell you how it grieves my heart to learn of your father's death. He was not always a wise king, but he did have good men in his service. I hope you will consider retaining some of his*

Stewart Scotland — James IV
1488–1513
Major Sites

Castle Cathedral Battle

N
W E
S

Orkney &
Shetland
Islands

North Sea

Skye

Aberdeen

The Lordship of the Isles

MacLean

Dundee

Scone

Perth

Dunblane

St. Andrews

Stirling

Drummond

Dumbarton

Sauchieburn

Edinburgh

Glasgow

Duchal

Berwick

Crookston

Flodden
Field

Ireland

England

most able counselors. It could help you gain support for the Crown . . ."

"Always giving me advice," James grumbled.

Robert gazed at the letter. "Good advice, you must admit."

But James was reluctant to include anyone who had supported his father. How could he ever be sure of their loyalty? Margaret should keep to her own affairs.

Van Horn had told him, *"She has a sailor's instinct for treacherous conditions."* Those words annoyed him now. He would make his own decisions.

The army broke camp, and on the march back to Stirling Castle, James received a message from van Horn. He tore it open eagerly, hoping it contained news of the captain's return. The message was brief. *"Sir Andrew Wood still requires my assistance pursuing English pirates. I will join you as soon as possible. Praise the Saints for your victory!"*

James crumpled the paper. Despite his annoyance, he had wanted the captain's steadying hand in all that awaited him as the new king.

Go to your sanctuary; find its peace.

He heard the admonition as clearly as if the captain had spoken it to him, and the words softened his disappointment.

Once the royal procession reached Stirling, James began to realize the full extent of what it meant to be king. One of the first people to greet him was the Royal Exchequer of the king's treasury. The old man, who had served James's father and grandfather, pulled James aside and advised him to review the royal inheritance privately.

"Away from prying eyes, if you understand, Sire." He called James "Sire" as if he had already been crowned king and was no longer "Your Grace," the prince.

James gestured for Robert to accompany him, and they followed the old man to the secret treasury room deep in the bowels of the castle, one of the few places James had never been.

"The room holds some of the Stewart wealth your father and grandfather accumulated, Your Majesty." The old man gestured at the thick bound pages he carried under one arm. "And I have here an account of the remaining monies and a list of properties and land holdings."

As they entered the treasury room, James and Robert stared around them in disbelief. Artworks, tapestries, and jewel-encrusted weapons and armor glittered like Solomon's treasure in the torchlight. Tables set against the walls were laden with gold coins, candelabra, silverware, dishes, jewelry, and bolts of silk and velvet cloth, glistening with fine gold threads.

As the old exchequer led them around the room, James kept picking up and setting down one item after another as if trying to make it all real.

Finally the exchequer stopped at a table, moved aside twin basins of solid gold, and opened his book of accounts.

"As shown here, Sire, the crown also receives income from the proceeds of several monasteries, royal merchant charters, royal businesses, and tax revenues from the realm. The latest land holdings extend from . . ."

As best James could understand, the contents of the royal treasury and all the revenues were worth millions. When combined with the extensive land holdings, it meant the Stewarts were the richest clan in Scotland. In fact, in all of Britain—with only the king of England to rival them.

On the way out of the treasury room, Robert said in an awed voice, "I was wrong, James. A man's greatest treasure is *wealth*, not power. With wealth like this, you can buy power and anything else you might ever want."

James said nothing, thinking of how his father had never been content with the treasure he had accumulated. But for the first time, James was beginning to understand his father's obsession. Gazing on all that wealth made him wonder how much more there was to acquire.

James immediately assigned some of the wealth to pay for the coronation. He wanted the ceremony to be such a glorious rallying point for Scotland that it would overshadow any criticism about the death of James III. Though his father had been deeply unpopular, the rebellion against a king would never be taken lightly.

As expenses for the coronation mounted, James decided to keep his father's tax laws in place for a while to avoid drawing down the royal treasury too much. *Time enough for the laws to be changed later,* he thought.

He had to focus on the coronation and on a royal wedding, which he wanted to take place soon after he was crowned king. The way was now clear for him to marry Margaret Drummond.

But James soon found himself under siege from all sides. Several of the rebel nobles objected strenuously to his choice of Margaret and hinted they might withdraw their support if he didn't marry an English princess. Such an English-Scottish alliance, they argued, would resolve the southern border conflicts once and for all.

Lords Gray, Haile, and Angus advised him to send his two brothers, John and Jamie, to the Duke of Albany in France after the coronation. The duke was a distant relative of the Stewarts. "You don't want the royal princes to serve as pawns in any disputes, Sire." James was forced to agree.

A crowd of nobles and commoners with petitions descended on the castle and fought to present their grievances and issues to James. Lord Gray had to use the king's knights to send them away, explaining that until James was crowned king, he had no royal authority to hear petitions or decide disputes. Many refused to leave and instead camped outside the boundaries of the castle grounds to be first in line after the coronation.

Messengers brought rumors of trouble in the north. A few of the Highland clans did not accept the authority of the crown and were starting to gather an army to back up their declaration. Lord Gray and the other nobles urged quick action to bring the threat to an end, but James found himself unsure what to do. Every noble and royal courtier he talked with seemed to have different opinions and demands.

Feeling harried and besieged, James finally asked Robert, "How do I persuade them all to accept my reign and my decisions?"

Robert stared at him in astonishment. "James, you're the king! You can do what you wish."

The words struck deep and awoke the power of the crown like a dragon roused from its lair. James realized he no longer needed to persuade or convince. He could simply command, sweeping aside all objections from his path. He had enough money to raise as large an army as he needed to do his bidding and to enforce his decisions.

There would be no more objections to Margaret, no more trouble from the clans. There would be only one center of power in Scotland—the crown—and a chance for the country to know peace for the first time in generations.

James vowed that as soon as he was coronated at Scone, he would act. First, he would address Parliament immediately after the coronation. Its members should know right away that even though he was only sixteen, he was a king to be reckoned with and not the weakened monarch his father had been. Why else had destiny given him so much wealth and power? Why else had Captain van Horn and Master Zheng given him their secret knowledge?

Once he was king, he would also have to deal with the rebellious Highland clans. He sent for Lord Gray and began drawing up plans for an expeditionary force. Even though Lord Angus and Lord Haile had been appointed his official guardians until age twenty-one, James quickly let it be known that he would brook no interference with his decisions.

Lord Angus complained loudly, "He acts as though he's already free of all guardianship. I find out what he's going to do after he's done it!"

Lord Gray, rubbing his face to hide his smile, said, "Have you discussed his status with him?"

Angus threw his hands up. "Have you ever tried to tell a Stewart anything? He's even put Sir Lennox in charge of the king's knights. Now they will take orders only from him!"

Gray said, "When you helped make him king, you forgot to tell him he shouldn't act like one."

James next sent word to Margaret and her father to visit him at Stirling. It was time they started planning their royal wedding. After experiencing Margaret's love for him in the tower, James had assumed she would quickly agree. But to his surprise, Margaret was not as keen to announce their betrothal as he was.

She asked him, "James, do the nobles who wanted you to marry an English princess agree to our union?"

"They don't have to," he retorted. "All they have to do is stay out of our way. There are enough allies on our side who will support us!"

"Our side?" she echoed. "I thought you wanted to eliminate warfare, not inflame it!"

"Why are you so concerned about those who oppose us?" he said angrily. "I'm not a prince any more, I'm the king! *They* have to answer to *me*, not the other way around."

Margaret gripped his arm. "These are the men who put you on the throne, James! Do you think they will step aside and let you do what you want?"

"They wouldn't have a king if I hadn't agreed to join them! They would be slaughtering each other for the crown, and they know it!" He pulled out of her grasp. "They will yield in this matter."

"For how long?" Margaret asked, eyes dark with worry. There was a hardness to James's face that had not been there before. "We Scots have deep and bitter memories, James. When wronged, we don't forget or forgive it."

Exasperated, James left her and sought out Lord Drummond and the archbishop to negotiate his betrothal to Margaret. The announcement of their marriage banns would be made after the coronation. He told himself that she would realize this was the right course when he was king. As for any threat to her from the nobles, Stewart wealth would buy all the protection she would need.

From then on, plans for the coronation so filled his days that James put aside, unread, all the letters from Margaret. Sounds of the preparations reverberated through the castle day and night as a ceaseless parade of workmen and servants carried out their tasks.

At night, James dreamed he was at the center of a great turning wheel, with the ability to bend all others to his will. Energy seemed to flow through him, and his body felt strong as a clenched fist.

"Hold fast to your sanctuary," the captain had said.

James felt he was doing so even without focusing within. By raising the power and image of the king, he would force the warring clans to make peace and bring all of Scotland under his rule.

On June 26, 1488, only fifteen days after his father's death, James was crowned at the ancient site of Scone where the kings of Scotland's distant past had been crowned. Thousands of people lined the road from Stirling to Scone as the royal procession passed by, led by James and his entire royal family—including his two brothers—escorted by church leaders and the Stirling knights.

They were followed by the families who had supported James against his father and by those Highland clans who had come over to his side after the battle.

The splendor of the procession and the ceremonial grounds prepared at Scone surpassed anything the country had ever seen. The processional line stretched nearly half a mile, carrying the flags and banners of many noble families and clans.

James's royal armor shone like burnished silver and gold. Beneath it, he wore a velvet tunic and leggings and white leather boots. His charger, chosen for its spirit, pranced like a show horse, neck arched and hooves stepping high.

Ambassadors from England, France, and the Netherlands had managed to arrive in time to attend the coronation. In their eyes, all of Scotland seemed to welcome the young king.

The coronation ceremony took place at the Scone sanctuary. Once the crown of Scotland was placed on James's head, he turned to face the crowd, and a deafening roar broke out from the people massed around him. The church bells rang out over Scone, and the court musicians began playing a sacred hymn, though it was drowned out by the crowd.

James could feel the weight of the gold crown pressing on his head, but it was a weight that seemed to belong there. He saw Robert cheering with the rest and Margaret looking up at him gravely.

And close behind her stood the one person he most wanted to see: Captain Jacob van Horn.

Chapter 10

The Third Scroll

The captain had not had an easy time catching up with James. His service aboard the *Yellow Caravel* had put him in the center of a fierce battle against five English warships. England was trying to take advantage of the rebellion to gain control of the North Sea. Van Horn's knowledge of the sandbars, tides, and currents along the Scottish coast of the North Sea proved one of the deciding factors in the Scottish victory.

Only after the battle, when the *Yellow Caravel* put into port for repairs, did van Horn learn of James's victory. He immediately caught passage on a river boat and sailed inland to Dundee port, where the harbormaster greeted him happily.

"Great things are happening in the country, sir! Old King James the Third got himself killed, and now it's his son James the Fourth who's king! If you hurry, you'll see the coronation at Scone. The lad knows his history, he does! Wouldn't be surprised if the ghosts of Scotland's old kings show up to bless him."

The captain set out for Scone in the fastest carriage he could hire. Along the way, he heard similar talk from everyone he met. It was evident the change in monarchs was widely regarded as a blessing for the country.

People speculated in awe about how much James was spending on food, drink, and tent lodgings for the thousands who had gathered around Scone. They wondered which of the crown's enemies he would strike first. Rumor had it he had already started to recruit and outfit his own personal army.

If even half these stories are true, Master Zheng, I'm not a moment too soon, the captain thought. *Men twice his age have been corrupted by sudden power and wealth.*

Van Horn reached Scone on the day of the coronation and searched among the throng of nobles, clans, and commoners until he found Lord Drummond's family.

Margaret was greatly relieved to see him. "James needs his true friends, Captain. He is quite changed."

Van Horn stood with the Drummonds as James was crowned king of Scotland. With his inner vision, he saw the light of sanctuary in James, which pleased him. But he also saw dark lines of power and ambition, like ribbons of smoke, swirling around the young king, lines that hadn't been there a year ago.

By the saints, he thought, *I'll have to act quickly.*

It took James nearly two days to arrange a secret meeting with the captain. He hadn't realized how hard it would be as king to get away alone. He had to postpone meetings with the archbishop, have Robert distract the royal bodyguards, and make his valet swear on pain of death not to divulge his absence.

At last he was able to join van Horn at his lodgings on the outskirts of Scone. Van Horn had been fortunate to acquire even this meager shelter. A small fire burned in the hearth and shed its soft light in the room, which had only a small chair and one thin pallet. He sat in the chair while James, unable to remain still in his excitement, paced back and forth in front of him.

"You were right about everything!" James said. "The inner sanctuary, the game, the scrolls—everything! There were times when I thought I had failed, and then something would happen that turned it all around. I even thought I was going to die in the tower, and then this calm, this certainty came over me that I would live. I felt you so close—and then Wullie came . . ."

The captain merely listened, the firelight illuminating his face as he watched James carefully. The dark lines were growing thicker, more compact as they circled about the young king.

This will take careful handling, the captain thought, *or he'll turn the wrong way. He is young and full of himself.*

"And the wealth of the Stewarts!" James's eyes shone. "It's far more than anyone could ever imagine! It will give the crown so much power, and a king needs power above all else. With it, I can overcome all opposition and truly rule the kingdom instead of trying to convince everyone—"

"And do you still believe that love is the greatest treasure?" the captain asked quietly.

James stopped pacing at this, his excitement somewhat deflated. "I . . . well, of course . . ."

"Do you? Then allow me to pose an old Chinese riddle, Your Majesty."

James hesitated and then reluctantly sat down on a small woolen rug by the fire. "What kind of riddle?"

"This one: There are two things in this world that the more they eat, the more their hunger grows. What are they?"

James thought of all the animals he knew, but each one of them had a limit to how much it could eat. What never stopped eating . . . in fact, its hunger grew larger the more it ate? It couldn't be an animal . . . something else. A mythical creature? No, the captain had said these two things existed in this world.

He gripped his head in frustration, his anger building. Then he saw the flames dancing in the hearth and inspiration struck.

"Fire!" he cried. "Fire never stops eating, and the more you feed it, the hungrier it grows."

"You are right, Sire. And the second thing?"

James pondered more deeply, but everything he thought of had a limit, and none, like fire, grew hungrier as it fed. This time his anger flared more quickly. *There's no time for this foolish riddle. We need to discuss my rule and how to make it stronger—*

"Tell me," he snapped. "What is the second thing?"

The captain's eyes narrowed. "Something you are feeling now, I think, a hunger that burns. Look within you."

James didn't want to look inside himself, but the captain was staring at him in a way that made him feel he had no choice. He breathed more slowly, deeply, and for the first time in many days, felt the area around his heart grow warm and still.

He shifted into his sacred place, stepping out of his role as king, and almost at once saw what van Horn meant. A hunger crawled inside him, like fire smoldering before it burst into flames. This hunger had a name, and it rose unbidden in his mind. *Greed.*

For a long moment, he said nothing. Then in a low voice, "That's it. The second thing that never has enough: human greed."

The captain said. "Greed withers all it touches. Wiser and stronger men than you have been destroyed by it." He stirred the fire with an iron poker and gazed into the hearth. "Someone once told me, Your Majesty, that 'without love, wealth buys an empty room, and power earns only hatred.'"

James recognized his own words, spoken on a day that seemed a lifetime ago. He was appalled to find that greed for wealth and power had taken root in him before he had even known it. He broke into a sweat, though the night was cool.

I am more like my father than I ever thought.

And with that bitter truth, the hunger slowly died within him.

Van Horn, moved by his stricken look, said gently, "Do not judge yourself too harshly, James. The Soul has a deep root in your heart, or you would not have recovered yourself so quickly."

James bowed his head. "Everything I did, everything I said—I thought myself the savior of Scotland . . . and Margaret, I told her . . ." The painful memory of their quarrel stopped the words in his throat.

The captain said, "Many a poor wretch has thought the same of his enterprise, only to do more harm than ever he intended. It is a strange paradox, James."

The captain opened his traveling valise and pulled out the small cedar chest. He carefully took out the third scroll. "Perhaps with this, it's a paradox you can resolve."

James read:

THE THIRD SCROLL: Let the Soul Guide

In your sanctuary, Divine Love connects you
To all Creation, to the eternal Source of life.

But if tempted to fulfill only your own desires,
You break your connection to others and
Lose touch with your Soul.

Allow the Soul's Divine Love to guide your path.
Use your power to establish justice,
Use your wealth to promote generosity,
Let your life, like a great river, nourish others.

I will remember who I am. Where I come from Where I will return.
I will let the Soul's Divine Love guide my life.

James read the scroll several times and then stared wordlessly into the fire. The captain said nothing. He could see the dark lines around James had greatly diminished but not disappeared entirely. *Steady as she goes,* he thought. *Let him come to the knowledge.*

He turned to van Horn. "I had no warning that I faced a choice. Why did you not tell me this when you gave me the second scroll?" James tossed the scroll on the rug. Van Horn glanced at it but did not pick it up.

"The scrolls are to be given one at a time," he said evenly. "Just as they came to me, as they come to all who are to receive them."

"And the Soul," James said heatedly. "If it is truly from the spiritual realms, then how can it let our desires rule us? Surely its purity would prevent that."

"So it would compel us to do good?" the Captain asked.

"Yes!"

"No need to make a choice?"

James struck his knee. "We are too blind and weak! Better we are compelled than left to ourselves. Look at the harm we do in the world. Why allow us to do more of it?"

"You refer to the harm your father did . . . that you might have done?"

James stared at him, sickened by the truth of his words. The man seemed to have an uncanny knowledge of his innermost fears and faults.

Van Horn picked up the scroll. "When you begin to build your sanctuary, James, at first it is only a way to recall who you are, to remember your Soul. But as you continue, you create far more than that. You create something like a beacon that attracts energy from the spiritual realms. As this energy pours in, it magnifies all of who you are, not just one part. Thus, you must choose whether the Soul or your own desires will guide how you use it."

James looked away. He ran a hand through his hair in exasperation. "But this seems unjust. How can we choose when the Earthly desires are still so strong? They will compel us down the wrong path. I felt this energy, but I had no idea I was misusing it."

The captain remained silent, keeping his face carefully neutral.

"And you were gone," James added angrily. "I had no one to advise me, no one to talk with."

The captain said, "I believe a certain Lady Margaret tried."

"Yes . . . yes," James sputtered, "but . . . I . . . I . . . didn't listen," he finished miserably.

"There is another ally you have, James, even closer to you than Lady Margaret; one that cannot lie to you."

"What do you mean? Who is it?"

101

"Your own body. It is not just a vessel for spiritual energy. It can also tell you the truth about what you are choosing."

He smiled at the look of utter bewilderment on James's face. "Tell me, when you were wielding the energy as king, did you sleep well? Did you feel at ease in yourself?"

James shifted uncomfortably. "No . . . in truth, it seemed I was always preparing to do battle with someone. I felt—"

"Like a clenched fist?"

"My very thought! How did you know?"

"Look at your hand now."

James looked down, startled to find his hand curled into a fist. When he opened it, there were fingernail marks in his palm.

"When your Earthly desires wield the energy, your mind and body are strained. The body is tight, like a fist, and finds it difficult to rest, to be still. There is a hardness in the face and eyes. Your mind is filled with restless thoughts, suspicions of those around you, compulsions, sudden anger or fear. Whatever you have or gain is never enough."

James thought back on the past fortnight and found the captain's description fit him far too well.

"When the Soul wields the energy, the body is at ease, the mind and heart are open to others. A light shines in the face, the eyes."

Van Horn took a deep breath and let it out slowly. "There is no strain in what you do, no hardness in your thoughts. As for fear and anger—they have no place in you. And though the future may be uncertain, your success unsure, you are at peace."

He pointed to James's heart. "Enter your sanctuary, and let go of all else. Then you will feel what the body has to say."

Silence stretched between them, broken only by the crackling of the fire. After a moment, James held out his hand without a word, and the captain passed the scroll to him.

He read it over again a few more times. "I believe I understand . . . but how do I choose to let the Soul's wisdom and compassion guide me?"

"In the same manner as before—by going to your sanctuary. In that quiet place, you will hear your Soul's wisdom and compassion. That's why you must make this sacred place strong, James. Build it daily. In time, you will be able to enter more quickly, and your choices will become easier."

James frowned, tapping his chin.

"Something still troubles you?"

"Why can't we make one choice and be done with it for life? Why must we choose over and over? What is the purpose?"

The captain pursed his lips, as if weighing his answer. "The purpose? In a word—*mastery*, James. Each time we choose, we give our Soul greater dominion over this Earthly life until we complete our purpose for coming here. Earthly desires only take us further and further from this great enterprise—"

"Therefore, build your sanctuary, let the Soul guide you," James said, as if completing the captain's words.

"You have it!"

To James, his earlier complaints now seemed like the words of a petulant child. He thought about how he must have appeared to others in the past several days.

"When I let my desires rule, Captain, it was as if I had fallen into a feverish state."

Van Horn chuckled in sympathy. "The scrolls are like a medicine. They treat the illness of the king while it is still mild."

"If only my father could have—" James broke off. He had not spoken of his father since the battle. Mentioning him now made his throat ache and his eyes sting painfully.

"I made them all swear not to harm him, Captain, all the nobles." His voice trembled. Van Horn had to lean in to hear him. "They signed an oath . . . I tried to save him . . ."

The captain said gently, "His death was not your doing, James. It was his own."

"He died alone by the road, away from everyone," James said hoarsely.

"By the saints, a tragic end for a king."

The grief James had locked away suddenly swept over him. He leaned his head on the captain's shoulder and wept for his father.

Van Horn held James as he would a son. The dark lines he had seen around the boy were gone at last.

Now, the captain thought, *he is ready to be king.*

Chapter 11

The Challenge

The two of them talked long into the night as James told van Horn what had happened in his absence. In turn, he wanted to hear about the captain's sea battles, noticing for the first time the wounds on the man's hands and the side of his neck.

The captain put him off. "Another time, Your Majesty. It's a tedious tale of cannon fire and sword fights. We have more pressing concerns to discuss."

As the conversation turned to his duties as king, James realized that the Third Scroll had planted new ideas in him about how to rule both himself and the country.

"Justice and generosity—these qualities are sorely needed. I remember the inequities in the law I witnessed when traveling with my father. And the misery of those impoverished by the nobles above them. We must change this."

The captain smiled. "So, Your Majesty, the king must be a medicine for the country."

James got to his feet in his excitement and started pacing again. "There has to be a universal system of laws to replace the whims of local lords and officials. And the country's wealth should do far more than just enrich the nobles or pay for the excesses of the crown. It should help the arts and sciences flower in Scotland, and build a strong navy so other nations will seek peace with us . . ."

Van Horn beamed at him more like a proud father than a mentor.

He said, "It's a wondrous thing, but the Soul brings about not only what is good for you but what is good for all those around you."

James continued to outline what he would do until the captain reminded him he must return to Scone before dawn, or his absence would be discovered.

The young king was still shaken by how close he had come to repeating his father's mistakes. It was proving more difficult to remember who he was than he could have imagined. Every time he overcame the pull of desires in one area, he lost himself in another. To rule wisely, he would have to practice letting his Soul guide him every day.

The Scone settlement was stirring awake with the dawn light when James slipped into Margaret's room. It would be the only time for the next few days they could talk in private. Her lady-in-waiting, Lena, stirred at his approach, but he put his finger to his lips. The young woman smiled and nodded. James knew she would tell no one of his visit.

He shook Margaret lightly, and she awoke, squinting up at him in the dim light.

"James?" Her voice was blurred with sleep. Then she came fully awake and sat up abruptly. "What are you doing here? Someone will see you!"

"Shhh. I came to apologize. You were right once again. I was foolish not to heed your warnings about our marriage."

She smiled and pushed her hair back. "You should listen to me, James. It would save us both time." She grew serious, seeing in his face a familiar light. She rested her palm against his cheek. "It's good to see you are yourself again. I feared we had lost you."

He knelt by the bed and grasped her hand. "As for our marriage, I'll enlist Lord Gray's help with the nobles. They may not bless our union, but if they can accept it, that will be enough."

Margaret touched her forehead to his. "Thank you."

For a moment he closed his eyes, breathing in the scent of her.

"Pulse of my heart," he whispered, and kissed her before he left.

When James and his retinue returned to Stirling, he had the chance to put his ideas into action almost at once. Part of the final coronation ceremony at Scone had been to receive a pledge of fealty from all the clans. But the Lord of the Isles and several northern clans who disputed James's right to be king had been conspicuously absent. This public defiance was James's first royal challenge—with all of Scotland watching to see what he would do.

Lords Montrose and Grey advised him not to deal with the Lord of the Isles for now, a clan leader who ruled over the western islands off the coast of Scotland.

"Your great-grandfather and grandfather tried to rein in this Lord," Grey said, "and they had no success. Leave him alone for now. If you want to unify Scotland, start with the northern clans. At least you'll be fighting closer to Stirling, which will make your supply lines easier to defend."

James had been ready to answer the challenge of the northern clans with force, but now he saw another way. He called Angus and Argyll, along with Captain van Horn, to join him with Grey and Montrose to learn what he could about these clans.

Lord Angus said, "They've resisted the authority of the crown for generations and can put more than 6,000 men in the field to back up their defiance."

"Their leader is Ross MacLean," Grey added, "who considers himself lord of the region. He has a reputation not only for battle but for dispensing a rough justice on the people of his estates. He once hanged a man for stealing a chicken."

James's face hardened at this. After a moment he asked, "Tell me, do the clan leaders play the game up there in the north?"

The earls looked at each other in bewilderment. Montrose finally spoke.

"They do, Sire. Lord MacLean has even built himself a course. He once had the arrogance to invite James III to play on it."

James had to smile at this. He could well imagine his father's reaction.

Lord Gray snorted in contempt. "We've played on his course, Sire. It offers some challenges but nothing like the course the Douglass clan has built."

James turned to the captain, "Have the Dutch made any improvements in the game since last summer?"

Van Horn inclined his head. "Indeed they have, Your Majesty—a most cunning club designed to get a ball out of tall grass and other hazards. I have ordered two of them sent here by the next ship."

Angus tried to control his impatience. "Begging Your Majesty's pardon, but this is a time for war, not for playing the game."

"I agree, Lord Angus," James replied. "Two weeks ago, I sent word to Lord MacLean that I wished to meet with him and the other clan leaders to discuss our differences. MacLean refused."

There was a general outburst at this, and Angus thundered, "Such arrogance must not be tolerated!"

"Not tolerated?" James said. "On the contrary, my lords, I was counting on it. I intend to challenge him to a duel, using an old Celtic battle tradition."

Lord Angus frowned. "And what tradition is that, Your Majesty?"

"Flyting, Lord Angus—a duel of battling poets."

James smiled at the confounded looks on the faces around him. "Our ancestors were men of imagination and spirit, gentlemen. When there was a dispute, at times they sent out not their best warriors but their best poets to battle one another in a war of words and wit. This duel was called flyting, and the winner settled the matter—at times, so decisively that the armies retired. Other countries like Sweden, Finland, Norway, even our English cousins have held the same contests."

Lord Argyll laughed shortly. "I hope you're not battling MacLean with words, Sire."

"No, but the Celts are his direct ancestors, and he'll likely recognize the tradition. This time, I'm challenging him to a duel involving the game—just the two of us. I'm hoping his arrogance will push him to accept my challenge."

James glanced at the Captain, whose broad grin told James he approved of this strategy.

James stood up, and the others rose with him.

"Until then, gentlemen, we have a great deal of work to do."

Grey lingered behind as the others left. "I have an idea that might help guarantee your victory, Sire, but I will need Lord Angus to help us plan it."

"Indeed?" James said. "Your ideas always interest me, Lord Grey."

Within the week, James heard back from Lord MacLean, who accepted his challenge on the appointed day in July. The duel would take place on MacLean's course, which had twelve holes.

Robert was dumbfounded when James told him about his plan.

"You've challenged him to the game?" he said. "Are you mad? What if you lose?"

"You're going to be one of my seconds, Robert. And I'm grievously wounded you think so little of my skills. Besides, had I challenged him to anything else—swords, battle axes, jousting—he would have beaten me, rather soundly. At least now I have a chance."

"How can you jest about this, James? Just take an army and defeat him."

"And then what? If he survives, his enmity will be stronger. If he's killed, his allies' lust for revenge will be a sword hanging over the crown."

Robert set his jaw stubbornly. "This has something to do with that Captain van Horn, doesn't it?" When James didn't answer, Robert threw up his hands. "I knew it! Tell me, how can you conquer an enemy this way?"

"I don't want to conquer MacLean; I want to convert him." James slung his bag of clubs over his shoulder. "Come on, we'd better start practicing. It will be very bad for the country if I lose."

News of James's forthcoming duel with Lord MacLean traveled quickly around the region. A lively trade in betting for and against the crown sprang up and preoccupied many in the local pubs.

To help himself prepare, James had a six-hole course built not far from the castle and spent every spare moment practicing.

It was not enough.

Even with the earls and the captain to help, James found that his game was not improving as much as he had hoped. At one point, when he had missed yet another putt, he looked over at Captain van Horn, who shook his head slowly.

James understood. There was nothing more the captain could do for him. He had to solve this one on his own.

That night he told the priest in Stirling Chapel that he wanted to pray alone. Once the man left, James sank to his knees, utterly humbled by the task he had set himself. He slowed his breathing and entered his sanctuary.

The familiar warmth and peace surrounded his heart, and he pleaded silently, *Tell me what I must do, and I will do it.*

For a moment only silence answered him. Then in his mind a clear image of Margaret appeared, smiling at him in that knowing way of hers. The message that accompanied the image was equally clear.

Seek her help.

He emerged from his reverie bewildered.

Later James asked the captain, "Seek Margaret's help? But she knows nothing of the game. What can she possibly do?"

The captain was firm. "Follow the message, no matter how foolish it seems. The wisdom of the Soul is beyond our knowing."

The next day, James rode to Drummond Castle on the pretext of consulting with Margaret's father about parliamentary issues. After an hour or two with Lord Drummond, James managed to draw Margaret aside and walk with her to his carriage.

"I'll need more than skill to win this duel," he told her ruefully. He gestured at his bag of clubs and golf balls in the carriage. "These are my only weapons. It will take divine help for me to defeat a Highland chief."

Margaret reached in and picked up one of the golf balls, examining it closely. "This is what you use in the game?"

"Yes, these are the best that Captain van Horn could give me."

She frowned and studied the leather sphere in the sunlight. "They don't seem very well made. They aren't round at all, and look at the needlework. The stitches are larger in some places and smaller in others—very poorly done."

He hadn't noticed such details but now saw that she was right. An imperfect sphere, he mused. How would that affect the flight and roll of the ball?

A light of inspiration gleamed in her eyes. "James, what if we could make better ones? Would it give you an advantage?"

"I suppose so, but I don't see how you can—"

"I would need Wullie to help me. Lord Gray says he knows more about working leather than anyone else. Can you send him to Drummond for a few days?"

"Yes, of course, but Captain van Horn assured me—"

She was already turning away with that absorbed look he was getting to know. He left Drummond wondering what she could possibly have in mind.

A few days later, Margaret and Wullie arrived at Stirling and asked James to take them, along with Robert, out to the royal course. Wullie lagged behind, singing a wheezy tune; James caught a few of the words.

". . . the king's fair maiden, who brings a secret treasure . . ."

When they reached the first hole, Margaret handed him three new balls.

"Wullie and I have labored hard over these, James. We think you will find them a great improvement."

He and Robert studied the leather spheres intently, and James rolled one between his palms. He stopped in surprise. "What is this on the leather—wax?"

Margaret smiled at Wullie, who bowed his head shyly.

"As Wullie pointed out, leather stretches when wet, which makes the ball 'soggy,' he says, and it falls apart much too soon. It just seemed common sense to make the leather proof against water. So Wullie concocted a fine lacquer and painted it on the ball."

Wullie reddened and scratched his head. "Well, now, the Captain gets the credit for that. He spent time in the Far East, you know, and picked up some useful knowledge about lacquers. Right clever he is about such things."

James shook his head in amazement. "Of course he is. And you, Margaret—'common sense' you say, only no one ever thought of proofing the leather against water before."

He looked more closely at the surface of the ball. "This is uncommonly round and even. And the stitching—I've never seen any so finely wrought."

"That would be Lady Margaret's handiwork, Sire," Wullie said, bowing in her direction.

Margaret smiled. "All those hours I thought wasted on needlework! It turns out Sibylla and I have a new use for the skill. And we boiled and chopped the feathers more finely so we could pack them tighter into the covers. That makes the balls more solid."

She gave him a shove. "Well, go on, James, try them out!"

James put one of the balls on his tee, set his stance, and swung. He heard a solid *thwok*, and the sphere soared in a long curve down the fairway, landing close to the green.

Robert shaded his eyes against the sun. "Straight and true as a cannon shot!" he exclaimed.

James looked down at the club in his hands. The solid feel of it hitting the ball was unlike anything he had experienced before.

"Let me try one," Robert said. His drive produced the same results, though his ball landed well short of the green.

James eyed the distant circle.

"Let's see how well they work for the short game."

As they walked down the fairway, Margaret glanced at him hesitantly. She finally asked, "James, you are so changed since the captain's arrival. How did he work such magic?"

"I've asked him the same, Lady Margaret," Robert said. "He won't say a word."

But James made the mistake of looking into Margaret's eyes. He felt his promise to the captain weaken. Surely he could say something without revealing the scrolls.

"He told me to build a sacred place within me where I could hear my Soul."

Robert cuffed him on the shoulder. "I could have told you as much," he said, half joking. "Why didn't you ask me?"

"A sacred place where you can hear your Soul," Margaret said. She studied James with a measured look, but he had recovered his resolve and said nothing more. To his relief, she didn't question him further.

They reached the green. James carefully lined up his shot to the hole, some twenty feet away. The other three watched as he hit the ball with a firm stroke. It traveled evenly over the grass, losing little of its speed, and dropped neatly into the hole.

For the first time in days, hope flowered in his chest. Perhaps heaven would favor his chances after all. He took the last ball out of his pocket and handed it to Margaret.

"How many of these can you make before I leave?"

She smiled proudly. "I think a dozen or so. What do you say, Wullie?"

"It can be done, Lady Margaret."

"I owe a great debt of gratitude to you both. And to the clever fingers that did such work." James raised Margaret's hand to his lips.

Wullie gave a hacking cough that covered the words, "Visitors,

Sire." James released her hand and straightened just before Gray, Montrose, and the captain emerged from the small woods that bordered the course.

A fierce light shone in Margaret's eyes. She leaned forward so only James could hear. "We've given you an advantage, James. *Now win the duel!*"

He was struck by her force of will. "If MacLean saw you now, he would surrender immediately!"

James turned to grin broadly at the men coming to join them. "Gentlemen, Lady Margaret and Wullie have devised a clever improvement of one of my dueling weapons. I believe it will help us prevail in the Highlands!"

The captain glanced from James to Margaret and back to James again. He nodded once in acknowledgment. The young king smiled at him.

The Soul's wisdom may appear foolish, Captain, but it is wisdom nonetheless.

Chapter 12

The Duel

James found that the new golf balls gave him a consistent advantage on the fairway and the green. Even when wet, each ball's lacquered cover stayed tightly bound around its spherical, feathered core, helping him drive the ball further down the fairway.

Van Horn and the others did all they could to help prepare the young king for the duel. The captain tutored him with the new club in the fine art of hitting out of sand traps, water hazards, and rough grass. Lord Gray gave James sage advice about his Highland opponent.

"Ross MacLean is a man who admires skill in the game, Your Majesty, whether from friend or foe. He has a passion for winning, but he's not a subtle or finesse player. That should give you an edge in the short game."

Montrose and Argyll, Robert and Sir Lennox helped James prepare in a different way—trying hard to throw him off his game. They rang cowbells as he was about to putt; shouted before he teed off; drove sheep across the course; let a flock of chickens loose on the fairway. They kicked his ball deeper into the rough or threw it into the water and claimed he had hit it there.

They insulted him, his parents, his grandparents, and his patron saint. They challenged him to play in all weather conditions, readying his body and mind against anything nature might bring on the day of the duel.

James endured it all by entering the sacred place within him again and again until he could reach it through every distraction, no matter how subtle, outrageous, or creative. In the end, the men marveled at his power of concentration.

"You're like a monk, James," Robert said. "The Devil himself couldn't shake you on the course."

James wiped the sweat off his face and replaced his driver in the bag. "You forget, Robert, a Highland chief can be more cunning than the Devil."

Two nights before they left for the Highlands, Van Horn taught James more about the Soul and its subtle energy. He brought out several charts and laid them on the table, lighting more candles to brighten the reading light.

"The Orient has a wonderful knowledge of human life, Your Majesty. They have discovered that our subtle energy flows like rivers through our arms and legs, through the torso and the head."

He unrolled a chart that showed a series of lines drawn on the human body. James bent over the image, intrigued. He traced the lines with his finger.

"How did they come upon this?" he said. "It's a wondrous design. Look—these rivers you speak of run parallel on each arm and leg, and on each side of the body. Mirror images of one another."

James straightened. "Are you certain we have this in our European bodies?"

The captain thumped the chart enthusiastically. "Every human is born with the same system, James. You can use it to restore your body from fatigue. We don't know what hardships you may face on the journey to the Highlands or what conditions may prevail on the course."

"What other hidden matters does the Orient hold? I want to learn them all!"

The captain laughed. "For that, you would need several lifetimes! Let's begin by teaching you how to gain energy from nature. It may prove a handy skill against a man who's spent years in battle and has the strength of an oak!"

"What do you mean, gain energy from nature? What alchemy is this?"

"The alchemy of the Soul." At the young king's bewildered look, the captain merely said, "You'll see, James, you'll see."

It took several days to travel from Stirling to the northern Highlands. On the appointed day of the duel, James and his retinue arrived at the border of Ross MacLean's estate.

The Highlands had a majestic, austere beauty different from the forested lands around Stirling. Their craggy, rolling hills spread out to the base of distant mountain ranges, lined up one behind the other until they faded into mist. Cloud shadows driven by a strong wind raced across the land like the spirits of ancient Celtic warriors.

Even in August there was a coolness to the air, as if the sun could never quite warm this place. The people who lived here, James thought, must be as tough and enduring as the gnarled trees that clung to the soil.

They saw MacLean's castle in the distance, its high walls set on a knoll overlooking the surrounding land. As they rode toward the castle, James and the others gazed, astonished, at the crowd gathered near the course to watch the duel.

MacLean's course wound its way across the landscape, broken here and there with sand pits, a small pond, and a meandering stream. Armed men from the clans lined the first two fairways to keep people and stray animals off the cropped grass.

Lord Montrose surveyed the crowd. "The game appears very popular, Your Majesty. It seems the entire population of the Highlands is here."

James smiled in grim satisfaction. "It's better than I had hoped."

Halfway down the long road to the castle, James could see Lord MacLean and his retinue waiting for them. There would be no courteous reception in the castle hall.

James turned and called out, "Sir Lennox, have the knights show their best form! We want Lord MacLean and his allies to see the spirit of Scotland in our party."

"Aye, Your Majesty!" Sir Lennox called back.

James urged his horse to quicken its pace, and the bay charger stepped out eagerly, its coiled, muscular power evident in every stride. The rest of the retinue followed, with the knights bringing up the rear. Their black horses, dress armor, and royal banners flying in the wind made them look like men riding out of a myth.

Robert rode alongside James and heard people murmuring and whispering as they passed by. He doubted they had known James was so young. His fair looks and the air of quiet authority about him were already making an impression.

Lord MacLean, however, sat his horse unmoved as he and his men watched the king approach. Montrose and Argyll had been able to tell James more about the clan leader, including that he spoke fluent Gaelic. This made James's heart leap. He would have the advantage of surprise there.

James pulled his horse to a stop only a few feet from MacLean. Neither man bowed as they studied each other.

Lord MacLean had coarse, red-brown hair tied back with a leather thong, a full red beard, and deep-set eyes that regarded the young king with mixed curiosity and contempt. Broad and thick as Lord Angus, MacLean sat his horse with the confidence of a man at home in battle. He wore a deep-green tunic with a plaid cloak of red, gold, and black fastened at his throat by a gold pin. He had pushed up the sleeve on his right arm, revealing a vivid scar running from elbow to wrist. Even without armor, he seemed invulnerable.

James broke the silence in a clear, strong voice. *"Cha d'fhuaireadh am facal Beurla.* Greetings to you, Lord MacLean."

The men around MacLean, who had been staring at James in stony silence, shifted in their saddles and glanced at each other, startled. A king who could speak the Old Language!

MacLean turned his head to the others and said, *"Tha coachladh cuir air clò Chaluim."*

His tone was amused, as if James were a child mimicking adult speech. The men laughed. James caught the meaning: "He's full of surprises."

"The day may be full of surprises, Lord MacLean," he said in Gaelic. "Let's confirm the terms of our duel."

The two of them dismounted, surrounded by their seconds. The usual duty of the seconds was to try to reconcile the duelists, but in this case the issue would be settled on the course.

It was agreed that only one man would accompany each of them. James chose Captain van Horn. MacLean chose his son Hamish, who was only a little older than James. MacLean's men at arms and the king's knights would stand as guarantors for the safety of both men. The two groups eyed each other warily.

The stakes of the duel were high. If MacLean won the game, he and his allies would be able to rule over their own estates without the king's interference. This would set a dangerous precedent that other clans would be likely to follow, crippling the power of the crown.

If James won, the clans would pledge their fealty to the crown for the first time in three generations. They would also agree to abide by the laws of the land, including taxation and the legal system. This would be a bitter loss of power to swallow.

With the terms settled, the four of them approached the first fairway. MacLean, as the one challenged, went first. James saw with satisfaction that the ball the clan chief used was roughly made, and he silently thanked Margaret and Wullie for their innovations.

While MacLean was lining up his shot, James gazed out over the course. It was exactly as Montrose, Argyll, and Gray had described.

They had mapped out every fairway, green, and hazard for him, describing the lay of the land at each point, how the greens slanted, where the uneven ground lay, what the hazards were like. They drew sketches and discussed whether a green ran fast or slow and where the trickiest shots were likely to be. At this point, James felt he could walk the course blindfolded.

The wind blew harder, tugging at his clothes, and brought his mind back to the duel.

The captain murmured, "Which way is the wind blowing, Your Majesty?"

James laughed. "From the north, in a steady breeze." He looked meaningfully at van Horn. "But I think it might turn in our favor to the south before the day is over. What do you think?"

"There's a very good chance, Sire."

A rousing cheer from the crowd drew his attention to MacLean. The man had hit his ball far down the fairway, the wind pushing it to the right.

MacLean swept his arm toward James in a mocking gesture. "Your turn, young Stewart."

James, ignoring the man's arrogance, stepped forward. He took out one of the new balls and placed it on the tee, then set his stance. He appeared outwardly calm, but despite his best efforts to reach his sanctuary, his mind was racing.

He felt the pressure of the crowd and the watchful eyes of MacLean and his men on him, and for the first time had an attack of nerves. What if he just nicked the ball, what if he sent it flying into the crowd, what if he lost his grip on the club and sent *that* flying into the crowd?

In the midst of this inner chaos, he swung his club up and back, then whipped it down. . . and missed the ball completely. A great roar of laughter erupted from the crowd, with MacLean laughing loudest of all.

His face burning, James heard the captain say quietly behind him, "Steady as she goes."

All right, he told himself, he'd done his worst. Anything he did now could only be an improvement. This time, he closed his eyes, breathed deeply, slowly, and felt his heart grow warm and quiet. He had an uncanny sense of merging with the club in his hands, the turf under his feet. The noise of the crowd faded; what was at stake in this game dissolved.

All that mattered was this moment as he swung the club back and swept it down, knowing even before the club head connected that the ball would end up close to MacLean's.

He watched the leather sphere sail through the air to land within four feet of MacLean's ball. The crowd fell silent. Only Robert, the two earls, and the king's knights cheered the shot.

MacLean said loud enough for James to hear: "Luck makes a fool look wise."

James smiled. "Lord MacLean, wisdom makes its own luck."

He caught the wary look MacLean gave him. Full of surprises, indeed.

From that moment on, both James and MacLean played as if they were possessed, answering one uncanny shot with another.

At the third hole, where a water hazard blocked the green, MacLean hit the ball in a high arc over the pond. It bounced once onto the green, then seemed pushed by some invisible hand to within a foot of the hole. The crowd cheered wildly, and MacLean grinned in triumph, saluting the people.

The wind suddenly picked up, blowing so hard James had to brace himself to keep his feet. He would need a low, straight shot to keep the ball out of the crosswind. But the moment he swung, he knew with dismal certainty the ball would fall short and end up in the water. He tried hard not to show his dismay. The mistake would likely cost him two strokes and put MacLean in the lead.

Just as he feared, the ball, traveling in a low, straight line, struck the surface of the pond. But to his astonishment, it then skipped twice like a river stone over the water and rolled onto the fairway just outside the green. The lacquer coating—had it repelled the water?

His hopes soared, and James made an effort to hand his club calmly to the captain, as if the play had been nothing unusual.

A few whispers arose from the crowd, but people seemed too awed to talk out loud. While MacLean's shot had been a marvel of skill, this shot had a touch of the supernatural about it. The clan chief's amused contempt vanished, and for the first time he looked a bit worried.

By the fourth hole, everyone knew something extraordinary was happening on the course. If MacLean blasted his ball through a thicket onto the fairway, James launched his ball out of a blind ditch onto the green. If James sank a 40-foot putt, MacLean sank a 60-foot one.

The crowd began to cheer for both men. At some point, MacLean's men at arms and James's knights abandoned keeping watch on each other and joined the crowd, eagerly following every play.

As the game intensified, the duel became one of wits as well as skill. MacLean and his son tried to disrupt the young king's game. Hamish dropped his bag of clubs just as James was about to putt. The two men laughed loudly and shouted to the crowd, who took their lead from the clan chief and began to harass James as well.

The young king was deeply grateful for everything his friends had put him through in training. It was fairly easy to enter his sanctuary and block out all distractions.

At the end of the sixth hole, halfway through the game, MacLean paused to take a drink from an elaborate silver flask and offered a dram to James. The young king knew that according to Highland customs he could not refuse and still hope to gain MacLean's respect and the crowd's support.

He glanced at the captain, who nodded briefly, and took the flask. The drink went down like liquid fire, much stronger than anything Sir Lennox had ever given him, and it required a mighty effort of will not to cough and sputter.

James turned back to the captain, his eyes watering and his head feeling slightly detached from his body. The club was like an iron stick in his hand.

The captain took one look at him and fished a small flask out of his pocket. "Drink this quickly."

James downed the thick, spiced liquid. Within a few seconds, it had put out the fire in his throat and cleared his head.

Van Horn capped the flask and grinned. "Master Zheng's brew. I thought it might be needed."

James wiped his eyes and said hoarsely, "Your foresight, as always, is uncanny."

MacLean and his son watched him closely as he lined up his shot, almost as if waiting for him to topple over. James thought about retaliating—it would be simple justice if he did.

No. The higher justice was to win free and clear. Besides, MacLean had had to replace his ball three times already. Each new ball acted differently when hit, affecting the clan leader's shots. So far, James had been able to use the same ball.

From that point on, James focused on his game even more. He wanted to give MacLean no excuses for defeat. The captain helped him stay anchored in this decision by offering a steady stream of advice along the way.

When James's ball landed in a small crater in the sand trap: "Work your feet into the sand. That's it. Now you'll be solid on the shot. Strike the back edge of the crater around the ball."

When the ball landed in tall grass in the rough: "Play well back in your stance, James. You'll get the most contact with the ball with the least grass."

By the ninth hole, James was winning by three strokes.

But MacLean was not one to give in or let up. On the tenth hole, the wind caught his long drive and sent it 250 yards down the fairway. James had to take two shots over the same distance and lost a stroke. By the eleventh hole, MacLean was only one stroke down.

The twelfth and final hole started with the advantage to James. MacLean hooked his drive, landing in the rough behind a pile of stones. James drove straight down the fairway and was starting to feel more confident about winning until MacLean made an impossible shot. His ball arced over the stones, struck a small oak tree, and ricocheted onto the fairway.

The roar of the crowd made James lose his focus for an instant; he jerked his club and watched, sickened, as his ball went sailing past the green into the rough at its edge. He was over 70 feet from the hole, but it might as well have been a mile. Not even the captain's consoling words helped.

MacLean's next shot put him on the green 30 feet away from the hole on fairly level ground.

The crowd had fallen deathly quiet, the only sound the wind whispering through the grass. James and the captain studied the wicked twists and turns of this last green. James's heart sank like a stone.

The green was shaped almost like a bowl on his side, curving up and then breaking sharply down before leveling off to the hole. He knelt to look at the terrain more closely and noticed an unevenness to the surface. That would make the shot even harder.

James and van Horn cleared the debris from the green as best they could. The wind sprang up fiercer now, as if to challenge James even more. It was down to this one shot. If he took two shots to sink the ball, and MacLean made his putt, MacLean would win. If James could put his ball into the hole with one shot, the game was his.

The captain stepped back; it was up to James now.

The young king approached the ball, but he felt a curious weakness, as if the pressure of the moment were draining his strength.

He stilled himself, reaching deeper within than ever before, and then, as the captain had taught him, drew in the energy of Earth through the soles of his feet. He seemed to be pulling the power of flowing water into his body, refreshing and strengthening it.

His mind, his heart grew quiet as breath; he focused on the weight of the club in his hands, the living feel of it. As had happened before in key moments of the game, a path to the hole seemed to appear in the grass. All he had to do was send the ball along that invisible line.

His vision narrowed until all he could see was a leather sphere in a small patch of ground. He swung the club back, trusting that his body would know what to do, and struck the ball a sharp, decisive blow.

At first he thought he had hit it too hard. The ball shot forward, almost skimming the grass as it crossed the wide green. He sent a silent command after it: *Slow down!*

The ball, heedless, continued to speed toward the top of the green. Another foot and it would be in the rough. James stopped breathing, the blood pounding in his ears.

Turn, he begged it. *In the name of God, turn, turn!* To his immense relief, the ball obediently followed that invisible line and curved downward toward the hole.

The murmur of the crowd grew louder and louder as the ball, still heading straight for its target, began to lose speed in the bumpy grass. James leaned to one side, trying to keep it going, and threw out a plea. *Margaret, help me!*

In answer, the ball started to bobble the last few feet.

He felt the rivers within him turn to ice; the crowd seemed to disappear. His vision narrowed to the small sphere that carried all his hopes. *Keep going, oh, keep going . . .*

The ball hopped right and then careened left before reaching the lip of the hole. It hung for a long, agonizing moment. And at last fell in.

A thunderous cheer exploded from the crowd, even MacLean's men joining in with the king's knights. James almost dropped to his knees in gratitude and felt the captain's strong arm steadying him. He heard Robert, Montrose, and Argyll all shouting. Then the crowd's cheer died away, as if people suddenly realized what James's victory meant.

MacLean's face was pale. The duel was lost, but tradition demanded that he finish the hole. He stared bleakly at the distance stretching between his ball and the cup.

Van Horn leaned in toward James and said softly, "It might be time for the Soul's generosity, Your Majesty."

James didn't understand at first. Then he looked at MacLean again. The man, already badly shaken, would be doubly humiliated if he missed this shot. James nodded to the captain and walked onto the green.

He spoke so all could hear. "Lord MacLean, we have both played with skill and fortitude. Fortune favored me this day, but on another day, I have no doubt it would have favored you. Therefore, I concede your skill in making this shot and propose we declare the duel concluded. What say you?"

The look on Lord MacLean's face was hard to interpret. The man's eyes bored into James as if weighing every word.

The young king had the sudden feeling that if MacLean detected the slightest mockery or disrespect, there would be bloodshed. James knew the defeat was a bitter wound for him, especially suffered in front of his allies and his own people. Clan pride ran deep.

Out of the corner of his eye, James could see MacLean's men at arms gripping their weapons. Even though they had cheered the young king, they would split him in two at a nod from their clan chief. Sensing the change, Sir Lennox and his knights started to move toward James. He stopped them with a lift of his hand, still looking calmly at MacLean.

The silence stretched on until James could feel sweat trickling down his back. At last MacLean slowly bent down and picked up his ball, held it for a moment, then tossed it up and caught it deftly.

His voice rang out. "I say our duel is concluded."

At his signal, the other four clan chiefs stepped forward and gathered around MacLean. They reminded James of stags at bay, still dangerous even in defeat. James studied their rugged, battle-scarred faces and the proud set of their shoulders. These men could be bitter enemies or fierce friends of the crown.

The wise use of power would set the tone for the relationship between these clans and the crown for a long time to come.

"Gentlemen," he said in Gaelic, addressing them as near equals. The men were quick to notice this gesture, and their hostility seemed to ease. "You are free men of the north. Your word alone is guarantee of your honor. We need no other bond between us."

James had just let them know he did not require them to kneel before him, something he was sure they would have refused to do. Right now, he wanted to avoid a clash of wills at all costs.

MacLean looked at the men around him. After a moment, he folded his arms and said quietly, "And if we choose to contest the outcome of this duel?"

It was a response that Gray and Angus had anticipated. In answer, James turned to the high ground above the course and waved his arm. Lord Angus, who appeared as if conjured out of thin air, waved back, and suddenly the knoll sprouted a long line of warriors. MacLean and his allies, along with the crowd, gaped at that bristling line.

James turned back to MacLean. "The other clans were eager to watch the duel as well, but I didn't think your course could accommodate four thousand men. I told them to wait until the final hole was played."

MacLean studied the men on the knoll and then gazed thoughtfully at James as if debating whether to be angry or amused. At last, to James's great relief, his laughter boomed out over the crowd. The other clan chiefs joined in.

MacLean bowed his head briefly in respect for James's final play. "Wisdom as well as luck. Truly, you are full of surprises," he said.

He raised his voice until it rang over the course. "According to the terms of the duel, the northern clans of MacLean pledge their fealty to the crown. We swear to honor this pledge until death, Your Majesty."

Your Majesty.

Everything James had risked to gain was in those two words. It was a moment before he could reply. Then he said simply: "Gentlemen, it is a proud day for Scotland that I call you allies."

Chapter 13

Among Equals

The king's knights and MacLean's men-at-arms escorted James and MacLean across the course to the castle road. Along the way, the crowd cheered as if the two men were victors returning from battle; all enmity toward the crown had vanished.

James could hardly feel the ground beneath him, still overwhelmed that his gamble had paid off so spectacularly. He was dimly aware of reaching their horses on the road, of speaking with Robert, and of the people pressing around him.

James mounted his horse and in that moment, his vision shifted strangely. As he looked at MacLean and the clan chiefs, at Robert, Angus and Gray, at the king's knights, he saw a light within each of them glowing like a bright flame.

Astonished, James gazed at the herders and farmers thronged on either side of the road, all those who wore ragged cloth, rough wool, and tattered boots or no footwear at all. In every one of them, the same light burned as brightly, regardless of rank or status, young or old, male or female.

This discovery shook James to his core. All his life he had been told that it was divine order for a select few to rule over all the rest, who by nature lacked the qualities of their superiors. Yet the evidence of his own eyes now told him this teaching was false. How could this be?

Dazed by the revelation, James turned to the captain, who was

128

riding close beside him. He found the same light in the captain, but much brighter than in the others. Van Horn stared intently into his eyes and smiled.

"Do you see it, James?" he asked quietly. "What lies deep within us all?"

James replied in a hoarse whisper, "What am I seeing?"

"The Soul's light—our true self."

As if the captain's words had broken a spell, the noise of the crowd abruptly returned, hitting James with a wall of sound. At the same time, his eyes could no longer see the light in people. But the revelation it had awakened remained.

As they entered the castle grounds, MacLean proposed that James and his retinue stay as his guests for a few days, and James decided to accept the invitation. The clan chiefs seemed as eager to prove their hospitality to the crown as they once had been to declare their independence.

James saw to it that his men were settled in the castle and sent word to Angus to dismiss the army he had brought northward. Not until evening could James meet with the captain in his chambers. Robert had reluctantly moved into Lord Gray's room for the night, grumbling, "One day, you had better explain what this is all about, James."

James closed the door and turned to face the captain. "Now tell me—what was that light I saw?" he demanded.

The captain sat down slowly in one of the heavy oak chairs by the fireplace. "The first time it happened to me, I thought I was going mad . . . everyone ablaze as if they had candle fire in them? I didn't know what to think."

He stretched out his legs, easing the tightness in them. "Then Master Zheng told me that a kind of inner eye had opened up, allowing me to witness the Soul's light in all people. I was seeing our dual nature, he said, the indwelling Soul in an Earthly body . . . in everyone, without exception."

"Yes!" James said. "The servants, the farmers, the nobles all had the same light. They looked . . . that is . . . as if they were . . ." His voice slowly trailed off.

Van Horn waited and then said, "I believe the word you are searching for is *equal*."

James nearly shouted, "That can't be! That's . . . that's not the way heaven has ordained it. There are rulers and ruled, superiors and inferiors. It's how the kingdom is arranged, how nature itself is ordered!"

The captain remained silent as James struggled to regain his footing.

"If. . . if we were all equal, things would fall into chaos. The lowest peasant would be equal to a king—that's not possible!"

"And yet," the captain said quietly, "the same light is within you both."

James flung himself into a chair and grasped his head. The room seemed to be spinning, and he couldn't stop it. Van Horn laid a hand on his shoulder.

"Aye, it's a hard learning, James, especially for one who must be king. You have centuries of tradition against you if you want to act on the truth about our human race. Yet your very Soul tells you it is real."

James dropped his hands and stared at the man bleakly. "Who would listen to such talk? Everyone is equal? The nobles, the church—they'd think I've gone mad, and God's truth, I couldn't blame them."

The captain gazed at him sympathetically. "Give the knowledge time to become part of you. The fact that your sight opened here means you are to talk with MacLean about your vision for Scotland."

James could feel his confidence fading. His goal had seemed so clear before: win the duel and gain the fealty of these clans; then persuade the Highlanders to join a united Scotland.

130

Now, with his own mind in turmoil, the task seemed beyond his power. If the Highlanders refused to be part of a unified Scotland, word of that refusal would travel rapidly throughout the country. Other regions would be emboldened to resist, threatening his reign before it even began.

How could he face Margaret and bear the disappointment in her eyes?

"Forgive me, Captain, but to persuade MacLean, heaven itself would have to give me the words."

Van Horn's eyes sparked with humor. "Well, James, since you have heaven itself within you, that shouldn't be too difficult."

The look of despair on James's face sobered the captain. *Ah, he's lost himself. No wonder, given what he's seen. Well, Master Zheng, I've comforted the boy, now I need to call to the man.*

"Your Majesty," he said firmly. He saw James straighten at the words, jolted by the title van Horn rarely used between them. "Your Majesty, this task is well within your power. You don't have to persuade all the Highlanders, just their leader. Let MacLean bring in the others."

James suddenly felt like a child caught out of school. His fear diminished, and the world seemed to right itself again.

"You have always acted as more than a father to me, Captain, recalling me to myself. How can I ever repay you?"

Van Horn glanced away and had to clear his throat several times before he could speak. "Yes . . . well. . . 'tis a mutual feeling, James. Just attend to your Soul. That's payment enough."

He rubbed his hands vigorously. "Now, let me give you some advice about men like MacLean. He may be easier to win over than you think."

It was some time before James could act on what the captain had advised him. The next day, MacLean and his chiefs arranged a feast that drew in clan members from throughout the region. The chief seemed determined to show James and his retinue the grandest traditions of the Highlands to dispel common beliefs about the "rough, backward" north country.

Musicians, poets, and artists crowded into the castle, eager to impress the royal visitors. The rich smells of roasting boar and ox filled the castle as great slabs of meat turned on the spits in the main kitchen, intermingled with the pungent scent of simmering stews and baking breads and pastries.

The preparations were overshadowed by the great banquet hall itself. Ablaze with torchlight and candle fire, the hall glowed like a cathedral as James and his retinue entered, escorted by MacLean, the clan chiefs and their families.

The banquet tables, arranged in a long U, were festooned with late-summer flowers, pewter goblets and, to James's surprise, heavy chinaware and gleaming cutlery—not the wooden bowls and truncheons he had expected to find.

"The chinaware is from the Low Countries," the captain murmured. "I recognize the pattern on the plates and cups. There's been trade between the Highlands and the Dutch before, James. The Scots probably offered wools, fur, salmon and cod for these fineries. Something you might use."

The crossbeams were draped with banners showing the MacLean heraldry, while huge tapestries hung on the towering walls. In most castles, the tapestries depicted scenes of hunting or highlighted a clan's great leaders and their battles against rival clans.

But here James noticed that over half the tapestries portrayed religious themes—the Garden of Eden, the Great Flood, the crucifixion and ascension of Christ. He saw that MacLean himself, along with his wife and children and the other leaders, all wore elaborately fashioned crosses that blended Celtic designs with the Christian image.

James recalled part of the captain's advice: "Notice what

symbols dominate the castle hall. This will give you a clue to the heart of the man."

An earnest and deep faith, that's the heart of him, James thought. But as yet he had little idea what use to make of this knowledge.

The Highlanders themselves were dressed in finery that would have put to shame many of the town burghers in Stirling or Edinburgh. They wore not only fine woolen cloth but silks and velvets, trimmed in ermine and fox fur. The women's braided hair flashed and sparkled with silk ribbons and jeweled combs. The assembled poets recited sophisticated tales from Celtic myths and Biblical stories. Far from "barbaric," the Highland culture was as complex as any James had seen in the rest of Scotland.

He was glad he had brought his finest clothing and insisted the others do the same. As Margaret had said, "You cannot be outdone by the people you're trying to impress."

A sudden longing to have her by his side seized him. She would have been the brightest jewel in the room. Robert caught his eye and smiled. James could tell he was thinking the same of Sibylla.

As the meat and drink were served, talk around the tables quickly turned to the duel. Men and women both replayed every move, telling and retelling the more remarkable shots made by the two players. One man swore he had seen a saint come out of the pond and send James's ball skipping across the water, while another recalled a marsh spirit flinging MacLean's ball out of the rough. The legends grew with each retelling.

James didn't mind. The more they embellished the story, the more power the crown would have in this region. He knew from reading history that myth far outweighed fact when it came to winning over a people. Besides, as he had seen at court, once a story caught fire in the imagination, there was no putting it out.

Several times over the next two days, James started to speak with MacLean, but each time his Soul counseled him to wait. Instead, he accompanied MacLean on a tour of the region, not only the castles of the clan chiefs, but the small farms, cottages, and tiny villages scattered across the countryside.

James could see the soil was poor and thin, broken up by stony outcroppings. Fields of oats, barley, and wheat seemed to grow only through the sheer will of the farmers. Flocks of sheep and long-horned cattle picked their way along the rocky ground, their thick coats a sign of the harsh weather they endured most of the year.

But it was the people who made the deepest impression on James. Before, he would have simply looked past them to the fields and flocks they tended. But ever since seeing the light that each carried within, he couldn't think the same way. Now his gaze kept returning to their lined faces, the stoop of their shoulders, the worn look of them.

They stared in disbelief at his royal cloak, his fine velvet tunic and boots, and the Stewart tartan draped over his shoulder, even the trappings his horse wore. When he stopped to ask a question or two, some were so awestruck they could barely stammer out a reply. MacLean, impatient at their slowness, struck a few of them with his staff and shouted, "Answer the king!"

Most took the blows without complaint—the clan chief was absolute ruler on the estate. But in a few faces, James caught a flash of anger. *They know they're worth more,* he thought, *even if they don't know why.*

The same scenes were repeated at each estate he visited. Most of the people either worked at the castle or tried to scratch out a bare living from the land.

He was beginning to understand why the clans fought each other as a way of life and resisted the crown's authority so bitterly. Taking over a rival's estate was one of the few ways they could increase their own wealth.

And with most of the population living on the edge of poverty, taxes would be a great hardship to pay. If the tax collector seized land or livestock as payment, the victims would starve. It was enough that the clan chief took his share, often leaving farmers and herders with barely enough to survive.

It was clear that as king he needed to do more than unify Scotland. He had to transform it. For such a task, he needed strong allies. James knew barons loyal to his father were already scheming to oppose him.

His resolve sharpened into a decision; he would talk with MacLean that night.

As it turned out, the clan chief himself gave James the chance he had been waiting for. That evening as the feasting neared the end, MacLean stood up from the table and gestured for James to follow him. "I'd like to show you something, Your Majesty."

The captain, conferring with two men nearby, overheard MacLean. He glanced up at the clan chief, then nodded to James as if to say, *Now is the time.*

James stood up, glad to find he was still steady on his feet. Thanks to Master Zheng's potion, he was one of the few revelers still halfway sober.

Most of his men and MacLean's clansmen lay scattered about the hall. Robert was sprawled near the fireplace with two of the king's knights. Angus and Gray were waving their pewter goblets and singing a drunken ballad with two clan chiefs.

MacLean led James up steep, winding stairs to the top ramparts of the castle. The slanting rays of the setting sun flooded the rolling land below them, turning the heather a deep purple on the hillsides. To the north, the distant mountain peaks glowed with the last light of day.

MacLean stretched his arms out wide as if to embrace the land. "Look at it. The MacLean clan has been here for over four hundred years. I'm the nineteenth generation—my sons will be the twentieth."

James studied MacLean's slightly reddened eyes and strong face, deeply lined by wind and sun. "You belong to the land, Lord MacLean, as much as it belongs to you. Anyone can see that. As for the Stewarts, to hear my great-grandmother tell it, we sprang out of the ground like dragon's teeth and have been here ever since."

MacLean laughed. "'Dragon's teeth!" He gave James a look of measured respect. "She might be right . . . from the mettle her great-grandson has shown."

They were silent for a moment. James was glad MacLean couldn't hear his pounding heart. He was as nervous as before the duel. If his Soul had tested him then, it was testing him far more now. So much depended on his relationship with the clan chief.

James stepped beside MacLean, looking out over the vista below them, and tried to keep his voice deliberately casual.

"I've heard it reported that you once hanged a man for stealing a chicken. Is that true or has the tale been exaggerated in the retelling?"

MacLean folded his arms across his chest. "It's true, Your Majesty. A clan chief is judge, jury, and executioner. It's always been that way."

"It seems a severe punishment for the theft of a chicken. Shouldn't your power be tempered by compassion?"

"By weakness, you mean? If I showed compassion toward one thief, it would only encourage the others, and there's enough thieving going on as it is. Before long the tenants would lose respect for their clan chief and be selling the secrets of our castle stronghold to rival clans. No, there are those meant to rule and those meant to serve. That's the way Heaven has ordained it."

James flushed, hearing his own words repeated back to him. He breathed slowly, deeply. *Let the Soul choose my words,* he prayed, *let it speak for me.*

The rays of the sun caught the cross on MacLean's chest, and James found himself asking: "And what if Heaven has ordained a different order?"

MacLean unfolded his arms. "What do you mean?"

"According to the Lord of Heaven himself, we all come from the same source, do we not?"

MacLean's face reddened as the words sank in. "Are you saying that a common thief enters the world the equal of a clan chief or a king? That's going against what the Church teaches, that we are each assigned a place in this world. To strive above our rank is to go against Heaven!"

"Yet Scottish history is rife with those who fought each other to be king."

"And why not? Why shouldn't those in higher rank strive for all the wealth and power they can get? They deserve it. They have the cleverness and nerve to win the right, while those of a lower rank could never succeed."

"Why strive for personal gain only?" James asked. "Why not use power and wealth to build a kingdom that ensures advancement for many, not just a few?"

MacLean gestured toward the rolling hills stretching below them. "You talk about wealth and power. Look at this land—how poor it is. Heaven itself has treated it in a paltry way. Here wealth and power don't come from tilling the land but from ruling it. Everyone in the region knows this, which is why we build our castles to withstand raids from one another."

He faced James. "We clan chiefs and our men can be a powerful fighting arm for you, Your Majesty, but don't ask us to stop raiding and sow the fields or tend sheep. That's what the tenants are for. It's their lot in life."

"And you believe Our Savior ordained it this way?"

"Aye, and so it is."

James stepped closer. "Then answer me this: Why did He choose His twelve followers from among 'tenants' like those? Not a single ruler, noble, knight, or clergy among the twelve. In truth, you and I, Lord MacLean, with all our wealth and power—He would not have chosen us. What did He see in them?"

MacLean stared back, anger and puzzlement flickering across his face like cloud shadows.

James looked into his eyes. "What did He see in them?" he asked earnestly, as if he and MacLean were trying to solve the mystery together. The light in the faces he had seen still haunted him. "And when we look at them, what do we see? The men and women around you, what do you see?"

When MacLean remained silent, James said, "Perhaps He had a different view of power and wealth."

MacLean turned away, the dying light lingering on his face. "It's easy for you to consider such things, Sire. You are young yet, and haven't suffered much in the world nor had to hard-scrabble for yourself."

James moved even closer to MacLean. The words flowed from deep within him. "You are a laird of the manor, a chief of your clan. This is a heavy responsibility. But I must be a king and guide a country—and I will answer with my Soul for the welfare of all her people. I need men who can help me forge a new vision for Scotland. Are you among those men, Lord MacLean?"

The hair prickled on MacLean's neck. He had the sudden, eerie feeling that something more than human was speaking through this young man. Suddenly he recalled a vivid dream he'd had only two days before James arrived. In it, an ancient shield lay shattered on the floor. A voice commanded him to assemble it, but he was unable to do so.

"What is your vision, Sire?" he asked, his voice low.

"We must draw all parts of Scotland together: the Borderlands, Middle Country, Highlands, the Western Isles into one great council—"

"And how would the Highlands fare among the wealthier cities and rich burghs? How are we to obtain an equal voice?"

James remembered what the captain had told him. "At one time your clans traded with the Low Countries across the North Sea. Not only wool and furs, but salmon, cod, and herring. These were prized in Europe."

"Yes! But since then raiders and pirates have destroyed our harbors, our ships. We cried out for help, but no one answered."

"I will answer!" James said, his eyes flashing. "My father left me a strong navy, and my admiral will sweep the sea clear of raiders. We can restore your trade and bring wealth into your clans. And that wealth will be a boon to all your people, easing their lives.

"Our destiny lies in becoming one nation, Lord MacLean, like a great shield protecting all our people. Only then will other nations respect us, only then can all of our people prosper."

Like a great shield . . . a chill shot through MacLean. Had God sent this young king the same dream? James's face before him appeared to glow with an inner light, like a mythic king returned and calling for men to follow him.

"And how does Ross MacLean answer?" James asked suddenly.

Overcome with emotion, MacLean slowly knelt on one knee. "It's God's will, Your Majesty . . . I must follow you."

For a moment, James couldn't move. He heard the captain's words: *Men like MacLean have but one defense—breach that wall, and he will join you.* Somehow, his Soul had known just how to do it.

James reached out and laid a hand on the man's shoulder.

"Rise, Lord MacLean. Heaven has made us brothers in this endeavor."

As Captain van Horn had predicted, James had to do little to persuade the other clan chiefs to accept the vision of a united Scotland. MacLean's arguments and forceful personality did the work for him.

"This is God's will for our clans!" MacLean thundered. "The English will fear us, and our enemies will look elsewhere for conquests. We will make a nation to rival those of Europe!"

Robert leaned toward James and murmured, "You've made quite a convert. What did you promise him?"

"I take no credit. My Soul found the heart of the man."

"I would appoint your Soul chief counselor from now on," Robert said. He glanced toward Van Horn. "That is, if he will allow it."

James heard the jealousy in his friend's voice but didn't respond to it. Instead, he merely replied, "Rest assured, Robert, he will allow it."

James decided to seize the moment and propose a code of justice for the tenants and farmers, their plight still fresh in his mind. But at this the Highlanders balked, claiming, "Fealty to the crown does not include losing power over our estates!"

James was afraid he had risked too much and threatened his new alliance, but the Soul kept urging him on. As he pressed the chiefs to reconsider, he had to return to his sanctuary over and over when his anger and frustration pulled him away. Didn't these men understand the burdens placed on their people, the fear they lived with?

At such moments, the captain's presence was like a steadying hand on his shoulder. Finally James rose and addressed the clan chiefs, trusting he would find the right words once more. His eyes fell on MacLean's stubborn face. James heard himself asking: "Tell me, Lord MacLean, who is it you love above all others?"

MacLean sat back in surprise and stared at James. The other men seemed to recede from James's sight, leaving only the two of them facing each other in the room. MacLean's hand closed around the Celtic cross at his throat. *My Lord and Savior,* the gesture said.

James asked, "And would you willingly give your life for Him?"

MacLean never broke his gaze, his devotion showing clearly in his eyes. The silence around them was complete, as if the others had stopped breathing.

James said, "Our Lord's true power is rooted not in what He took, but in the life He willingly gave. He showed us how to wield power here on Earth." James looked at the other chiefs; he had their full attention now. He leaned forward, meeting each man's gaze as if speaking to him alone.

"If we willingly give our people true justice, they will freely give us their love and loyalty—even their very lives. Think of it, my lords! Your people willing to die for you! Such power would make you the strongest clans in the Highlands!"

Silence greeted the end of his words. For a long moment James thought he had failed. Then MacLean, his face flushed with emotion, glanced around him at the others and growled, "God's wounds, Sire, you could sway the Devil from sinning."

Their laughter broke the tension enough that a few men started to throw objections at James.

"What if the tenants and farmers keep stealing deer from our lands?"

"Establish a hunting season so theft is not required to feed their children," James shot back.

"What if a man commits an offense numerous times?"

"Set increasingly severe penalties—and publicly honor those who keep your laws. That will bind them to you even more closely."

James countered every objection with a wisdom that came from the depths of his Soul. He had a vague impression of Robert staring at him in astonishment.

At last the chiefs relented and agreed to establish a legal system that would codify offenses. Everyone on their estates would know both the laws and the punishments for breaking them. Such a code would go a long way to freeing people from the whims of clan chiefs and nobles.

After a final night of feasting, James and his retinue prepared to leave the next morning, gathering with MacLean and his men in the castle courtyard. As a parting gesture of his regard for MacLean, James made a gift of the golf balls Margaret and Wullie had given him.

"May they bring you the good fortune they brought me," James said quietly.

MacLean studied the spheres with a wry smile. "If I'd had these, our story might have ended differently." His eyes met James's. "But then I would be the poorer for it, Your Majesty."

"As would I, Lord MacLean."

The chief glanced over at Angus Douglass and then skillfully drew James away from the others. He switched to Gaelic. "You have given me a gift, Sire. I offer you something in return—a warning."

James waved a hand, inviting him to speak freely.

"I've fought such men as the Earl of Angus for more years than you've been alive. They're like a coin with *friendship* stamped on one side and *treachery* on the other. I beg you, Sire: set a watch on these men more than on your enemies."

James studied the man's rugged face for any hint of guile but found none. He nodded. "My thanks for your gift, Lord MacLean."

The chief bowed his head briefly. The young king's safety mattered more to him than he cared to admit. *"Dia air do chrann! Beannachd Dia dhuit."* God protect you. The blessings of God be with you.

"Beannachd Dia dhuit," James replied.

He mounted his charger, and behind him the others swung up on their horses. James started forward, but as the castle gate opened, he halted in surprise at the sight that greeted him.

The pathway to the main road was lined on either side with herders, farmers, and villagers. But there was a striking difference about this crowd. Instead of cheering and shouting as they had on the course, every man and woman stood in silence. James heard Angus say to the knights, "Stay on your guard, lads."

James shook his head. "No, my lord. They mean us no harm."

He kicked his horse forward, and the others followed, the royal banners rippling in the morning light. The ring of the horses' bridles and the steady hoof beats sounded unnaturally loud in the eerie silence.

As James passed by, the people knelt, slowly at first and then one after another like a wave rippling down the line. Robert, riding beside

James, saw the careworn faces turned up to the king and heard the quiet tributes as he passed by.

"God bless you, Sire."

"May Our Lady keep you safe, Sire."

"Remember us, Your Majesty."

Robert caught something in their faces he had not seen before, a spark of hope. They must have heard about the code of laws the young king had drawn up. One look at James, and he could see the young king was deeply moved.

The group reached the end of MacLean's lands, and James paused to look back at the crowd still standing in the chill air. His gaze shifted to take in the castle behind them and the wild, haunting landscape of the Highlands that stretched to the horizon. For the first time, he felt the full weight of his kingship settle like a mantle on his shoulders.

"We must help them, Robert," James murmured. "All of them."

Watching the two young men, the captain thought, *Well done, Your Majesty. Master Zheng would be proud.*

They turned their horses away and began the long journey back to Stirling Castle.

Chapter 14

Margaret's Duel

Sibylla burst into the women's sewing room, startling Margaret and her lady-in-waiting Lena.

"It's James and Robert! I heard from Wullie!" Sibylla stopped, clutching at her side, completely out of breath.

Margaret's blood ran cold. "What about them?" she demanded. "Are they alive? Tell me!"

"James—defeated—Lord MacLean!" Sibylla gasped. "He won, Margaret!"

"Oh, thanks be to God!" Margaret cried, the needlework forgotten in her hands. She jumped up to hug her sister and then hugged Lena.

Sibylla began to recover her breath. "Lord Angus's soldiers are spreading the story everywhere. They're saying every play was a miracle!"

Margaret laughed. "It was our golf balls! They brought him luck, I know they did! What would Lord MacLean say if he knew a woman and a servant had made them?"

Then a new fear clutched at her heart. "James's success will make his enemies more determined. They'll want to strike before he gains even more popular support!"

The talk at the noon family meal showed Margaret her fears were well founded. With her father away at Edinburgh, Lord Fleming dominated the table's conversation. He seemed to take pleasure in pointing out every danger to James he could imagine.

144

"A few of the old king's supporters want to topple the boy from the throne. Despite his father's unpopularity, the killing of a king doesn't sit well with them, nor with some of the merchants and burghers in the cities. There have been mutterings about 'dark designs behind the rebellion,' even claims the Devil himself was involved in the 'foul crime of a son killing his father.'"

Margaret sat rigid with anger. James had not killed his father. The poor man had done himself in with his foolish actions.

Lord Fleming cut a slice of beef and droned on. "And I hear that Lords Crichton and MacKenzie and others like them resent the men in James's inner circle who are seizing lands, appointments, and royal titles for themselves. Crichton might be willing to fight to rid the court of these carrion feeders.

"And this duel—James must fancy himself now a David slaying Goliath! The flatterers around him will only inflame these boyish delusions."

Margaret fought to remain silent. She needed to hear all of what this strutting rooster had to say as he named names and recounted grievances.

She glanced at her sisters. Sibylla's face had gone pink with anger, like her own, but Euphemia looked pale and distracted, staring sightlessly at her plate. *How far had Lord Fleming gone in dampening her spirit,* Margaret wondered. Another reason to despise the man.

Sudden sharp pains lanced through her hands. Margaret looked down to discover her fingernails had cut blood-red crescents into her palms. Her hands would bear the wounds, but at least she had controlled her temper!

That night in the Drummond chapel, Margaret's fear drove her to kneel before an icon of the Virgin Mary to pray for James's safety. While he was in the Highlands, his enemies might move against him. It could bring civil war and tear Scotland apart once again.

Nightmarish images kept invading her mind—James attacked and left dying in the road like his father, or slain in his bed at night, the sheets stained red with his blood.

She bowed her head, her heart beating hard and fast. Her eyes stung with tears. How could she bear this fear?

Our Lady, help me! But even the Blessed Virgin seemed unable to comfort her now.

Then Margaret remembered what James had told her before he left for his duel. *I have built a place within me where I can hear my Soul.*

What had he meant? She wiped her eyes and tried focusing on her heart, breathing slowly, quietly. After a moment, it seemed to soothe her fear and create a new calm. . . *a place where I can hear my Soul.*

And into that calmness came the words: *Stand and wait.*

She felt a flash of anger. Stand and wait—for what?

Stay calm, she told herself. *Listen to your Soul.*

She breathed again slowly, deeply until the anger faded.

Then in her mind's eye the vision of a spider's web appeared, bejeweled with dew and glowing in the early morning light. She caught her breath at its beauty.

As she watched, the web's long, supporting spokes glowed brighter, and their drops of dew began to flow, one after the other, toward the center.

Like messengers, she thought. Was this what the vision meant? Messengers coming to her from all directions?

But something else waited at the center, something that cast a dark shadow. She felt a chill shoot through her. Like a spider, did death wait there as well?

Slowly the glowing web faded, leaving behind a calm resolution in her heart. She must do everything to help James stay alive. Shadow fears about death mustn't stop her.

Margaret rose to her feet, a daring plan forming in her mind.

Men aren't the only ones who can fight a duel, she thought.

The next morning Sibylla was awakened by Margaret's whispered command: "Meet me and Wullie in the workroom. I need your help."

She left before Sibylla could ask any questions. Sibylla tossed back the covers and called for her lady-in-waiting to help her dress.

She was worried about Margaret. Over the past few days, her sister had been acting very oddly, muttering to herself and spending a great deal of time sketching strange designs like spiderwebs on parchment.

Sibylla had managed to catch a glimpse of one of the drawings. The names "Stirling, Crichton, Dumbarton" were written on points around the web. The names of castles. This only deepened the mystery. Either her sister was going mad, or she was up to something.

Sibylla hurried across the castle courtyard toward the stables, raising her skirts slightly to keep them out of the mud. The moment she arrived at the open workroom door, the thick, cloying smell of boiling chicken feathers struck her like a blow. She choked and covered her nose and mouth with her shawl.

Peering into the small room, Sibylla saw Wullie bent over the hearth fire, patiently stirring a boiling kettle. A battered, stained worktable stood in the center of the room, covered with bags of freshly plucked chicken feathers and strips of leather. Fragments of feathers floated in a shaft of sunlight streaming in from a side window.

Margaret suddenly pulled Sibylla into the room and shut the heavy oak door behind them.

"I told Euphemia we're making more golf balls for James. I had to get us away from any prying eyes and ears in the castle."

The heat in the room was making Sibylla feel light-headed.

"Margaret, please, what is this about?"

"First, you must swear not to repeat what we say here to anyone— anyone. Not even Euphemia."

"But she's our sister—"

"Who is married to Lord Fleming. If he suspects anything, he'll try to stop us."

Wullie coughed discreetly. "Very wise of you, Lady Margaret."

Sibylla fell silent. It was true. Lately, Lord Fleming had made cutting remarks not just about James but about Robert as well. "He has neither wit nor manners. My cousin is a far better suitor for you."

Sibylla had met his cousin. The man talked incessantly about his falcons and stared at a point above her head whenever he deigned to notice her. She would rather join a nunnery than marry such a man.

Margaret led her sister to the stained table, where they perched on two wobbly stools. Margaret's face shone with a fierceness Sibylla found almost alarming.

"James is not yet safely on the throne. You heard Lord Fleming. There are certain men who would be willing to fight to regain the crown."

Wullie nodded. "Aye, m'lady. We hear such talk in the markets. The names of lords Crichton and MacKenzie are bandied about as their leaders."

Sibylla paled. "Then Robert is in danger as well. But what can we do? We can't take up arms, like men. And Father cannot invite these men to Drummond. They know he supports James. So we have no chance to overhear them anymore."

"There is a way to know their plans," Margaret said. She leaned toward her sister. "We must build our own web of spies."

Sibylla gasped and looked at Wullie. His eyes were shining in silent approval. Obviously the two of them had talked about this before.

"Margaret! That's . . . that's . . . so *dangerous*. If we're caught—"

"If we want to help safeguard James and Robert, we have no choice. Which is why you must swear an oath—not a word of this to anyone. I mean it, Sibylla, not to friends, servants, anyone!"

For a moment Sibylla didn't answer. Then a change seemed to come over her, as if her soft features had suddenly sharpened. Margaret was pleased to see a rebellious spark in her eyes.

"I swear," Sibylla said firmly. "No one will know from me."

Wullie wheezed from the fireplace: "May my tongue blacken and my eyes shrivel—"

Margaret said dryly, "A simple 'yes' will do, Wullie."

The old servant lowered his upraised arm. "Yes, my lady."

Sibylla grasped her sister's hand. Margaret could feel her trembling with excitement and fear. "But how do we start? Who do we ask?"

"Wullie will help us. He's worked in some of the Borderlands and Middle Country castles during his youth. He still knows many of the servants there."

Wullie shrugged modestly. "I've a few acquaintances and relatives, your ladyship."

"But what if they are caught?" Sibylla asked. "They could be killed . . . or worse . . ."

To her surprise, Margaret smiled. "Yes, it's true, but you are forgetting something. To most of the high-ranking men, like Lord Crichton and Lord Lyle, women and servants are invisible, seen only when we are needed. We can turn that to our advantage. No one will suspect frivolous girls who stay in their chambers, servants who work in the background."

"You have thought about this in a marvelous way," Sibylla said.

Margaret dabbed the sweat off her face. "I've thought of little else. As I told Wullie, the people we recruit will be those who hear valuable information but are unnoticed by their masters. And they must be able to leave the castle occasionally without attracting suspicion. With God's help, we may prevent a civil war."

Wullie bowed to them both. "Leave it to me, Lady Margaret, Lady Sibylla. I will begin on the morrow and see what can be done. We must choose carefully, as you say. These days, t'ain't easy to tell false friends from true."

"Take care," Margaret said. "We will be trusting our lives to these friends." She pulled a sack of feathers toward her.

"Stoke up the fire as we talk, Wullie. The more chicken feathers we boil, the more their foul smell will keep others away."

149

Sibylla wrinkled her nose in disgust. "In truth, not even the butcher would enter here!"

Wullie was as good as his word. Within a week, he had recruited spies in the households of three castles where Lord Crichton and his retinue were known to visit. In a stroke of luck for the conspirators, one of Wullie's many cousins worked in Lord Lyle's stables.

"The laird talks with his captain while they ride," Wullie confided. "My cousin is a hostler, so he overhears everything the buggers say— begging your pardon, m'lady."

Margaret grimaced. "If I weren't a lady, I'd call them much worse. We need more spies, Wullie!"

As if Providence itself had heard her, the next day, Margaret and Sibylla received an unexpected invitation from one of their cousins at Donne Castle, a few miles to the south.

"It's been far too long since we did needlework together. You must join me on Tuesday, and we will remedy this oversight. Your loving cousin, Aileen."

Sibylla frowned. "We saw her last week at Lord Haile's castle . . ."

Margaret shook her head in warning as the chambermaid entered the room. Sibylla finished loudly, "But one can never do enough needlework. It shows a lady's quality."

When the two of them arrived at Donne Castle, Aileen greeted them warmly and suggested a walk in the castle gardens first. She led them to a tattered gazebo at the far end.

"Only thistles grow here. The servants hate this spot." She smoothed her skirts as she sat down and said casually, "Cousins, I had a dream about you both the other night."

"Did you?" Margaret said, her face carefully neutral.

"Yes. I dreamed that you and Sibylla were writing a treatise . . . about the history of Scottish rebellions."

A spike of fear sent Margaret's heart racing. She struggled not to look at Sibylla. What did Aileen know?

When the two sisters remained silent, Aileen fixed them with a knowing look. "In the dream, I asked if you needed information for this work."

Margaret plucked a purple flower from among the thistles close to the gazebo. "If we were to do such a treatise, we would always be glad of details . . . number of soldiers, time and place, that sort of thing."

"A fortunate coincidence. My uncle, Lord Huntley, has been speaking of these very matters lately. Perhaps I might hear something you could include . . . if you were writing such a work."

Margaret inhaled the faint scent of the thistle flower. "You have very prophetic dreams, cousin. We have indeed started such a work."

Aileen exhaled as if she had been holding her breath. "I was hoping you would trust me enough to accept my help. My lady-in-waiting confided in me that an old servant from Stirling Castle had approached her. She knows my sympathies are with the new king and thought I might be able to help."

Aileen glanced around them. "We can't stay out here long. The duchess who works for my uncle will be suspicious if we don't start our needlework. I had enough trouble getting permission to ask you here in the first place."

Margaret said, "Your help is deeply welcomed. But we can't keep visiting one another every time you have a message."

"We don't need to, cousin." Aileen smiled. "My mother taught me a secret language in needlework that she and her sisters used. I can teach it to you both. We can send messages back and forth through our embroidery samples without arousing any suspicions. What man would look twice at needlework?"

"None that I know of." Sibylla laughed. "How clever!"

"Why are you helping us?" Margaret asked. "Your family has stayed out of this royal fray until now. You are taking a great risk to choose sides."

Aileen's frowned. "I must do something! My uncle is a violent man, and he's pulling my brothers into his schemes. And if the rebels win, he has promised me as a wife to the Earl of Edding—a man who can barely stand upright!"

Aileen glanced to the path behind them and raised her hand. "The Duchess is coming! Quickly, cousin, I must tell you that every day, more men join my uncle's cause. Just a fortnight ago, the Duke of Bothwell came to offer his services and his troops."

Margaret crushed the thistle flower. "The duke? Does he bear a reddish scar on his neck?"

"Yes. Do you know him?"

Sibylla replied, "He's been to Drummond several times. I believe he is one of the Douglass clan."

"The Duke of Bothwell is more than that," Margaret said. "He is the brother of Lord Angus."

As the duchess approached, Margaret whispered to Aileen, "You must teach us this secret language right away. James's friends could prove more treacherous than his enemies."

Chapter 15

The Second Rebellion Begins

After the morning Mass, Lord Crichton lingered in the nave of the small church near his castle until most of the nobles and their families had left. He caught the eyes of Lords Lyle and Jameson, who held back as well.

All three had grievances against the circle of nobles closest to James IV. The three had been supporters of King James III, but in the end believed the man had lost his hold on the kingdom. They had not committed their full forces at the battle of Suchieburn, helping to ensure the success of the rebellion.

Now, after the coronation of James IV, their service was being ignored by men like Gray, Haile, and Angus.

When the last of the worshippers had departed, Crichton closed the church doors, dismissed the priest, and spoke to the two men. "We must act soon, my lords, or we will be shut out of the king's circle entirely and lose all power to influence the court."

Lyle scowled. "I didn't think Haile would seize so much land so quickly. He must have been planning this well before the rebellion."

Jameson glanced around them and lowered his voice. "Lord MacKenzie already charges that the Drummonds will rise above all other families and clans in the new court. Lady Margaret has caught James's fancy, it seems."

"MacKenzie holds an old grudge against the Drummonds," Lyle said. "And the path he takes, Lord Forbes and the others will follow."

Crichton nodded grimly. "We did not hold back our hand in the rebellion to have our rivals cut it off now."

"What do you have in mind?" Jameson asked.

"I will gather my men at Dumbarton. The castle is more fortress than home. We can plan our strategy there. Our campaign must be well thought out before we strike."

Lyle said, "There are others who will join our cause. I know Lord Forbes could be persuaded. He considers killing a king a great sin, and he favors an English alliance, as we do." Lyle's eyes flashed. "It's time we put an end to Drummond's ambitions and signed a treaty with King Henry! James IV must marry an English royal!"

None of the men noticed that an old church caretaker, sweeping the stone floors nearby, was listening to every word.

As James and the others approached the city of Stirling, they discovered that stories of the Highland duel had preceded them. The tales they heard bore little resemblance to what had actually happened. In one version, the ghosts of the ancestral kings David and Alexander had appeared to help guide James's final shot into the hole.

Lord Angus grumbled, "It's the army we sent back, Your Majesty. They've spread folktales like gossiping women."

James was amused. "Aye, but you have to admire their invention!"

In every village and town, crowds flocked to greet them, and innkeepers and hostlers competed fiercely to offer them shelter, food, and care for their horses. Some of the local nobles even raised their golf clubs in salute as James and his retinue passed by, clubs once banned under his father's decree.

Robert pointed them out, laughing. "You'll have to make the game legal, James. There will be golf balls flying everywhere now!"

But they noticed another effect of James's victory. In every gathering, the commoners, men and women both, called out to him,

"Protect us, Sire!" "Give us justice, Your Majesty!" It was clear that what he and MacLean had talked about had spread south just as rapidly, like a fire burning beneath the land.

By the time they reached Stirling Castle, a dense crowd of barons, earls, and dukes waited for them, all eager to be seen with the king. The captain had warned James that from now on he would be watched, flattered, spied on, and constantly surrounded by those seeking their own advancement.

Behind the nobles, James spotted an army of petitioners waving their parchments and calling out to him. The king's knights tried to keep them away, but the petitioners kept pushing forward, desperate to catch his eye.

On the far edges of the crowd, the commoners strained to see the young king. They cheered and waved, holding their children up to glimpse the royal party.

James was struck by the irony of the situation. Up north, in what many would consider uncivilized country, the commoners had been able to speak directly to their king. Here in the center of the kingdom, they couldn't get near him.

How to hold onto his Soul in the face of all this? It would take Heaven and Earth to help him.

The moment James entered the castle courtyard, he spotted Margaret smiling down at him from a tower window, her face rosy in the brisk wind and a dark-green cloak wrapped around her. All his concerns vanished like smoke.

Sibylla stood beside her, waving at Robert, who had gone scarlet in the face the moment she caught his eye.

James's years of court training stood him in good stead as he dismounted and went through the ritual of greeting the castle steward and the royal staff lined up to welcome him home. The steward kept up a steady stream of news as James moved down the line.

"Three ambassadors from Europe are waiting for an audience, Your Majesty. Lord Haile will return to Stirling in a fortnight. Quite upset he was about your departure. Says there are rumors of a rebellion against the crown . . ."

James smiled and nodded but took in very little. It could all wait. He was burning with impatience to see Margaret. At last he was through the line and could enter the throne room, with Robert, Gray, Angus, and the captain following him.

Lords Montrose and Argyll greeted him first, beaming as if James were a prodigy who had performed beyond their expectations. They had the right, he thought. They had helped train him in the game. He heard their hearty congratulations and said something he hoped made sense.

Then he spotted Margaret, and everything else in the room faded. He didn't know when he crossed the distance between them; he just found himself standing in front of her. On the edge of his vision he was dimly aware of her sister Sibylla and their father, Lord Drummond. A cluster of attendants stood behind them.

Margaret bowed her head. "Welcome home, Your Majesty," she murmured as she curtsied.

He held out his hand to lift her up. When she took it, his heart leapt into his throat. She rose to her feet, and he was acutely aware of his travel-worn clothes, the dust covering his face and hair, and the smell of horse sweat that lingered around him. Why hadn't he cleaned up first?

"Lady Margaret," he said, his face burning. "Thank you for your welcome."

"We were glad to hear of your victory, Sire. It must have been a truly memorable battle."

"That it was, Lady Margaret. And our superior weapons played no small part in that victory."

Margaret leaned toward him and murmured in a voice soft as breath,

"See me at Drummond. You are in grave danger!"

When her eyes met his, a shudder swept through him. A shadow had flickered across her face, as dark and vivid as if a raven's wing had blocked the light. It left him reeling. What had happened to her in his absence?

But two days later, when he and Robert finally managed to visit Drummond Castle, the dark shadow was gone. Margaret shone as bright and animated as ever.

"I want you to see where Sibylla, Wullie, and I are making golf balls to replace the ones you gave away to Lord MacLean."

He didn't care where she took him as long as he could be with her. Margaret glanced around at the king's knights escorting them and asked, "Where is Captain van Horn? I've rarely seen you go anywhere without him."

Robert said, only half-joking, "He does occasionally let James out on his own."

James, ignoring him, said to Margaret, "I made certain promises to MacLean that Captain van Horn is helping me to keep. They involve cod and salmon—fish, you know, and maybe wool, between the Highlands and—" *Why was he babbling like this?*

"I'm sure the captain will succeed," she said, smiling.

His heart swelled in gratitude. She didn't think him a complete fool.

As they entered the courtyard and made their way toward the stable area, a rancid stench hit Robert and James so forcefully that it stopped them in their tracks. Robert covered his nose and mouth with his scarf. The knightly escort behind them backed away, coughing and gagging.

"What is this?" James gasped. "The Devil's workshop?"

Margaret laughed and tugged him toward the shed in front of them. "You were curious about how we made the golf balls. Well, now you'll see!"

Once they entered the hot, steaming room, Margaret pulled James away from the open door and out of sight of his men. She was breathing hard, as if she had been running. He was aware of the loose strands of hair curling around her neck, her high color, and the fierce light in her eyes.

How he had missed her! Even the pestilential stench in this small room couldn't dampen his love, although it was making his eyes water.

She spoke quickly, her voice low and intense. "A rebellion against the crown is well underway, James. Even now, the rebels are gathering at Dumbarton Castle. You must act quickly to stop them!"

James spat out a feather and brushed away another floating in the air around them. What was she talking about?

He protested, "Lord Haile said there were only rumors, and Lord Angus—"

"Lord Angus," Margaret said scornfully. "Be wary of that one. His brother has joined the rebels."

"Lord Bothwell has—*how do you know all this*?" James demanded. "Have you spies at Dumbarton?"

"Aye, she does, Your Majesty," Wullie's cracked voice wheezed.

Margaret glanced back at him and Sibylla. The two sat frozen in the act of chopping chicken feathers; Robert stood with his arm around Sibylla's waist.

A smile played around Margaret's lips when she turned back to James. "What Wullie says is only partly true. We have spies in *all* the castles," she said. "All the ones that matter."

For the next hour, James and Robert listened in astonishment as Margaret, Sibylla, and Wullie laid out for them the extent of their spy network. Margaret unrolled a large embroidery nearly three feet square that showed all the most important castles and the landscape surrounding each, along with an array of animals and flowers that decorated each castle ground.

"It's a spy language, James," Margaret explained. "Our cousin taught us how to use symbols for language, and we made up some of our own."

She pointed to Dumbarton Castle. "The thistles represent the number of soldiers gathered there—one thistle for each two hundred men. And each type of flower represents a noble who has pledged his support to Crichton."

Sibylla pointed to a barking dog. "Except for that one. Margaret made that one for Lord Bothwell."

"The man's a mangy cur," Margaret said tartly. "The laurel is Lord Lyle, the dandelion is Lord Forbes, the holly is . . ." She went on until the last noble had been accounted for.

James sat down and stared at the embroidery in awe. The sheer amount of work it had taken to create it and the intelligence it contained made him lightheaded. He counted ten thistles at Dumbarton—2,000 men! If that were true . . .

"Who are these spies, and how accurate is their information?"

"Who are these spies? Tell me, James, on our way through Drummond Castle, how many servants did we encounter?"

"Well, I . . . I suppose a few." He didn't want to admit he hadn't noticed any of them.

"I can tell you. At least twenty—in the courtyard, in the chambers, the great hall, the corridors. Every one of them knew when we passed by and heard what we were talking about."

"We servants hear a great deal, Sire." Wullie nodded humbly. "Whether we wants to or not."

Sibylla said, "Just this morning we learned that Lord Forbes has joined the rebels—"

"And that King Henry has promised to sign a Borderlands truce with them," Margaret said. "You must stop these men, James!"

James looked over at Robert and could tell he was thinking the same thing. How could they go to Lord Gray or Lord Haile and say, "We learned of a rebel plot from the Drummond sisters, who have all the details embroidered on a cloth . . ."

Then he looked at Margaret again, and there was such certainty about her, the way she stood her ground, the courage that warred with her fear. It persuaded him.

He rose to his feet, grasped her hand, and kissed it fervently.

Pulse of my heart, the feeling seemed to flow through his fingertips into hers.

"I believe you, Margaret."

"Thank God!"

Then his duty as king asserted itself. James released her hand and leaned over the embroidered cloth, his attention as sharp and focused as the point of a sword.

"Lord MacLean warned me against men like Angus. Now, tell me again the nobles who have joined this rebellion and how many men are under their command."

Later, James asked Robert to remain at Drummond Castle to learn more from Margaret's spies. He returned to Stirling and found Lord Haile and Lord Gray waiting for him in the throne room.

Before either could say a word, James launched into his report. The two men listened in incredulous silence, glancing at each other in a way James hoped didn't mean, "The king has gone mad."

Lord Haile bowed briefly. "Begging your pardon, Your Majesty, but where did you get such detailed information?"

"From an impeccable source, I assure you."

There was that glance again between the two of them. James was beginning to find it infuriating. Did they think him a gullible child who believed every story?

Lord Gray cleared his throat. "Sire, forgive us, but we are more than amazed by the knowledge you possess. The treachery of Crichton and Lyle we know, but not that the Earl of Forbes had joined them."

James issued an order. "We must send envoys to lords Lyle and Crichton at once and demand they abandon this course and accept their new king and his royal court!"

Lord Haile said hesitantly, "I'm . . . afraid the time for envoys has passed, Your Majesty. If we do not attack the rebels now, we will be fighting them at the gates of Stirling."

James struck the table beside him. "Are we never to be rid of this plague of war?"

He turned away from the men, despair roiling inside him, and gazed out the castle window at the peaceful countryside below. He closed his eyes briefly, trying to calm the turmoil within. Reaching his sanctuary was like pouring cool water on a raging fire.

What had the captain said? *"If you must go to war, the Soul can tell you why. To stop a conflict, to prevent greater loss of life."*

And something more. *"Put the strengths and weaknesses of those you are to rule to a new purpose."*

A plan started to form in his mind, showing him the way forward. He turned back to Haile and Gray.

"My lords, forgive my outburst. You are right. It appears this time we must take swift action. But afterward . . . afterward, I assure you we will gain a victory far beyond any won on the battlefield."

It was nearly midnight when James finally retired to his bedchamber. He had asked Gray and Haile for every detail of their strategy and how many men would be deployed against the rebels. Besides troops, they had also sent the royal siege cannon to shatter the castle walls at Duchal and breach the thick fortress that was Dumbarton. Lord Drummond was to hold his men in reserve while the first assault continued.

James opened the door to his chambers, his mind filled with dark memories of the battle against his father and the bloodshed it had brought.

Then to his great relief and joy, he saw van Horn standing by the fireplace waiting for him. "I heard of the trouble, James, and got here as quickly as I could."

James crossed the room in three strides and embraced the captain tightly, then held him at arms' length, unable to stop grinning. "I thought salmon and cod commanded all your attention."

The captain laughed. "Well, everything considered, fish are rather dull, don't you think? They don't go around staging rebellions. But I'm a boring subject. Tell me, how is the charming Lady Margaret?"

James shook his head. He raised a hand and let it fall in awed resignation. "She is astonishing, Captain. You would not believe what she can do with embroidery."

Van Horn's eyebrows arched in surprise. "Really . . . I had no idea the young lady was so talented."

It was clear the Captain sensed there was more to the story, but James said nothing. Best to wait until they were safely away from the castle. Someone might be watching and listening even this late at night, and he would never endanger Margaret or her spies.

The captain caught his mood and changed the subject. "From what I hear, war with the rebels has already begun."

"Yes." The burden settled on James once again. "There's no chance of a duel for this fight, though I wish with all my heart we could manage it."

A servant entered and placed two mugs of mead on the table, then withdrew. James took a deep draught from one of the mugs and sat back, more tired than he wanted to admit. The captain left his own drink untouched.

"Well, then, this may be the right moment . . ." Van Horn withdrew his hand from his jacket pocket and held out a small roll of parchment tied with a silk ribbon. James sat up, his heart beating faster. *The Fourth Scroll.*

"War can bring many sorrows, James. This may help you when the time comes . . . and for other times. You may not grasp all that it says just yet, but hold the knowledge in your heart."

There was a somberness in his manner toward this scroll that made James hesitate before he took it. He slowly pulled the silk ribbon loose, feeling an unaccountable dread. As he straightened the scroll, a shadow fell across its surface. He shivered; it was like the shadow that had crossed Margaret's face.

Chapter 16

The Fourth Scroll

James suddenly remembered a dream he'd had on the road back from the Highlands. In it, he was caught in a battle and heard Margaret calling out to him. Yet no matter how hard he searched, he couldn't find her.

James broke into a sweat and glanced up at the captain. "You said war can bring sorrows. Am I to lose someone I love because of this war?" He found it impossible to say Margaret's name.

The captain said gently, "Take heart, James. Read the scroll."

The young king's hands shook as he held the parchment. His chest felt constricted by a band of iron. He could barely make himself read the words.

THE FOURTH SCROLL: The Dark Crisis

There may come a time of great sorrow, great loss
That seems to extinguish all light of the Soul.
An endless night descends; you feel abandoned by
Everything and everyone you have ever known.

Yet know this: what happens in this Earthly life
Is not what matters, for much is beyond your control.
What matters is how you transform it.
This alone you choose, this alone you can control.

In this dark crisis, despite your despair, surrender to your Soul.
Its light dispels abandonment, the terrible separation.
Follow where the Soul leads, do whatever it asks.
Guided by its light, you are free.

I will remember who I am. Where I come from. Where I will return.
I will surrender to my Soul in the darkest times.

Every word seemed to pierce his heart. James looked around in a daze. *A great loss . . .*

"I ask you again, Captain," he said, his voice hoarse. "Am I to lose someone I love because of this war?"

"I can't answer for all those you love, James, but if you mean Lady Margaret, then I can put your mind at ease. She will be far from the battlefield."

James clutched his head in despair. "You don't know her. She would ride to battle like the Irish Queen Boudiccia if she thought it would help me."

The captain smiled. "I'm sure she would. But as I said, she will be far from the battlefield."

Relief made James slump back in his chair, feeling he had escaped some black fate. But he was angry the scroll had provoked such fear in him, and he reread it with a more critical eye.

"Here it says a great loss *can extinguish the light of the Soul.* How can that be? The Soul always remains untouched, indestructible. You've told me this over and over. And this part here," he pointed to the first stanza in the scroll, "about being *abandoned by everything and everyone you've ever known.* How can that be true?"

The captain listened as James picked apart the rest of the scroll ("*How you transform it.* Yes, of course, this is obvious"), but all the while van Horn was thinking furiously.

He's young, Master Zheng. He doesn't know great loss yet. How to show him . . .

Then the captain's eye fell on the tapestry hung over the fireplace mantel. The woven scene memorialized Robert Bruce's heroic charge against the English at Stirling Bridge, the same bridge that James had crossed fleeing the king's guards. In the firelight, the soldiers' faces looked contorted into a kind of madness.

"And seeking the Soul, I am always seeking the Soul—"

"James," the captain cut in abruptly, "you'll likely see some of the fighting in this rebellion, unless Lord Haile keeps you away."

James looked up from the scroll impatiently. "If he tries, he'll not succeed," he shot back. "A king should lead the men who fight for him."

"Then perhaps war can give you a sense of what it's like to lose everything. Look at the faces in that tapestry, James—all good, God-fearing men who are honest and fair, who would protect their women and children. But look at their faces!"

James turned to look at a tapestry he had seen all his life. But now the soldiers in Bruce's army seemed transformed, their faces twisted and savage.

"You need to know, James, there is a kind of blood rage that can overtake men in the heat of battle. It's a madness that robs you of yourself. For a time you lust for only one thing. To kill as many as you can. There is no mercy in such a feeling, no human sentiment, but rather a Devil's curse that inflames your mind and limbs."

James stared, appalled at the vision the captain was conjuring.

"A man in the grip of this madness would kill his own family and not know he did it. This is what it means to lose everything and everyone you have ever known."

James sat riveted to his chair, unaware he was crushing the parchment in his hand.

Van Horn leaned forward and said earnestly, "The despair of great loss can be like this, wiping out all comfort and knowledge of the Soul. Keep the words of this scroll in your heart against that time, James. Know that none of us is exempt from such dark madness and despair. Do you understand?"

James stared wordlessly at him, his fist still clenching the parchment. Van Horn let out a long, slow breath and leaned back. *He doesn't understand fully yet, but at least that anger is gone. He won't reject the knowledge the scroll has shown him.*

James looked down at his fist and slowly opened it. He spread the parchment on the table, smoothing out the creases in its pale surface. "God's truth, Captain, you have an uncommon power to make me see what I wish to avoid."

Van Horn smiled ruefully and took a draught from his mug. The drink warmed him as it filled his stomach.

"Master Zheng was an excellent teacher, James. He said to me on more than one occasion, 'Those who do not listen must learn through experience.' I suppose I am trying to save you such hard learning."

James kept smoothing the parchment, feeling a certain comfort in the simple motion. The words flickered in the light as his hand passed over them again and again. They seemed to set themselves in his mind without effort, as if he had given them permission to enter. But he did not want to talk further about their meaning. The chill they put in him was enough.

He spoke without lifting his gaze. "In two days, I ride with Lord Haile to Duchal Castle. I must see for myself the battles to end this rebellion."

"And when you are victorious, what then?"

James glanced at him, half smiling. "You seem sure that I will be."

"The tide is with you, James, and those who try to sail against it will break on the rocks. And then what will you do?"

James remained silent, not sure where the captain was going with his questions. At last he said hesitantly, "I suppose . . . we will celebrate the union of Scotland."

"Will you? No one wins when brother fights brother. Take an old soldier's advice, James. In war, treat victory like a funeral. To delight in victory means you delight in killing. And if you delight in killing, you have lost touch with your Soul."

The memory of the first rebellion came unbidden to James and left a taste like iron in his mouth. "When my father and his forces were defeated, I didn't feel like celebrating. I felt . . . ashamed. All those good men lost—"

"Yes!" Van Horn thumped his empty mug on the table. "That is a fitting response to war."

Buoyed by the captain's response, James blurted out the plan that had been forming in his mind. "I'll offer those shipwrecked rebels a safe harbor. They are all passionate men who served my father long and well. Perhaps there is a way to bring that passion and loyalty into my service."

"Yet some of your nobles will want revenge. You know this."

James' eyes met the captain's. "Only the king can decide a rebel's fate."

Van Horn bowed his head slightly. "Indeed, Your Majesty."

James gently rolled up the creased parchment as if it were gossamer and likely to crumble under his touch. He re-tied the silk ribbon and handed the scroll to the captain without a word.

Van Horn saw the Stewart fire flare in his eyes. The young king's thoughts were as clear as if he had spoken them aloud.

I will keep this knowledge in my heart, Captain, but you had better be right about Margaret.

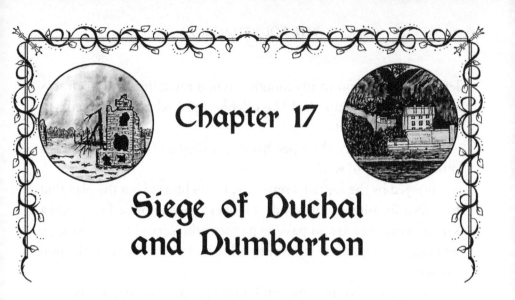

Chapter 17

Siege of Duchal and Dumbarton

The next day, Robert returned from Drummond and showed James the latest embroidery from Margaret. Two more nobles had joined the rebel cause.

"I swear, James, the two sisters' knowledge is greater than any general's. Every day their spies brought news."

"Every day?" James said angrily. "How can Margaret be so foolish! Someone will notice all these servants coming and going—"

"The sisters are very cunning. They've started sewing new clothes for the fall and winter festivals, so they keep ordering supplies, you know, cloth, thread, buttons, ribbons. And the servants—"

James smiled in relief. "The servants deliver them, along with their news."

"Drummond is as crowded as a mid-summer's fair." Robert laughed. "Even if someone suspected the servants, in all that melee no one would know who was a spy and who wasn't."

James rubbed his jaw. "If those two ever join the rebellion, my crown will be forfeit in a month."

"Margaret would never think of it. She talks about you all the time, even to the point of driving her older sister out of the sewing room."

James smiled and leaned against the table. "And Sibylla still favors you?"

Robert tugged blindly at the embroidery threads. "Well, before I left, she was pulling chicken feathers . . . I mean . . . we talked about her father . . ."

"So, between embroidery and chicken feathers, Sibylla talks about her father. This doesn't sound encouraging, Robert."

"You have a devil in you, James, you know that?"

"Rest assured, I am as bewitched by Margaret as you are by Sibylla." He pushed away from the table. "But action may be a remedy. Tomorrow you'll ride with us to Duchal Castle."

"We'll join the battle?" Robert asked eagerly.

"Lord Haile will try to keep us well out of it, but we'll have our own chance. I'd best send word to Margaret where I'm going—"

"I'm sure she already knows. After all, doesn't Wullie's cousin work in the kitchens here?"

James laughed ruefully. "From now on, I'll simply step into the corridor and speak aloud what I want her to know." He rolled up the embroidery cloth. "Come with me to the armory. We need to choose our weapons."

It was a two-day ride to Duchal Castle, and Lord Haile insisted on taking the full complement of the king's knights, fifty in all, to accompany them.

"We'll be passing through territory where some nobles are sympathetic to the rebels," he cautioned. He made James and Robert don part of their armor as well. The two endured the bulky breastplates and helmets, along with Lord Haile's dire predictions of ambushes.

But as they drew close to Duchal Castle, the only people they saw were a few sheepherders, who gawked at the royal party riding by. The idea of war seemed at odds with the peaceful countryside around them. Early fall had tinged the hills with broad swaths of purple heather that blanketed the fields on either side of the road.

Hills towering to the north gleamed white from the first snows, while hawks circled overhead, held aloft by the rising winds.

James wondered if such beauty reflected a watchful presence in Nature, something he could invoke to protect Margaret and her sister.

"What do you think, Robert? Does the natural world care for us as God does?" he asked.

His friend eyed him curiously, glancing around them to see what might have provoked the question. "Perhaps on such days as this." Then he shrugged. "At other times, it can kill us cruelly."

James's face clouded. "More cruelly than we kill one another?"

Robert said nothing, and James made an effort to shake off his mood. "Thinking of battle brings memories of my father."

"It's not good to dwell on such things, James. This rebellion is very different, as Lord Drummond said. The rebels want to overthrow those around you. They do not dispute your right to the throne."

"I'm hoping their fealty to the crown is something I can use—"

A series of deep booms, like the roll of distant thunder, cut across his words. The two pulled their horses to a halt as a second roll of thunder echoed off the hills around them.

"Cannon fire," James said. "That would be Lord Montrose."

Lord Haile and Sir Lennox caught up to James and Robert and drew alongside them.

Sir Lennox said, "Lord Montrose is making short work of Lyle's castle, Sire. By the sound of it, there won't be two stones left standing."

James wanted to ride on, but Sir Lennox made him and Robert suit up in the rest of their armor. "Best be ready for battle when you join a siege, Your Majesty."

A third series of booms echoed in the still autumn air. James mounted his charger, who snorted and began pawing the ground as if eager to join the fray.

Lord Haile reached for the horse's reins. "I urge you, Sire, to let the knights ride ahead while you remain—"

The charger swerved to avoid Lord Haile's grip, and James urged the horse into a gallop, with Robert following close behind him.

"Your Majesty!" Lord Haile's voice faded behind him, and James heard Sir Lennox shout for the knights to follow the king.

He had to stop Montrose. It would be hard to convert an enemy if his family was rendered destitute.

As they topped the rise above Duchal Castle, James's heart sank. Montrose's artillery, arrayed on two sides, had blasted the castle's entire front walls and iron gates into rubble. Only the back part of the castle remained standing. Shards of glass glittered like crystals among the debris, a mocking symbol of the Lyle wealth.

Neither the courtyard buildings nor stables had been spared; their oaken beams stuck out of the wreckage like splintered bones. A few bodies lay scattered about the ruins, Lyle's men or Montrose's, James couldn't tell at this distance.

Sir Lennox said grimly. "The price of rebellion."

Montrose's soldiers clustered around the cannon, some still holding their archers' bows, others their swords. James's gaze shifted to the field where Montrose had set his command tent with the soldiers' tents scattered behind it, and finally to the thick woods that marked the edge of Lyle's estate.

A strange movement caught his eye, a line of tall brush in front of the forest swaying as if in a strong wind. But there was no wind. A glint of sunlight flashed among the branches. Then James saw an entire line of soldiers, swords drawn, emerge out of the brush and move quickly and silently across the field toward the tents.

Montrose's men, focused on the castle and unaware of the danger behind them, would have no time to turn their cannon before the soldiers were on them.

Without hesitation, James drew his sword and shouted to the knights behind him. "FOLLOW ME!"

He charged down the hillside straight at the enemy force, with

Sir Lennox and the king's knights pounding after him, holding the royal banner high. Robert and Lord Haile tried desperately to catch up.

Sir Lennox took half the knights and cut off the soldiers' retreat to the woods, while the other knights followed James as he plunged among the tents, determined to keep the attackers away from Montrose's men. He was vaguely aware that some of the knights were riding close around him, but the clash of battle soon overwhelmed everything else.

His charger attacked soldiers who came near until James had to clutch the saddle to hang on. He saw one soldier pull a knight off his horse and swing up into the saddle. Another attacker broke through the knights and rushed toward him, only to be cut down in mid-stride.

James blocked a sword thrust at his horse's neck and felt his own sword strike something solid. A spurt of red stained his blade and spattered his armor.

His hearing and vision narrowed to only a few feet around him, and he swung his sword at every soldier who came within reach, fighting with a strength he didn't know he possessed. If even one solider got through, someone would die.

Then, as abruptly as the battle had begun, it was over. James seemed to wake from a fugue state to find a few wounded men on the ground around him. Some distance away, the surviving enemy soldiers had been surrounded by the knights and forced to throw down their weapons.

Only then did he hear someone shouting his name and turn to find Robert beside him, his face red with anger.

"—riding off like that! You're lucky I caught up with you or you'd have no arm instead of that scratch! I'm begging you, James, never do that again!"

James looked down in surprise at his blood-soaked sleeve. When had he received that blow? It had been powerful enough to take off part of his armor, but he had no memory of anyone striking him.

Robert, breathing hard, railed on. "Yes, I cut down the man who gave you that. And if I hadn't, what would I tell Lady Margaret—that you died a reckless fool? She fears for you enough as it is—"

"It was an ambush!" James snapped. "There was no time to debate strategy."

He whirled his horse around and rode toward Lord Montrose and his men, standing with the king's knights, their drawn swords and arrows trained on the attackers. James jerked off his helmet and addressed the prisoners.

"Who leads you? Are you Lord Lyle's men or do you answer to another?" he demanded.

One of the men stepped forward defiantly. "I am Sean Hughes, and we are Lord Lyle's soldiers who fight for his estate."

"He has no estate!" one of the knights shouted. "It's all forfeit. Kneel to King James!"

His men cheered, but James shouted above them, "HOLD YOUR TONGUES!"

His charger reared and forced the men back. Even the enemy soldiers seemed startled. James reined his horse to a standstill.

His voice rang over the field. "There is no victory when brother fights brother! There is no cause for cheering."

A deep silence followed these words. James let it extend, gazing at the men until they lowered their eyes, acknowledging his authority. Only then did he speak to Lord Montrose. "What of Lyle's family and servants?"

Montrose replied, "They surrendered two days ago and are prisoners at Edinburgh Castle, Sire."

"And how many dead and wounded from that fight?"

"Of theirs, only a handful who refused to surrender. I lost five men to the castle archers."

James looked at Sir Lennox, "And here on this field?"

"Two knights wounded, Sire, none slain I know of. We'll have to make a count of Lyle's men—the dead and wounded."

James slowed his breathing, trying to master his racing heart and merge with the peace rooted within. What he did now would set the course for his rule after the rebellion. He needed to buy time to decide the right path.

"Lord Montrose, hold these men here. Sir Lennox and Master Hughes, gather those who fell and place them in the tents, one for Lord Montrose's men and one for Lyle's. And let both sides tend to their wounded."

"Aye, Your Majesty." Sir Lennox bowed. The set of his jaw showed his disapproval of treating Lyle's men as equals.

Hughes seemed uncertain how to respond. He settled for a stiff bow of his head. "As you say, Your Majesty."

James gestured to Montrose, Haile, and Robert. "Gentlemen, attend me in Lord Montrose's tent."

He rode ahead of them to the command tent and dismounted slowly. His armor seemed to weigh twice as much as before, and his wounded arm ached. The energy that had driven him on the field had spent itself, leaving his hands trembling. The squires in the tent sprang forward to remove his armor and cut away his sleeve.

"Tis but a scratch, Your Majesty," one of them said, smearing a thick balm on the wound. "We'll fix that right up."

The man was tying a linen cloth around James's arm when Robert and the two lords entered the tent. Lord Haile began chastising James the moment he saw him. "You take too many risks, Sire. Far too many!"

Lord Montrose joined in. "Sire, I agree with Lord Haile. Sir Lennox is a skilled leader in battle. There was no need for you—"

"A king should lead the men who fight for him," James replied. The men fell silent, but Haile seemed ready to explode again. "Besides," James half smiled and flexed his wounded arm gingerly, "the field was far too rough for golf."

The squires choked back their laughter. Lord Montrose stood with his mouth open. Then he and Robert burst out laughing.

Only Lord Haile continued to scowl at James. "Someone must restrain your excesses, Sire," he muttered sourly.

"Leave that to Heaven, Lord Haile," James said. *And to a certain*

Dutch captain, he thought. He sat down on a camp stool. "Now, gentlemen, how should I deal with Lyle's men—with all the rebels' men?"

"Hang them with their leaders!" Haile snapped, handing his sword to one of the squires.

Montrose said, "Send them to Edinburgh's dungeons."

"Pay them to fight for you," Robert put in. "Money would turn most of them."

"So . . . execute, imprison, or bribe them. Hmmm." He tapped his chin for a moment, then asked, "What if I talk to them instead?"

He could see by their expressions this idea had never occurred to any of them. He hoped Lyle's men would be equally caught off guard.

Over the next day, James spoke with Lyle's captured men in groups of three or four. They all knew it was within his right as king to do whatever he wished with them, including seizing all their goods and sending them and their families away with nothing but the clothes they wore.

Instead he asked for their names, what they did, who were their families. He asked what kind of master Lord Lyle had been. He heard a grim tale of a man who squeezed them dry through taxing, punished them for even the slightest offense, and demanded absolute obedience.

To each group James offered amnesty if they would join the royal cause. He spoke about dividing Lyle's estate into smaller farms, about giving them more control over their livelihoods. From there he talked about Scotland united under one banner—the king's—instead of every petty lord having his own fiefdom.

Most of all, he talked to them about justice, a fair system of law that would treat all people the same.

Robert saw the men's faces change from defiant to puzzled to inspired as they listened to the young king describe a new future for the country and the role they could play in its emergence. More than once, as James spoke, Robert thought of MacLean and the Highland chiefs. By the end of the day, most of the men had agreed to join him.

As the sun drew low on the horizon, James knew there was one more duty he needed to perform. He rose from his camp stool and said to Lord Montrose, "Show me those who fell in battle."

Montrose led James over to the two tents that housed the dead. He pulled the flap open on the first one to reveal five of his men lying next to one another. James entered and knelt beside their heads, studying their faces frozen in death. Three had heavy beards, streaked with gray, and looked as old as his father had been. The other two appeared only a little older than himself. Their clothes were stiff with blood, showing where the arrows had pierced them.

He remembered the captain's words. *Know why you go to war. To cut short a conflict. To save lives.* He had felt the exhilaration of battle, but not the madness the captain had mentioned. Surely this battle was justified.

He rose and moved into the tent where Lyle's dead soldiers lay, stacked like cordwood. There were more than three times as many as in Montrose's tent.

Something about their faces struck him deeply. He remembered in the Highlands how the commoners worked the fields and did the hard labor. It was the same on many of the nobles' estates here. These men would not return home. Who would do the hard labor now? How would their families survive?

War can bring many sorrows, the captain had said. James was beginning to learn who bore most of those sorrows.

When James emerged, he found the soldiers had gathered at a discreet distance behind Montrose and Haile. Some wore bloodied bandages, others bore gunpowder burns on their clothing, still others were streaked with grime and gore from the battlefield.

James pointed to the tents behind him, and his voice reached the farthest row of soldiers and knights.

"I will see to it that all those who have fallen are buried with honor by the Church. Those who are wounded will receive care, and all of you who pledged loyalty to the crown's service will be rewarded. Finally, I decree that the families of those who have fallen will receive a pension from the crown. You have the king's word on this!"

The men broke out in a loud cheer and pressed forward to surround James.

"Long life and good health, Sire!"

"Long live King James!"

"God grant you protection, Your Majesty!"

They seemed eager to touch him, to receive a word or two from him, as if he offered a royal blessing by his very presence.

Observing it all, Robert thought in wonder, *These men no longer belong to Montrose or Lyle. Now they belong to him.*

Wullie stood at the door of the work shed. "My Lady, Lord Forbes and his soldiers have left their castle. No word of where they have gone!"

The color drained from Margaret's face. "Quickly, what villages lie near Forbes's castle?"

Wullie looked stricken. "None, m'lady. It's all nobles who side with Lord Forbes. T'was a stronghold for King James the Third— they took it ill when he was killed."

"Then where is Lord Forbes likely to go with his men? Dumbarton, Crookston, Duchal?"

Wullie took an agonizingly long time to reply. Margaret's heart pounded with fear, her mouth dry. *James is in the field. What if he falls into the path of Lord Forbes?*

"Hard to say, m'lady. But Lord Forbes wouldn't want to kill the king—just take him prisoner."

"Just take him prisoner," Margaret said in despair. "And then what? We must discover where they have gone. Think, Wullie, think! There must be some priest, some herder, someone who can help us!"

Wullie stared mutely back at her, and Margaret shivered at his silence. Was this the dark center of the web she had sensed in her vision—the place where death waited?

No, she thought fiercely. *We'll find them, and with God's mercy, it will be in time.*

She grabbed Sibylla's hand and started pulling her back to the castle.

"We must let Cousin Aileen know about this right away." She spoke to Wullie over her shoulder. "Send word to all your people— find Lord Forbes!"

At Dumbarton Castle, Lord Argyll waited until every cannon in his artillery line was loaded. He raised his arm, then brought it down sharply.

"FIRE!" he bellowed.

The row of cannon belched smoke and flame and split the air with an ear-shattering roar. The heavy weapon near him recoiled as smoke curled from its gaping muzzle.

Argyll and his men watched a rain of black cannonballs arch over the river and strike the stone walls of Dumbarton Castle, but the thick walls blunted their impact. Only a small shower of stone flared from where the cannonballs hit. The wall was riddled with shallow scars, and Lord Crichton's banner still flew defiantly above the ramparts. Rebel archers sent a volley of arrows back across the river to vex the cannon crews.

Argyll spat on the ground as an arrow struck near his feet. "Three days' bombardment, yet this castle looks as if it's suffered nothing worse than a case of cowpox!"

The knight beside him folded his arms across his chest. "We

need more artillery. Perhaps Lord Montrose or Gray could send us theirs."

Argyll glared at the castle. Dumbarton had been constructed to withstand heavy siege, set against towering rock walls, flanked on three sides by stone, and protected in front by the river. Crichton had chosen his rebel headquarters well. It would take considerable firepower to force him and the other rebels out of the fortress.

He could wait them out, but that would take time, and the longer the rebellion went on, the worse it would be for the king and his court. Every delay would encourage others to join the rebel cause.

"A rider is coming, Lord Argyll!" a knight called out. "He wears the king's insignia!"

The rider sped at a gallop through the camp and pulled his sweating horse up before Argyle. "King James sends his compliments, my lord, and wishes you to know that Duchal Castle has fallen!"

"Duchal is ours? Then tell the king to send us Lord Montrose's men at arms and heavier artillery!"

"Aye, my lord. I'll make sure he knows."

In the inner tower, Lord Jameson watched the cannon muzzles flash from across the river, then a moment later heard the dull impacts on the outer castle wall. Lord Crichton joined him at the window.

"Let's hope Lord Forbes acts soon," Jameson said. "My men are restless confined to the castle."

"Assure them they have not long to wait!"

Another round of cannon fire struck the wall but produced not the slightest tremor where the two men stood watch.

"Fire as you will, Argyll," Lord Crichton said. "There is a judgment coming for you and your kind."

Chapter 18

Battle for
The Kingdom

The short journey from Duchal Castle to Dumbarton was slowed by the horse-drawn cannon bringing up the rear of the march. James dismounted from his horse and used the time to walk with Montrose's men up and down the line. He asked them about their lives and their families and committed to memory much of what he heard.

Gradually the soldiers lost their awe of being in his royal presence, though their deference never deserted them. They still bowed when James drew near, still held their caps respectfully in their hands as they conversed, but to Robert they looked more and more like the Highland people who had no fear of speaking to their sovereign.

Montrose rode his horse alongside Robert's. "The king has a touch with his subjects his father never had."

"But he has cunning as well," Robert said. "He told me the English privateers have been attacking our ships, but Admiral Wood sank three frigates in the North Sea. Wood sent an English captain as a prisoner to Stirling. Do you know what James did? Instead of hanging the man, he gave him a gift and sent him back to King Henry!"

"Why?" Montrose asked. "He could have ransomed him instead."

"James told me he wanted England to know 'we view this rebellion as a minor disturbance, hardly worth our time.'"

Montrose rubbed his jaw. "By the Blessed Virgin, he may be the best of the Stewarts. Pray that he escapes the family curse of dying young."

They saw James walk over to his bay charger, held by a squire. He grabbed the horse's mane in one hand and, in one fluid leap, swung up into the saddle. There was a general murmur of admiration from the men.

Robert snorted. "That's meant to impress Lady Margaret. He's been practicing for weeks. I think the horse agrees to stand still if James makes the saddle in one try."

Montrose laughed and called for his men to close up their lines. The soldiers glanced at James before they obeyed, as if waiting for a signal from the king.

Already they'll follow him wherever he leads, Robert thought.

When the group rode into Dumbarton camp, the soldiers cheered to see the royal banners waving past their ranks. Gray and Argyll walked out to greet them, and James leaped down from his horse to embrace both men.

"What of Crookston Castle?" James asked Gray. "We've heard nothing on the road."

"We took the castle and its defenders five days ago, Sire. We just now arrived and heard of your victory at Duchal."

"And your men? How many lost and wounded?"

"Fewer than feared, Your Majesty, but the defenders lost nearly a hundred soldiers."

The number made James pause. He turned slowly to Argyll. "And the assault against Dumbarton?"

"As you see, Sire." Argyll waved wearily at the scarred fortress. "By the time we breach the castle, we'll be too old to fight."

James heard his bitterness and was quick to point out, "Yet you prevented the rebels from attacking us at Crookston or Duchal."

He turned to include Montrose and Haile as they joined the group. "That's worth a great deal, wouldn't you say, gentlemen?"

"That I would, Sire," Montrose said. "And none could do it better."

Argyll straightened at the praise and gestured toward his command tent. "Accept our hospitality, Your Majesty, my lords."

The men reclined on the thick carpets and cushions that covered the tent floor while the servants brought food and drink. James hadn't realized how hungry he was until he started eating. Next to him, Robert was already halfway through a loaf of bread and a leg of mutton. The talk quickly turned to strategy.

Argyll said, "If Lord Montrose can spare me his men and cannon, that will better our chances of taking this fortress."

"They're yours," Montrose said. He grinned. "Our king has already turned Lord Lyle's soldiers to our cause. Perhaps he could do the same with Crichton's!"

The others laughed, but Lord Haile flung down his knife. "'Tis no time to jest, gentlemen! There are others who may join the rebels—the Master of Huntley near Aberdeen, for one. Many in that region supported James the Third."

James sat up, a stab of fear cutting through him. "If Huntley raises an army, he could threaten Drummond Castle from the north."

"Aye," Lord Gray said, "but he'll have to get through loyalist territory to do so, and he's not likely to want that much of a fight."

James sank back, but the words did not reassure him. He had seen firsthand that a slight change of fortune could swing a battle one way or the other. Despite what Gray thought, Drummond and Margaret could still be in danger.

Argyll cut in, "And there's the matter of Lord Forbes and his men. Is there any word of where and when he will strike?"

Gray, wiping his hands on a towel, shook his head. "The rebels at Crookston told us nothing of his intentions."

Montrose said. "I wonder if Forbes has proven as false to his friends as he has to the king."

Argyll's face tightened. "I know the man. He's not one to change his course. He commands some three hundred knights and as many peasant soldiers and can raise more men from the nobles surrounding his estates. The loss of Crookston and Duchal will surely goad him to battle. I would give a great deal to know when and where he intends to fight."

James and Robert exchanged a look. By now, Margaret might know. It was another reason to return to Stirling.

James thoughts sharpened into a decision. "Lord Gray, if Lord Argyll does not need your men, we can use them and Lyle's soldiers to reinforce both Stirling and Drummond."

"A wise idea!" Lord Haile said, relieved. "What say you, my lords?"

Argyll replied. "We have enough artillery now and can call on nobles loyal to the crown in Glasgow, if need be. Besides, our men may not trust Lyle's converts. There's likely to be trouble if they are idle too long."

Gray looked less than enthusiastic. "Your pardon, Sire, but I think you are being overly cautious. I think the greater danger lies here in this region." He saw the determined look on James's face and knew the young king would not yield. "Nevertheless," he bowed his head, "I will do as you ask."

"Then it's settled!" James said. "Tell Sir Lennox we leave at break of day."

In the sewing room, Margaret scrutinized her large embroidery with the intensity of a general studying a map. Next to the symbol of Forbes Castle, she had stitched a briar with large thorns to represent Lord Forbes.

"Where are you?" she murmured in frustration. "How could you hide so many men?"

"Perhaps he's a mage," Sibylla said behind her. "Perhaps he's turned them all into ravens."

"Don't laugh!"

"Margaret, Lord Forbes wouldn't dare attack Stirling."

Margaret sank back in her chair, closing her eyes wearily. James was safe, she kept telling herself, but it did little good to calm her fears at night. Only a fortnight ago, she had dreamed about him charging recklessly into battle. So like him to be so heedless!

Her head was beginning to throb painfully. *Where could that devil be?*

A quiet knock on her bedchamber door made her throw the embroidery over its frame so that it blended in with the other fabrics. Lena answered the door and turned to Margaret. "It's Wullie, m'lady, and he's got a lad with him."

"An' it please you, Lady Margaret," she heard the familiar wheezy voice say. "We know where Lord Forbes and his men have gone."

Without the cannon holding them back, James could drive the men harder toward Stirling and Drummond. He seemed to have inexhaustible energy. He was the last to lie down and the first up before dawn. Even hardened soldiers like Gray had difficulty keeping up with him, while Lord Haile finally took refuge in one of the baggage wagons.

James rode up and down the line, calling out his men by name to encourage them. The effect was striking. Those who had been lagging wearily suddenly seemed to gain a new energy. Robert realized that James could be a great military leader if he wanted to be. He could make men believe that when they followed him, they were part of something greater than themselves.

When Sir Lennox asked Robert, "What drives the king so?"

Robert replied only, "Lady Margaret."

Sir Lennox studied him for a moment, understanding growing in his eyes. From that moment on, he urged the king's knights to help James keep the others moving.

On the third day, Stirling Castle came into view, its bluff rising above the city like the prow of a ship. James told Gray to settle the men into the soldiers' quarters and have the royal hostlers see to their horses.

When he and Robert had reached the king's private chambers, they didn't have to wait long to hear from Margaret. A chambermaid quietly entered the room and delivered a rolled package to James.

The maid left just as quietly, and James spread the embroidered cloth out on the table. Robert crowded next to him to see the design.

"By the saints," James marveled. "They found Lord Forbes and his men!" He pointed to the symbol for Forbes on the embroidery. Next to it was a thistle with the number 4,000 stitched into the fabric.

"Forbes has gathered four thousand men?' Robert exclaimed, "How does Margaret do this? Her spies are like ghosts flitting everywhere in the Middle Country."

James frowned in concern. "Forbes and his men are in a valley only a few miles north of Drummond Castle!"

He folded the embroidery cloth and placed it in his rucksack. "I'll tell Lord Gray to rest the men and horses and then follow us to Drummond. You and I, Robert, and a few of the king's knights will ride for the castle within the hour!"

If James had expected to talk with Margaret alone, he was disappointed. Drummond Castle resembled a military encampment, with farmer-soldiers crowded into the courtyard and surrounding grounds. The air rang with the metallic clang of swords as the men drilled in battle formations, and archery ranges had been set up in the courtyard. Margaret waved to him from her chamber window and gestured that she and Sibylla had been confined to their rooms. Obviously, Lord Drummond wanted them out of harm's way as the men prepared for the coming fight.

Lord Drummond ushered James and Robert into the Great Hall, where he had spread a large map of the surrounding terrain across the main table. By then, Lord Gray had arrived with the king's army. He stood with James and the others as they studied every feature of terrain the map revealed.

A slight movement in the shadows of the room caught James's eye. To his amazement and joy, he glimpsed Margaret watching them, peering from behind a marble column as the men talked. As usual, she had found a way around her father's orders. *Did she have no fear at all?*

Lord Drummond said, "Providence has given us a timely advantage. The valley Forbes has chosen is one where my uncles and I hunted for years. I know every rock, tree, and path in it."

Gray's demeanor sharpened. "How many in Forbes's army?" he asked.

James answered, "About four thousand, at best estimate." He glanced covertly back at Margaret, who nodded slightly.

Gray said, "We brought eight hundred from Stirling. Lord Drummond, how many men have you raised in your army?"

"Close to two thousand."

Gray stroked his chin. "Add Angus's men to that, and Forbes still has the advantage over us. We'll never get the royal artillery there in time."

"We have the element of surprise," James said. "And Lord Drummond's knowledge of the terrain."

"But Forbes will see we don't have enough men," Robert said.

Gray folded his arms and gazed around at the group. "Not if we attack at night. I believe there's a full moon in two days' time."

James grinned at Gray. "Lord Drummond, summon your court astrologer. We need to know when the moon will be at its brightest."

186

In the shadows, Sibylla had joined Margaret to watch the council. The girl's nervous hands twisted the ends of her shawl into tight little knots. Her eyes were fixed on Robert.

Margaret said quietly, "Father has promised me he will keep James and Robert out of the battle."

"You know how stubborn James is," Sibylla whispered. "If he joins the fray, Robert will follow him."

Margaret's gaze fixed on James as the men walked out of the hall. As if he could feel her eyes on him, he glanced back at her once.

"Listen to your Soul," she whispered, her voice so low Sibylla didn't catch the words. "Promise me you will."

Two nights later, the bright light of a full moon shone on the tents of Forbes's army, casting deep shadows on the grass and shrubs around them. Two disgruntled sentries guarded the cavalry horses penned tightly together in a rope corral. The men flapped their arms against the autumn chill.

"I'd like to see one of them fancy nobles freezing his balls out here in the cold."

"There's a bad feeling to this place. We should attack. What's Lord Forbes waiting for?"

"That's why you ain't in charge! His lordship is waiting for Lord Crichton to join him."

"Still, last night I dreamed about ravens picking at our eyes."

"Ahh, everytime we're on a march, you dream about ravens—"

Suddenly the corralled horses behind them began snorting nervously. Some tossed their heads, their eyes glinting in the moonlight. The two sentries raised their long pikes and searched around them to see what had caused the disturbance.

A muffled drumming came on the night wind, almost as if the very Earth were vibrating beneath their feet, and then a solid black line of the king's horsemen burst over the top of a small ravine and swept down on the two men before they could shout an alarm.

Swords flashed and the men fell, their pikes cut in two. A few more strokes and the rope corral lay in pieces. The spooked horses stampeded toward the camp, driven by the black riders, whose hair-raising battle cries rent the air.

The herd swept through the rebel camp, trampling soldiers who raced out of their tents, pikes and swords in hand. The horses scattered wood fires and set the tents ablaze, ripped out tent poles, and struck at men trying to catch and mount them.

Following close behind, the riders descended on Forbes's army like avenging furies, cutting down everyone in their path. The soldiers' long pikes were useless against the swords and maces of the cavalry, and the men grasped any weapon they could wield in close quarters.

Amid the cries and clash of arms, the attackers swept like a scythe through half the camp, leaving the dead and wounded in their wake. Led by Lord Gray, a group broke off to surround Forbes's command tent and repel the soldiers who rushed to defend it.

Suddenly, from the opposite side of camp, a second wave of cavalry charged out of the night, with the infantry close behind them. Soldiers trying to fend off the first attack turned to find another howling force, swords raised high, bearing down on them.

James paced furiously as he watched the battle rage below, angry that he could not join the men. But all the leaders and Robert had been firmly united against him.

"We can't have you killed!" Robert had finally shouted. "That would be the death of everything you hope for and the ruin of the country!"

He had sensed his Soul agreed, but how could he stand idle while others risked their lives for him?

Lord Gray swore they would do everything in their power to capture Lord Forbes alive. "He has a great deal to answer for," Gray said, his eyes flashing. "He can't do that if he's dead."

Only then had James agreed to stay behind with Lord Drummond, Robert, and a bodyguard of knights. From their position, they watched the tents burn like torches throughout the camp, a fog of white smoke rising in the moonlight. The sharp, acrid smell of burning canvas reached them, and they could see dark figures outlined against the fires, fighting one another in desperate battle. A thick knot of horses and men surrounded Forbes's tent. James hated to think what this victory might cost.

Chapter 19

Healing The Realm

By early dawn the fires had died out, leaving only smoking ruins in the camp. Stray horses wandered aimlessly among the bodies of the dead and wounded. Only Lord Forbes's command tent and a few others remained standing. The king's infantry had rounded up the last of the rebel army.

James rode with Lord Drummond, Robert, and his escort of knights down the hillside to the battleground. True to their word, Lord Gray and the others had captured Forbes alive, though his face was blackened by smoke and his clothes torn and stained with blood. James rode up to the command tent where Forbes was being held and dismounted, his heart hammering in his chest.

He confronted the man, keeping a tight hold on his temper. "Lord Forbes, you have committed high treason against your king. How do you answer for your actions?"

Forbes did not yield. "You have surrounded yourself with traitors to the Scottish people, Sire. These men," he pointed at Gray and Drummond, "seek only their own gain."

Gray started forward in rage, but James flung his arm out and stopped him. He spoke to Forbes instead. "Then you should have come to me and presented your grievances."

He raised his voice so all could hear him. "You and all the nobles who have taken part in this rebellion are charged with high treason against the crown. You will be escorted to Stirling Castle and held there pending trial. All of your lands and possessions will be forfeit."

He turned to Sir Lennox. "Take these men to Stirling and see they are imprisoned in the castle hold."

The knight eyed Forbes darkly. "Aye, Your Majesty, we'll see to it."

Now that the battle was over, James felt bruised and drained. He spoke wearily to his own nobles. "My lords, we will bury our dead, tend the wounded, and then return home. There is much to be done before we can declare this rebellion over."

As a final act, James gathered the peasants and herders who had been summoned by Lord Forbes to fight against the crown. These men were not soldiers but commoners pressed into service. James addressed them all, announcing a general amnesty.

"You are free to return home," he said. "Your fields and families need you. It will be winter soon."

The commoners gaped at him in astonishment, unwilling at first to leave, lest the amnesty be a trick. Then slowly they began to disperse. A few kept looking back as they crossed the valley floor, as if to reassure themselves the king's word held true.

At that moment, James longed to return to Drummond and see Margaret again, but Gray and the others urged him to lead the army back to Stirling.

"The rebels are still a threat, Your Majesty," Gray said. "You need to show the country that Stirling is the center of royal power."

They were right. He would have to delay seeing Margaret until the rebellion was fully quelled. He could imagine her in the Drummond chapel, praying for just such an end.

Once James and the others reached Stirling, two messages were waiting, one from Argyll. James eagerly tore open Argyll's letter first. "He tells quite a tale," James said, reading it over. "It seems a rebel force surprised them at Dumbarton, and Montrose had to pull their artillery out or risk losing it. But with help from the burghers in

Glasgow, they won a victory. Crichton and Jameson are now isolated, and Argyle expects Dumbarton to fall within the month."

He passed the message to the others and opened the second one, from another noble in the field. As he read silently, James's eyes widened in wonder. "Hear this, gentlemen. Forbes's allies were travelling to join him here when a contingent of Highlanders led by Lord MacLean's son entered the battle and Captain van Horn was with him! They defeated the rebels—"

"MacLean!" Haile exclaimed. "How did he hear about our troubles?"

Gray replied, "Most likely from van Horn. I've never met a man who could travel so fast and be so well informed."

When a group of rebel prisoners from the north arrived at Stirling, James fully expected the captain to be with them. Instead, van Horn had sent a letter with the commander of the troops.

"Returning with MacLean's son to the Highlands . . . have burghers' agreements in hand . . . terms to be negotiated . . . arrive in Stirling as soon as possible . . ."

So, again, the captain wasn't coming. Yet James discovered he did not feel the man's absence as keenly as before. *Perhaps I'm growing in my own strength*, he thought, *as he said I would.*

James treated all the rebel prisoners, regardless of rank or standing, with cold severity, declaring their lands and estates forfeit and informing them they would stand trial for high treason. Only to Robert and Margaret did he confide his true course—giving the rebel nobles a second chance by including them in his court and government.

Margaret responded, *"I'm glad to see you are taking to heart my advice about including some of your father's men . . ."*

James smiled. "Always giving me advice." But the love and strength she had shown him were never far from his mind.

Robert was more skeptical about his plan. "How are you going to persuade the others in your court to agree? They won't forgive treason, James—or the loss of their men in battle."

"I will find a way," James said. "Else . . . what did all those men die for?" But Robert heard another question behind his words: *Else what did my father die for?*

James campaigned hard to get support among his closest circle and found that Montrose, Haile, and Argyll were the easiest to convince. But Gray and Angus refused. They were outraged by his proposal of amnesty for the main rebel leaders and, even worse, giving them positions of power in the king's court and in the government.

"Begging your pardon, Sire," Gray said heatedly, "but this is telling everyone that rebellion is the road to advancement. I cannot countenance this! Particularly not for Forbes! Make an example of them, as your father—"

"As my father would have done?" James asked.

Gray fell silent. He seemed acutely aware that his temper had led him onto sensitive ground.

James continued. "Isn't that the kind of king you yourself rebelled against? Why did you put me on the throne if not to forge a different path?"

Lord Gray shifted uneasily, and Angus stared down at his boots. Then Montrose's calm, steady voice glided smoothly into the stillness.

"I think, Your Majesty, they were hoping you would lift the ban on golf."

Angus shouted through the burst of laughter, "But, Your Majesty, they rebelled against the crown—"

"They were not rebelling against the king," James replied firmly. "Only against those who, in their eyes, disgraced the crown."

He leaned forward, his gaze boring into Gray and Angus. "Gentlemen, think on this. No matter how bitterly your two sides view one another, you share the same virtue: a love of Scotland's honor. Search your hearts, gentlemen. Surely we can build on that common ground."

He saw the struggle in their faces and silently prayed that their Souls could lift them above hatred and strife. If all men could make this choice . . .

Gray spoke reluctantly. "We will try, Your Majesty, for your sake."

For my sake. Well, James thought, *it's a beginning.*

Over the next few days, James consulted with his inner circle and with other members of his court about the various positions the former rebels should be given. He had not fully realized the tangled maze of checks and balances he had to consider among the noble families. If he gave too prominent a position to Forbes, for instance, he might offend the Haile family. If he gave too low a position, Forbes would likely regard it as an insult to his family's reputation and cause trouble in Parliament.

And there was the matter of the petty lords and burghers who had sided with Forbes and the others. They could not be given any prominent positions, yet they couldn't be ignored.

James called on his Soul over and over again to maintain his equilibrium and found himself more than once longing for the steadying influence of Margaret and Captain van Horn.

Yet it was also true that it seemed easier to reach his Soul than ever before. Perhaps, as the captain had said, the decisions were giving him mastery, anchoring the higher qualities in him more deeply every time he followed his Soul's guidance.

Finally, the bickering and negotiating ended and the group reached an agreement. The major leaders of the rebellion would retain their estates and be given positions in James's court where he could keep an eye on them. They would become members of a new, unified Parliament that James would form from both sides.

The rest would be assigned minor functions in commerce and

trade, the Church, and the courts. In exchange, they would all pledge their fealty to the crown and to the government James would lead.

When the young king gathered the rebel leaders before him in the throne room and delivered this declaration, Robert had to stifle a laugh. These men of rank and power looked as dumbfounded as had the lowest peasants.

But as the realization sank in that they would not lose everything they owned, nor be tried and hanged, nor have their families exiled, a general feeling of relief and gratitude swept through them.

They all knelt willingly to James and signed agreements to lay down their arms and pledge themselves to the king's service. There could be no better symbol of the new unity in Scotland.

James let out a long slow breath. *We have done it.*

True to Argyll's prediction, Dumbarton Castle fell three weeks later. To celebrate the end of the rebellion, the young king announced a great feast at Stirling Castle. He hired musicians, entertainers, and poets from around the region to amuse his guests throughout the night. A steady stream of mutton, venison, pork, and beef, along with salmon and cod, mounds of bread, and what seemed like an endless parade of confections, kept the tables brimming.

James had Sir Lennox and the knights keep a wary eye on those who might be too inflamed with drink to remember they were allies now. Over the objections of some, James had declared all weapons be left at home.

Through most of the feast, James was at the center of the revels, telling stories, listening to tales of Scotland's past glory, mingling with the guests to avoid favoring any one family over the others.

But close to midnight, he found Margaret and skillfully brought her away from the main hall to one of the upper balconies, where they could overlook the celebration. He wanted to be alone with her, after what had seemed like an eternity of separation.

"This new Parliament, James," Margaret was saying, "they are calling it the Healing Parliament. Everyone is praising you, even Lord Fleming. Though he looks as if he's eating sour mash when he says it."

James smiled but said nothing. He didn't want to talk about himself or politics right now. He watched the glittering company of men and women below. By all counts, the feast was a great success.

The poets had dueled among themselves to create the best verses about James, the country, and the reconciled nobles. During the evening, their high poetic tone had descended into bawdy poems that set the company roaring with laughter. Revelers danced to the musicians' tunes, while children crowded around the jugglers and acrobats. Women in their gowns and jewels sparkled in the candlelight as men competed for their attention.

But the same melancholy that had affected him after winning the duel was settling over him again. Would this happen each time he penetrated the realm of the Soul? If only he had the captain's counsel to help him understand what was happening.

The scene below seemed distant, as if he were watching a crowd of sleepwalkers. How could he ever awaken them from their anger and fear, from their illusions?

If only he could show them the radiance they carried, teach them how to merge with it as he had done and see how immense it was, far beyond their mortal life, yet so close, anchored in their flesh.

Margaret noticed his silence. "James, what's wrong?"

He gestured to the crowd below. "I may be able to unite them, but I can't free them."

She didn't understand what he meant, but she sensed his isolation and sadness, as if he had failed in some inexplicable way.

"You can *lead* them, James. They will listen to you, just as you listen to your Soul."

Her earnest face in the flickering light and the warm scent of her skin sent a fierce wave of love through him. He drew her into the shadows where no one could see them.

"*A chuisle mo chroi*," he murmured.

For Margaret, the feel of James's arms around her broke the tight hold she had had on herself for so long.

She burst out, "James, I was wrong before! The barons, the earls—It doesn't matter what they think of us. I will marry you. I'm no longer afraid!"

A powerful desire to protect her rose up in his heart, a feeling so new and fierce, it startled him. His arms tightened around her, and he poured all his fear and love and longing into that embrace.

I swear I'll keep you safe.

On the balcony staircase below, Sibylla turned abruptly to stand in Robert's path.

"Don't look! They're kissing," she whispered. She was relieved that no one else had come in search of the king.

"They're kissing?" Robert tried to peer around her, but Sibylla firmly pulled him back down the stairs.

"I said don't look! They have little enough time alone as it is. Give them this moment."

As the two walked down the stairs, Robert said, "James talks about her in his sleep, you know. He's always warning her about something, telling her to hide."

To his surprise, Sibylla's eyes filled with tears. "She worries about him as well. She fears someone will try to kidnap or kill him. This has happened to so many kings."

Robert risked a quick look over his shoulder. James and Margaret were so close together they looked like one figure. God have mercy on anyone who tried to come between them.

Chapter 20

Fate and Will

After Margaret and her family returned home, James assigned Sir Lennox and a squad of royal knights to Drummond Castle as bodyguards. Margaret wrote:

"I know why the knights are here, James, but I assure you there's no need. Recall the men to ensure your own protection. May the Blessed Mother watch over you night and day."

James had no intention of recalling them, but neither did he want to trust Margaret's safety solely to the protection of men or even Providence. He would talk with the captain. Surely with the man's knowledge of the East, he would know secret ways to safeguard her.

As if in answer, a message arrived from van Horn: *"Returning to Stirling soon . . . we have much to talk about."*

As Sibylla had predicted, James and Margaret had little time together after the feast. James had wanted to send his steward to her father to start negotiating her dowry and send word to the archbishop to publish their marriage banns in the Church, but Margaret had persuaded him to wait. She had regained her practical nature, though there was a new tenderness to it.

"I feel as you do, but such actions would cause a storm of gossip," Margaret said. "You know what the royal court is like. You don't need people pestering you for wedding details night and day right now. It would drive you mad, and you must establish yourself as king."

James had reluctantly agreed. Instead, with his customary high energy, he threw himself into setting the foundation for his reign. He asked for Lord Drummond's help in drawing up a list of nobles who might serve as ambassadors to the courts of Europe and England. They would carry not only diplomatic instructions but also orders to seek out the finest books, scholars, and artists and send as many back to Scotland as they could.

"Other nations are ahead of us in all areas," James said, "and we must make up for lost ground."

But how to choose the best candidates on the list—and how to choose the best men for the countless other positions to administer his kingdom? He remembered what the captain had said about golf revealing a man's character. He had already built the royal course. All that remained was to invite the men to play on it.

James was both surprised and pleased when most of them flocked to Stirling with clubs in hand, eager to display their skill before the king and their peers. He sat back and, with a few trusted advisors, watched the men try the course.

He found the challenges of the game did indeed reveal the true nature of each man. The Earl of Campbell, who always presented a calm, controlled demeanor, lost his temper whenever his stroke went wrong and refused to let anyone advise him. A man who could not listen to advice or instruction would make a poor ambassador.

Lord MacKenzie blamed the sun, the wind, the club, bird sounds, the time of day, in short, everything but himself for his poor play and eventually left the course in a rage. Not a good candidate as a commander of men.

"You'll want to watch MacKenzie," Lord Drummond told James. "He'll likely make trouble in court or in Parliament."

Lord Gray added, "And his family are notorious English sympathizers."

Still another noble revealed a reckless streak that compelled him to bet on every hole. He should never be given a post in the treasury.

Gradually James began to determine who might be trusted and who might prove false; who could learn from experience and who couldn't; and who could stand firm against adversity and who weakened under pressure. With his advisors to help him, he used this knowledge to match the best man with the best position.

Within a short time, the court and the government took shape, and James began to acquire a reputation as an astute judge of character.

When he wasn't on the course, James sat in the king's chambers and heard an endless litany of petitions and complaints from nobles, merchants, and the poor, asking for his intervention. This task challenged him beyond his knowledge and his years, and he pulled on his Soul like a drowning man clutching at a log.

Every morning, he attended early Mass in Stirling Chapel and used the time to quiet his heart, enter his sanctuary, and listen to his Soul. The words of the Third Scroll reverberated in his mind: *Use your power to establish justice; Use your wealth to promote generosity.* Such guidance helped him judge disputes and devise remedies that were regarded by others as unusually fair and even-handed.

But James's true awakening came when he asked local bailiffs and sheriffs to report on the criminal cases in their areas. James was dismayed by the number of crimes that poverty alone compelled people to commit—theft of food to avoid starvation; of clothing to weather the elements; of money to pay rent or taxes.

Every case provided James with a grim lesson about the true state of his country. It was clear that if he sought to reduce such crimes, he would have to ensure a greater prosperity in the nation.

Now the voices pleading for justice and protection haunted him even more now. He assigned clerics to review Scotland's laws, which were based on Roman codes, with an eye to creating a modern, universal system of justice that could be applied throughout the country.

Not content with letting clerics do the work, he immersed himself in Latin, French, and English texts on common and civil laws to find out what other nations had devised. The task so consumed him that everything else, even Margaret, faded from his mind. Robert and others grew alarmed by what seemed like a growing obsession, but James curtly dismissed their worries and redoubled his efforts.

One afternoon, as he was parsing out the rights of ingress and egress on lands bordering a water source, a familiar voice came from the doorway of his chambers.

"Sire, it took your ancestors several centuries to create the nation. Allow yourself at least a few months to change it."

James's head jerked up. "Captain!" He leapt up from his chair and embraced the man. "Come, sit down, sit down! As you said, there are so many things to talk about."

James hurriedly moved a pile of scrolls off a chair and pushed it toward Captain van Horn. The man sank into it while James tried his best to tidy up the room.

The captain looked around him at the scrolls covering every chair and all the weighty, opened books on the table. An empty mug lay half-propped against a candlestick, while the shriveled remains of a meal had been set aside on the window seat. Tunics, leggings, boots—all had been flung on the bed like casualties of some scholastic battle.

Apparently James had not allowed his valet, let alone the chambermaid, to enter this room in some time.

The captain pushed one of James's mud-stained boots aside with his foot and remarked casually, "Robert tells me you hardly eat anymore, and you never seem to sleep!"

James stopped, his arms full of clothes. "I confess, it's true." He threw the clothes into the armoire and slammed the door before they could fall out. "I've been using the techniques you taught me, drawing energy from nature, which is inexhaustible! When fatigue sets in, I do the practice, and it's as though I had slept all night and eaten two meals!"

The captain sighed. "You cannot abuse such practices, James. You will consume your body's heat and find yourself susceptible to melancholy."

James, who had been settling into his chair, froze at these words.

"Ah," the captain said quietly. "You have experienced this already, then."

"In a way." James eased himself down. "It's one of the many things I wish to ask you."

The captain saw with satisfaction that the light within James glowed more steadily now. *He must have overcome some formidable tests, Master Zheng, and done so without my presence. We must help him stay the course.*

Aloud he said, "Why don't I tell you how the Highland chiefs and I are getting on, and you can tell me everything that's happened since we last parted."

James learned that many burghers in the Low Countries were more than willing to re-establish commerce with the Highlanders, now that the shipping lanes were protected. There was a ready-made market for Scottish salmon and cod, as well as the durable Highland wool and fine leather.

They were also intrigued by the new king, listening to van Horn's stories of the golf duel with relish. "Expect an invitation to play on their courses," the captain said.

Having secured a few letters of commerce from the burghers, the captain had traveled to Aberdeen to negotiate with Scottish wool merchants. He arrived in time to hear about Lord Forbes and his northern allies.

The captain had immediately sent a message to MacLean, who responded by sending his son and two hundred battle-hardened clansmen to fight for their king. The Highland warriors had decimated the rebel army.

When the battles were over, van Horn had ridden back to

MacLean's castle, carrying offers to buy Highland wool. The terms weren't totally agreeable, the captain admitted, but at least the two sides had started to negotiate.

"Lord MacLean and his men regard you as a monarch who keeps his word. That means a great deal to them, James. You have solid friends for life in those men."

He folded his hands across his stomach. "Now, tell me what has been happening here in my absence."

James's face, which had been lit with pleasure at the captain's good news, became sober again. "God's truth, where to begin?"

The captain listened closely as James described the events from the first battles of the rebellion to the fact that Margaret had withdrawn her objections to their marriage.

Van Horn beamed with satisfaction. "I always thought she had the most sense of anyone around you! You've done well, James, far beyond what I could have expected, and you've grown stronger in your own judgment and spiritual power. Now, what did you wish to ask me? It's not about Lady Margaret, is it?"

Fear flickered across James's face. The captain was quick to notice but held his peace, waiting for the young king to speak.

James's heart beat faster, a knot twisted in his stomach, and his mouth seemed to go dry as sand. They had come to the heart of what he wanted to know. He both hoped for and dreaded what the captain might say.

"These are still dangerous times, Captain, and I fear for Margaret's life. Tell me there is some magical way to keep her safe. You've said the Eastern mages talk of a person's fate. They must know ways to change that fate should it show death at an early age!"

"Can we bend fate to our will, do you mean?" the captain asked.

"Fate, God's will—whatever you wish to call it. Do you know something that can protect her?"

"James, the fear of losing Margaret—"

"I must not lose her!" he exclaimed. The thought was like falling from a great height to the rocks below. His hand balled into a fist.

"She is the pulse of my heart, Captain, you have no idea how much! Without her, the throne is empty."

Careful, van Horn thought, *we are entering treacherous waters here. He needs an answer that he's not going to like.*

The captain said gently, "I can make talismans to protect her, James, but know this: Your fear is the greatest threat to her safety."

He held up his hand to forestall a protest from James. "Hear me out. The human mind can become so distorted by this emotion that you lose the ability to see clearly or act wisely. The great tragedy is, you may bring about the very thing you fear the most.

"My advice—go deep in within yourself, listen to what you hear, and you will discover the best way to protect Lady Margaret."

James waited, hoping for another answer. When none came, he slumped back in disappointment.

"Go to my sanctuary," he said dully. He could sense the truth in the captain's words, but his feelings warred against it. What if that voice gave him the wrong answer? It was Margaret's life in the balance.

Yet it had never proven false before. If, as the captain had said, the Soul knew what was right not only for him but for all those connected to him, perhaps he should simply trust it, as he had in the past. Perhaps he didn't need to understand how it worked.

"All right, Captain," he said slowly. "I will be ruled by your advice."

Van Horn relaxed. "I'm glad to hear it. Now I'll show you how to go deeper within yourself than ever before. I urge you, James, hold fast to what you hear, no matter what may happen."

But as James reached deeper into his sanctuary, the answer he heard was not the one he wanted.

Do nothing more. Trust that all will be well.

Every nerve screamed at him to do more. To hold fast to that deeper answer was going to take all the strength and discipline he could muster.

The captain watched flashes of red and black, like smoldering coals, flicker around James, something he had seen in him only once before. Van Horn knew it signified anger and fear driven by an iron will. It could easily pull James away from his Soul.

Whatever James decided to do, all his spiritual force would pour into that action, for good or ill.

Treacherous waters indeed, the captain thought.

At Drummond Castle, Margaret had to sit though yet another attack by Lord Fleming against James. Even at breakfast, the man seemed unable to keep any opinion to himself.

"They say he's taken up embroidery!" Fleming's voice skated a thin line between amusement and contempt. "Will we all be required to learn a woman's craft in the new Scotland? And he is intruding into areas best left to older and wiser counselors. Seventeen years old and he debates judges, daring to correct them on points of law! It's said he has ideas about natural sciences, medicine, even alchemy— it's unnatural! Everyone knows that too much knowledge overheats the brain and distorts the judgment."

Oh, that is enough! Margaret put a hand to her forehead and found it easy to assume a pained look as she rose to her feet. "Excuse me, Lord Fleming, Euphemia, but I am not feeling well. I think I should retire."

Sibylla rose. "I'll attend you, sister. In truth, you do look ill."

Lord Fleming waved a dismissive hand, and the two sisters escaped the dining room. Margaret stalked through the corridor, brandishing a napkin, still clutched in her hand, like a dagger.

She hissed, "That preening, over-stuffed, weak-kneed—"

Sibylla stifled a laugh, then said, "You must admit, Margaret, it's astonishing what James can do. If he weren't king, people might even suspect him of meddling in witchcraft or trading his soul to the Devil to gain knowledge."

"People are ignorant!" she snapped.

But when they reached the sewing room, Margaret's anger

vanished. Wullie was standing by the door, holding a basket and talking with two of the knights who guarded the sisters' rooms.

Seeing Margaret and Sibylla, Wullie held up the basket and said, "Scones from your cousin Aileen, m'lady."

Once they were inside the room, Margaret took a rolled-up embroidery cloth from the basket and spread it carefully on a table. It was beautifully made, its exquisite embroidery so skillfully wrought it looked as if elvish hands had done the work.

In an outer circle, Aileen had placed the familiar symbols for the castles of Crichton, Angus, Lyle, and Drummond. But there were two other symbols the sisters didn't recognize: a bear and a ram. In the center of the circle, Aileen had stitched a goshawk, a bird of prey. A red lion stalked beneath the whole image.

Entwined all around the symbols was an elaborate, twisting pattern of vines and leaves that filled in the rest of the cloth. Here and there, the glint of silver thread shone beneath the pattern.

But what was its message? The two sisters and Wullie stared at it in bewilderment. After a moment, Sibylla touched the goshawk in the center.

"That's our Drummond symbol, but why would she put two symbols for us in the work?"

"And whose are these?" Margaret pointed to the bear and ram.

Wullie scratched his head. "Well, now, the bear would be MacKenzie's clan. My nephew's girl works there. And the ram— probably the Jameson clan."

"Jameson," Margaret said in surprise. "He bears us an old grudge, but so far most of his clan has stayed neutral."

She leaned closer to study the twisting patterns of vines and leaves. Aileen was very cunning in the way she had stitched the vines, creating beautiful Celtic knots, using darker thread for some lines and lighter thread for others.

As she examined the vine near Drummond Castle, her eyes stopped on a small black spot. A spider—their symbol for an enemy spy.

"Look, Sibylla," she said. "An enemy spy is crawling away from our castle."

Margaret remembered nearly two years ago James had told her about a spy at Drummond, one who had reported his words to his father. After the king's death, the spy seemed to disappear . . . but perhaps he had simply lain dormant.

"Look there," Sibylla said. "Another spider near MacKenzie's castle . . . it's crawling away from the castle as well."

"If my old eyes t'ain't fooling me," Wullie said, "there's another spy crawling toward Lord Angus's castle."

Margaret frowned. She put her finger on the Drummond spider and began to trace its vine forward, following where the spy was headed. The vine took her through several convoluted Celtic patterns, past MacKenzie's castle, and ended at Crichton's.

A sudden idea struck her. "Sibylla, Wullie, trace your spider's vine. Find out where it comes from or where it's going."

They bent to their work. After several moments, Sibylla said, "MacKenzie's spy ends at the lion—England's symbol!"

Wullie looked up. "My Angus spy started from Crichton, m'lady."

It made no sense. Why would these nobles be spying on one another when they were on the same side—except for Angus, who played both sides. And what was this Drummond spy up to?

Margaret hung the embroidery on a needlework frame and stepped back slowly, trying to see the pattern from a different perspective. Several feet away, she stopped in her tracks, a chill shuddering through her.

At a distance, the light and dark patterns no longer made a twisting vine. They formed a spider's web, the silver threads connecting it all to the center. And at the center, the goshawk.

Suddenly the message fell open in her mind. The goshawk wasn't Drummond.

It was her.

The spiders were carrying secret messages about her.

"Sibylla, Wullie! Quick, come see this! It's a spider's web!"

The two stood beside her and stared in astonishment at the design. "It's a warning, m'lady," Wullie said. "About all those who want no joining between you and the king."

"We didn't know until now about MacKenzie and Jameson," Sibylla said.

Margaret gazed at the cloth, her mind racing. "And the spy at Drummond is in league with them all. Aileen must have risked a great deal to learn this, else she would not have disguised her message so."

"Wullie should take this cloth to James."

"Not yet. If we were in immediate danger, Aileen would have sent a different message. James must finish what he's doing with the laws. It's like some sacred duty. But we can heed Aileen's warning. It seems we need to uncover a spy at Drummond."

She turned to Wullie. "Sibylla and I will arouse suspicion if we try. But you can roam the castle without being noticed. Do what you must, but find out who this spy is, Wullie."

The old servant's face took on a sharp, cunning look. "Aye, m'lady. I've a good idea where to start!"

Lord Crichton had more than hunting deer on his mind when he invited Lord Angus to ride out with him. He knew the man wouldn't be able to resist. Angus had hunted deer in the king's woods since he was a boy and loved the sport.

Crichton pulled on his riding gloves and paced anxiously while Angus drew on his boots. A pack of hounds and their handlers started down the road toward the distant forest. Crichton realized he was taking a calculated risk with Angus, but he had to try. If Crichton himself couldn't get close to the king, he needed an ally who could.

A squire led Crichton's horse to him, and the earl swung up into the saddle. "Tell me, Lord Angus, what do you think of Lord Drummond's influence on the king?"

Angus mounted stiffly and squinted at Crichton.

"Why do you ask?"

"It appears he has the king's ear not just on matters of diplomacy but on most of the Church, civil, and military appointments. We pledged to serve the king—not to be overshadowed by the Drummonds."

"I agree," Angus said flatly. "I wanted my nephew to be appointed commander of the Edinburgh garrison, but Drummond's cousin was placed there instead."

"And now this family, which has furnished two queens to Scotland, may be about to furnish a third. That doesn't bother you?"

Angus shifted uncomfortably in the saddle. It did bother him. If the recent rebellion had succeeded, James would still be king, but the treaty with King Henry would have secured Angus's border estate against English claims. It was one of the reasons he had tried to remain neutral.

But a marriage to Margaret Drummond would finish that hope. There would be no leverage to bargain with King Henry.

Crichton said casually, "And what if the king and Lady Margaret shared a close ancestor that makes them, in effect, first cousins?"

Angus, astonished, pulled his horse to a stop. "You have such information?"

Crichton bowed modestly. "From one of my informants close to the Drummonds. He is searching through records that may prove it. He thought I might like to know."

Angus felt a stirring of hope. "If true . . . they would need a special dispensation from the Pope to marry. That could take months to acquire."

"In that time, the king might be persuaded to accept a Tudor princess on the throne, yet still retain Lady Margaret's affections."

"As his mistress, you mean? You don't know him, Lord Crichton."

Crichton didn't answer. Instead, he called out to the hunting party ahead of them. "Take the dogs up to that line of woods. Give us time to circle around and then send them in to flush the deer!"

He turned back to Angus. "I will be blunt, my lord, since you have a stake in the matter as well. If James marries a Tudor, King Henry is still prepared to sign a treaty of perpetual peace with Scotland. He remains at war with France, and he can't afford an enemy on his own border. He will also settle all disputes regarding the Borderlands, which include, I might add, your estate and those of several other nobles."

Angus mulled this over. At last he muttered, "In faith, such a treaty would benefit both countries."

"That it would. Undoubtedly the king has his heart set on Lady Margaret, but he is, after all, the king and must consider the best interests of Scotland. Remember, James was betrothed to an English princess when he was born. We would only be carrying out what his father wanted for the country."

"Aye, that we would, that we would . . ." Angus felt torn. He had a genuine fondness for James. On the other hand, kings came and went, but a family's land, its true wealth, would outlast generations of royalty. That thought tipped the balance.

"What would you have me do, Lord Crichton?"

"Help the king make the right choice for Scotland. There are many willing to support you in this effort."

They had reached the far side of the forest, where a deer trail led out of the woods. The two men dismounted. Each notched an arrow in his hunting bow.

"All right, I agree," Angus said. "God willing, the king will see his duty."

"If he does not, I fear there are those who will take the decision out of his hands. Do not fail in this, Lord Angus."

They heard the faint baying of the hounds. A few moments later, a large buck bolted out of the forest. The two men, moving almost as one, drew back their bows and shot at the deer. Both arrows struck their mark, and the buck collapsed to the ground, mortally wounded.

Chapter 21

A Secret Union

"Lord Angus told you what?" Robert said.

James's horse shied at Robert's outburst, and James had to settle the animal before he could answer. The two of them were trying out two Barbary stallions sent to James as a gift from the king of France. The horses were reputed to have uncommon speed and endurance.

"That Margaret and I might be first cousins," James said. "He claimed he was only trying to protect Lady Margaret from gossip and slander. And he pointed out that as king, I have a duty to marry well for the sake of the country."

Robert glanced back instinctively, though he and James were riding well ahead of his bodyguard of knights.

"But if it's true," Robert said, "then the Church won't allow you—"

"—to marry. I know." James grinned. "You forget, I just appointed the Archbishop of Glasgow. He can petition the Pope to grant us a dispensation." His jaw set in determination. "Then we will be free to marry."

That fierce need to protect Margaret rose up in him again, yet each time his Soul whispered, *Do nothing. Trust that all will be well.*

He was finding that harder and harder to believe. If anything happened to him, the nobles would put one of his brothers on the throne and marry the boy off to one of King Henry's daughters.

Worse—Margaret's enemies would likely wipe out the Drummond family for good measure. Such bloody deeds had often happened in the country's history.

Unless . . . James lifted his head, struck by an idea so daring that he could scarcely hold it in his mind. "Robert, I have a plan, but I'll need your help and the captain's."

"What do you have in mind?"

"I'm going to wed Margaret in secret."

Robert's eyes widened in shock. "You've gone mad, James! Lord Drummond would never agree. And the nobles who are barely your allies would—"

"Don't you see?" James snapped. "Once we're married, Margaret will be the legitimate queen of Scotland. If anything happens to me, the country will rally around her, and she will rule in my stead. I'm not only protecting her, I'm protecting Scotland! I'm sure the captain will agree."

He spurred his horse into a swift gallop back to the castle. Robert had to urge his mount to keep up.

But when James revealed his plan, the captain simply stared in disbelief. "Say it again. Surely I didn't hear you right."

"I intend to marry Margaret secretly," James said firmly. "I want you, along with Robert and Sibylla, to witness for us."

"Does Lady Margaret agree to this?"

"She will, I've no doubt."

"And where did this idea come from?" the captain asked. "You swore to trust the answer your Soul gave you, regardless."

"The threat to her is more serious than I thought. Even now, men are conspiring against our union."

"Listen to me, James! I once tried to go against fate. Out of fear, I sent my sister and her daughter away to escape a plague, but I sent them to the very city where both were struck down."

"Plagues are an act of God," James fired back. "Men are helpless against them. But acts of men against Margaret—those I can prevent!"

"You don't know that!" Van Horn took a deep breath and tried to speak reasonably. "Don't you understand, James? My action brought about the very thing I feared. If you want to know how we lose connection with our Soul, this is how!"

James shot to his feet, shaking with anger. He had never felt more certain of anything. When he spoke, it was with the authority of the king.

"Either you are with me in this or you are not. Which will it be?"

The captain could see the red and black colors swirling around James again—that powerful Stewart will! Going to his sanctuary had not resolved this conflict.

He said solemnly, "I am always with you, James."

"She will be safe once we are wed. I am sure of it."

James sat back down, and an uncomfortable silence stretched between them. The captain said nothing, watching as the young king's temper cooled, and he started fidgeting in his chair.

Finally James said, "I . . . I apologize for my outburst, Captain. I should not have doubted you."

"With loyalties blowing one way and then another, you are justified in your suspicions, Sire."

"Yes, but never toward you."

The captain bowed his head in acknowledgment but said nothing. *He has his whole heart set on this young lady. I'd best step softly here, or I might lose him.*

Rain battered against the closed windows of Lord Angus's hall. It was a wild night that fitted the mood of the two men visiting his castle. He waited until the servants had set the meal and left the room. Only then did he speak to MacKenzie and Crichton.

His voice low, Angus said, "I haven't been able to persuade the king to set Margaret Drummond aside. I hear he's already sent to Rome for a dispensation."

Crichton looked at him in dismay. "We can forestall that, surely. Waylay the messenger, destroy the Pope's letter—"

"Which messenger? The archbishop sent three of them, all by different routes." Angus tore a piece of bread from a rye loaf. "I'm beginning to understand how Lord MacLean felt when he dueled with James."

MacKenzie, who had been listening with a growing fury, slammed his fist on the table.

"*A Drummond will not sit on the throne while I live.*"

The two men stared in alarm at MacKenzie's white face, his eyes filled with hatred.

"Drummond treachery nearly destroyed the MacKenzies. They locked half our family in a church and burned them alive! A Drummond will never sit on the throne."

Angus felt a chill ripple down his back. He had not known this simmering hatred lived in MacKenzie. After all, the atrocity had taken place nearly eighty years ago. Almost every family had committed similar crimes against their rivals. It was an unfortunate part of Scottish history.

He glanced at Crichton and saw the man had much the same thoughts. MacKenzie's volatile nature could be a liability to their purpose. Perhaps it would be prudent to shift the focus away from Margaret.

Before Angus could speak, Crichton said, "In light of our change of fortunes, we might go about this in a different way."

MacKenzie eyed Crichton suspiciously. "What do you mean?"

Crichton clasped his hands in front of him. "I've recently received a proposal from one of King Henry's men. He suggests that instead of trying to separate the king from Lady Margaret, we kidnap James and take him to England."

MacKenzie stared at Crichton in astonishment, but Angus felt a glimmer of hope at the idea. After all, James's father had been kidnapped twice and both times ransomed and returned from England without harm.

Crichton continued. "Part of his ransom would be a Tudor on the throne and a peace treaty between England and Scotland. The treaty would include a generous settlement along the border in Scotland's favor."

Angus seized on the idea. "With a Tudor queen, the Drummonds would lose their influence, and our estates would be secured. What say you, MacKenzie?"

Mackenzie hesitated, unable for a moment to let go of his anger. Finally, he growled. "If we do this, we must act quickly. Other monarchs in Europe have petitioned for the hand of Henry's daughter when she comes of age." He still looked doubtful. "But how do you propose to seize the king when he is surrounded by bodyguards?"

Crichton turned to Angus. "You can ask him to go hunting with you on your estate. He'll be glad to get away from the court for a time. Petitioners are besieging him night and day. We can act while he's separated from his men."

Angus didn't like being cast in this role. And there was something more. Lately it seemed that just being around James was having a curious effect on him—as if he were being urged to become a better man in some way, almost against his will.

Thinking about it now colored how he felt about his border estates. Although dear to him, perhaps they weren't worth betraying the young king.

Angus let out a long, slow breath and rubbed his forehead wearily. Such noble sentiments were all well and good, but he had already cast his lot with these men, and he had to see it through.

"I suppose asking him to go hunting with me might work. We did so before, when he and my sons were younger. He might remember those times."

Crichton said, "We must put our plan into action at the earliest moment. Let us know the day and time you and the king go hunting. We will prepare the English court to receive us."

MacKenzie glowered. "And if this doesn't work, be assured there are other ways of dealing with the Drummonds."

MacKenzie had little trust in Angus. The man had shifted sides once. What was to keep him from doing it again? Besides, Providence had already given MacKenzie another weapon. A spy at Drummond had made himself known only a few days ago, saying, "There is a way to strike at the heart of the Drummonds. Say the word, and it will be done."

Perhaps, rather than count on a man as weak as Angus, it would be better to let the spy do his work.

Chapter 22

The Goshawk and the Unicorn

Wullie managed to smuggle a new embroidery from Aileen into Margaret's rooms. But he could tell her nothing about the spy at Drummond, though he was working hard on this puzzle.

"I gave a quiet word here and there to folks I trust. 'Watch out,' I says, 'for anyone who might be doing something odd, out of their usual ways, so to speak.'"

But the only person who seemed to be doing anything at all was Father Ewin, who had traveled two or three times in the past week from Drummond to see Lord Crichton. If he continued on that road, Wullie told her, he would also reach MacKenzie's castle, and a few miles beyond that, Lord Angus's estate.

"Find out what that priest is up to, Wullie," she said. "And I don't care what you have to do."

"Aye, m'lady. That I will."

After Wullie left, Margaret examined every inch of Aileen's new embroidery. Her cousin never included anything idle in her needlework. She had stitched in symbols for the castles of Crichton, MacKenzie, and Angus and woven a complex web of vines around them all, vines that ended in the center, where she had put a unicorn.

A unicorn . . . part of the Stewart royal coat of arms.

This warning was about James!

Margaret spotted two vines leading out from the center of the embroidery. Aileen had made these harder to trace, as if to hide her news so only the most discerning eye could catch it. Margaret tracked one tendril with her finger all the way to a lower corner of the embroidery.

And saw a gold lion crouched behind a thicket.

England!

The meaning of the embroidery leaped out, and anger swept aside her fear. The three treacherous lords intended to betray James to the English—kidnap him, most likely, and hold him for ransom. She could guess what the price would be for his return.

James had to know about this right away, before these men could put their plan into action. Margaret wrote a short note to him, wrapped it with the embroidery in a thick package, and then sent for one of her most trusted couriers.

"Take this to the king. Deliver it to his hand and no one else's! Stay off the main roads, and ride like the devil himself is after you!"

The courier bowed, and Margaret closed the door and sat down at her bureau, her heart beating hard in her chest. The threats against her and James seemed to be multiplying.

She shivered at the thought and moved to the window, where sunlight poured into the room and warmed her chilled body. In the distance, she could see the forest that surrounded Drummond, its red and gold autumn leaves standing out against the deep green pines.

Overhead, white clouds towered like the sails of ships against the morning sky. And farther to the southwest lay Stirling, its snow-capped mountains sheltering the castle and James.

The tranquil scene was so beautiful that for a moment all her fear dropped away, and a strange euphoria slowly enveloped her. It had happened before when she had prayed to the Blessed Virgin.

She hadn't told anyone, not even Sibylla, about these spells. When they occurred, the immediate world around her, with all of its sounds and sights, receded, as if she were looking through the wrong end of a spyglass. Another, vaster world pressed close and brought such joy and peace that she longed to step into it fully.

A place where you can hear your Soul . . .

If everyone could feel this hidden radiance, surely no one would fear death . . . It was so close, if she could just cross over. Was this what James had felt?

At the thought of him, a surge of love filled Margaret's heart, an echo of that radiance. Her whole body ached to be with him. She still could feel his lips on hers, raising a fire in her body that left her restless at night.

James, if you asked me to marry you now, I would do it right here in this room!

"We can hold a royal ball here at Stirling," James said to Robert, "and keep everyone dancing and feasting while Margaret and I are in the chapel. No one would notice our absence."

Robert frowned, considering the plan. James was pacing, too excited to sit still.

"Wouldn't Lord Drummond notice? After all, he keeps a close eye on his daughters—"

A knock on the door interrupted him. James flung the door open to find a courier bearing a small package. "Lady Margaret sends her compliments, Your Majesty. She told me to deliver this to your hand."

James gave the courier a gold coin and tore open the package. An embroidery, along with a note from Margaret, fell onto the table. James read the note outlining the suspected plot against him, gave it to Robert, and turned to look carefully at the needlework. Robert came up beside him and studied it as well.

"Do you see the meaning?" James asked.

Robert nodded slowly, and James folded the cloth. "We need to see Lord Gray."

Lord Gray listened in silence as James and Robert explained the threat to the crown from Crichton, MacKenzie, and Angus, although the young king was careful not to divulge the source of his news.

Gray tugged at his beard. "It appears that Angus has switched his loyalties, Your Majesty. You've no idea what they are plotting to do?"

"I can hazard a guess from my father's experience—it might involve a kidnapping. But it would be only a guess."

"Hmmm. Then permit me to give you a lesson in strategy, Sire. If you don't know what the enemy is up to, let him tell you. Whichever of these three men contacts you first will expose their plan."

A few days later, an invitation came from Lord Angus, asking the king to join him in a boar hunt on his estate.

Lord Gray waved the invitation in triumph.

"What did I tell you? Your guess about a kidnapping is on the mark. Angus's estate is a good secluded place to do it and then whisk you off to England. But they don't know we have the advantage. By the saints, Sire, your spies outdo my own! How do you learn of these things?"

"If I told you a goshawk brings me news, would you believe it?' James asked.

Gray gave a short laugh. "No, Your Majesty, I would not. Keep your secrets, then. We have an old rebel to arrest along with his conspirators! I recommend we leave at dawn, Sire."

James said, "Get everything ready. Robert and I will meet you in the courtyard at sunrise. But there's something I need to ask the captain before we leave."

That night in van Horn's quarters, James came straight to the point.

"I want you to go to Drummond and stay with Margaret until we can be wed. I have Sir Lennox and some of my knights there, but I would rest more easily if I knew you were guarding her as well. I trust you more than any other man, even Robert."

James gazed out the window to where the moon was rising in the east. "I have never felt like this about anyone, Captain" he said softly.

"I think about her so much. I hear her voice giving me advice . . ." he smiled briefly, "always sensible, of course. Sometimes I can feel her next to me, the way she has of taking my hand, reminding me who I am." He flushed and looked down. "I suppose I sound foolish."

The captain said, "Like every man since Adam and Eve. I will go to Drummond, Sire. It will be my honor to watch over Lady Margaret."

Chapter 23

Fall of the Drummonds

Wullie wheezed, "M'ladies, the priest went to see MacKenzie early this morning and returned about two hours ago. But MacKenzie allowed no servants in the room when the priest was with him. I'm sorry, Lady Margaret."

"No need to be sorry, Wullie," she said gently. "But if Father Ewin is the spy, I suspect Lord Fleming is his master."

Margaret sat back from her embroidery frame. She and Sibylla had taken up work in the sewing room so they could speak with Wullie alone. Few servants came to this part of the castle during the morning hours.

She said, "With that cur Fleming gone to Edinburgh, perhaps we can send someone to search his bedchamber and private rooms."

"Margaret!" Sibylla gasped, then colored and laughed. "You are a devil when you suspect someone!"

Wullie's eyes gleamed. "We'd have to get around his valet and Lady Euphemia, but it might be done. I'd wager we'd find something!"

Once they had caught their spy, maybe then James would finally recall the king's knights to Stirling, where they could protect him.

Suddenly they heard a frantic voice calling from the corridor, "Lady Margaret, Lady Sibylla!"

The voice grew ever louder until Euphemia's lady-in-waiting appeared in the doorway, her hair in disarray and her face so pale her eyes looked almost black.

"My ladies, come quick!" she gasped. "It's your father—he's taken seriously ill. Lady Euphemia needs you right away!"

Margaret turned sharply to Wullie. "Fetch Sir Lennox and have him meet us at Father's bedchamber."

Euphemia was waiting for them outside Lord Drummond's rooms, her face worn and gaunt. "Father asks for you both whenever his delirium lifts."

When Margaret embraced her, she could feel her sister trembling.

"Tell us what happened?" Margaret said. Sibylla clung to her arm, too frightened to speak.

"He was in the conservatory all morning—Oh, Sir Lennox!" She exclaimed. "Thank God you are here!"

Margaret turned and found herself staring not at Sir Lennox but at the tall, ruddy-faced man following closely behind him. It took a moment for her to believe who it was.

"Captain van Horn!" She almost sobbed in relief. "Providence has sent you to us! Lord Drummond is desperately ill."

Van Horn lifted the leather satchel he carried. "T'was James who had a premonition of danger. If I may be of assistance—"

Margaret said, "Yes! Our own physician is useless!"

Van Horn asked, "When did this illness come on him?"

"Only a short time ago," Euphemia said. "He had taken his noon meal in the conservatory, and some angel put it in my mind to visit him there. I found him on the floor, barely alive."

"You still have the remains of what he ate?" the captain asked.

"Yes," Euphemia said. "His tray from the conservatory is here."

Van Horn turned to Sir Lennox. "Stand guard here. Let no one pass through these doors—no one! And put guards on the ladies' bedchambers as well. We don't know yet who their enemies are."

"Aye, Captain," Sir Lennox said. "We'll make sure no one gets by us."

As Euphemia opened the bedchamber door, Margaret and Sibylla both gasped at the scene. Lord Drummond lay back on his pillows, his face a ghastly grey and twisted with pain. The heavy curtains had been drawn shut, and the flickering candlelight made it seem the shadow of death wavered over him.

Margaret recovered first and hurried over to her father's side, followed by the captain, who took one of the lighted candles and held it close to Drummond's face. With his other hand, he carefully lifted the man's eyelids one at a time. He felt the gray, dry skin, and listened to his chest. Margaret watched as he took her father's pulse, using not one finger but three on each wrist.

"Mushroom poisoning is my guess," the captain muttered. "Where are the remains of the meal?"

Euphemia showed him her father's tray with a bowl of half-eaten soup and asked in anguish, "The antidote—do you know it?"

"Only if I know the mushroom." The captain examined the soup carefully. He finally pulled out a short brown stem with part of the mushroom still attached.

"It's a roll-rim mushroom. Praise God, it takes a while for the toxin to accumulate." He opened his leather satchel and pulled out a vial of yellow powder. "We'll need a pitcher of water, a glass, and a bottle of whiskey!"

A servant quickly brought the three items requested. As the captain mixed the powder and water in the glass, he had Euphemia and Margaret help their father sit up to ease his breathing. He then put Euphemia and Sibylla to work rubbing their father's legs to keep the circulation strong.

"Margaret, while I spoon this mixture into his mouth, massage his throat gently to help him swallow. With any luck, the potion will neutralize the poison before it does lasting harm."

They worked for what seemed like hours, until Margaret's back ached and her arms could barely move. Finally the glass was empty.

"Now we wait," the captain said. "In the meantime, I suggest we question the kitchen staff about the mushrooms."

Under van Horn's careful questioning, one of the kitchen maids broke down, sobbing hysterically and swearing that though she had gathered mushrooms for the soup, she had not picked the roll-rim.

"I know it's poisonous, my lady. I would never use it. May God strike me dead if I'm lying. I beg you, don't send me away."

Another kitchen maid spoke up timidly. "My lady, Father Ewin came into the kitchen, but he's the only one I saw there besides us." Margaret exchanged a quick look with Sibylla.

She said, "I'll tell Sir Lennox to arrest Father Ewin and confine him to his monk's cell. We'll question him when Father is out of danger."

A few hours later, Lord Drummond's color began to return, and he fell into a peaceful sleep. The bottle of whiskey, it turned out, was for the captain, who poured himself a generous drink to celebrate the patient's progress.

The captain urged the three sisters to rest, assuring them that he would keep a watchful eye on their father. Margaret stayed back as her two sisters wearily departed. The captain gestured to the chair beside him.

"Keep an old man company, Lady Margaret." He raised his glass to her. "My compliments. You have a soldier's steadiness in a crisis."

Margaret said, "This poisoning is too convenient by far. I fear my brother-in-law Lord Fleming has gone over to the English side, but I will have to prove it before I can tell James. These days James sees dark designs everywhere."

The captain poured himself another round. "You would make a formidable inquisitor, Lady Margaret."

Margaret looked at her father and steeled herself to ask the question that the nearness of death had provoked in her. "Captain, have . . . have you told James something about my fate?" She turned to face van Horn. "Is that why he is so fearful of losing me?"

The courage that shone in her face moved the Captain deeply. *By the saints, Master Zheng, if James were not the one to receive the scrolls, I would give them to her!*

"Do you feel your own death is near?" he asked gently.

She pondered the question. "I have experienced something, as if another world is beckoning to me. James has seen it, I think . . . and perhaps you as well, Captain."

"You are very discerning, my lady."

"What is it I am seeing?"

"Where we come from," the captain said. "Where we will return."

Margaret said nothing. His words carried a haunting meaning, but one that remained just out of her grasp.

"As for James," the captain said, "there's a strange truth, my lady. We will trust our Soul in all things, even our own death. But not when it comes to those we love. To trust those lives to our Soul's care is beyond the reach of many, including, I'm afraid, our James."

"Then I will help him."

He smiled at her with a touch of sadness. "I've no doubt you will."

"Thank you, Captain, for saving our father." She rose, and he stood up with her. "And for being like a father to James. It's very fortuitous how you have entered his life, almost as if you had been sent to find him."

He bowed. "I am at your service, Lady Margaret. I suggest that when Lord Drummond is strong enough, you and your sisters accompany me back to Stirling. With a spy on the loose here, it's not safe. I'm sure Sir Lennox will guard you until then. And we can have a food taster test any dishes you are given."

Margaret said, "I am indebted to you, Captain, for everything."

As van Horn watched her depart, his eyes stung with sudden tears. He sensed a thinning of her life, as if she were already partly in the other world.

What if her greatest help to James would come not through her life but through her death? It would be a bitter lesson. One that James might not be able to master.

The attempted kidnapping of James collapsed before it had even begun. Once Lord Angus saw James with Gray and his men riding toward his castle gates, he seemed to lose whatever resolution he might have had and quickly confessed to the plot, naming Crichton and MacKenzie as accomplices. It was then an easy matter to capture the hired brigands who had been waiting in the forest.

Lord Angus was so repentant and contrite that James hadn't the heart to arrest him. The man looked as if his conscience had been tormenting him night and day. Instead, James took Angus's knights prisoner and ordered the earl confined to his castle until a judgment could be rendered in court.

As they rode back toward Stirling, Lord Gray confided to James, "I'll have to admit, the old warrior isn't a true criminal. I'm surprised he joined such an ill-conceived venture."

"MacLean said men like him have friendship on one side and treason on the other."

"Minor treachery, yes, but real treason?" Gray shook his head. "Let him stew in his castle for a time, pondering his sins. Then I would recommend you take him back into your trust, Sire. In my judgment, the old man will be loyal to you for life now."

Robert laughed. "As long as we count the gold whenever he leaves Stirling."

"MacKenzie and Crichton, now," Gray said grimly. "There's another matter altogether."

James's face hardened at the names. "They will be arrested and tried for treason. We need to know whether they acted alone or whether there are others in league with them. A poor use of the second chance I offered them."

Robert added, "And I'd wager they know the spy at Drummond. All these foul devils know each other."

"Wullie will ferret him out," James said. "He knows how to catch a rat, even if it wears a priest's robe. Besides, with Sir Lennox and the captain at Drummond, Margaret and Sibylla are well guarded."

"A priest's robe, you say!" Gray said. "Well, if that's the case, it wouldn't be the first time the clergy has proved treacherous! I heard of a monk once who trained a pet raven to drop poison pellets into his lord's ale. When the lord's sons uncovered the plot, they hanged the raven alongside the monk!"

The men laughed, and Gray added, "But look to family members first. A brother, uncle, cousin—there's your poisoner or assassin, nine times out of ten."

James said, "God's truth, Lord Gray. My father's own brothers tried to remove him from the throne."

As if summoned by such dark thoughts, a shadow suddenly swept over the group. The men instinctively flinched, and James looked around wildly for its source.

"There!" One of the knights pointed to the tall grass by the side of the road. "It's a hawk!"

The large raptor appeared to be dragging one wing, as if injured. The fierce bird cocked its head from side to side as if searching the group.

"It's bewitched!" one of the knights cried. "Shoot it!"

Before anyone could draw a bow, James shouted: "Hold! Don't harm it—it's a goshawk!"

The moment he uttered the words, the hair stood up on his neck. Symbol of the Drummond house.

As if waiting for James to understand, the goshawk gave a loud cry. With two sound wings, it flew off northward where Drummond Castle lay.

They were two days' ride from the castle, but James didn't hesitate. He shouted to Gray, "Lead the men to Stirling! Robert and I will ride for Drummond. Something has happened to Margaret—I know it!"

Lord Gray pleaded, "Don't be headstrong, Sire. We'll ride with you!"

"No! You'll only slow us down. Get the prisoners back to Stirling!"

Without another word, he and Robert set off at a hard gallop. James gave a silent prayer of thanks they had chosen to ride their Barbary horses. Gray roared for three of the king's knights to follow them, but within a mile or two, Robert and James had left the men far behind.

It was the worst ride of James's life, haunted by the feeling they might be too late. He focused all his strength on willing Margaret to live. After all he had done, all he had risked, he wasn't about to let fate steal her from him.

Robert had to urge him to rest the sweating horses now and then to keep the animals from collapsing under them.

At the last roadside inn, James and Robert commandeered new mounts and kept going, feeling neither fatigue nor hunger. Fear drove James relentlessly, and for the last few miles, the sense of doom increased until he could hardly breathe.

He felt as if his heart were being torn out of his chest.

God in Heaven, let me be in time to save her!

It was nearly noon on the third day when Robert and James spotted the distant turrets of Drummond Castle through the bare winter trees.

They whipped their horses up the main road and through the gates, clattering to a halt in the courtyard, where James saw a scene to fit his worst nightmare.

The courtyard was crowded with people dressed in black, the women shrieking and wailing and milling about as if lost.

Lord Drummond, distraught with grief, shouted for his horse and his sword as several courtiers tried to wrestle him back into the castle.

James pushed his way toward him, only to find the captain blocking his path. Before he could speak, the captain threw his arms around him.

"I'm sorry, James, I'm so sorry."

The young king tore lose, his whole body shaking.

"Margaret—" he said hoarsely.

The captain shook his head, looking old and beaten. "She and Sibylla, Euphemia, they're gone . . . all three . . ."

Sudden rage blinded the young king, and he roared, "WHAT GOOD ARE YOUR SCROLLS AND YOUR TEACHING? *WHAT GOOD ARE THEY?*"

"James—" the captain began.

But James whirled, seized Robert's arm, and dragged him toward the castle. They had ridden as if possessed to get here. He had to see Margaret.

Chapter 24

Blood Rage and the Captain's Risk

A frightened monk led James and Robert toward the chapel, where Margaret and her sisters lay in state. The monk cast a furtive glance at James. The young king's eyes blazed with such fury it made the man's blood run cold.

"Tell me how she died," James demanded.

The monk swallowed thickly. "It . . . it was poison, Your Majesty. An—an assassin put poison on wild grapes. No one suspected this. All three sisters ate of them—"

James grabbed the man's cassock. "Who did it? Who killed them?"

"We—we d-don't know, Sire," the monk stammered. "Some say it was the priest, Father Ewin, but he has disappeared."

The monk broke loose and hurried on ahead, as if afraid James would seize hold of him again. When they reached the chapel, James saw Sir Lennox and two of his knights standing guard by the door.

The moment Sir Lennox caught sight of James, the color left his face, and he fell to one knee.

"Your Majesty," he said hoarsely. "You charged me to protect her, and I failed. I offer my life in forfeit."

James shook his head. "You are not to blame, Sir Lennox. You could not guard against so cunning a threat. Not even the captain—"

he stopped, unable to speak. After a moment, "Take the king's knights and Lord Drummond's men and arrest MacKenzie and Crichton for treason and murder. Bring them to me at Stirling."

Lennox's head came up like a wolf catching a scent. The expression on his face matched James's mood exactly.

"I will leave at once, Your Majesty."

James caught his arm. "I want them delivered alive, Sir Lennox."

The knight controlled himself with an effort. "As you wish, Sire." He bowed and left quickly down the corridor.

The monk pushed the chapel door open and stepped aside to let James and Robert enter.

The sisters lay on three raised biers, each bier intricately carved with the Drummond crest and symbols of the goshawk. Sunlight streamed through the stained-glass window, and smoke from incense burners twisted and curled in the light.

Several women in mourning clothes were sitting vigil in the pews. Upon seeing the young king and Robert, they bowed and withdrew, silent as shadows.

James saw none of this. To him, the room was dark except for one face. He walked toward the middle bier where Margaret lay. He could hardly breathe against the searing pain that gripped his chest; he felt dazed and light-headed. Dimly he heard Robert crying behind him.

She was so still, dark hair framing her marble-white face, her graceful hands folded on her chest. This could not be real. Margaret was never still. She would wake and see him, and they would return to Stirling, where she would be safe. He covered her hands with his own to let her know he was there and bent to kiss her forehead.

But when he touched the dry coldness of her flesh, her death struck him like a black wind that tore away his sanctuary, his knowledge, his faith. He gasped and bent over Margaret, his eyes clenched tightly as the devastation ripped through him. Suddenly he was sobbing, one arm flung across her body.

The monk, in a clumsy attempt to comfort the king, moved

forward and murmured, "Your Majesty, she will be buried in the Drummond family cemetery with her sisters—"

"NO!" James shouted and drew his sword in one swift motion, a mad light in his eyes. "No one will touch her!"

The monk backed away so quickly he tripped and sprawled onto the stone floor. James stepped forward and pointed his sword at the man's heart.

"She was to be my queen, and she will be buried like one. I swear, all of Scotland will mourn her. Send for the Archbishop and the chief members of my court."

The monk gaped up at him mutely.

"DO IT NOW!"

"Of—of course, Your Majesty, I—I will send . . ." The monk scrambled to his feet and hurried away, his sandals slapping loudly on the stone floor.

A fierce purpose took hold of James, pushing grief aside. If the conspirators had thought to defeat him by killing her, he would turn that act against them. They would become the most hated men in Scotland.

He went to Robert, who was staring bleakly at Sibylla's lifeless form.

"I was wrong, James," Robert said, his voice thick with grief. "*Power* is the most important thing. Use it to burn their castles and send those murderers to a fiery hell."

The hunger to do it coursed through James's blood. The power of the king—he had never been more aware of it than now. He would send for MacLean and his men and unleash the Highland clans to annihilate his enemies.

He put his arm around Robert's shoulders. "The whole country will know how we loved them, Robert. And then, I promise you, we will have justice."

Word of the tragedy at Drummond had already reached Stirling when Gray and the king's knights arrived at the castle. The news struck Gray like a blow and silenced the men around him. When they learned how the three sisters had died, Gray had to restrain the knights from turning on their prisoners and slaughtering them.

A few of the men whispered about the goshawk that had met them on the road.

"T'was sent by God to let the king know."

"Aye, there are spirits at work here."

Gray cut short such talk and instructed the leader of the king's knights, "Secure the prisoners and have lords Argyll and Montrose come to Stirling. I'll ride for Drummond and see to the king. With Lady Margaret gone, there's no telling what he'll do."

At Drummond Castle, James threw himself into the state funeral arrangements like a man possessed. He put Robert in charge of overseeing the elaborate funeral carriage, livery, and coffin.

"She must be carried like a queen. Do whatever is necessary to make the carriage fitting for her."

Whenever anyone tried to console him or talk about Margaret, he turned abruptly away. Their words threatened to awaken his grief, waiting like a black emptiness that could swallow his life. People quickly learned not to mention Lady Margaret's name around him.

He was tormented by memories of her that flooded his mind: the way she laughed, the feel of her skin, her voice murmuring in his ear. To keep the memories at bay, he redoubled his efforts to prepare for the funeral.

In the midst of this, James gave orders to bar Captain van Horn from his presence. He had no desire to hear his words of wisdom or advice on what he ought to do. "The captain is free to go where he wishes, but he will have no audience with me."

Robert asked him why, but received no answer. He did not ask James again.

The only other person James allowed close to him was Wullie, who had cried like a child over Margaret's death.

The funeral procession would convey Margaret to the royal cathedral in Dunblane, where she would be interred. When the time came, he would be buried beside her. "Together as we should have been in life," he told Robert.

Sibylla would be laid to rest on Drummond land, beside her sister Euphemia.

When the Archbishop arrived, James commanded him to announce the marriage banns that would have been made between himself and Margaret. The country must know it was the future Queen of Scotland and her sisters, not just the daughters of Lord Drummond, who had been treacherously slain by the king's enemies.

Only in the quiet times of night did James visit the chapel, where the women of Drummond sat vigil over Margaret and her sisters. He would kneel by Margaret's side, his face white and hard as stone, and after a few minutes, depart.

The women wondered among themselves why, if the young king loved Lady Margaret so much, he never wept for her.

Prohibited from seeing James, Captain van Horn watched events unfold with growing dread. He stood on a shadowed balcony overlooking Drummond Castle's great hall while below him James argued with tradesmen about a cloth of gold that would cover the carriage.

The captain could see the strain of the past three days in the gray smudges under James's eyes and the sunken look to his face. Wullie had told van Horn that James barely ate or slept, and when he did sleep, he suffered nightmares.

The captain thought, *The path James is on now will drag Scotland into murderous violence again. He must choose another way . . .*

"I see you watch the king as we do, Captain."

Van Horn turned to face Montrose and Argyll as they reached the top of the stairs. The two men looked as worried as he had ever seen them.

Montrose said. "You know he's called the Highland clans to fight for him."

"So I've heard," the captain said.

Argyll added. "It's put a chill over the country, and just when people were beginning to hope for a time of peace. Many fear that his promise of justice and the rule of law will be forgotten."

Montrose shook his head. "Already, feuds settled under James's amnesty rule are starting to flare up again. If you could only make him see—"

The captain let out a slow breath. "I would try, gentlemen, but he has barred me from his sight. I'm afraid I have no influence at all."

"I wouldn't be so certain, Captain," Montrose said thoughtfully. "Had he truly wanted to be rid of you, he would have ordered the king's knights to put you on the next ship to the Low Countries. Yet he allows you to stay here under this roof."

For the first time in days, van Horn felt a spark of hope. "A fair point, and one that I had missed. My gratitude for your insight, Lord Montrose."

"Do what you can, Captain. He will not listen to us. Nor is Lord Drummond of much use in this. The death of his daughters has plunged him into a black grief. It's said that he has not left his chambers in several days now. It's said that Lord Fleming is in mourning as well, keeping a vigil for his wife in the chappel."

Van Horn watched as James restlessly paced the room below. Glowing red and black swirled thickly around him now. But deep within him the Soul's light still shone, faint but persistent, an ally he could call on.

There is a terrible knowledge he does not want to see. When the state funeral is over, I fear it will break through to him. And then he will need the Fourth Scroll more than ever.

On the seventh day after the deaths of Margaret and her sisters, the royal funeral procession began its slow journey from Drummond Castle to the cathedral at Dunblane. Those in the procession gaped in astonishment at the masses of people gathered along the roadway between Drummond and the cathedral.

News of Margaret's tragic murder had spread rapidly throughout the countryside. Robert realized with awe how popular James had become among the people and how much they felt his loss as their own. James's vow to have all of Scotland mourn for Margaret and Sibylla seemed to be coming true before his eyes.

A priest ringing a bell led the procession, the bell's rhythmic tolling sounded like a mournful heartbeat. James and Robert rode behind him, followed by the Archbishop and officials of the church.

The funeral carriage, drawn by four bay horses, gleamed in the sunlight with its embroidered cloth of gold draped over the frame. Within the carriage lay a slender cedar coffin, ornamented with the Stewart and Drummond crests. A long line of noble families rode behind the carriage, followed by commoners walking on foot, many of them crying openly.

After so much effort, James felt detached and numb, like a ghost leading the procession. Lord Drummond and Lord Fleming rode behind him, but he barely noticed their presence. Even the packed crowds lining the road seemed unreal to him. Their mouths moved, yet no sound reached his ears. Like silent mummers, they were all weeping, or crossing themselves, or throwing flowers in the procession's path.

Only the bell penetrated, its steady tolling mournful and unrelenting. *Pulse of my heart.* The thought flickered in his mind and faded.

James had little memory of reaching the cathedral or of the ceremony. At one point he smelled incense and looked around vaguely, searching the faces near him, but the one he looked for wasn't there. The sounds of liturgical Latin wove back and forth in the cathedral hall. As the monks chanted a haunting requiem, the cedar coffin was carried from the bier and placed into the vault prepared for it. Masons set the stones to close the opening.

And she was gone, shut away from him forever.

Only when the funeral procession returned to Drummond for the two sisters' burial did James wake from his trance. In the courtyard, Lord Drummond tried to speak to him, but James walked away without answering.

He found himself in the castle, climbing the staircase to Margaret's bedchambers.

At the sight of the room without her, the black grief he had held at bay came sweeping over him.

I can't live without you, he had told her. He hadn't known how true those words would be.

In blind rage and pain, he grabbed letters, quills, clothes, icons, everything he could lay his hands on from the tables and shelves, and hurled them to the floor. He threw chairs across the room, hearing the satisfying crack of breaking wood and the splintering of shattered mirrors.

When there was nothing left to destroy, he sank to his knees in the wreckage with his chest heaving and tears streaming down his face. Hatred burned in his heart; all he wanted now was to kill the cowards who had murdered her.

The next day, James and Robert prepared to ride back to Stirling Castle where they would join the Highland clans and the nobles' armies. MacLean had already sent a message to James: *"We stand ready to fight, Your Majesty, a powerful arm to wield swords in your name. Your Lady Margaret and her sisters will be avenged."*

James showed the letter to Robert and said coldly, "These men know what I want. There won't be a stone left standing in the traitors' castles. And then we'll destroy their estates in the Borderlands. I'm going to burn everything they own."

From Stirling, James would launch his attacks against the castles and estates of lords MacKenzie and Crichton. He could feel a power surging through him to accomplish his deepest desire. It made him feel invincible.

As Robert buckled on his sword, he kept glancing at James, worried by the changes he saw. It was not just the gaunt look of him but a coldness in his eyes and around the mouth. The Stewart black temper seemed to be taking over his nature, molding it to a hardness that Robert feared might become cruelty.

He also knew that Gray, Montrose, and Argyll were not fully behind the king's decision.

"If we object too much," Gray had told him, "the king might simply replace us. If we stay, at least we have some chance of restraining him." Only the Highlanders seemed eager to carry out the king's revenge.

Suddenly a familiar wheezy voice penetrated the door to James's room. "Your Majesty! Sire, if I might have a word before you leave?"

James paused in the act of buckling on his dagger and glanced in annoyance at Robert, who shrugged and shook his head.

"Not now, Wullie," James snapped, and pulled his belt tight. "It will have to wait."

"An' it please you, Sire, a moment is all I ask."

A hoarse cough like a death rattle followed these words. James rolled his eyes heavenward.

"Oh, very well." He flung the door open and froze. Wullie had moved aside, leaving James face to face with Captain van Horn.

The man's eyes flashed dangerously, and the power radiating from him was so strong James took a step back before he caught himself.

"No one summoned you here," he said defiantly. "You will leave—now!"

The captain moved past him and seemed to fill the room as he entered. He looked steadily at Robert and the king's valet.

"I will speak with James alone." The quiet voice carried such authority that the two left without a word or a backward glance.

James felt a stirring of alarm. He pushed down the feeling and folded his arms across his chest. "I have no need of advice from you."

The captain held out the Fourth Scroll. "I have come here to remind you who you are."

James's face went scarlet with rage. He snatched the scroll and flung it across the room. At that moment, his face looked like the blood-crazed soldiers in the Stirling tapestry

"I know who I am!" he shouted. "I am the king!"

"YOU ARE FAR MORE THAN THE KING!"

The voice cracked like thunder, silencing James instantly. Van Horn took a step closer, his eyes boring into him.

"Be warned: the path you take, a nation will follow. Choose with great care."

James had never before felt fear in the captain's presence. Yet even with his heart pounding and his mouth dry, he couldn't let go of his anger and pain. They kept the darkness away; even hatred was better than a bleak nothingness.

"I have sworn to seek justice."

"It is not justice you seek but *revenge*," van Horn said sternly. "And what of your code of laws? Would you establish the rule of law and then declare yourself above it?"

James shot back, "What meaning is there to the law? To fate? All your wisdom and scrolls, all your learning could not save her."

The captain was now only inches away from James's face. "And your actions, James—did you save her?"

The words knocked the breath out of him and summoned a truth James had been desperately trying to avoid. "You will bring on you the very thing you fear," the captain had warned him.

His legs gave way, and he sat down heavily and buried his face in his hands. The hatred and rage that had driven him for so many days began to ebb from his heart, revealing the bleak ruins where his beloved sanctuary had once been.

He looked up at van Horn in anguish. "No, I couldn't save her. Why did she have to die? Why could you save Lord Drummond and not Margaret?"

His words pierced van Horn like arrows. The captain had asked himself the same question over and over since Margaret's death. The only answer that came to him was, *It was fated to be.*

He shook his head in sorrow. "Her assassin used an old Roman trick—putting the poison on wild grapes cut for the table. No one suspected they would be tainted. The venom used has no antidote. It attacks the heart, and the body dies within minutes."

James stared at him, his eyes hollow and sunken. The man could see that the red and black colors around James had subsided, but a uniform gray had taken their place.

"I am nothing without her," he said dully.

"Lady Margaret would disagree."

James mustered a final rebellion. "The Highland clans are waiting for me. They expect to march when I return to Stirling. How can I change the course I've taken?"

"If you do not, you will be lost . . . and the country with you. Remember the Fourth Scroll. Everything depends on what you choose."

For a long moment, the desire to lash out at his enemies battled with what James knew to be true: Margaret would not want him to take revenge. Finally his shoulders slumped, and he nodded slowly.

The captain could see there was still a truth James held at bay. But for now it was enough to have brought the young king out of his blood rage and turned him from a deadly course of action. Perhaps the scrolls would also help heal his grief.

After the captain left, Robert rejoined James and was struck by the profound change in the young king.

"What did Captain van Horn tell you?" Robert asked.

"It's a private matter, Robert," was all James would say. His movements were slow and heavy as he unbuckled his dagger and let it fall to the floor.

His hatred and anger were gone, but in their place, he felt nothing at all.

Chapter 25

The Fifth Scroll

Once they reached Stirling Castle, James announced to his commanders that they would not be riding against the estates of MacKenzie and Crichton. Instead, the two lords, along with any other conspirators, would be tried in a court of law and punished according to the verdicts rendered.

As James spoke, Robert noticed that Gray and the other nobles seemed relieved there would be no campaign of revenge. Montrose confessed that it had been difficult to hold the army together for the past few days. After fighting to quell the second rebellion, the men were weary of battle and longed to go home, especially as colder weather settled in.

The nobles left the king's chambers, but Gray stayed behind and warned James, "You'd best see to your Highland allies, Your Majesty. They've been sharpening their swords for the past two days."

MacLean did not take the news well. He argued hotly for battle, pointing out that if the king did not make an example of the conspirators, such treachery would continue.

James merely listened; the numbness inside made MacLean's anger seem distant and futile.

Finally the clan chief threw up his hands in exasperation. "You test a fealty greatly, Your Majesty. More than any man I've ever known."

"I am charged by Heaven to follow this path, Lord MacLean. As I have been reminded, I cannot establish a rule of law and then declare myself above it. If I hold to it now—though I have great provocation for revenge—the nation will follow and respect the law. I ask you to stand with me in this."

MacLean regarded him in silence. He saw an emptiness in James's eyes that had not been there before. After years of Highland warfare, the clan chief knew that look all too well.

At last he said quietly, "If my wife had been slain by my enemies, I doubt I could make the same choice, Sire." He took a deep breath and exhaled slowly. "But if this is what you choose, I will stand with you."

"You have my deepest gratitude, Lord MacLean," James said. "You and your men will not return to the Highlands empty-handed, you have my word."

He walked with MacLean to the Highland troop quarters, where the clan chief paused before entering. "It won't be easy, Sire, to tell the men there will be no battle. Revenge is a Highlander's call to arms."

"Tell them . . . tell them the king will need their swords against the Lord of the Isles. The northwest regions must come under the royal banner."

"The men will be with you there. We have strong grievances against that lord's clan."

James added, "As for revenge, say that I follow the old Gaelic proverb: *ge milis am fion, tha a searbh ri dhiol.* 'The wine is sweet, but the price is bitter.'"

"Aye, Your Majesty," MacLean said. "Some would agree with that."

The next day, Wullie appeared before James in his chambers with a small burlap bag on his back and a fierce gleam in his eyes. "Sire, I believe we have caught both our spy and our murderer."

He set the bag on the floor and pulled out a metal box, then produced a key from his tunic pocket. James watched as he unlocked the lid and opened it. Within lay several corked vials of powder held securely in their metal sleeves.

"Poisons, Sire," Wullie wheezed darkly. "Some of the Drummond servants showed me where to look after they had persuaded Lord Fleming's valet to tell them."

"Lord Fleming!" James said. Anger flickered in his eyes. A killer inside the family. "I'll send the knights to arrest him as well."

If this evidence held true, Lord Fleming would hang with the others for the murders. But even this thought stirred little feeling in him, as if Margaret's death had swallowed all others.

Within a fortnight, Sir Lennox and his knights brought lords Crichton, MacKenzie, and Fleming into the throne room, their clothing torn and their faces bruised.

At James's questioning look, Sir Lennox shrugged. "Not our fault, Sire. They needed a bit of convincing to come with us."

James turned to face the three lords. "Gentlemen, you are charged with conspiring to kidnap the king and murder Lady Margaret and her two sisters. How do you answer?"

"Your Majesty," Crichton managed to keep his voice level and calm. "I confess to the first charge, but I had nothing to do with the deaths of Lady Margaret and her sisters. I demand to answer that charge in court, where I can prove my innocence."

Lord Fleming spoke, "I am innocent of both charges, Your Majesty. It's obvious that Father Ewin has thrown suspicion on me to cover his own treachery. You cannot believe that I would kill my own beloved wife. I ask only for your fair judgment."

James rose and stepped toward the three men. In his detached state, he found that his vision shifted more easily now. He stared deeply within each one and was appalled by what he saw. The light of their Souls appeared dim and remote, obscured by a sickening gray-green color. His last remnant of anger died, replaced by a wrenching pity.

Then the thought struck him. *If not for the captain, I would be like them.*

MacKenzie felt sweat running down his back. No one had ever looked at him like this. A gaping emptiness opened within him, and a growing terror of it choked his breath. His thirst for revenge had brought him to the edge of his own grave.

Lord Fleming glanced uneasily from James to MacKenzie and Crichton, feeling his confidence ebb at the fear that marked their faces. Fleming had steeled himself for the king's wrath, determined to maintain a stalwart innocence in the face of it, but James's silence unnerved him. For the first time, he began to feel his life might be in danger.

James stepped back. "My lords, you will be formally charged and held in the castle tower for as long as the court requires. Sir Lennox, confine them to their rooms and set a guard. They are to have no visitors—family or friend—unless we grant permission."

Sir Lennox bowed. "As you wish, Your Majesty."

As the knights took the three men away, James said, "May the Blessed Mother have mercy on you all."

They would never know how much he meant it.

News of the trial spread rapidly, and when the proceedings began in the parliamentary chamber, spectators crowded the upper balconies to watch. James sat with the judges, betraying little of what he thought or felt. People whispered that he looked like the face of judgment itself.

The prosecutors brought their evidence before the court and then called on servants from the three families to testify against their lords. The uproar of the crowd at this turn of events made the bailiffs shout for order. Servants' testimonies had never before been accepted in a royal court.

At the end, lords Fleming and MacKenzie were found guilty of murder, while Lord Crichton was convicted of treason against the crown. The three nobles were sentenced to be hanged, their lands given to nobles loyal to the king, and their families exiled to Brittany.

People all through Scotland praised how the king had dealt with the conspiracy. "And him with every reason to go to war," many said.

But achieving justice did not heal James's grief. Stirling Castle held too many memories of Margaret, and he moved his court to the castle in Edinburgh. In his private chambers, he read the Fourth Scroll over and over but found no comfort in the words. "*In the dark crisis, despite my despair, I surrender to my Soul./Its light dispels abandonment, the terrible separation . . .*"

A lie. The separation from Margaret could not be more final—cold and permanent as stone.

Finally the captain and Robert persuaded James to leave his duties as king for a time and travel to a royal manor on the coast, accompanied by the two of them and a few servants. There, they hoped, the beauty of the landscape and the solace of nature would restore him.

But James walked the land day after day, shadowed by Robert, and felt only the bleak ruin inside. There were times lately when he could no longer remember Margaret's voice nor recall her face, as if his tormented mind was slowly erasing all traces of her.

Then one windswept morning, he managed to slip away alone and found himself at a cliff's edge with waves booming far below against the rugged coast. Overhead, the plaintive cries of seagulls gave voice to his despair.

James closed his eyes and let the darkness fill him. He finally admitted that his desire to have a secret marriage, driven by fear, had set in motion the events that led to Margaret's death.

He let go of all his pain, his longing, his love—no longer asking for reasons or answers, no longer wanting anything. The world faded from his sight, and as death drew near, he welcomed it.

In the threshold between worlds, he felt Margaret draw close to him, so clear and vivid that his heart leapt with joy.

The Soul's light slowly grew stronger and brighter until the vision of Margaret dissolved into a blinding radiance that poured through him like a river, so vibrant and alive it shook him from head to foot. A deep, ecstatic joy flooded his whole being.

Guided by the Soul's light, you are free.

No longer just words. A living truth within him.

The captain saw James walking back across the empty field toward the manor and could hardly believe his eyes. Gold light shone around him, radiating outward like a blessing.

Van Horn rubbed his face vigorously to clear his blurred vision. "Sentimental fool," he muttered sternly to himself. "You should have known she would come to help him."

Robert rushed out to meet James, about to yell at him for walking off alone. The vivid light in the young king's eyes stopped his words. The two friends stared at one another for a long moment; then James smiled, and Robert found himself smiling helplessly back.

"You don't need to worry about me anymore," James said.

That night in James's room, the captain mixed the last of a potion he had been giving the young king every day at the manor.

"See you drink it all," the captain admonished as he handed the cup to him.

James, propped up on his pillows, took a sip and made a face. "Why does it taste so bitter? It didn't before."

"That's a good sign!" the captain said heartily. "The worse it tastes, the more you're healing."

James downed the potion in one draught, coughing at its bitterness.

Van Horn took the cup and noticed with satisfaction that James's face had lost its grayish look. He had eaten his first solid meal in weeks, much to the servants' joy. They had been laboring to find something he wouldn't turn away.

James spoke quietly. "I am sorry, Captain, for how badly I acted toward you. It seems you have an unlimited capacity to forgive my lapses, for which I'm deeply grateful."

The captain laughed and brought his chair next to James's bed. He said ruefully, "Your actions resemble what I put my own father through! When I see him in the next world, I'm going to beg his forgiveness for all I ever did and said!"

"I owe a debt to Robert and Wullie as well . . . and the others."

"Many have been concerned about you, James. Your people love their king."

"And Margaret . . ." James stopped. He had not spoken her name since he had surrendered his desire for revenge.

The captain said nothing. James looked away, then back at him.

"She came to me . . . "

"I know, James."

"I feel her within me now . . . Is it true?" he asked.

The captain heard the deeper question he was asking. "That we don't die? Yes, James, it's true. We return home . . . where we come from."

"She hasn't left me."

"No, she hasn't left you."

James stared at the ceiling, absorbing this. "When I surrendered to my Soul, and Margaret came to me, I saw this radiant light. Yet I couldn't see it for long, and I remember little of it beyond the feeling it gave me. Why?"

"Your mind expects to see forms, landscapes, all the things it is used to. There is little of that in the higher realm. Once your mind is changed, you'll see far more. But you can feel that realm, and that plants the truth in your mind, makes you long to become who you really are—the Soul."

The captain stood up and pulled a familiar cedar chest out of his valise and brought it over to James.

"Since you've had a taste of that higher realm, I believe you're ready to read the Fifth Scroll. It's meant to help prepare you to return home. And, by all the saints, I hope that will not be for a good many years yet!"

James sat up higher in bed. *The Fifth Scroll!* His hands shook slightly as he lifted the scroll out of the chest and untied the ribbon. He began reading the parchment.

THE FIFTH SCROLL: The Return Home

We are all one in Divine Love,
Joined with the Creator, who cherishes us all.

As your Earthly life nears its end,
This higher realm draws close, becomes ever more real.
As the Soul, you know this place so well.

Turn inward to your Sanctuary and find the way home.
You leave behind all wealth and achievement,
All sorrows, failures, and losses.
The body's work is done—you let the Earth receive it.

The only treasure you take with you
Is how you have lived,
How much you have loved.

I remember who I am, where I come from, and where I now return.

James said nothing as he read the scroll over and over. It seemed like a map guiding him across a threshold he had crossed briefly. It was a great comfort to know what waited there.

He read it a final time and asked quizzically, "How you have lived?"

The captain tugged at his nose, wondering how to explain it. "Think of it this way for now. No one action, no matter how exalted or terrible, defines a life, James. It's the entire sweep of your life that matters—how you have lived."

"As the Soul," James said. A pleasant, drowsy warmth began to steal over him.

"Yes." The captain took the scroll from his hand, rolled it up, and returned it to the chest.

"The scrolls are yours now, James; they live within you. From this point on, you are their keeper until you pass them on to someone you deem worthy."

James rallied enough to ask, "And you, Captain? What of you?"

Van Horn laughed softly and placed the small cedar chest on the bedside table. "You won't be rid of me so easily. Now your real training begins!"

"I'm ready," James murmured.

He closed his eyes, and for the first time since Margaret's death slept without dreaming.

Part Two

Legacy of
The Scrolls

Chapter 26

A Fated Crossroads

Year: 1498
Master Zheng He's Monastery
Wudang Mountains, China

A white mist obscured the steep, rivered valleys below the monastery until only the tops of the mountains stood like sentinels above the fog. On the monastery's broad patio, Master Zheng felt the cool, moist air rising from the valley floor. He found the gazebo too confining that morning, and placed his small table under the open sky.

Captain van Horn's most recent letter lay open before him, but Master Zheng took a moment before reading it. The monastery's isolation offered a refuge from an imperial court infested with palace intrigues. Already the eldest son of the aging Emperor had told Master Zheng that he would not be welcome in the new court.

"You belong to my father's time," the prince had said. "I need younger men around me, with a bolder vision for China's empire."

A more reckless vision, Master Zheng thought. The young prince was already strengthening his father's military forces. It felt strange to be pushed to the outer circle of the court after so many years.

At last Master Zheng turned to the captain's letter and began reading it. He soon found that James was facing a similar challenge from a young prince of England.

"The current King Henry VII," van Horn wrote, *"has long favored*

peace over war. But his youngest son is eager for battle and conquest, and scorns diplomacy. When he ascends the throne, he will likely cause trouble for James."

The captain then went on to describe James's accomplishments in bringing peace and prosperity to Scotland. "He has made his country a power to be reckoned with in Europe—building up Scotland's navy with two massive ships. At home, he holds jousting tournaments to let the nobility fight without starting wars. He has brought the printing press to Scotland and established a uniform rule of law in this country that all must follow. James has even made education of the nobles' sons compulsory. 'How can they enforce the law,' he asked me, 'if they can't read it?'"

The letter ended with one of James's most recent victories. "Through diplomacy and the clever use of MacLean's Highlanders, James has managed to subdue the troublesome Lord of the Isles. For the first time in Scottish history, Master Zheng, the entire country is united under the crown!"

These last words resonated with the power of a warning. Master Zheng lifted his gaze to the mist, now closing in around the patio in a thick white cloud.

A united country might excite the fear and aggression of its neighbor. Would it eventually provoke the fiery prince of England to wage war against Scotland?

Master Zheng needed to find the answer. The fate of the Five Scrolls and King James IV could be at stake.

He retreated to his meditation room in the monastery and lit two candles and a long stick of incense that filled the air with the scent of cedar. He entered a state of deep calm and silence.

This was not the usual meditation, but one that would allow him to track the timeline of this situation. He focused on the images of King James and Prince Henry. A nexus of energy formed around the two of them. They were indeed linked in their destinies.

He then tracked the energy into the future, watching as it rose and fell, ebbed and flowed with the passing years until it reached

a point where it branched into two timelines. He followed the left branch and saw an empty throne in Scotland. When he followed the right branch, James still ruled the country well into old age.

Master Zheng sank deeper into the meditation, seeking to unravel the fateful point where death and life intersected. No matter from which direction he approached the crossroads, only James appeared and not Prince Henry.

So the actions of James alone would be the deciding factor.

Master Zheng attempted to discern more, but the timeline refused to yield its secrets, remaining impenetrable as the mist. He finally ended the meditation.

He would need to warn the captain about what he had seen. James would have to follow the teaching of the scrolls even more carefully, or there might come a time when he would forget himself and endanger his throne and his life.

Master Zheng rose and extinguished the candles. It now seemed fitting that he would have no place in the new emperor's court. Should the captain need him, he would be free to leave China and make the long journey to Scotland.

Chapter 27

The Captain's Promise

Year: 1502
Lord MacLean's Estate
Highlands, Scotland

The wind had picked up on Lord MacLean's golf course, and the sound of rustling grass made James lift his head and gaze at the sweeping Highland landscape that surrounded them. The wild hills seemed to echo a time when spirits roamed the land, and James felt his blood stir in answer.

It had been three years since the Lord of the Isles had been vanquished with MacLean's help. During James's current stay at the clan chief's estate, MacLean had challenged him to a private rematch of their first duel. Once again, James had chosen Captain van Horn as his second.

At age thirty-one, James had grown into his full maturity as a man and a king. His full, reddish beard and long hair that reached to his shoulders made him look more seasoned than his age. Even the foreign ambassadors admired his appearance, telling James that he would fit in easily in the fashionable courts of France or Spain.

That doesn't help me here, he thought. After eleven holes of golf, he was three strokes behind Lord MacLean. Now his ball lay in the rough grass at his feet, far from the green. If he lost, his Barbary stallion would be forfeit to the Highland chief, who had taken a great liking to the horse. If he won, MacLean would surrender his battle sword, a prized treasure of clan lore.

James saw Robert standing to one side with the king's knights and MacLean's men, watching every move of the two players. Robert knew of the wager and how much James would hate to lose.

Only one more hole to play. James glanced over at MacLean. The man was grinning as if he could feel victory in the wind.

Van Horn, steady as always, stood behind James. "Check the lie of the grass, Sire," he advised. "Is it growing toward you or away?"

James studied the surface. "Toward me," he said.

"Then hit under the ball. You'll lose some distance but gain in accuracy."

James stepped up and aimed his club to strike under the ball. It lifted high into the air, where the wind caught it and, improbably, carried it onto the green. MacLean's grin vanished.

"Well played, Your Majesty," he said, his strong voice carrying over the cheers of Robert and the knights.

But this time, despite James's skill and the captain's advice, the game favored MacLean. After the last putt, the clan chief remained two strokes ahead.

As MacLean's ball fell into the hole, James's heart sank with it. He had grown deeply fond of the Barbary horse since their desperate ride to Drummond Castle eight years ago.

When they reached the roadway, he handed the horse's reins to the Highlander.

"In honor of our wager, I award you your prize, my lord," he said.

MacLean gravely accepted. "A handsome animal, Your Majesty." He gestured toward the castle. "Why don't you tell me his finer points as we walk?"

He led the horse ahead of the others, and James fell in beside him, gesturing to Robert, the captain, and his knights to linger behind. When he and MacLean were far enough out of earshot, MacLean stopped and ran his hand over the horse's dark bay neck. The horse shied away from him and turned to shove James with his nose, a gesture of affection.

James stroked the stallion's head and regarded MacLean steadily. "You didn't draw me away to talk about the finer points of this horse."

"No, Your Majesty." MacLean glanced back at the others. "I've heard talk from a priest that the English king wants to put his eldest daughter on Scotland's throne."

James hesitated before answering, and not only because the Highlanders carried a long grudge against the English. In truth, the marriage proposal sent by Henry VII had been hard for James to consider at first. He still loved Margaret Drummond, and the idea of marrying someone else felt akin to a betrayal.

Yet he owed his country an heir to the throne, as many had pointed out.

He decided to answer MacLean with blunt honesty. "What you hear is true. In exchange for Margaret Tudor's hand, England is willing to sign a treaty of perpetual peace with Scotland."

MacLean's eyes flashed in anger. "I warn you, Sire, the only thing perpetual is their desire to rule Scotland. Do not trust their words. Should it come to blows, know that our swords are always at your service. You've only to call on us."

"*Cumaidh mi seo nam chridhe,*" James replied. I will keep this in my heart.

"There's something else, though I hope it is not too presumptuous." MacLean hesitated, then finally said, "Ever since your Lady Margaret Drummond left this world, I've had Masses said for her soul—as I've done for my first son, who died as an infant."

For a moment, James was too moved to speak. Years ago he had ordered the Bishop of Dunblane Cathedral, where Margaret was buried, to do the same.

At last he murmured, "I believe prayers said in the Highlands are closer to heaven than anywhere else in Scotland."

"Aye, we believe that as well."

The others were catching up to them. MacLean gazed at the

stallion, who stood with his head high, ears pricked sharply forward, as the company approached them.

"A mount fit for a king, not a lord, wouldn't you say?" MacLean asked. He held out the horse's reins to James.

"What are you doing?" James asked. "You won him in a fair contest."

"I return him to you as a Highland gift, Your Majesty. With the English so close, you may have need of his speed and strength."

James's first instinct was to refuse as a matter of royal pride; his word was his bond, not to be taken back. But his Soul stayed his hand. *Generosity lies not only with the giver*, it whispered.

He slowly reached out and took the reins. "I accept your gift, Lord MacLean. Your gesture honors us both."

"Even when you lose, you win. You have the devil's own luck, James." Robert pulled off his boots and warmed his feet by the fireplace. Their bedchambers within MacLean's castle offered refuge from the chill night air.

The captain, sitting at a nearby table, grinned broadly. "He couldn't very well insult a Highland chief to his face."

Van Horn had a thick book spread open before him and a half-finished flagon of malt whiskey at his elbow. He was peering through a magnifying glass to read the book.

James shed his heavy coat and stretched out on one of the three beds in the room. "Lord MacLean had a look about him, Robert, as if he knew I would need the horse in the future."

Robert snorted. "Yes, to chase King Henry and the English from the Borderlands."

Robert had a point, James thought. Skirmishes along the border had increased lately, one of the reasons he and King Henry VII were talking of ways to guarantee peace between England and Scotland.

Marriage between two royal families would help achieve that

goal. James had already indicated he would agree, though the irony of an English princess on the throne of Scotland was not lost on him.

He turned to gaze at the captain, who was still engrossed in his reading. They would be leaving the castle early the next morning to return to Stirling. It was already well past midnight, but James had a feeling the captain might consider this an ideal time for a lesson.

Over the past few years, van Horn had kept his promise and deepened James's instruction, showing him more about how to direct the energy that ran like rivers throughout his body. The practice not only strengthened James's health and bestowed on him a formidable endurance but also cleansed his senses and his mind, making it easier for him to reach his inner sanctuary and connect to his Soul.

The world appeared to be in sharper focus, as if a veil had been lifted, and he could see more clearly not only the natural world but the intrigues, motivations, and sincerity of the people around him. These skills were a great help when hearing cases in the courts and rendering judgments.

At one point, he had asked the captain if he could teach Robert some of what he was learning about how to strengthen the body.

"Show him what you wish," van Horn had said at last. "But I ask you not to teach him about the Five Scrolls just yet. If he is to learn that wisdom, you will know the right time."

In addition to these studies, James had also kept up his embroidery work, much to the amusement of many nobles. It kept him in the web of secret spies, a web still run by some of the noblewomen and their servants in several castles. The nobles soon learned it was fruitless to try to hide anything from the king, but how he obtained his information was a mystery.

When he officially lifted the ban on golf, James put Wullie in charge of producing golf balls, a task the old servant gladly assumed. With James's permission, he kept a picture of Margaret and Sibylla in his workshop.

"To inspire me, Your Majesty, since it was Lady Margaret's ideas that started it all. And Lady Sibylla was the best plucker of chickens I ever knew. Right game she was, given the stench."

Margaret's spirit seemed to be with James as well; at various times in court, he could hear her advising him on a case or a judgment. James smiled inwardly. *Give me all the advice you want, my love. I will listen.*

The captain's voice broke into his reverie, confirming James's intuition about an impending lesson.

"Let me show you both some of the deeper points of Chinese medicine. They are far ahead of Europe in this art."

James swung off the bed and joined the captain and Robert at the table. But MacLean's words about Margaret and his own thoughts had brought something else to mind.

"Before we start, Captain, I have a question to ask about death and remembrance. It has to do with something Robert and I have experienced recently."

The captain leaned forward. "If I can answer it, I will."

James continued. "Of late, we have both, quite by accident, come across things that Sibylla or Margaret gave us. The other day my valet found one of Margaret's pendants in my chambers. The sight of it dealt my heart such a blow that I wept like a child. Yet it's been eight years she's been gone."

"Ah . . ." The captain's expression softened in understanding. "Your heart is still not used to her absence, James, so grief can ambush you like that. Though the Soul knows eternity, this Earthly world does not."

Robert asked, "Have you had such moments, Captain?"

Van Horn gazed down at his book and then spoke quietly. "It's been twenty years since my sister and niece left this Earth, yet their absence can still wound my heart."

"Do you have a remedy for this?" James said.

"Yes. I focus on the love I bear them, which gives me comfort."

"And you find this is enough?"

"In time, yes. It becomes enough."

James said, "Then I will do the same, for I still love Margaret deeply."

"As I love Sibylla," Robert said, his voice a mere whisper. "That has not changed."

"Hold fast to that feeling, both of you," van Horn said. "It lies at the heart of everything else."

No one spoke. It was a moment before the captain gently cleared his throat.

"Well . . . let's begin, shall we?" He turned the thick book toward Robert and James. "You've learned about the Chinese five elements, but now I'll be teaching you from the ancient book of Chinese medicine, *The Yellow Court Canon*. This text above all others describes nearly every ailment that can afflict a human body and a treatment for each one. With this knowledge, you'll be wiser than the most learned physician in the West."

If he had intended to catch James's interest, he had succeeded. Long after Robert had fallen asleep in his chair, James was asking question after question about the book. The captain smiled inwardly. That insatiable curiosity was one of the things he loved best in James. At such times, he could still see the boy in the man, and it warmed his heart.

By the time the dawn light illuminated the room, James was already planning to found a college of surgeons in Scotland.

"Not even the English have such an establishment," he said. "Perhaps we'll discover a cure for their fever to rule Scotland!"

The captain raised his flagon. "God hear you and grant your prayer." He downed the last of his whiskey, then carefully tucked the ancient medical text into his rucksack.

James called for his valet to begin packing for the journey back to Stirling. His mind was alive with ideas. He couldn't wait to tell lords Gray, Montrose, and Argyll of his new plans for a medical college. Talk of marriage and a treaty with the English could wait. For now, with the captain's help, he wanted to bring his vision for a new Scotland one step closer.

Chapter 28

The Rose and the Thistle

May 1502
London, England

King Henry VII sat alone in the throne room, his thoughts dark as the night that blanketed the countryside. His eldest son, Arthur, the hope of the realm and the Tudor family, had died unexpectedly only a month ago.

Henry saw his privy councilor hesitating in the doorway, as if uncertain how the grieving king would receive him. Henry stirred enough to raise his hand, indicating the man should move closer.

"Your Highness," the privy councilor said softly. "King James has accepted your proposal offering Princess Margaret's hand in marriage. He is also open to signing the Treaty of Perpetual Peace."

The king merely nodded, as if the news were of little importance. Arthur's death meant the king's younger son, Prince Henry, would be the new heir to the throne. The king had never favored Henry, finding him too aggressive and graceless compared to Arthur. Now there would be no choice but to make him regent.

Finally the king spoke, his voice slow and heavy. "Send Margaret to me. I'll tell her the marriage proposal is now officially accepted."

"Yes, Your Highness. I'll fetch her right away."

The privy councilor backed toward the door, relieved to be

departing from the room. Perhaps speaking to his favorite daughter would help the king overcome his melancholy.

King Henry was aware of Margaret's presence only when she was near him. Her lady-in-waiting stood discreetly to one side, giving the two of them privacy.

"Father." Her soft voice touched his despair, lifting it slightly. "They said you wished to see me."

"Sit beside me, child." He studied her face, the strong Tudor features softened by her youth. "I wanted you to know that the marriage arrangements with the King of Scotland are moving forward."

When she remained silent, Henry reached out and stroked her hair gently. "Thirteen is a tender age to be a bride, Margaret, let alone a queen. You understand why you must wed the King of Scotland?"

The girl nodded slowly. "Yes, Lady Elizabeth said it would secure your throne for my brother Henry and bring peace between our two nations." She picked at the appliqué on her dress. "I've seen a picture of the King of Scotland, Father. He's so old!"

Henry smiled wryly. "He is younger than I am by many years, Margaret. It's the beard that makes him look older."

"Then I'll ask him to shave it off," she said decisively. "If he's a gentleman, he'll do it."

"I've heard that he is," Henry said. "I've also heard he is building a Great Hall at Stirling Castle just for the wedding. I'm told it will be very beautiful."

Margaret suddenly leaned her head against her father's arm.

Henry was silent for a moment, overwhelmed by the tender feeling she evoked in him. He said, "I am sorry so much has been placed on your young shoulders. Perhaps you can think of it as England and Scotland being wedded together in common purpose."

"Then I'll do it." Her voice was muffled against his velvet sleeve. "But still, I wish I could stay here."

Henry's throat tightened. "As do I, my dearest daughter."

He had lost one favored child and was about to lose another. He only hoped that James was as interested in peace as he was. England needed a strong alliance with Scotland to counter the rising power of the French, an old enemy.

The Scottish king had signed a preliminary peace agreement with Henry, although it was hard to trust the famously volatile temperament of the Scots. It was another reason he worried about Margaret. How would she fare among such people?

His thoughts turned to his younger son, and his mood darkened again. Of all his children, Prince Henry was the last one he would have put on the throne.

James entered his Privy Council knowing he faced a fight. His marriage to Princess Margaret had been received with general approval. Even Robert had growled, "About time you guaranteed a peaceful succession, James. We were beginning to wonder if you had embraced celibacy!"

But the Treaty of Perpetual Peace provoked vigorous dispute even among James's inner circle.

Lord Gray pointed out, "You have treaty obligations with King Louis of France through the Auld Alliance. Signing a treaty with King Henry would be like trying to ride two horses at once."

James replied evenly. "I assure you, Lord Gray, I can manage both horses."

Lord Montrose moved next to Gray. "The treaty could place Scotland in the awkward position of owing fealty to both England and France, who are enemies. If they go to war, who do we support?"

Lord Angus struck the table with his fist. "This proposed English treaty is backed by the Pope! If you break it, you'll be excommunicated—barred from burial in any sacred ground."

"Then I'll be sure to outlive the Pope," James replied.

He waited until the laughter subsided and then asked, "And you, Lord Argyll? What is your opinion?"

"I agree with the others," Argyll said firmly. "I advise against signing the peace treaty with Henry."

"Captain van Horn, what say you?" James asked.

Van Horn cleared his throat. "Alas, as a foreigner, I have no right to express an opinion."

A loud chorus of objections greeted this statement.

"You're an astute judge of politics—"

"We value your wisdom—"

Lord Gray laughed. "Since when does a master golfer have no say in our company? Give us your counsel!"

The captain threw up his hands. "All right, gentlemen. Then consider this. The marriage is more than a sound alliance. Should something happen to the Tudor line in England, the children of James and Margaret would inherit the throne of both Scotland and England together!"

"By all that's holy, he's right!" Angus exclaimed. "The entire island under a Stewart king!"

James's eyes gleamed. "And the Treaty of Perpetual Peace?"

The captain sighed heavily. "Ah, that. As was rightly pointed out, you already have a treaty with France requiring you to help her should England invade. If you sign the treaty with England, you cannot legally help France."

A frown flickered across James's face at this. With a sinking feeling, Van Horn sensed James had already made up his mind to accept the treaty.

The captain remembered again Master Zheng's letter warning of the danger should James begin ignoring his Soul and charting his own course. Van Horn had kept the letter and every now and then reread it to keep the warning fresh in his mind.

"Consult your inner counselor, Sire," van Horn said earnestly. "See what guidance you receive about this."

James gazed thoughtfully at him. The captain knew he clearly understood the veiled request.

Finally he said, "Good advice, as always, Captain. I will do as you suggest."

Still, van Horn felt a sense of foreboding. Lately, James seemed to have a growing reluctance to defer to his Soul. Exactly as Master Zheng had warned.

By June of the following year, the upcoming marriage was being hailed by Scotland's singers and poets as a romance of "The Rose and the Thistle." The thistle represented Scotland, and the red and white rose stood for the Tudor line in England.

Songs and poetry on this theme filled the air in the cities and towns James visited. It was a good sign that the people generally favored this union.

Under James's watchful supervision, the Great Hall and the renovation of the queen's chambers were finally completed in time for the wedding, set for the sixth of August. The hall's outer walls glowed white in the sun, while its interior resembled an Italian Renaissance palace. Elaborate tiles filled the ceiling with the portraits of figures from Scottish and English history and from Greek, Roman, and European mythology.

James was gratified at the astonishment of those who came to view it, particularly the foreign dignitaries he entertained at court. They were beginning to take Scotland seriously as a nation with a cosmopolitan culture.

James also began to orchestrate a show of pomp and pageantry on his frequent trips around the country. He dressed in the finest fabrics, brought musicians and poets along to entertain the people, and distributed his wealth among the commoners who rendered him any service, no matter how small. He spent lavishly on public buildings, waterways, and the Scottish navy.

As James told Robert and the captain, "I want people to see their king as part of something elevated and grand. And to see themselves as cosmopolitan and cultured, even if it's only through the royal office."

Robert tried to remind James that he was still a mere mortal by taking him out to the golf links and, occasionally, beating him at the game. But gradually, James found one excuse or another to avoid these outings, engrossed instead in planning the next royal tour of the country.

Robert sought out the captain and expressed his concerns. "He's determined to make every festival or tournament more resplendent than the one before it. He's even found a way to tax the Church so he has enough money to finance the royal treasury. It's as if he wants to outshine the courts of France, England, and Spain combined!"

The captain shared Robert's worries. He had noticed that James was beginning to take inordinate pleasure in his grand displays. A risky course, van Horn thought. The danger of creating such a powerful image was losing oneself in it.

Nearly two months before the wedding, Margaret Tudor left her home in London and began the journey north to Stirling with an entourage of ladies-in-waiting, servants, and court officials. Most of them felt they were leaving the sophistication of England for the rough country ways of the north.

James, dressed in his finest velvets and silks, mounted on his spirited stallion, presented a sight that changed many of the women's minds. He made sure that he encountered young Margaret's carriage and its long baggage train several times on the road towards Stirling. Each time, he greeted her with courtesy and grace, seeking to put her at ease, until the young princess began to look forward to his visits.

They entered Stirling together, riding on a gentle mare. Margaret sat behind James and held on tightly to his waist. The crowds along the way warmly greeted the young princess.

There were more courtship rituals to observe, and a long,

lavish wedding celebration held in the Great Hall. When James saw the young princess coming toward him down the processional aisle, escorted by her uncle the Earl of Surrey, his heart contracted painfully. It should have been Margaret Drummond, he thought, not this girl who was less half his age.

Then the moment passed, swept away by his desire to protect Margaret Tudor and help her learn how to be queen over his fiercely independent people.

Later that evening, after the ceremony and attendant ball, Lord Gray came to James in the king's chambers and discreetly mentioned that the young queen had asked if James would shave off his beard. "His face would look much fairer without it," she had confided. James agreed to the request, much to the young queen's relief.

But he did not share her bed that night. She was too young to bear the risks of childbirth. In fact, on the captain's advice, James decided to wait until Margaret was sixteen before they tried for an heir to the Stewart line.

Over the next three years, James kept informed about young Prince Henry through his spy network. The boy's English tutors and advisors were urging him to turn away from the peaceful course of his father. When he became king, they told Henry, he should embark on a course of expansion and conquest both in France and Scotland.

James took these warnings lightly. He felt confident that when the two of them met, he could charm the younger man and use diplomacy to get his way. In all his years as king, these qualities had never failed him.

By the time Margaret was nineteen, she had borne James three children, but each one had died in their first year. Although the young queen believed strongly that her children were in heaven, she still wept at the sight of the empty cradle. She wrote to her father frequently to express her grief.

James attended to her almost as diligently as did her own ladies-in-waiting and prayed with her for the care of each child's soul. Margaret was so touched by his devotion that she wrote to King Henry, "*Our husband grows more dear to us the longer we know him.*"

When two more children died, James desperately asked the captain if there was something in his Stewart line that prevented a child from surviving.

"I see nothing that would warrant such tragedy, James. Let me try a new herb with her—it may help. The best thing you can do is continue to show young Margaret great tenderness and care."

As he grieved each child's death, James sought comfort in his inner sanctuary. He knew that his children were alive in the higher realm. But seeing the sadness in Margaret's face and her loss of spirit made it difficult to feel truly comforted. Each child's death seemed to weigh more on her mind and heart.

James thought of the Fourth Scroll, which called him to transform his losses, a call he obeyed by looking after the welfare of the families in his kingdom. Perhaps it was his fate to leave this Earth without an heir, but at least he could ensure Scotland's future through the children of others.

Chapter 29

Henry VIII and James IV

In the midst of this sorrowful time, more sad news arrived. James learned from his spies that King Henry VII had died after a long illness. James didn't inform Margaret right away, not wanting to add to her grief. He would let the English ambassador, whom she had known since childhood, present the news.

A few days later the English ambassador Lord Hastings arrived at court, dressed in mourning clothes. The noble entered the throne room, bowed low, and delivered an official packet, bound with a black ribbon.

"I regret to inform you, Sire, that his majesty King Henry VII passed away on April 21 in this year of Our Lord, 1509. It was his desire that I present his last will and testament to you and his daughter Margaret. I was charged to inform you that King Henry's son, Henry the Eighth, will take the throne within the month."

Though James had been forewarned, the news still affected him as if a blood relative had left this world. "I am truly sorry, Lord Hastings. King Henry was held in high regard in our court—a man who sought the welfare of his people and ours. The queen will be deeply grieved at her father's passing. I'm sure she would wish to hear this news from you, since you have close connections with her family."

The ambassador bowed. "As you wish, Sire. Your regard for the queen at this time is deeply appreciated."

"King Henry's death may signal more than simply a change in monarchs, Lord Hastings. If you can speak freely, what is your assessment of the new King Henry's character?"

A dour look crossed the man's face, but he struggled to be diplomatic.

"He is more . . . aggressive than his father, Your Majesty, and eager to prove himself to the world. He has declared his intention to win back lands lost to France and gain more if he can. He is already increasing our army and navy to this purpose."

"I am grateful for your honesty, my lord. But I will detain you no longer. You will need to inform the queen of her father's passing."

James rose and escorted the ambassador to the door of the throne room. As they reached the entry, Lord Hastings paused. "I must warn you, Sire, the new king regards Scotland as a vassal country to England. He is only eighteen and rather full of himself, if you'll pardon my frankness. But he is in deadly earnest about this."

His words proved prophetic. James soon received messages from the young King Henry VIII, calling him a subordinate to the English crown. Despite his council's heated reaction to Henry's words, James followed his Soul's guidance to steer a middle course. He sent back a courteous but firm reply, leaving no doubt that Scotland was an independent nation equal in every regard to England and France.

Over the next two years, James tried hard to maintain peace between England and France and to preserve his treaties with both, sending his best ambassadors to England and writing personally to Louis XII and Henry VIII. He even sent Captain van Horn to the French court to try to maintain Scotland's neutrality with their old ally.

His efforts bore little fruit. Henry VIII refused all compromise and diplomatic solutions, eager to test himself on the battlefield. He continued to improve English artillery and weapons. James learned through his spy network that the English king was planning to invade

France in the summer of 1513, less than a year away.

He was not the only one who knew. The French Queen Anne of Brittany sent James a desperate plea. "I am calling on the Auld Alliance between our two countries, asking for your assistance against the English. Can you not create a diversion in England to draw some of Henry's troops away from French soil?"

When James called his council together, Lord Angus was solidly against the idea. "I've spent more time in the Borderlands than anyone else here, Sire, watching the English army. They're professional soldiers now, with new strategies and new weapons. If they decide to fight us in a pitched battle, we will be at a disadvantage with our civilian army."

His declaration drew a heated response from the others. Lord Argyll snorted in contempt. "There is no English army alive that can match us in man-to-man combat."

As the council began to shout at one another, James loudly called for their attention. "Gentlemen! May I remind you that the French queen is not asking us to fight a pitched battle, but simply to draw Henry's troops away from France."

Lord Gray, who so far had stayed out of the argument, quickly agreed. "We can strike with sufficient force in England to make it appear we are invading and then pull back into Scotland. This upstart Henry doesn't have enough supplies to pursue us all the way to Stirling."

"We win by yielding," James said. "As always, Lord Gray, you have hit on the ideal strategy."

"I don't like it," Angus declared. "Too many things could go wrong. We have no idea who Henry will leave behind and what capabilities they will have."

"Then, Lord Angus," James said, "I assign you the task of finding out."

Angus flushed under the men's laughter, and James softened his command. "I value your intelligence, my lord. Keep a watch on our old enemy."

"Aye, Your Majesty." Angus shot a dark look at the others. "The rest of you had best heed my warning. The English are better prepared for war than you imagine."

But within a few days, all thought of England, France, and war was driven from James's mind. Near the end of April, the queen gave birth to another son.

James hurried to Margaret's bedside where the midwife had just laid the swaddled babe in her arms. Margaret smiled wearily at him as James touched the baby's head lightly, as if in blessing.

Margaret whispered, "James the Fifth."

"Yes, James the Fifth." He kissed her hand and then reluctantly withdrew to let her sleep. The midwife was firm that the birthing room remain dimly lit and quiet.

But Margaret and the child were not strong. In his anxiety for their lives, James decided to leave nothing to chance. Besides using the captain's herbs, he made a trek on foot to one of the holiest shrines in Scotland to pray earnestly for the health and safety of mother and son.

Robert went with him and saw the looks of awe on the faces they passed along the road. James's piety touched them all deeply. Robert knew that another legend about the king was being born on this journey.

But this time, unlike the others, James's prayers were answered. Through the spring and early summer, he watched in joy as his young wife and son thrived in the warming sun that brought life back to the land. At last, he felt, the Stewart curse had been lifted.

James thought of all the things he would teach young James, all the wisdom he could share with him, including the Five Scrolls. In his mind, he saw his son grow up to be a strong, beloved king who ruled through the wisdom of his Soul.

Only when he received a message from Aileen in his spy network did James remember his charge to Angus. Aileen's small needlework showed a gold lion with a fleur-de-lis, the symbol of France, gripped in its jaws. The meaning was clear: England had invaded France.

Angus reappeared at Stirling two days later and confirmed the news. His stained clothes and dust-streaked face testified to his haste in returning to the castle.

He sank wearily to one knee in front of James. "Well, it's done, Sire. King Henry and his men have landed on the French coast. He's left a sizable army in England, led by the Earl of Surrey himself. The earl may be old, Your Majesty, but a more cunning soldier you'll never meet on any battlefield. I beg you to reconsider this diversion you've planned."

James helped the earl to his feet. "You have nothing to worry about, Lord Angus. We will discharge our promises to France and still maintain the peace with England."

At that moment, Margaret entered the room with the baby in her arms. To Angus's dismay, James immediately lost all interest in their talk and turned his full attention to his wife and son. He exclaimed over the infant's every move and sound as if he were the first child born to earthly parents.

Angus left the throne room feeling abandoned to his fears. The only way to change this fateful course, he decided, was to persuade the other nobles to listen to him.

By July, James began to prepare for the excursion into England. With the backing of his council, he sent out a general call to arms across the country that drew the flower of Scottish nobility along with MacLean and the Highland clans to his side. More than 25,000 answered the crown's call—the largest army Scotland had raised in centuries.

"We need a good fight, Your Majesty," MacLean said. "Since vanquishing the Lord of the Isles, we've had no battles worthy of the name."

James grinned at the chief's eagerness. "I am more glad to see you than I can say, Lord MacLean. I never doubted for a moment you and your men would be with us."

Lord Gray gazed around them at the general encampment and said dourly, "We had best start drilling the rest of the men gathered here, Sire. They need practice in how to fight together as one force or we'll make a poor showing on the field."

Under the able direction of lords Gray and Montrose, the men drilled day after day in the use of their 13-foot, wooden pikes, tipped with spear points. The nobles and knights honed their skills with swords, maces, and longbows. James had ordered a lighter, more flexible French armor from King Louis and made sure as many of the men as possible were fitted with the new armor.

After three weeks, Gray and Montrose declared the army ready to march south to England. The atmosphere was festive as the long column of men and horses left the castle grounds, the clan banners and flags rippling over them, and crowds all along the road out of Stirling cheering them on.

In the general confusion of departure, no one noticed Wullie climbing aboard one of the supply wagons and settling in for the long ride to the border.

But Lord Angus, right to the end, flatly refused to join in the campaign, driven to tears by his inability to stop the whole affair. His two sons, ignoring their father, chose to ride with their king.

The captain was also absent from the march, much to James's disappointment. From the French court, Van Horn had written earlier, "*I was about to set sail for Scotland when Master Zheng arrived unexpectedly in Paris. He has requested I stay a few days longer.*"

James had written back, "*Be sure to bring Master Zheng with you when you return. I have long wished to meet him!*"

The captain's reply came quickly. "*Pay close attention to your Soul, James. You are embarking on a voyage where the slightest change in the wind can have fateful consequences. Nevertheless, be assured that Master Zheng and I will be there when you need us most.*"

As James, Lord Gray, and Robert led the army past Stirling Castle, James looked up to see Margaret Tudor and five-month-old James watching them from a tower window. The queen lifted their son's arm to wave farewell to his father. James's throat ached; it was something his Margaret would have done.

During the first weeks of the campaign, the Scottish excursion unfolded as planned. James's army entered the disputed Borderlands, captured two English castles without much of a fight, and flattened two others with artillery fire.

Finally, as August waned, James took the fateful step and led his army across the border into English territory. They encountered little resistance from any of the surrounding castles, and Surrey and his army seemed reluctant to engage them. Perhaps the old warrior had decided to remain at court and keep an eye on Henry VIII's rivals.

But as the days wore on, James began to feel a strange sense of unease settle within him. Only then did he remember a story one of the nobles from Edinburgh had recounted.

"The night we left for Stirling, Sire, a strange omen appeared. Exactly at midnight, a mysterious figure dressed in black walked through Edinburgh's streets. He called out the names of every earl, lord, and baron in the city and commanded us all to appear before him in forty days. I sent men out to seize the crier, only to find he had vanished."

James had dismissed the story as mere fantasy, but now in his strange mood, it took on new force.

Even more disquieting, in the deepest hours of the night, his Soul now whispered to him, *Give Robert the Five Scrolls. Send him back to Stirling.* James had taken the small chest with him, as he often did when he traveled, but had not intended to pass it on to Robert. Still, the voice kept insisting he do so.

James didn't act on the command until word came that the Earl of Surrey and his army were on the march. James took the initiative by challenging Surrey to meet the Scottish army at Flodden Field on September ninth. He realized later that the date marked exactly the fortieth day when the mysterious stranger had commanded the men of Edinburgh to appear before him. It was an eerie coincidence.

On September seventh, two days before the battle, James led his army to Braxton Hill above Flodden and set up camp. He couldn't account for the way his confidence wavered, so different from his uplifted mood at the beginning of this excursion.

When the English army finally arrived and pitched their camp in the broad field below, James could no longer ignore his Soul's urging.

The wind is blowing from a different direction, he thought. He sent a messenger to bring Robert to him.

Chapter 30

The Eve of Battle

While he waited, James walked to the crest of Braxton Hill, bracing himself against the chill night wind, and gazed down at the campfires of the English army. The fires of his own troops lit up the hill behind him like a field of stars.

A ghostly bluish mist rose from the camp ground below and curled around the tents. The clouds parted enough to show the crescent moon, curved like a horn, hanging in the west. Even though the Scots held the high ground, the land between the two armies had turned marshy with recent rains—a disadvantage for men fighting on foot.

The sound of footsteps made him turn as Robert approached. James felt the sudden weight of this moment; he was about to make Robert his successor in a role far more important than wearing the crown.

"You wished to see me, James?"

James clapped him on the shoulder. "Yes. I'm going to fulfill a promise I made to you years ago and show you something you have long wished to see."

Robert's eyes brightened as he followed James into the king's tent. He was sure it was the secret knowledge that his friend had withheld from him for so many years.

After dismissing the servants, James knelt down by the baggage where his armor was stored and pulled out a small cedar chest. Its woody scent lingered faintly in the air as James carried it to the camp table. He laid one hand on the lid of the chest.

"Before I open it, let me ask you the question I posed so long ago. What is a man's greatest treasure: power, wealth, knowledge, or love?"

Robert pondered the question, struck by the earnestness of James's face, as if some great decision hung on his answer. Robert reflected deeply on his own youthful ambitions; the successes and bitter losses he had known, especially the death of Sybilla.

Earlier in his life, Robert had given different answers to this same question, but now he spoke with a quiet certainty. "Love is the greatest treasure, though some might consider me weak or sentimental for saying so."

"And why this answer?"

"I have lived long enough and seen enough in my life to know that without love, power is ruthless, even great wealth is empty, and knowledge grows heartless and cold."

James closed his eyes, feeling some of the weight lift from him. He had chosen his successor well.

"The very answer I gave the captain years ago. It's how I came to possess the most precious treasure anyone could ever have. Would God that I had been more worthy of it in the end."

Robert said quickly, "Don't speak ill of yourself, James. The people love you far more than you know. You have unified our country and protected the people from the lords and barons who would have them all kept poor and landless."

"Yes, but perhaps I should have paid more attention to my own pride." He looked steadily at Robert. "But I have not failed if I can pass on this treasure to another. Tonight, I will require a great deal of you, my friend, more than I have ever asked. Are you willing to give me your service?"

Robert said firmly, "For you, James, always."

James gazed at him thoughtfully. "We live in times of great change, and more is coming, Robert, you can be sure of that. The

Middle East may soon cut off the Silk Road for us, and wars on the Continent seem destined to continue without end. I sense that new ideas and discoveries coming from all over the globe will make the world of our children far different from the one we grew up in."

He gazed down at the cedar box. "But the knowledge in this chest transcends it all. I am entrusting this to you, not just for yourself but for the future. It's time for it to be given to the world, and you must help bring this about."

Robert's heart pounded too hard for him to answer. When James slowly lifted the cedar lid, Robert half expected to see some holy talisman or jewel-encrusted relic revealed. Instead, five small scrolls lay neatly in a row, each bound with a thin silk ribbon.

James carefully took out the first scroll and handed it to Robert. "You must read this one first and absorb its knowledge. Only when you have memorized it can you read the others. This teaching will guide you for the remainder of your life."

Robert untied the ribbon and unrolled the small parchment. The fine silk of the scroll's inner side caught the torchlight with an iridescent shimmer. Words written across its surface seemed to be in some ancient tongue, but as Robert looked more closely, he was surprised to see them written in Latin, a language he knew well.

He began to read and his astonishment grew with every word. He sat down on the campstool, forgetting in his wonder to ask the king's permission. He read the scroll over and over. Each time the words sank deeper until they seemed to awaken something hauntingly familiar within him.

When at last Robert returned the scroll, it seemed a great light was shining in his heart and mind. He saw the same light reflected in James's eyes. It was clear to him now where James had acquired the wisdom for all that he had accomplished in his life as king.

"James," Robert's voice was hoarse with emotion. "Where does this knowledge come from?"

"The scrolls were brought to China centuries ago from an ancient monastery in the Holy Lands."

"Why have you shown me this now?"

James put the scroll back into the chest and fastened the lid, then handed the chest to Robert. "I am sending you away from the battlefield, Robert Hume, to my queen and young son, James, who will be king long after me, God willing."

At this Robert bolted upright, his face anguished. He pushed the chest aside. "No! You can't send me away, James. You need every pike and sword for this fight."

James said firmly, "You will do as I command because I trust you above all others—"

"Don't ask this of me! I won't leave you now! Send me after the battle."

James thrust the small chest firmly into Robert's hands. "I have said there would be times when you must follow my commands without question. This is one of those times!"

"Why are you doing this?" Robert demanded. "You know you will return to Stirling!"

James continued as if Robert had not spoken. "You will pass the knowledge of the Five Scrolls on to my son that he may be a king worthy of the name. Use the game to teach him as well. And you will teach these things to others, regardless of birth or station. You will ask the same question I asked you, and you will know the ones you are to teach by the answer you receive."

Robert shook his head over and over, tears streaming down his face. "My place is at your side. We've endured so much together—" He broke off, unable to continue.

James smiled grimly. "Rest assured, my friend. I am giving you the hardest task by far tonight. You must do it for both of us, for my son, and for the world."

Robert argued passionately against the order, his love for James warring against the royal command and the fealty he had sworn. But the king remained unmoved. Robert knew that James's will, once set, would never bend.

At last, despite his grieving heart, Robert yielded. "God save me, I'll go," he said. "Though I'll regret it always."

James laid a hand on his shoulder. "Obey my command. That's all I ask."

He led Robert outside the tent. A squire stood holding the reins of the king's own stallion. Robert stroked the horse's shining neck.

James said, "Lord MacLean was wise when he returned this mount to me. He'll carry you to Stirling Castle, and no Englishman will be able to stop you. Remember, read the first scroll each day to keep its knowledge alive within your heart and mind. Only after you have memorized it, read the others, memorizing each in turn. God speed, Robert."

Robert mounted the horse, who tossed its head, eager to be off. The two men regarded one another, the silence between them holding all they couldn't say.

Finally Robert choked out, "God preserve you, my king. By His grace, we will see each other again."

He touched his spurs to his mount, and the horse sprang forward into a full gallop. James watched the night swallow horse and rider, and a deep sadness wrapped around him like a cloak. His valet urged him to come into the tent, but James turned away. He needed to be alone. The one person whose company he would have welcomed, Captain van Horn, was not with him now.

James felt his whole life converge on this place. The battle to come would pit England and Scotland against each other once again, but he hoped it might be the last battle.

As the eastern sky grew lighter, the melancholy that had descended in the night slowly began to lift. James came to accept that whatever happened, he would face it with courage and spirit. After all, his men outnumbered the English, and Braxton Hill was a formidable barrier for the enemy to scale.

A sudden thought made James smile. What if he and young King Henry had met in a duel on the golf course? He would have soundly beaten the Englishman, of that James was sure. The entire contest would have been settled, and all these fine Scottish nobles and countrymen would be safely at home. But the English didn't play the game, nor was it likely that Henry would have agreed to such a duel.

A light breeze fanned James's face, bringing with it the scent of wood smoke, wet grass, and sedge. Despite the ache left by Robert's absence, he felt a quiet joy that the scrolls were with the right person.

Robert has earned their wisdom. No one deserves them more.

As for himself, he had men to lead in battle.

Chapter 31

Flodden Field

September 9, 1513
Braxton Hill on Flodden Field

As the pale light of dawn lit the east, James saw most of the English forces preparing to break camp. He regretted dismissing Angus's warning about the English army. He could see by their armor and uniforms that these soldiers were not farmers or tradesmen, but men who had spent years in their king's service learning the skills of war.

Yet events here could still turn either way depending on the slightest of changes. James knew the English had marched nearly two days straight to arrive here, but he had seen little in the way of supplies or provisions for the men. Those troops will be exhausted and hungry going into battle. *Has Surrey no care for the men he leads?*

James shook his head and turned away from the sight as his own camp came to life. He strolled among the tents, talking with the men. He spoke quietly to the leaders and encouraged the farmers and yeomen who had answered his call for their service, addressing many of them by name.

Every now and then, James caught himself turning to speak to Robert, forgetting he wasn't there. It was like missing a limb.

"When do we take the field, Sire?" one man shouted.

"After the English finish their tea!" he called back, to general laughter. "They won't fight before that."

288

Lord Gray joined James and frowned as he watched some of the men still struggling to master their 13-foot pikes.

"I don't know if they'll hold their formations once the battle starts, Your Majesty."

"Fighting is bred into every Scotsman. They'll hold." James rubbed the back of his neck. "Though I admit, I'd give a great deal to have those cannon we lent to the French . . . and the artillery master I sent with them."

James glanced over at his seven bronze cannon that lined the hilltop. They were far heavier than the English artillery and much harder to align for firing.

Lord Gray shrugged. "Still, we have the high ground, Sire. We can stand fast and make them come to us."

"Make them come to us?" a rough voice growled behind them. They turned to see Lord MacLean approaching. "No! Charge them the moment Surrey's men get in range. Once we're in the thick of their ranks, they won't dare fire their cannon for fear of hitting their own men."

Gray shook his head impatiently. "There's too much open ground between us. Their cannon would take a bloody toll before we ever reached the first line of English soldiers."

"Gentlemen," James interrupted. He could see cook fires being doused in the field below. "The English are stirring. See to your men."

As the sun rose higher, the morning air was filled with the beat of drums and with voices bellowing, "Fall in, fall in!" James watched as more than half the English infantry began to line up to the left side of the field. *What is Surrey planning now?*

The English troops marched in loose formation for the Till River, which ran along the north side of the hill. They began to ford it at a low point some distance away.

"Fire on them, Your Majesty," Argyll urged. "You have them

in the open, where you can take out half their forces without losing a single man!"

"Slaughter them, you mean," James said; his mouth thinned in distaste. "Even if they take up a position behind us, they still have to charge uphill."

He turned to Montrose. "Set your men on our right flank. Argyll, you'll have the left. Gray and MacLean, take the center with me."

By the early afternoon, most of the English forces had established their positions on the north side of the hill. They had even managed to drag most of their artillery with them. In response, James ordered his seven cannon turned to face the new enemy line.

The English now stood between James and Scotland, while he and his men stood between the English and their countryside. Neither army could reach its own territory except by fighting its way through the enemy forces.

"Surrey and his officers are behind the lines," Gray observed. James and the others could see a small knot of riders clustered at the back of the ranks.

"The new English way of fighting," MacLean said contemptuously. "Those who direct the fight stay out of it, while the poor lads who do the dying are thrown to the front."

James studied the weapons the English soldiers carried: not the 13-foot pikes, but shorter staffs with an axe blade on one end and a hook on the other.

"They have new weapons," he remarked.

"Aye," Gray said. "But they'll have to get close to use them. Our pikes have a good four-foot range over theirs."

"Form up the ranks," James said. "It seems the English are ready to fight."

The leaders arranged their men into tightly packed wedges bristling with pikes whose spear points were leveled chest high at the enemy. James could only imagine what that fierce line must look like to the English troops below.

The men waited tensely, glancing at their leaders and the king for the signal to charge. In the silence, James heard the clan banners snapping like pistol shots in the wind. The English also hesitated, none too eager to charge up the hill.

In that moment, as James gazed at his men, all seemed timeless, as if they had done this over and over—the two armies facing one another, the gray sky, and the unsullied field that lay between them.

James felt the tight bonds of affection that bound him to his men and they to him. He looked down the line at the strong profiles of MacLean, Gray, Sir Lennox, at the others who stood fast.

A sense of peace settled over him. Whatever happened, he would bring them home.

Then the moment shifted into ordinary time, and he smelled the damp earth, and the sweat of men about to go into battle, the metal armor and swords. He looked down at the English lines and saw the infantry still hesitating.

Perhaps, James thought, he could prevent this battle even now. If he fired the artillery, that might drive the English back and open their ranks to a quick charge.

He turned to the artillery master. "Load the cannon. Let's see if we can break their lines before they take the first step."

"Aye, Your Majesty." The master called to his men, "Prepare to fire!"

The men sprang into action, loading in the gunpowder and cannonballs and priming the firing pans. The great bronze cannon were poised on the hill like siege weapons.

"Fire!" James called.

"Fire!" The command rippled along the line, and the seven cannon roared in rapid succession.

But they had misjudged the field badly. The cannon muzzles, unable to be lowered, were firing at too high an angle. Instead of ripping through the enemy lines, the cannonballs arched upward and struck the soft earth with a dull thump well short of the English front line.

James saw instantly that as weapons of war, the cannon were

useless. The English troops raised a wild cheer, and English cannon began to return fire.

The first volley tore through the packed wedge of men near James like a bolt of lightning. Splinters of wooden pikes flew like daggers through the air, wounding men nearby.

"Hold fast!" Gray bellowed.

James's first instinct was to pull the men back out of cannon range—but they were not trained to retreat in an orderly manner. Panic could easily turn such a move into a deadly rout.

A second round of cannon fire tore through another wedge, and the men began to falter. Down the line, James saw that some of the Scottish leaders and their ranks were already moving forward in a ragged line of attack.

If he didn't act quickly, they would break ranks and lose the advantage of a massed assault.

He raced out in front of the men, holding his sword and shield with the royal crest high.

"FOR SCOTLAND AND THE KING!" he roared.

"FOR SCOTLAND AND THE KING!" came the answer.

The ranks surged forward as one, their pikes in close formation. The English saw the massed wedges of bristling points bear down on them and for a moment pulled back. Their cannon fire faltered.

James felt a surge of hope. "KEEP ON, LADS. STRIKE HARD!" Leaders all around him were urging their men on as they raced down the hillside straight at the English ranks. He heard MacLean's voice strong and clear above the rest. The eerie battle cries of the clans sounded like demons of war. The English officers swore and cursed at their men, trying to drive them forward.

But near the bottom of the hillside a swollen creek cut through the meadow, scattering rocks and stones over its course. This small barrier broke the massed wedges, and James saw in despair the force of the Scottish charge faltering.

He shouted, "MACLEAN, GRAY—CLOSE UP, CLOSE UP!"

The English leaders were quick to notice the break, and their troops bore down on the center of the Scottish line. They attacked with a vengeance, their new weapon proving deadly against the pikes. The axe blades cut the shafts in two, while the soldiers used the hooked ends to yank the Scots off their feet. Once down, the felled warriors had little chance against the axe-wielding English.

James and the other nobles fought desperately to defend their men, but the English were cutting through the wedges like scythes slashing through wheat.

The battle raged around James—he hardly knew when his sword struck flesh or armor. The English seemed to be everywhere in his ranks, and soon he heard the booming charge of the English cannon. They had reached the high ground the Scots had left and were raking the rear of the Scots' line with cannon fire.

With English troops behind them, there was no retreat. Their only hope was to keep pressing on, fighting through to the rear, where they could capture the camp and the officers.

James wiped blood out of his eyes and saw Surrey on his horse, shouting to his officers. If they could reach Surrey—

"MACLEAN!" James shouted, and over the din of the battle, he saw the man turn to find him. James pointed his sword at Surrey, and MacLean understood instantly.

MacLean bellowed over his shoulder: "CAMPBELL, MACDOWELL—FOLLOW ME!"

The nobles fought their way to James, and the tight band attacked the English soldiers with renewed fury. If they could capture or kill Surrey, they might yet turn the battle.

James felt his shield ringing with blow after blow from the axe blades swung at him, but he kept moving forward. He heard MacLean swearing behind him as he threw one soldier after another out of his way.

Then the telltale hiss of an arrow burned past James's ear. The longbows! The English had begun to rain a thick cloud of arrows down on the Scots. The men behind him screamed as the arrows found their mark, and still they fought.

James re-doubled his efforts to reach the English general. Surrey stayed tantalizingly out of reach, no matter how hard James pressed.

Then suddenly a gap opened before him, a clear path to the bay charger Surrey rode. James sprang forward, unaware there was no one left of his small band to follow him. He struck aside an axe blade and leaped over a fallen body. He was now a mere sword's length away from Surrey. He saw the fear on Surrey's face as he realized James was nearly on him. The general tried to bring his horse around—

James never saw the English sword that struck him from the side, penetrating a break in his armor and piercing through his ribs. The pain of it knocked the breath out of him, and he fell hard on the bloodied ground.

Someone wrenched the sword out of his hand, and he saw flashes of light and dark as men leaped over him and kept on fighting. Arrows buried themselves in the ground near his head. It seemed they would never stop falling, the cannon never stop firing.

He struggled desperately to rise and keep fighting. Only one thought burned in his mind. His men needed him . . . MacLean, Gray . . . Robert . . .

Then the sounds of battle faded, and in the strange, unearthly quiet, two figures, led by a third, seemed to be moving across the field toward him. The third figure was smaller and more slender.

Margaret! . . . he called . . .

Chapter 32

Recovery and Forgiveness

The bumping, swaying motion of a wagon shook James awake. His body felt on fire, filled with so much pain he didn't dare move. Each jolt of the road sent a new wave of agony through him.

His vision cleared enough to see a canvas cover arcing overhead and a swaying lantern attached to one of the wooden ribs. The smell of incense seemed a connection to another place, but he couldn't remember where. *What's happened to me?*

Then a familiar ruddy face moved into view, illuminated by the lantern light.

"Ah, there you are, James. We were wondering if we still had you on Earth or if you had left us."

"Captain," he croaked.

"Just rest. Master Zheng has given you a draught to help with the pain of your wounds. It will make you drowsy, so save your strength and don't try to talk."

James vaguely recalled being in a battle and seeing three people approach him across a strangely quiet battlefield.

"But how . . . ?"

"How did we get you out? Well, you've always had someone watching over you. He found you while Master Zheng created a . . . diversion, let us say. Would you like to meet your guardian?"

James heard someone stirring in the background. Then an all-too-familiar face leaned over him, smiling. "God's grace to you, Sire."

"Wullie!" James exclaimed weakly.

The bent, wheezy old servant looked like a wiry angel now. As James's heavy eyelids closed, he took the image of that angelic face back into sleep.

Sometime later, voices reached him again. His lungs hurt and someone seemed to be sticking a knife into his side.

"We must get him out of Scotland quickly. . ."

". . . go to my family's estate in the Low Countries . . . he'll be safe there."

James tried to tell them he didn't want to go anywhere. He wanted to sink into oblivion and never wake into this world again. He longed for death . . . but he had to stay here, there was something he had to do.

Adding to his torment, nightmares pursued him in sleep. He saw his friends dying all around him as English arrows rained down in a deadly fire.

He remembered, then, that he had led them there. He was to blame for it all.

The battle dreams gradually faded, and the sound of ship's bells rang in his ears. He smelled old wood and sailcloth and heard sailors' voices and the cries of gulls. Someone held a cup to his mouth. He drank the liquid, which tasted like sweetgrass, and everything faded.

When he woke again, it was to the gentle sound of waves lapping against a shore. He knew he wasn't on board ship because the bed beneath him was still. The air was scented with roses.

James opened his eyes cautiously and saw a pleasant room of whitewashed walls, with a blue dresser and table, and a louvered window open to the sea breeze. White roses grew outside the window, their blossoms swaying and bobbing in the wind.

He tried to move and gasped at the searing agony in his side and chest. Something was wrong with his left arm and leg as well—he couldn't seem to move them.

"Let me help, Your Majesty!" Wullie hurried over to put pillows behind James's back to raise him up. "The captain says to keep you quiet. You must heal a bit more before you can set foot out of bed."

"What is this place, Wullie?" he asked.

"We're in the captain's house, Sire. He and Master Zheng brought you here a few days ago."

"We've left Scotland, then."

Wullie hesitated, then said softly, "Aye, that we have, Your Majesty."

"Don't call me that," James said. "I'm not the king any longer."

"You are to me, Sire."

Then an unfamiliar voice, speaking in an Oriental accent, came from behind them. "Wullie, I would like a word with James, if you please."

Master Zheng He! James's heart beat rapidly as he saw the master standing in the doorway, smiling at both of them.

His eyes shone with a strong, youthful light. All the more remarkable, because his grey hair and thin beard and the creased lines of his face spoke of considerable age. Master Zheng's long silk jacket and tunic, covered with embroidered dragons, rippled gently in the cool breeze from the windows.

Wullie bowed and quietly left the room.

Master Zheng's gaze seemed to pierce James's very soul and reveal all that lay there. James turned his face to the wall and squeezed his eyes shut in anguish.

Then, with a great effort of will, he slowly turned back to face Master Zheng. The truth had to be spoken.

"How can I ever pay for the death and suffering I've caused so many?"

Master Zheng said, "You are not defined by one action, James. Right now, we must help you heal so you can fulfill your Soul's purpose for returning here."

A memory came flooding back. The Fifth Scroll. "*The only*

treasure I take with me is how I have lived, how much I have loved." The words sounded like a mockery now.

"When you are ready, I will show you something few men ever see—the legacy you leave. Perhaps it will help you recover your health."

Surely his legacy would be a harsh one. Families would curse his name for generations, and the country would probably refuse to seat his son on Scotland's throne.

"You are wrong," Master Zheng said firmly.

But James, unable to believe him, turned away again.

Over the next few weeks, Wullie and Captain van Horn tended closely to James. The captain gave him herbs to help heal his wounds but could do nothing to shake him out of his melancholy. The memory of all the men who had died seemed to weigh on him more with time.

Every day was another battle to James, exhausting and discouraging. His world had shrunk to one or two rooms, and he found himself retreating from even the smallest exertion. Would he ever again be able to live without pain?

And what was the point of getting well if he was burdened with guilt for the rest of his life? He was foolish to think he could redeem himself through suffering. Such a monstrous crime as he had committed could not be paid for.

The captain began to notice a grayish light swirling around James.

"I'm afraid the challenge may be too great for him," the captain said to Master Zheng. "He's lost himself."

Master Zheng was silent for a moment. Then he asked, "And his wounds?"

"He's still young enough and strong." The captain shook his head. "But the body can't fully heal without his mind."

"Then it is time we help to heal his mind. Think of when you first met him, Captain. What of that encounter might help him remember who he is?"

Van Horn frowned uncertainly. Then his face brightened. "I believe I have a remedy . . . at least I hope so."

"I leave him in your hands and Wullie's. Until he remembers, he will not listen to anything I have to say."

"Sire, we're going to get you dressed for a short ride," Wullie said briskly. He flung open the curtains to let the bright sunlight stream into the room. "The captain has something he wants to show you."

James flung his good arm over his eyes. "Leave me alone."

"Just a short ways, Sire. You can't lie abed forever."

"I'm not going. Just leave me alone."

No matter how Wullie cajoled and wheedled, James refused to move. Finally, in desperation, Wullie began to recite his many sacrifices in the king's service.

". . . and as I climbed the high tower to rescue you, fear of the king's men froze my limbs every step of the way, but I kept on . . ."

His body seemed to shrink and his voice took on the wheezy tone James knew so well, punctuated with a racking cough or two. Every word prodded James like a sharp stick.

At last he could stand it no longer. "You should be a lawyer," he growled. "You are an expert at blackmail."

"No idea what you mean, Sire," Wullie said mildly. He laid out a set of clothes and began to help James dress, careful not to cause him too much pain. "I just think a bit of air would do you good, is all. There . . . that's it, Your Majesty."

Wullie stepped back to survey his handiwork. James wore a pleated white shirt, dark waistcoat, dark brown breeches, tan leggings, and buckled shoes. "If not for the reddish hair, you'd be the right picture of a Dutchman."

James said in disgust, "Robert would laugh like a fool if he saw me like this."

Wullie glanced sharply at him. It was the first time he had mentioned Robert's name.

"Ah, a good disguise, James!" the captain said as he entered the room. "We can't have someone who looks like the king of Scotland wandering about my estate. I'd have to start rumors you're a ghost!"

Van Horn helped James to his feet and, with Wullie on the other side, walked him slowly out the louvered doors to where a cart and horse waited. James gritted his teeth against every movement. Even that small a distance left him gasping. Each breath seared his throat as if he had been burned from the inside.

When he reached the walkway, he was startled to feel the wind brush against his face. It stirred a brief spark of life before the gray melancholy returned. The captain noticed that subtle change and nodded briefly to Wullie.

They settled James in the cart, and the captain slapped the reins on the horse's back. They moved forward at a gentle walk.

"Just a little way, James. There's something you must see."

They drove past the estate gardens, alive with red and gold as autumn made its first, early appearance. James looked dully at the wide expanse of the bay, where small boats plied the waters for fish. Gulls wheeled and dipped above their decks, eager for scraps.

But none of it seemed real. His head ached, and he broke out in a sweat, though the day was cool. He was about to ask the captain to turn back when they topped a slight rise and van Horn pulled the horse to a stop.

At that moment, James forgot all about his aching head, his wrecked body, and his melancholy.

Stretched out below them was the most beautiful course he had ever seen outside of Scotland. The fairways rolled and curved over a gently rugged landscape. Each green lay like an emerald circle set carefully at every fairway's end, while patches of white sand traps, sparkling water hazards, and a border of tall grasses appeared placed artfully throughout the course.

Captain van Horn said, "I had some of the Scottish courses in mind when I built this, James. It seemed like a good thing to show you first. It reminds me of a young man I met a long time ago."

For James, the sight provoked vivid memories of a more innocent, peaceful time when a king's burdens had rested lightly on his shoulders. Good friends playing the course, laughing at each other's jokes; the wild, challenging holes at St. Andrews—

And then the strongest memory of all arose, a fourteen-year-old boy and a Dutchman walking across a makeshift field in Scotland, so many years ago. His throat tightened as emotion swept over him like a sudden storm. He bowed his head against the captain's shoulder and wept.

Afterward, a sense of peace settled deep within him, and a memory of his sanctuary stirred, offering the first tenuous link to his Soul.

Remember who you are.

Perhaps his life could be redeemed; perhaps forgiveness was possible, even for him.

Chapter 33

The King's Legacy

From that day on, James grew stronger, often walking the course with Captain van Horn and Wullie, and even playing a few holes now and then. Gradually, strength returned to his left arm, though it would never be fully restored, and only a small limp reminded him of the wound to his leg. His lungs healed, even if the deep wound in his side continued to pain him at night.

He even dreamed every now and then of being with Margaret Drummond, although he could remember little of the dreams when he woke. It was enough to feel her close again.

As his interest in the world revived, James began asking about Robert, Queen Margaret, and his son, James V. The captain told him that Robert had reached Stirling safely with the scrolls and now served the queen, who treated him as a close friend of the family.

"Robert will teach your son the wisdom of the scrolls, and if Master Zheng's vision is true, he will teach your grandson the scrolls as well."

"My grandson? Master Zheng can see that far ahead?"

"He can see what will clearly come to pass—and your grandson is part of that future."

James's heart constricted painfully as he realized he would never see his son grow up and become a man, in turn having sons of his own. James was beginning to grasp what his absence from Scotland would mean to those left behind—to a boy growing up without a father to guide him.

"Can we not let Robert know that I live?" James asked. "Can't we let anyone know?"

The captain's gaze softened. "You will have to ask Master Zheng about that."

James flushed. "I confess I have been avoiding him. I couldn't bear to look him in the eye—"

"Master Zheng does not judge you. Go to him, James." The captain laid an affectionate hand on his shoulder. "It's hard to obtain forgiveness from others, but far, far harder to forgive yourself. Let him help you. Let him show you the truth."

It took a few days for James to work up the courage to follow van Horn's advice. When he did, Master Zheng greeted him warmly and suggested they walk outside.

The brisk winds of autumn scattered brightly colored leaves over the captain's course. The two men strolled in silence along a creek winding like a serpent through the grass. James waited nervously for the councilor to speak first.

At last Master Zheng stopped on a curved bridge that spanned a pond on the course. James leaned against the railing and gazed at their reflections in the water. Any moment, James thought, he's going to ask if I want to see my legacy.

But the master surprised him. "You must have been curious about an old man the captain kept mentioning. What questions do you have for me?"

James hesitated. It seemed too soon to ask about letting people know he was still alive, so he broached a safer subject.

"I've been wondering for some time—how did you manage to get me off the battlefield? The captain and Wullie have been vague on the subject."

Master Zheng smiled, took a small biscuit out of his pocket, and crumbled it for the fish who had gathered below. "Let us say . . . the minds of those around you became confused. They may have been lost in a thick mist, or perhaps they forgot where they were, while we slipped in and carried you off. Afterward, they may have believed that another man was the king and brought that body to King Henry."

James gaped at him. "Someone else is buried in my place?"

Master Zheng dusted the last of the crumbs from his fingers and thrust his hands back into the sleeves of his jacket. "No burial has taken place, James, nor is one ever likely to happen. This mysterious body will disappear at a future time . . . or perhaps it already has. Such things are hard to know precisely."

"What are you saying? There's no tomb for the king?" James asked. "Then . . . what do people think happened to me?"

Master Zheng said, "I hear that all over Scotland, people whisper you didn't die on the battlefield but were carried away by spirits and are living as an ordinary man somewhere. Other rumors say you sailed west for a distant land and live there still."

James asked, his stomach cold as ice, "And the people . . . do they curse my name for the disaster at Flodden Field?"

"No. They grieve that such a king was cut down before his time and so many were lost with him. But they know you wished to protect the country against its enemies--not to gain power for yourself, James. Their affection is part of your legacy."

James flinched at the word "legacy." Yet hadn't the captain said to let Master Zheng show him the truth? He took a deep breath and steeled himself.

"My legacy, Master Zheng. What is it?"

"Ah, to see that, we must go to a meditation room the captain has set aside for me. I believe you are ready for this knowledge."

Inside the small, dimly lit room, James had to seat himself carefully in a chair lined with cushions. Master Zheng lit two oil lamps and a strongly scented incense. He sat down easily on a silk cushion and told James to relax.

"There is nothing you need to do. I will guide you. Simply allow yourself to see what appears in your mind."

Later James tried to recall exactly what happened next. He remembered the room around them seemed to disappear until only the incense smoke remained, curling upward toward the ceiling as he watched it.

He heard Master Zheng's voice. "Scotland enjoyed twenty-five years of peace and prosperity under your reign, longer than under any other king. That alone is a worthy legacy, but there is much more, James."

The smoke cleared slowly, and he saw a large, cathedral-like building where figures in black robes crowded the steps. He recognized the university he had founded in Edinburgh.

"This university, James, will become the birthplace of ideas and inventions that will change the world. They will be used far across the Atlantic—in a nation that does not yet exist."

James gazed, transfixed, as image after image arose and vanished before his eyes. The surgeon's college, the arts he had fostered, architecture, engineering, and sciences, all of it spreading out like the roots of a great tree through Scotland, England, and into the world.

Gradually the images faded, and the room coalesced around them once again. By now the incense had burned down to its holder, and the oil lamps shed only a dim light. Master Zheng regarded him kindly, the humor bright in his eyes.

"It may be difficult to believe now, James," Master Zheng said, "but your grandson will be the first Stewart to rule over a united England and Scotland. He will be known as James I in British history."

"How can that be?" James said hoarsely. "We were at war—a war I started!"

"Flodden Field was the last major battle fought between England and Scotland. The Tudor-Stewart line inherits the throne."

"And the scrolls? What of them?"

"They are passed on from generation to generation, but through Robert's line, not yours. This is how you fulfilled your destiny as king, James. Robert was meant to carry them at the end, and you ensured it would happen. Perhaps their future will become clearer in time. After all, your friend has not yet found the woman he will marry.

"You may also like to know that the game you made a royal pastime will sweep the world as well. Players will come from many countries to challenge the course at St. Andrews. I'm afraid it will show no mercy to any of them."

James laughed in spite of himself. He well remembered how St. Andrews had beaten the best players of his own time.

"It's good to know that some things won't change."

A silence stretched between them, and in that pause, James asked the question weighing the most on his mind. "Can't we let anyone in Scotland know that I'm alive?"

Master Zheng studied him closely before replying, "Let me pose a question to you. You have seen your legacy as king. If you were offered the chance, would you return to Scotland and take the throne again?"

James straightened. Was the man serious? He thought for a long moment. It was clear he had some purpose to fulfill on Earth, or he would not have survived the battle.

A purpose, yes, but not as king. He understood that now.

"No, Master Zheng, let Scotland's fate be in the hands of others. I intend to spend the rest of my life making amends for Flodden Field. As the Fourth Scroll says, it's not what happens to you but how you transform it that matters."

Master Zheng's eyes gleamed in approval. "Indeed. Then it is better to let things remain as they are, do you not agree?"

"Yes . . . I agree."

Master Zheng rose and refilled the lamps, brightening the room. He resumed his seat next to James.

"Let me propose a way for you to fulfill your Soul's purpose for continuing here. In two weeks—before the winter storms begin—Wullie, Captain van Horn, and I will set sail for Africa and from there to Asia. Our work is finished here in Europe, and it is unlikely we will return."

He looked deeply into James's eyes. "I invite you to come with us. If you are willing, I will teach you the ancient healing arts. You have learned a great deal from your own struggles to heal yourself. You know now the patience and effort it takes, and how it can obscure the memory of who you are. And you have overcome guilt and shame and learned to forgive yourself.

"You would have much to offer others. The Western skills you have acquired would be of great value where we are going. I offer you a chance to save ten, perhaps a hundred lives for every one taken on Flodden Field."

James said nothing, his heart racing. Accepting the offer meant in all likelihood he would never see Scotland again; he would leave behind everything and everyone he knew and loved. But by now, he accepted that the entire kingdom believed he was gone—if not killed on the battlefield along with the others, then spirited away somewhere.

In that instant, James felt the last shred of attachment to his role as king fall away. There was nothing holding him here.

I will remember who I am. Where I come from. Where I will return.

The words of the scrolls were no longer a mockery but a promise. James bowed deeply to Master Zheng.

"I would be honored to be your student."

Chapter 34

The Journey Home

A month later, the four men boarded van Horn's ship Cathay and set sail for Asia, never to return. They settled in the Wudang Mountains, where Master Zheng began to instruct James in the healing arts. James threw himself into this new purpose with the same energy that had astonished the people of Scotland. Within a remarkably short time, he was assisting Captain van Horn with his patients.

"People don't know what to make of him," the captain confided to Master Zheng. "But they can't argue with his results. If he keeps this up, I may be able to retire in a few months!"

Yet throughout his studies and practice, James never lost his interest in the fate of Robert and the Five Scrolls he carried. After several years, Master Zheng was able to show James how the ancient wisdom would live on through Robert's descendants. James saw Robert marry a Scottish girl—the youngest sister of Margaret's cousin Aileen—and raise four children.

One of Robert's descendants served as mentor to James I of Great Britain, who had the Latin Bible translated into what became the King James Version. The king tried vainly to instill the values of the scrolls in his court and in his subjects. Unable to pass on the knowledge, he returned the scrolls to Robert's family near the end of his life.

Another of Robert's descendants took the scrolls overseas to the new British colonies in North America in the early 1700s. There,

Robert's great-great-great-grandson, George Wythe, a gifted Virginia lawyer, became the beloved teacher and advisor to Thomas Jefferson, James Madison, and Henry Clay.

All who knew Wythe admired his integrity and tireless work for the new nation. Under his influence, some of the concepts of the ancient scrolls were incorporated into the new nation's founding documents.

Although Wythe fought against slavery, he was not able to eradicate the practice nor keep it out of the Constitution. Yet as he wrote to friends, "I have faith that the ideal 'we are all created equal and endowed by our Creator with certain unalienable rights' will be realized by future generations."

For the next fifty years, James lived in a small cottage with several of his students and continued to learn and teach the deepest medical arts of China. He became renowned as the red-bearded healer of Wudang Mountains. With each patient James saved, the memory of those lost at Flodden Field dimmed until their faces dissolved altogether.

His knowledge of the higher realms unfolded and pervaded his every word and action. It was said that those who understood his lessons lost their fear of death, utterly certain of their survival beyond the body. They lived lives that blessed others.

James himself lived to be well over a hundred years old, long enough to see Wullie, the captain, and Master Zheng leave their Earthly lives and return home.

As the time neared for James to return as well, his interest in the Earthly world began to fade. He turned most of his duties over to his assistants and apprentices and spent more time in meditation as he felt the other realm draw near.

Once, after a particularly long meditation, he was asked by one of his students what it was like to be in that realm.

"Let me answer this way. Is there someone you love?" James asked.

The young man leaned on his straw broom. "Yes, Master James," he said shyly, "Jung-Li, the girl in the village herb shop."

"And when you think of her, are you aware of where you are or what you are doing?"

The student, embarrassed, lowered his gaze. "No, I . . . I lose myself thinking of her voice, her eyes . . . the others have to remind me of my chores."

James smiled. "Going to the other realm is similar. Your body is here, but you are elsewhere, in a place where you are cherished beyond imagining. One day you will return there . . . as I will, not too long from now."

Word soon spread throughout the countryside that Master James was about to depart this Earth. People traveled for miles to his small cottage to express their gratitude and affection. Those who attended his last days remarked that his room seemed filled with an otherworldly light.

In his final moments on Earth, each person James had known and loved paraded through his mind: Robert, Gray, Angus, Montrose, Argyll, and MacLean . . . Sir Lennox, the captain, Master Zheng . . . so many who had touched his life.

And when at last he let go of his body, to his great joy he saw Margaret Drummond coming to meet him.

Epilogue

The Five Scrolls

This first-person version of the scrolls was written by one of Robert Hume's descendants. The version was passed on through the family line, along with the original Five Scrolls.

THE FIRST SCROLL: The Soul and Divine Love

The Soul descends from Divine Love,
Dwells within my Earthly body, and fills it with light.

But as I embark on my Earthly life,
The Great Forgetting begins,
And the Soul's light dims.
I become lost in desires, trapped in fear and anger,
Waging endless war with myself and others.

Yet the Soul is never lost.
When I remember who I am,
All wars cease, and the Soul's light of peace
Is radiant within me.

I am a Soul filled with the love of the Creator,
Through me, Divine Love dwells on Earth.

I will remember who I am. Where I come from. Where I will return.
I will express Divine Love in all I do.

THE SECOND SCROLL: The Soul's Sanctuary

The Soul seeks a sacred place to dwell within me,
A sanctuary where it can remain,
Despite the storms of desire, anger, and fear.

I will build this sanctuary in my heart.
Here the Soul can deepen my Love for
The Creator, for others, for myself.

Each time I remember who I am,
I strengthen this sacred place within me,
Allowing the Soul to fill my life with Divine Love.

I will remember who I am. Where I come from. Where I will return.
I will build within me a sanctuary for the Soul.

THE THIRD SCROLL: Let the Soul Guide

In my sanctuary, Divine Love connects me
To all Creation, to the eternal Source of life.

But if tempted to fulfill only my own desires,
I break my connection to others and
Lose touch with my Soul.

Instead, I allow the Soul's Divine Love to guide my path,
Using my power to establish justice,
Using my wealth to promote generosity,
Like a great river, my life nourishes others.

I will remember who I am. Where I come from. Where I will return.
I let the Soul's Divine Love guide my life.

THE FOURTH SCROLL: The Dark Crisis

There may come a time of great sorrow, great loss,
That seems to extinguish all light of the Soul.
An endless night descends; I feel abandoned by
Everything and everyone I have ever known.

Yet know this: what happens in this Earthly life
Is not what matters, for much is beyond my control.
What matters is how I transform it.
This alone I choose, this alone I can control.

In this dark crisis, despite my despair, I surrender to my Soul.
Its light dispels abandonment, the terrible separation.
I will follow where the Soul leads, do whatever it asks.
Guided by its light, I am free.

I will remember who I am. Where I come from. Where I will return.
I will surrender to my Soul in the darkest times.

THE FIFTH SCROLL: The Return Home

We are all one in Divine Love,
Joined with the Creator, who cherishes us all.

As my Earthly life nears its end,
This higher realm draws close, becomes ever more real.
My Soul knows this place so well.

I turn inward to my Sanctuary and find the way home.
I leave behind all wealth and achievement,
All sorrows, failures, and losses.
My body's work is done—I let the Earth receive it.

The only treasure I take with me
Is how I have lived,
How much I have loved.

I remember who I am, where I come from, and where I now return.

Historical Notes

King James IV was arguably one of Scotland's most enlightened and successful kings. For nearly 25 years during his reign, the country enjoyed a time of relative peace and prosperity unmatched in its history.

Only sixteen years old when he took the throne in 1488, James IV made great strides during his reign to unify the country, enforce an equitable system of justice, initiate an impressive building program, enlarge the Scottish navy, introduce the first compulsory education laws, found the first college of surgery, bring in the printing press, support the arts and sciences, and strengthen the power of the crown versus the nobility.

He spoke French, German, Flemish, Danish, Italian, and Spanish, and was the last monarch to speak the old language, Gaelic. James IV was also the first king to strike down the ban on golf and pave the way for it to become a national pastime.

His faults have also been well documented, confined mainly to the realm of lavish spending on royal outings, card gambling, and grand public displays, such as jousting tournaments and entertainments at court.

Even in the midst of such excesses, his contemporaries noted that he was remarkably moderate in food and drink. He also had an unfortunate tendency toward impulsive actions on the battlefield, a tendency that in the end may have cost him his life.

In 1603, Scotland and England were united; and James VI, the grandson of James IV, was placed on the throne. James VI became the first Stewart-Tudor to rule Great Britain and was crowned King James I. However, he did not inherit his grandfather's touch with people and was never a popular monarch.

Prologue

Zheng He: The Chinese admiral Zheng He was one of the most accomplished and famous members of Emperor Yongle's court. There is some evidence he even led an expedition of the emperor's ships across the Pacific to the Americas. However, the emperor after Yongle abandoned exploration, and Zheng He's fleet never sailed again. Although the historical figure Zheng He died in 1433, when his tomb was opened, it was found to be empty, His body was never recovered. In our story, he lived on as the mystical sage of Wudang Mountains.

Captain Jacob van Horn: The Netherlands produced some of Europe's finest navigators and sailors, which served as a model for Captain van Horn. These men hired themselves out to the English, French, Portuguese, Spanish, and Viennese to sail in their fleets. There is reason to believe one or two of them might have sailed as far as Madagascar or even India and China.

Christianity in China: In the A.D. 800s, Christianity was brought to China by a Syrian monk. The evidence for this event is contained in a series of documents recently unearthed in China that describe the monk's arrival and missionary work. In *The King's Way Home*, the spiritual wisdom brought by the monk is condensed into the Five Scrolls, which were then given to Master Zheng.

Chapter 1: Politics and the Game

James III had banned an early version of golf, which by the 1470s was becoming increasingly popular. The first clubs were made of ash with heads hollowed out at the back and filled with lead to give them heft. The handles were wrapped in several layers of leather thong to give players a better grip on the heavy clubs.

The first balls were either wooden or stitched leather spheres that were stuffed with boiled, chopped feathers and covered in several coats of paint. These leather balls remained relatively unchanged for nearly four centuries.

Before the establishment of greens, golfers aimed for a striped stake or poll at a set distance from the tee. However, some form of green was likely developed by individual clans or nobles in Scotland for their own courses. James IV lifted the ban on golf, which became Scotland's national pastime and one of the world's best sports.

Chapter 3: The First Scroll

Captain van Horn refers to an actual Chinese text, *DongXuani*, from the Song Dynasty, A.D. 960–1279. Some scholars have claimed that the game described in the book may be the origin of golf. Illustrations show the emperor and his nobles using club-like equipment to hit balls into holes set in a greens-like enclosure.

The captain's chopsticks would have been an exotic utensil to Europeans. Even by the late Middle Ages, forks had yet to be introduced into Scotland. The main utensils were spoons and knives.

Chapter 4: Margaret and the Crown

The Stone of Scone mentioned in the chapter, also known as the Stone of Destiny, was once kept in the Abbey of Scone near Perth, Scotland. It was used for centuries in the coronation of Scottish kings.

In 1296, the stone was captured by the English King Edward I and taken to Westminster Abbey. The stone was stolen back by a small group of Scottish students in 1950 but returned to England in 1951. At last, in 1996, it was formally returned to Scotland—700 years after its capture.

Today the stone remains with the Scottish Crown Jewels in the crown room in Edinburgh Castle.

Chapter 8: Battle for the Throne

The victorious rebels were eager to bury the king and coronate James IV as quickly as possible after the battle. In the Middle Ages, regicide was regarded as a grave crime, no matter what the provocation. Those who brought about the king's death, whether intentional or otherwise, had to pacify public opinion or risk losing their victory.

Chapter 11: The Challenge

The tradition of battling poets, or "flyting," that James refers to existed from the 5th to the 16th centuries in Scotland, England, and in some European countries. Poets from opposing sides would duel in court or on the battlefield. In some cases, the winner of these contests would also decide the outcome of a conflict, sending the armies home. Flyting gradually faded after the 16th century. Today, modern rappers continue this tradition, engaging in poetic duels that are referred to as "battle raps."

The medieval court system in Scotland was a complex maze of royal and ecclesiastical courts, legal burghs, sheriffs' courts, and estate or baronial courts. On many estates, for example, the laird was absolute ruler and meted out judgments or punishments as he saw fit. The medieval court system in Scotland was a complex maze of royal and ecclesiastical courts, legal burghs, sheriffs' courts, and estate or baronial courts. On baronial or highland estates, for example, the laird was absolute ruler and meted out judgments or punishments as he saw fit.

James IV rightly saw the need to hold the multi-tiered court system to a higher standard and ensure that it functioned as efficiently as possible. This policy would become one of the hallmarks of his reign. His work laid the foundation for the Scottish Court of Sessions, the supreme law body in the nation.

James's passion for justice also led him to issue a compulsory education decree that all the sons of nobility be educated in the law. It was the first order for compulsory education in all of Europe.

Chapter 12: The Duel

James IV was the last monarch to speak Gaelic, the Old Language still spoken in the Highlands, which gave him an advantage when he wanted to acquire the loyalty of those clans.

When leather gets wet, it tends to stretch and lose its tension. This would have made these balls harder to hit any significant distance or roll very far on the ground. Coating them with lacquer instead of paint would have the advantage of waterproofing them. The Chinese had developed lacquering to a fine art, and the captain might have known some of the secrets, passing them on to Wullie.

Chapter 13: Among Equals

From the A.D. 600s through the Middle Ages, the Church defined all relations in both the natural and supernatural realms. The total dominance of the Church in all areas of life—religious, civil, and cultural—would be hard to overstate.

The Church had established a philosophical and spiritual "great chain of being," with the Church hierarchy at the top, followed by the king and nobles, and with the other classes in descending order: knights, merchants, burghers, common laborers and farmers, servants, criminals, and heathens/pagans.

To suggest that all people were equal would be considered heresy. The "divine right of kings" to rule had not yet become orthodox doctrine, but the king was considered an instrument of the Church under the Pope's guidance and a channel for God's purpose on Earth. The Pope was still considered the highest Earthly authority, even over kings. However, that doctrine was slowly changing during the time of James IV.

Chapter 14: Margaret's Duel

The tradition of a secret language among women has been documented in Europe and Asia. In Scotland, as in other countries of Europe, women had a secret language of flowers they used to communicate among themselves.

It would have been a small step from that tradition to develop other symbols for communicating intelligence, as Margaret's cousin Aileen does. Embroidered messages would have been ignored by the men, who regarded such women's work as beneath their notice.

The intermarriage among clans and families would also give women, and the servants who accompanied them, a natural network among castles. Since both women and servants were often "invisible" to the men around them, the spy network could operate under their noses.

However, the danger to the participants in such a network was real. Servants caught spying would be tortured and executed without a second thought. Women in the family might be imprisoned within the castle, sent to a nunnery, married off, or removed to a distant town or land, forever separated from their families.

Chapter 24: Blood Rage and the Captain's Risk

The triple poisoning of Margaret, Sibylla, and Euphemia is historic fact. All three women died at Drummond Castle. The idea that Lord Fleming was responsible for the deaths has some historical validity. Sources also cite that James was grief-stricken at the death of Margaret Drummond and mourned her for years.

Chapter 28: The Rose and the Thistle

The marriage between James and Margaret Tudor took place on August 8, 1503. It was commemorated by the great Scottish poet William Dunbar in his poem "The Rose and the Thistle." The rose with five white inner petals and five red outer petals stood for the House of Tudor (uniting the families of York and Lancaster).

James made the wedding one of the social and royal highlights of his reign, building the Great Hall at Stirling for the ceremony and sparing no expense for the wedding celebration. It's also historic fact that Margaret Tudor asked him to shave off his beard and that he graciously complied with her request.

She and James suffered the deaths of five children before James

V was born and survived. James V was only about eight months old when his father died at Flodden Field in 1513. This made Queen Margaret the guardian of a king who would not come into his full majority for another eighteen to twenty years.

Chapter 29: Kings Henry VIII and James IV

The story of the town crier calling out the names of all the barons, earls, and noblemen of Edinburgh is based on historical record. According to the account, the crier commanded these men to appear before him in forty days. When guards attempted to arrest the crier, they found he had vanished.

The battle of Flodden Field took place forty days after the incident in Edinburgh. Of all the men whose names the mysterious crier called out, only one nobleman returned alive to Edinburgh. The rest were killed at Flodden Field. Legend has it that the crier was Pluto, lord of the underworld, calling his own to come with him.

Chapter 31: The Battle of Flodden Field

This account of the battle fought on Braxton Hill is based on several sources that provide corroborating details of how it unfolded. Lord Surrey, the uncle of Margaret Tudor, had a keen understanding of James's chivalric tendencies. He rightly gambled that the king would not fire on the exposed English soldiers as they crossed the River Till.

Yet even when the Scots lost the advantage, they continued to press forward. The English officers later recorded they were astonished at how fiercely the Scottish warriors fought even when struck by several arrows or slashed by sword and axe blades.

The final casualty count for the Scottish army ranged from 15,000 to 20,000 killed or wounded on the field. The Scottish song "All the Flowers Have Gone Away," was written to commemorate this great loss of the king, the flower of the Scottish nobility, and thousands of their men. All of Scotland mourned a king cut off in his prime.

Chapter 33: The King's Legacy

Remarkably, the story of James IV being taken away from the battlefield has its origin in legends of the king's fall. In one story, he is taken off the battlefield by mysterious figures and another man is left in his place. This false king is then taken to King Henry VIII in England, but the body disappears. In another story, James manages to escape and make his way out of Scotland. In both stories, James is rumored to be alive in a distant land.

There was no burial for the king. The body that was delivered to King Henry VIII eventually disappeared, and James's body was never conclusively identified, just as Zheng He's body was never found. It seems fitting that the two men were linked by a common mystery after their deaths.

George Wythe, the supposed descendant of Robert Hume, was also a historical figure who lived in the North American English colonies at the time of the Revolutionary War. Wythe helped write the Constitution of Virginia, signed the Declaration of Independence, and helped craft the U.S. Constitution.

Acknowledgements

It takes many people to bring a book into the world. First of all, I want to thank my good friend and fellow writer, L. Sue Baugh. Her historical research, input, and writing/illustration skills made my book come to life—I am in your debt.

A special appreciation to all those who read drafts of the manuscript and gave their feedback to make the work better. A heartfelt thank you to the designer, Jericho C. Hernandez; the copyeditor, Judith Gallagher, who devoted many hours to improving the book: and the proofreader, Norm Zuefle, whose sharp eyes helped perfect the final text. Also, a salute to Mike Nash, Wayne Gurowsky, and many other golfers who helped us understand the finer points of the game for the story.

My deepest gratitude to my family for giving me encouragement and honest feedback throughout this long creative process. I couldn't have done it without you.

Finally, I want to express my great respect and admiration for James Stewart IV, whose vision and achievements form the core of the book. He remains one of the most accomplished and beloved kings Scotland has ever known. It's fitting that in the story, James is the one to ensure that the legacy of the Five Scrolls continues.

Thomas Pizur

Author and Illustrator Bios

Thomas Pizur was a young child when his family moved to a poor, working-class neighborhood in Youngstown, Ohio. What he found there left a lasting impression.

"I still remember the love and warmth of the people in that neighborhood. I felt like I could go up to any house, stranger or not, and be cared for and fed with the best that house had to offer. Many of these strangers gave my family food off their own tables. Together, we were all poor and lived under the threat of eviction. Whether we were black or white didn't matter. In that neighborhood, I learned about unconditional giving and love."

After a few years, his family moved to a factory town in Illinois, a place that had "tough people for a tough town." The contrast with Youngstown was clear.

As Tom grew older, he began searching for that same unconditional love he had experienced. His path led him to explore various spiritual traditions, such as Catholicism, Buddhism, and Daoism, He studied and taught many forms of martial arts. But the deep sense of belonging and purpose eluded him. Then in the 1980s, Tom watched as his older brother, a Vietnam vet, struggled to receive veterans' benefits and fought the Veterans Administration to keep them.

"I decided our country's veterans and their widows needed some help. Since 1987, I've been fortunate enough to assist thousands of U.S. vets." Listening to the stories of these veterans and their families, the idea for *The King's Way Home* was born. "These people had love, then suffered devastating losses, and recovered love again through the difficulties of their lives. That's the hope, that's the core of my story."

L. Sue Baugh has worked as a writer, editor, and illustrator in the publishing industry for many years. Her clients include Scott

Foresman, Pearson, McGraw-Hill, Holt McDougal, and Houghton Mifflin Harcourt.

She also helps individual authors develop their manuscripts for publication. "I consider *The King's Way Home* one of the best stories I've worked on." Like Thomas Pizur, she has also studied both Eastern and Western spiritual traditions.

Ms. Baugh has written eight books, including the award-winning photo/essay book *Echoes of Earth: Finding ourselves in the origins of the planet*. She took the photos and created many of the illustrations for the volume.

Made in the USA
Monee, IL
18 September 2023